FIRE of HEAVEN

R.J. LEENMAN

Ark House Press
arkhousepress.com

© 2022 R.J. Leenman

All rights reserved. Apart from any fair dealing for the purpose of study, research, criticism, or review, as permitted under the Copyright Act, no part may be reproduced by any process without written permission.

Unless otherwise stated, all Scriptures are taken from the New International Translation (Holy Bible. Copyright© 1996, 2004, 2007, 2013 by Tyndale House Foundation. Used by permission of Tyndale House Publishers Inc., Carol Stream, Illinois 60188. All rights reserved.)

Some names and identifying details have been changed to protect the privacy of individuals.

Cataloguing in Publication Data:
Title: Fire of Heaven
ISBN: 978-0-6454596-5-4 (pbk)
Subjects: Fiction
Other Authors/Contributors:

Design by initiateagency.com

I.
Rejection

CHAPTER 1

The sound of shouting and dogs barking woke Selim, and his gritty eyes opened to the darkness of the room. Throwing himself out of bed, he lit a lamp and quickly pulled on some clothes and boots. Bursting into the corridor, he wrapped his sword belt around his waist and ran to the front door. Outside, men were running for the walls. Some were bracing the fort's wooden gates and others could be seen on top of the wall, pointing and shouting, firing arrows and throwing spears. Selim darted up the steep stairs to the top to see who was attacking. He could make out horses and riders, but in the dim light they could have been from any of the tribes who lived in the Sarmadee Ranges.

Selim couldn't yet determine why the attack was happening, and had little time to think with arrows whizzing over his head. He fired a number of arrows in response, but none hit either horse or rider. Selim wasn't keen on hitting the horses, with either arrow or spear, as he took no joy in their pain or death. He knew they were only obeying their riders and were innocent of hatred and anger towards his tribe.

The gates were holding up against the attack as horses and riders made repeated runs toward it, directing arrows and clay pots filled with burning oil towards the defenders on the wall.

REJECTION

Loud calls rang out from high on the wall as oil from a fire pot sent up waves of smoke from one of the gates.

"You there," called Selim, pointing to a couple of young men running past, "get some water and put the fire out!"

As the gates were opened to wet down the fire, a group of intruders on horseback burst towards them. A barrage of arrows flew from the quickly growing number of defenders, causing the riders to make a hasty retreat. Their horses were travelling fast, and Selim saw only one horse injured. An arrow had skidded off its haunches, leaving a shallow groove he hoped would heal quickly. The horse squealed in shock and pain and retreated out of range of the arrows.

Looking at the riders retreating, Selim was puzzled by how unlikely this type of attack was.

An urgent call was heard from one of his tribe members. "Selim, come over here."

Peering over the wall, Sekeen pointed to the road leading into the Sarmadee Ranges. Selim saw three riders on horses who were motionless and obviously intent on the battle, directing the attack.

"What are they doing? Why don't they attack?" Selim asked.

"Just what I was thinking," Sekeen said quietly. "Maybe this attack is a diversion."

On the western side of the fort, two men were scaling its steep walls, puffing and straining to find hand and footholds, making no noise beyond the scrape of leather on rock. Nearing the top, they were desperately hoping the attack on the gates had drawn the guards away. Quickly, both men slid over the top of the wall, hiding in the shadows. Creeping carefully along the wall, they reached a passageway leading downward, and made their way inside the living quarters of Selim and his family.

Finding the right door into Selim's bedroom, they opened it and peered through the doorway. Staying at the entrance, one of the men signalled for the other to go on. Moving in quickly, he lit a small candle, holding it up as he scanned the dim light within the room. Knowingly, he felt along the wall to the right of Selim's bed, his hands moving over the wall searching for cracks in the cement. Finding the cracked outline of a brick, he carefully removed it from the wall. He put his hand into the hole and pulled out a rectangular wooden box, intricately carved with palm trees, gazelle, flowing rivers, and galloping horses, beautiful images of desert life. Inside and out, the box was adorned with the thinnest of gold leaf. Ignoring the craftmanship, the thief opened the box, taking out an object from inside. It was wrapped first in the soft, supple skin of a young goat and then enfolded in a rich, thick cloth. Intrigued, the guard at the door came over to help. Delicately removing the layers, their eyes widened as the hidden object was revealed.

Staring back at them was the handle of a sword. A short, jagged blade extended from the well worn handle. Lying next to it were various age blackened shards of the original blade. After returning the securely wrapped sword back inside, the two men placed the box into a bag for safekeeping and retreated back into the passageway.

Out on the eastern wall, Selim suddenly made sense of what was happening. He jumped from the wall and cried out to Sekeen as he ran, "I think they're after Al Maksour. You're right, it's probably a diversion."

Less than a heartbeat behind, Sekeen joined in the race toward Selim's home. Bursting through the front door, both heard a high-pitched scream coming from deeper within the house. Entering the passage, they found Selim's sister on the ground in front of two men, each with a dagger and a sword in hand. Jumping over his sister, Selim drew his sword, rage welling up inside him. The two sinewy thieves had no answer for the man coming toward them. Though there was little room to make a swing, Selim closed in on the first man, cutting his arm with a short slice of his sword. The man's dagger and sword fell to the floor and he grabbed at his arm, crying out in pain. The second man threw his weapons down and drew back, calling out "Mercy Lord, mercy."

Selim's rage was now burning hot. "Selim! Selim!" called out Sekeen in desperation. Selim pulled himself up at the sound of his name, and stood with his sword thrust out, quivering.

"Get something from my room to tie their hands Sekeen," Selim barked, with far more anger than he intended. Together they threw the men to the floor and bound their hands. Selim's mother and servants came rushing in, and then led Ansim away. Sekeen searched the men and found what he was looking for in their bag. He took the box out and gently unwrapped the sword.

"All's well. There's nothing missing," he said to Selim.

"Praise the gods, it's safe," replied Selim.

"I'll take these two up to the top of the wall. It will show their comrades their little surprise didn't work," said Sekeen with a glint in his eye.

Selim made his way to the sitting room to check on Ansim and found her and his mother there along with some other women who had heard the commotion.

Ansim was sitting on some cushions, with one held tightly to her chest. "Are you hurt at all?" asked Selim.

"No, I'm alright. He frightened me, that's all. I just wish I had my sword with me ... then I could have frightened him," she replied with passion.

"Always the hero," said Selim, "even with your life in danger. There were two of them, you know. Were you going to fight both of them?" replied Selim with exasperation.

"Well, you would have come eventually, and I could have held them off till then," Ansim said bravely, flicking her hair off her forehead.

"Ansim, what are you saying? How could you have protected yourself from those two men? Be serious! Why do you always want to be like a man?" cried out Almas as she stood up in anger.

"I can fight as well as any man," replied Ansim defiantly.

"Maybe. You certainly don't lack courage. But why put yourself in danger? We don't want to see you hurt, you know," said Selim with a softer tone.

Ansim looked up at him, somewhat surprised at his response. "I can't really argue with you, can I?" she said with a smile.

"Well, someone's changed," said Selim.

Ansim raised her eyebrows at him and turned her head away.

"Maybe, she is growing up," thought Selim.

Taking his leave from the women, Selim went up to the wall and joined Sekeen who was standing there with the two intruders. He looked out to see a rider from a group who hadn't been involved in the attacks move slowly toward the fort and stop his horse just out of range of the arrows. The rider looked intently at the two captured men then whirled his horse sharply in the sand and galloped back again, speaking to a man on a chestnut horse with a wide blaze. Holding up his hand, he signalled to the riders. They galloped off leaving nothing but dust and a black scar on the fort's gates. Holding up their spears and bows, the men of the fort gave a deafening yell, and rejoiced with each other in their victory.

Jubilation quickly turned to anger as the story spread around the fort of the attempted stealing of Al Maksour. A number of tribesmen scowled at the two thieves as Sekeen brought them down from the battlements. As Selim followed them along, he noticed that although they had the skills to climb they were thin and wore dirty, discoloured clothing. Only one was hurt but both had a look of dread and despair. Stopping at the fountain, Selim took a seat on its side while Sekeen sat the two men on the ground in front of him.

"What are your names and which tribe are you from?" Selim asked.

The uninjured man spoke for them. His voice trembled with fear and humiliation.

"I am Abdul, and this is Farag. We are from the El Wabib tribe far to the north of the Sarmadees. We are slaves stolen in battle, both us, and our families. They will punish our families if we fail to bring them Al Maksour. Please sheikh, spare our lives and have mercy on us."

"Hmm," thought Selim, "they say they have been forced into this act of thievery. Not only were they in danger, but so were their families. That is why they were so desperate and fearful." Yet, he spoke sharply to them.

"You expect mercy when you break into our fort and try to take away our heritage and belongings? How can you expect mercy when you threaten a harmless girl?"

The men bowed even lower to the ground and the air thickened with tension. Selim turned away, too angry to go on. He finally turned back and asked, "Which tribe sent you?"

Abdul, not lifting his face from the ground, replied, "The Al Bedi."

Selim was not surprised. He had heard of the Al Bedi. They were a greedy tribe who ransacked caravans and constantly sought to find trouble with other tribes. They lacked any sense of mercy and he could well believe that the Al Bedi would carry out their threats towards Abdul and Farag.

Would he behave in the same way to protect his family if he were in Abdul and Farag's position? Selim knew he would have to act with some mercy if their claim was true, but he couldn't forget his tribe had been attacked and that an important part of their history had nearly been stolen. Who knew what the Al Bedi would plan next? However, he was sure they knew his tribe would strengthen the guard on the fort, particularly on the western side of the bluff that he had thought was impenetrable.

Selim waved to the guards Sekeen had assigned for Farag and Abdul and they took them away. The crowd of men slowly dispersed, whispering their own judgements on the two prisoners.

"Sekeen, Ibrahim! I need you to come here," called out Selim.

Unwrapping the pieces of the sword, the trio carefully examined the remains. Al Maksour was undamaged. Selim twisted the pommel in his hands and though almost as old as the mountains the broken blade still managed a dull glint in the sun. The hard, wooden pommel fitted snugly into the palm of his hand as though it belonged there. Wound around the worn wood was a strip of leather, dark with age and tattered in places. A metal cross-guard stretched out on either side of the sharp blade. It was pitted and dented from ancient sword fights. Just below the cross-guard some faint markings could be seen. No-one knew if they were part of a picture that had largely worn away or just scratches gained over time. Every time Selim looked at Al Maksour, he wished the marks were words he could understand, hoping the sword would reveal some of its history. The faint markings added to the mystery of the sword, as well as to its importance. Al Maksour had passed through a hundred generations and had given birth to as many stories over the years, stories passed down and added to over each night's fire.

"It's still a plain looking sword," said Sekeen. "Every time I see it, I wonder how it could do what the stories say," he added.

"I know," replied Selim. "You're not the first person to say that. When I hear Ibrahim's stories about it, I imagine it to be beautifully decorated. But here it is, looking worn and broken, and not anything like the sword of legends or of great leaders and warriors."

Ibrahim, having satisfied his curiosity over Al Maksour, looked at Selim and Sekeen intently.

"How did the Al Bedi know where to find Al Maksour?"

Selim looked at Ibrahim speechless, as the truth of what he had just said struck him. He was right. How did they know where to find Al Maksour?

Sekeen answered Ibrahim, "But wouldn't our sheikh's bedroom be a logical place to look?"

"But how did they find the hole in the wall?" Ibrahim added.

"Someone must have passed this information onto them. But who?" said Sekeen.

"Yes, but who?" said Selim.

"Let me question the thieves again, Selim. They will give me an answer," Sekeen said as he wrung his hands together, making the muscles in his arms bulge.

Selim didn't reply immediately as his mind was occupied by the question, "Who, in the tribe would betray us?"

Then Selim spoke, "Sekeen, question the men again, but don't harm them." Sekeen left with a disappointed look on his face.

Speaking up, Ibrahim said, "I don't think Sekeen will get much from them. They would only have been told what they needed to know in case they were caught, as has happened."

"You're right," answered Selim. "But whatever their story, they will remain here in the fort as servants."

"I'll send word through the tribe to find out if anyone has heard of a person talking about Al Maksour to someone outside of the tribe," said Ibrahim. "There isn't much opportunity for this except when the caravans come through. We'll have to instruct the tribe to think back to the times the caravans have been here," he added.

Selim nodded and Ibrahim left, taking Al Maksour with him. Selim made his way toward the stables, deep in thought. As he walked, he realised just how shocked he was to find out that someone had actually broken trust with the tribe and passed on the knowledge of Al Maksour's hiding place. Who would do this and why?

However, the morning's events rekindled his thoughts and questions about an older issue. The issue was Al Maksour itself, the sword their tribe called "The Broken One." What sort of history and power did it really have to cause a tribe to attack them for it? Did the Al Bedi believe the stories they had heard? It had been part of the heritage of Selim's tribe for so many generations that he and others had lost count. Did the Al Bedi really believe it more than he did?

Many said that it was the sword of Nimrod the hunter, the first man to set eyes on the mother of all horses, Al Hadiyeh. It was thought his family had passed it down from son to son and that many generations ago it had been shattered when the last of the great aurochs was struck down. Many of the tribes around attributed the strength and blessing Selim's tribe enjoyed to Al Maksour, even though it was shattered and unusable. Somehow, women were more fertile, crops were bountiful, hunting was prosperous and their horses swift, hard-boned and courageous. There was no doubt his tribe was favoured, but was it because of Al Maksour, "The Broken One"?

Other stories told of Al Maksour being forged by a group of jinn, crafted with all manner of spells in the deepest caves of the Sarmadees, fashioned with metal only a jinni could delve for. Somehow, the sword had been lost by the jinn and ended up belonging to his tribe. What Selim was sure of was that the sword was the cause of jealousy among some of the tribes of the region. They envied the blessings Al Maksour was believed to have given to his tribe. He could understand the jealousy, as life in the desert and mountain regions was harsh. The land was unforgiving, and tribes battled to survive.

As Selim neared the stables the mixed smells of fresh, green lucerne and manure turned his mind to his horses. The younger men had already been there to feed them and were grooming them as they finished their food. Other men were returning from the walls of the fort, putting away weapons and buckets used to put out the fires. They nodded as they passed Selim, and he nodded in return. The men of his tribe revered and respected Selim, despite his young age. They had honoured his father, Rasheed, whom they loved and many of them saw the same deep-thinking spirit in Selim. Rasheed had settled many arguments with wise words and a quiet expectation that matters were to be resolved among his people.

Selim didn't think he could ever be like his father. He felt awkward at times, leading men who were older than his father, and responsibility for the tribe did not sit lightly on him. However, he knew the tribe expected him to act as their leader and that they would follow him because he was their sheikh, knowing their survival was in his hands. It had always been the same and Selim could not and did not want to change this. He did, however, want to lead well and at the same time feel comfortable about it.

Selim called to one of the younger men coming out from a stable. "Go to the women and tell them not to go to the fields till they have been checked. I want to make sure there is no danger from the Al Bedi down there."

REJECTION

The boy picked up the bottom of his robe and ran to find the women as though jinn were chasing him. Selim smiled to himself. The attack had excited everyone. Even the dogs were still barking at noises in the fort and their hackles had not settled back into place. Selim made his way into the storeroom of bridles, halters and saddles. It smelt strongly of leather and oil as well as smoke. The smoke came from lanterns hanging from the rafters, which lit up the cave-like room. It was a room hewn from the rock, and it was cool and dark. Selim found the tack for Narji, the bay mare he was to take. As he was going out, three other men entered. Hijari, the smallest of the three, spoke to Selim.

"We'll join you in checking the fields. Ibrahim thought you might be going down there. He's sent for some others to join us as well. They're coming from the northern walls."

These were not young men. All were battle hardened and experienced. Selim would have picked these men to join him if Ibrahim hadn't.

"Excellent," said Selim, "it will make the job quicker. Take your bows and arrows as well as your spears, just in case the Al Bedi were only pretending to retreat. I think it's unlikely, but it's better to be prepared."

The three men gathered the tack for their horses and Selim made his way to Narji's stable. He found her searching through the straw to find the last stalks of lucerne. Her eyes and nostrils opened slightly at the sight of Selim, but she showed no fear. Her dark coat shone brightly, and Selim rubbed her head as he always did before putting a bridle on. He spoke soft words to her and as he did, her eyes started to close. Selim had no trouble putting the bit in her mouth and securing the bridle. Narji was eleven years old and she had covered many dusty tracks over those years. Selim led Narji out into the sunlight and saddled her, walking and trotting her around in circles as he waited for the other men to saddle their mounts. He led them all out of the fort, down the road toward the river and their farming land. As he spurred Narji into a canter, she lifted her head, her tail sprang up and her eyes brightened. She sucked in the morning air and her nostrils widened at the smell of fresh grass and lucerne. Reaching the boundary of the fields, Selim said to them, "Look for any damage the Al Bedi may have done. They could have filled in channels or destroyed formwork. Check the crops for they may have ridden over them. Anything you see, report it to me."

Selim trotted Narji around the edges of the millet field but couldn't see any damage and this confirmed his suspicions about the Al Bedi attack being a diversion to get hold of Al Maksour. The men soon returned and reported there to be no damage and he breathed a sigh of relief.

"What a way to start the day!" Selim said lightly to the others as they rode back.

Despite sounding casual, his mind was spinning with thoughts about Al Maksour. He needed to find out more about the sword.

CHAPTER 2

Climbing over the mountain, the sun's spreading rays enveloped everything in its path. First, the stonewalls of the fort, and then the fort square, slowly moving on to engulf the fountain in the centre of it. Finally, the light crept up on the sun-beaten doors of the old stable, creating sparkles on some of the blue and turquoise mosaics decorating the walls. These mosaics had felt the heat of a thousand times a thousand suns. The lustre of youth had worn off, yet here and there a tile rubbed by a jacket managed to catch the sun, throwing it back in a sparkling spike.

The mosaics told of ancient battle, the clash of strong steeds, of victory and death. Brave warriors and hunters sat on the most exquisite horses the sun had ever laid its rays upon. But now the sun reached beyond the pictures and pierced the dark and dust of the stables. Its light reached in and touched the soft, satiny coats of the horses. They shuffled in the straw and blew the dust from their nostrils, lifting their heads to greet the sun.

Elsewhere within the walls, dogs were opening an eye as they lay on the floor to see the stirrings of their masters. Women rekindled the grey coals in their fireplace and set about preparing the morning meal.

Selim was already striding down the well-trodden stone stairs from his family's home to check on the horses, however, he was never the first one to reach the stables. Ibrahim, the horse master, was already moving through the stables, removing straw from manes and forelocks, and rubbing a leathery hand over cannon bones and hooves to feel for any bruising or heat. Selim greeted Ibrahim and was rewarded with a wide smile, showing a mouthful of yellow, worn teeth. Around them, young men were finding grain and lucerne for the horses and gathering their brushes and combs for their morning's work.

Selim loved this part of the day. It was still cool and to look upon the horses framed in the stable doorways after a long night was like balm to sand-beaten eyes.

The horses were as exquisite as their ancestors in the mosaics and they were renowned throughout the entire region. They had been bred in his tribe for generations and were worth more than their weight in gold. They were the pure-bloods of the desert, the jewels of the region of Nejd. None could reach back into the ancient past to recall how men first touched these proud and independent animals or determine where they came from. There were stories about their origin and their taming by men, but who could ever know the truth?

Selim loved to hear these stories of old as he sat around the fire at night. As the storyteller of the tribe, Ibrahim would often spend the night retelling the stories he had heard as a boy, ones he had soaked in and locked away so many years before. When he was a boy, Selim had often crept wide-eyed out of bed to hear these stories being told. Over the years he had grown to believe that these horses were a living link to his ancestors and to the history of his tribe. His appreciation of these animals was not just due to their strength and beauty but also because of their historical link to the past. They were a part of the deeds of his dead ancestors, of losses and gains in power and prosperity.

Selim could never get enough of the stories of his tribe's history or spend too much time with his beloved horses. He drank in their smell in the fresh, morning air and feasted his eyes on the beauty reaching out over each stable door.

A lightly flea-bitten grey whinnied at him. "Yes, Aisha I know you are there, your turn will come," said Selim.

He turned to the first stable and unbolted the door. A chestnut stallion nuzzled him, searching for a handful of lucerne or grain. Selim rubbed him on the neck and straightened his mane. He pushed the stallion away to give him the opportunity to soak up the full picture. To Selim, this stallion was the closest to perfection his tribe's breeding had achieved. His name was Faraj.

Immediately, Selim's gaze was not drawn to Faraj's beautiful head, but rather to the lie of his shoulder. It was angled in such a way as to give the most pleasure and satisfaction to the onlooker, whether he was a mere technician of conformation or a hard-worn rider looking for both speed and comfort. Selim knew what sort of a shoulder a Nejd horse should have and Faraj's was exquisite. It tied in beautifully with strong high withers, and from it flowed a long, arched neck, curved beautifully at the poll. Two small ears which turned in toward each other at the top sat on his head. Faraj's head had now outgrown the immaturity of a colt. His face was slightly scooped between the forehead and the nose; so typical of the Nejd. His head, from muzzle to ear was short and his nostrils seemed to be made of silk. But it was his eyes that reflected his spirit. They were large and round, deep and black. They seemed to have the wisdom of creation in them, independence and arrogance, yet a willingness to learn to be loved and to love in return. In them was the soul of his ancestors and to Selim they were spellbinding.

Selim turned his attention to Faraj's front legs. He noted Faraj's circular hooves, his short cannon bone and large knee joints. Nodding in appreciation at the proportion of forearm to cannon bone, Selim knew there was strength and endurance in those straight legs. His eyes moved to Faraj's elbow. Succeeding generations had brought about an elbow which was ideally over half the length of the shoulder. It was beautifully angled, and Selim knew from seeing Faraj move that it was free to move with the leg. As the shoulder lifted the elbow swung easily and allowed the forearm to be carried forward as far as it could, giving both athletic ability as well as a longer stride. If Selim wanted anything, it was to see his horses have enough power in their shoulders to lift the front legs both up and forward. This, he knew, was how the Nejd horses were able to travel for days over sand and rocks.

Selim's eyes swept over Faraj's short, strong back and well-sprung barrel. Faraj was built to ride. There was no weakness in his back or loin and his strong back tied in tightly to a long, deep and well-balanced hindquarter. His hindquarters were balanced by the length and depth of his shoulder, and his hind legs were well angled, strong and hard with bones as dense as desert rock. They were well muscled in order to pull themselves out of the sand and the hard tendons were cut deeply into his legs. These qualities gave Faraj the power to move for hours over the sand and rocky plateaus.

But above all, Faraj was smooth. It was this that appealed so much to Selim and his tribe, as they were accustomed to having horses pleasing to their eyes in beauty as well as in proportion.

Selim called Faraj to him and rubbed his neck. Faraj responded gratefully and thrust his muzzle into Selim's hand, half hoping for the tidbit he didn't get when Selim entered. Faraj's coat shimmered in the soft morning sun, even though it had not yet had its morning brush. Selim lovingly swept his hands over it. Aisha, however, was not to be denied. Her call rang out again and Selim smiled. How she tried to have him be her servant, to scratch her when she was itchy, deliver food when she was hungry, and come to her when she felt bored. She could be a dominating mare, a demanding queen, but how he loved her.

Leaving Faraj's stable he greeted Aisha. Her head stretched out over the stable door as he approached, exposing her deep, round jowls and wide nostrils. Selim ran his hand over her flea-bitten grey coat. At five years old she had lost the blackness of her foal coat but not the liquid ebony of her eyes. They were the eyes of a soft, soulful and friendly mare, but there was also a spark of mischief in them. Her beauty was undeniable, but somehow it was her demanding, haughty attitude which reached out first. At times it could be annoying, but this attitude also gave Aisha an aura about her whenever she was let loose for exercise and play. She would trot around as though she commanded the world, snorting her frustration at not being let out earlier. She held her head and tail high as she stood out in a corner of the paddock. Her spirit also lent her a determination and a steely heart, which kept her racing over mountain slopes and deep drifting sand when many other horses were spent. Aisha was certainly ready to take her part in the hunt for gazelle today.

In search of food for his growling stomach, Selim began to make his way back toward the house. Inside him was a peace and contentment that almost rose out of the dust beneath his feet and the air within the walls. This feeling of belonging came from listening to the sounds of his horses and from smelling their aroma, from the clang of the silversmith, and from the smoke and noises rising from within the fort's walls. It was this atmosphere which hugged him closely and filled his heart with life.

Selim jogged back up the steps to his family's house, his soft, leather boots hardly making a sound as he moved into the dim interior of the house and into the living room. The morning meal was laid out and his mother, sister, and brothers were just beginning to eat. He greeted them cheerfully. Some returned it but others grunted, unhappy to be roused from the comfort of their bed. Selim smiled and dished himself up some of the sweet, steaming millet Ansim had made.

"Is the hunt still on today?" Jusef asked.

"Yes," replied Selim. "We still need more meat and skins."

"Great," said Jusef. "I can try out my new spear," he added.

From among the clang of spoons and knives on bowls and plates came the soft, pleading voice of Ansim. "Selim, can I go on the hunt too?"

Selim looked down into his food and shook his head slowly. "You have asked that question more times than I can count, Ansim. You know our customs. Females don't go on hunts, no matter how skilful they are."

Ansim dropped her head and her hair fell around her face covering her disappointment. She knew how hard it was to get any of the men to let her go on a hunt, let alone her own brother. Selim looked up at his mother, Almas, who reflected Ansim's disappointment but said nothing.

Selim had decided to take Aisha on the hunt, and she was eager. She was dancing on the spot and snorting, dust flying from her feet and from the other twenty or so horses around her. Selim took the reins from Aisha's young groom and spoke some soft words in her ears. "Aisha my darling, save yourself for the gazelle and the deep sand. Be still."

She reined in her enthusiasm and settled quickly so Selim could mount. However excited she became, Aisha knew the gentleness of the voice and hands of her master, and because of the love he had shown her since her birth she could not help but listen and obey.

The hunters made a noisy yet colourful charge through the gate and down the hill on which their fort stood. Brightly dyed cloaks whipped in the wind. Marking pennants on their spears and the mix of horse colours—black, grey, chestnut and bay—all added to the spectacle. They cantered down the road toward the fields and made their way up the other side of the valley. They were heading to the hunting grounds on the plateau in the mountains south of their valley. The mountain range was named the Sarmadees, the eternal ones. These mountains had endured countless days of sun and wind yet they had remained unchanged for as long as there was knowledge and memory of them.

Ibrahim led the band through the rugged tracks and soon the horses were beginning to sweat even though it was still early morning. Reaching the plateau, they slowed and halted just before the crest. Ibrahim dismounted and went ahead on foot, careful to keep his head low so as not to be seen by any prey grazing there. Carefully screening himself behind some shrubs, Ibrahim looked out onto the plateau. He could see the flicking white tails of the gazelle as their heads were down grazing. They hadn't noticed or caught his scent. Things looked good so far. He motioned to the others who readied their spears and bows and divided into two groups, one going to the right and the other to the left to wedge the gazelle between them. This strategy would give them a short opportunity to release their arrows and spears before the gazelle outpaced even their fast and eager horses.

Together they broke from their cover and showered the slope with stones and dirt. One of the men holding Ibrahim's horse swept past him and without slowing Ibrahim threw himself up into the saddle, grabbing the mane of his mare. He let out a whoop and charged toward the edges of the herd of gazelles. The young men on their first hunt wore both intensity and excitement on their faces, wanting to wait for the biggest gazelles they could find. Their horse's nostrils were wide as they quickly moved to full pace. They galloped after the spooked gazelle, enjoying the run and chase as much as their riders.

Many of the gazelle bounded in front of each other as wild horses came at them from both sides. On his bay colt, Jusef was straining hard, eyeing the large buck he had picked as his target. His spear was poised, and he was about to throw when the buck darted back sharply and came straight at the side of his horse, Rakkas. With deadly horns charging toward him, Rakkas' eyes opened widely in surprise. To his credit Rakkas didn't break stride. Jusef adjusted quickly and threw his spear at the buck. The spear flew between the curled horns, digging deeply into his back. The spear sliced nerves and tendons in its backbone and the buck's front legs crumpled, his head dropped toward the dust. His horns pierced the ground and stuck so tightly that the momentum catapulted his body over his head and he was flung heavily onto the ground. The fall broke the spear, leaving the buck lying with his legs pointing to the morning sky.

Jusef pulled hard on the reins and Rakkas circled quickly back to the buck. Jumping off, Jusef quickly regained his broken spear and thrust it into the ground. It stood there quivering while his personal pennant fluttered in the breeze

Meanwhile, the others raced past him, eager for their own trophy. Time was running short as the gazelle flattened out their bodies for full speed. Jalab, a nephew of Selim, had already pulled down a young gazelle. Wily Ibrahim had also placed an arrow into the front of a good-sized female, while Selim and Aisha were still trying. Selim had fired a number of arrows, but they had missed the fleeting gazelle. Already they were outpacing their hunters and

Selim realistically had only one more chance. He urged Aisha to extend herself further and readied his bow. A doe and her young were the last of the herd, straining to keep up with the others. Selim took what aim he could on his flying horse and loosed his arrow. As he did Aisha stumbled and threw Selim onto the front of the saddle and over her neck. He grappled to keep himself on as Aisha instinctively slowed. Pulling up, Selim saw through the dust that the doe and her young one were quickly disappearing into the rocks.

He swung Aisha around and cantered back to check what the final tally had been. He found the men readying four gazelle, three does and Jusef's prize buck. Selim jumped down to congratulate Jusef on his first impressive kill.

"Well done, Jusef. You and Rakkas make a great pair."

Jusef grinned widely in return, turning back to the younger men who were re-enacting their hunt and boasting of their skill, laughing and pointing as though they had killed a ferocious beast.

Ibrahim patted the back of one of the younger men. Atroub was still dusting his clothes from the fall he had taken when his horse Aamin (which means "to be kept safe") had knocked her foot on a large stone and fallen. Ibrahim called out to Selim with a grin, "Atroub has just been initiated into the hunting, men. He has eaten so much mountain dust he won't need to eat tonight."

The other men laughed and one added, "Maybe he should change his horse's name to Darthroo ("to stumble"). He might catch a gazelle by having his horse fall on it."

A pained look came onto Atroub's face, while loud laughter erupted from the others. They were in high spirits after the hunt and were satisfied with the kill. Atroub muttered to himself about the will of the gods and then went to check Aamin's legs. He found no damage, just dust. The river would clean off the dust, but nothing would prevent his friends joking about him for the next month at least.

Slinging the gazelle over their saddles, the men slowly began the trek back to the fort. Spurring Aisha on, Selim called out to Ibrahim, "I'll meet you back at the fort." Aisha moved to a canter as they headed west, deeper into the Sarmadee Ranges. Selim enjoyed the peacefulness of the mountains and being with Aisha. He came to a steep part of the mountain, strewn with boulders of irregular sizes. Leaving Aisha tethered there, he climbed the boulders and headed toward a cave opening about forty-five metres from where Aisha stood. The cave was cool but not particularly large. Sunlight played gently on the back wall and highlighted a stunning array of drawings. Selim drew in a deep breath, affected by the colour and life of the drawings. They were in stark contrast to what lay outside the cave.

There were drawings of animals, tall trees, dark green bushes, flowers, and an amazing amount of water—more water than he had ever seen at one time. There were also pictures of men, women and children sitting along the banks of the water. However, the strangest part of the picture was a rectangular box that appeared to be made of wood, which floated on the water. Selim could not understand what it was or what it did. He marvelled at the animals as he had never seen some of them alive. A herd of horses was shown galloping over the desert, but the desert had no yellow sand, only green, rich grass. The horses looked fat and sleek and fast and they carried their tails in the air, flagging their joy for all to see.

He recognised other things as well, certain trees, jackals, gazelle, and a spotted mountain cat. This reminded him of the skin of a spotted mountain cat that hung on the wall in his room. His great-grandfather had killed one with his spear many, many years ago. So much beauty and life had disappeared since then. Sand, so small, yet so plentiful had swallowed up the water and the grass, leaving it barren and dead.

Aisha's whinny suddenly cut through the air and echoed off the rocks. Looking down at her, Selim saw her prancing on the spot, neck and head held high, throwing up dirt and snorting with her tail curled up over her back. Something had frightened her. Selim called to reassure her and scrambled down the rocks towards her. He untied her and climbed into the empty saddle. Aisha danced and spun her way down the trail back to the road. She continued to whinny and Selim suspected there must be other horses nearby. As they neared the intersection of the track and the road, Selim began to hear the neigh of horses and the loud, deep call of camels. Making its way up the narrow road was a caravan of horses, camels and donkeys, and an array of colourfully clad people. Driving Aisha on, he galloped to the front of the caravan. Selim picked out their leader and a large man raised his hand and waved to him.

"Welcome Feluj. It's good to see you again," said Selim.

"Ah Selim, it's so good to see your face and to know we have pleasant company, a warm fire and fine food for a time," replied Feluj. "I have been wearing a hole in this camel saddle, but yes, I've looked forward to returning."

"You are most welcome and as always our place is yours," answered Selim. "We can't wait to hear what is happening in the rest of the world," he added.

"And I can't wait to tell you," Feluj replied with a wide grin.

Aisha was not particularly fond of camels and the strange smells of the caravan, and though held in tightly by Selim, she cantered very slowly, snorting and flicking her tail as if warning the camels to stay away. Loosening the reins, Selim waved to Feluj, signalling that he would speak with him back at the fort.

Aisha's powerful hindquarter pushed her back hooves deeply into the dirt and thrust her and Selim forward at an astonishing pace. In the space of a few seconds she was galloping at full speed toward the road up to the fort, eating up the ground in her swift strides. The staccato beat of her four feet was a sound Selim loved to hear as he rode balanced between Aisha's flying mane and bannered tail. Aisha was excited and slowing her down as they approached the river crossing was not easy. Using his voice and the reins, she began to respond and her speed lessened. Her nostrils and eyes were dilated, and she snorted in frustration. Jumping from her back, Selim led her toward the river.

At the sandy bank he removed her saddle and took her into the water. Aisha was always a little anxious about entering the river but once in she splashed her front feet up and down while Selim threw water on her back and neck, washing away the sweat and dust from the ride. Revived by the wash, they made their way slowly back to the fort.

The road the caravan had travelled in on wound through the fields and then rose upwards toward the fort. The fort sat on a large outcrop of rock, which was part of a spur running out from the Sarmadee mountains and deep into the river plain.

The fort was many hundreds of years old and new generations had gradually added onto the existing structures. Stone walls rose many metres above the rocks, ending in battlements, and small windows dotted the walls. Every fifty metres there were bastions built to house weapons and soldiers when they were needed. In the highest bastion above the main gate sat a lookout which was manned at all hours of the day and night.

Reaching the inside of the fort, Selim found the men busy at work skinning the gazelles. Handing Aisha's reins over to the stable boys who would groom her and put her back in her stable, he made his way home, knowing others would take care of settling Feluj and his caravan into their usual spot. He looked forward to hearing what was happening outside of the desert.

CHAPTER 3

The foal paddocks drew closer and Selim heard the chatter and laughter of children swinging on the fences as they tried to entice the fillies and colts to come over to them.

"Come on baby, come over. I've got some nice cake for you," one of them called.

Most of the foals and even a mother or two had their eyes on the children and stood intrigued but were less than confident to approach them. Selim called out to the children and they turned and waved. Running up some of them grabbed his arms and pulled him along. "Help us get the babies to come to us," one said. "You can lift us onto their backs," another told him.

"They're scared of little children," he said, laughing at them. "They'll buck you off faster than I can put you on," he added.

"No, they won't," said one boy confidently. "I'll stay on their backs forever!"

The others chimed in with their own objections but realising that they were unable to change Selim's mind, they soon returned to their spot on the fence. Selim made his way through to the horses. A dark chestnut colt poked its head and tail in the air and began to prance away. Selim smiled at his perkiness.

Most of the foals were a few months old now and had gained the confidence to go galloping far from their mothers. They came up close to Selim but not close enough for him to touch. Their little noses stretched out toward him,

REJECTION

sniffing, and their ears twisted and turned. Every now and then one would take off suddenly and run a lap of the paddock before rejoining the group. Others began to copy them and in no time at all they had all broken into a canter, stirring up the dust beneath their feet. The children who had ventured to the other side of the fence scampered to safety as the foals flew by.

As the group raced around the paddock, Selim noticed the bay colt of Bashasha leading the way, yet he didn't seem to be putting a great deal of effort into his running. Every now and then he put his head down and exploded in a burst of speed, quickly increasing the distance between him and the others. Selim hadn't seen the colt display this type of talent before and he locked it away in his memory. He reminded himself to talk to Ibrahim about the colt's display of speed.

"They're looking good, Selim. Probably the best your tribe has produced. The bay colt is a beauty!" Feluj called out from the fence.

"Feluj, I didn't see you come. You've set up camp then? Yes, this colt is one that Faraj has sired. His foals have better structure than their mothers, as well as more quality," replied Selim. "A little longer in the leg and powerful hindquarters as well as a large overstep," he added.

"He is doing well as a sire then! Will you still enter Faraj into the annual race at Al Huraydah?" said Feluj.

"Yes. We've decided he deserves to race. He's the fastest horse we have and the whole tribe wants to see him run and win," answered Selim.

"I wonder if you should. He'll be the envy of all the tribes once they see him and you don't want any harm to come to him," Feluj replied.

"Surely no-one would want to harm Faraj," said Selim with some indignation.

"It's a big race and the prize money is substantial," added Feluj. "Who knows what a tribe or person might do to make sure they win?"

"Yes, I suppose," replied Selim with some doubt.

"Are *you* riding him in the race?" asked Feluj.

"Absolutely!" said Selim. "We've been training him for months now. Just slowly though. We've been increasing the length and speed of his workouts and he's really enjoying it." He hesitated, and then added, "I don't think I've seen his best yet, so when the race comes and he is pushed by the other horses I think we'll see something spectacular from him."

"Well, I wish you all the best and may the gods protect you," said Feluj with solemnity.

"Come on Feluj. Don't be so serious. Let's go and eat."

The children had already wandered back home. After their run the foals were snuggling in for some milk and the mares could be seen picking up the last tidbits of lucerne from the ground, snorting the dust out of their nostrils.

Darkness was gathering around as they made their way back to the central court of the fort. The sound of lively music and the laughter of men drifted towards them as they walked in the direction of a large fire. They smiled at the children chasing each other and joined the other men sitting around the fire. Loud laughing caused by the retelling of Atroub's fall faded away as Ibrahim clapped his hands. Immediately the music stopped, and the group grew quiet. In anticipation, the older children ran and sat down with their parents. Ibrahim stood, spread his hands theatrically and cleared his throat.

"In the time of the giants, many, many generations ago, the jinn of the Sarmadees gathered together to join their power. They met by the side of the large river Nadji. It was lush and fertile, and the jinn lacked nothing. There were many caves nearby where they could sleep or hide if men came by.

Remember my people, the Creator does not allow jinn to have relations with men who can overpower and capture them. They usually avoid us except when they believe they have a new way to bring us harm."

All eyes were now on Ibrahim. "This meeting of the jinn was not a common event as jinn were selfish beings not given to sharing things, especially power. Yet the one thing they had in common was a dislike for mankind. They wanted to turn their combined power against men. Having a hatred for men, they wanted to create a creature who would be a burr in their sandals or a thorn in their saddles, a dangerous creature. For many days and nights, they debated about what they would create. They finally decided to take the character and strength of the Sarmadees and blend it with the spirit of the south wind, which was fickle and taunting but rarely damaging, and then give their creature a twisted and unstable mind.

It was thus that the first mare of creation was to be born, the mother of all horses. She was to be born on the slopes of the Sarmadees when the moon was white and full. The jinn were to name her "Al Hadiyeh," the Gift, and she was to be presented to humans from creation.

In their craftiness the jinn took the mountain rock and shaped it into four hard hooves. They used the strength and density of the horns of the mountain aurochs to form the bones of the mother of all horses, giving them a shape both pleasing and powerful. To the bones they added muscles of both speed and endurance. The softness of the down of a young ostrich was added to the forelock, mane and tail. The jinn then clothed the mare with skin made of desert moonlight and sprinkled it with soft, short hair which glistened like purified silver in the sun. They added eyes as dark and as deep as the mountain caves and below them gave her nostrils as soft as the petals of a desert flower.

As the jinn were readying themselves to give life to the mind of Al Hadiyeh and to twist it into hatred and anger toward men, the Creator appeared. The jinn drew back in fear and some even fled at his presence as the Creator was immensely powerful. He was a spirit who could not be challenged and his very presence demanded awe. His voice was soft, yet it held immense authority. He scolded the jinn for their intentions, telling them they were going too far in their hatred of men. And he stopped them from going on with their plans.

However, the Creator was left with the lifeless form of the mare. He did not want to leave her cold and spiritless on the mountainside. So at dawn of the determined day of birthing, he caused a part of the west wind to blow. He commanded it to give of its spirit and grant her its speed. He also willed that her tail be touched so she carried it like an oasis palm pointing skyward, singing the praises of the Creator. Last of all, he willed the west wind to fill her mind with a mixture of the fear of man and an ability to trust and love him with every quivering fibre. Then, as the sun rose in the east, the west wind opened her nostrils and blew into her lungs, giving her life. She rose from the cold stone and shook herself. The morning sun glittered on her coat. Slowly she looked around, drawing great draughts of air in to fill her lungs and to give life to her blood. She stamped her feet and pawed at the mountain rock. Life was now throbbing through her veins and she was impatient to be off. She lifted her head and her first loud cry rang out across the Sarmadees, heralding her presence. Even the Creator was surprised at the beauty and wonder of this creature. How could the jinn have formed such a being? Seeing her as he did, he realised both predator and man would desire her. He could not let her loose into the world without some protection, some wit and understanding. The Creator placed his hand over Al Hadiyeh's forehead. As he pulled his hand away the jinn stepped back in awe and horror. Within the eyes of Al Hadiyeh appeared a depth of wisdom they knew only lived within the Creator. Some of the jinn screwed their fists in frustration as they saw their creature turned into something even more beguiling and beautiful than they had imagined, but lacking the hatred and twistedness of their own hearts.

Finally, at the nod of the Creator, Al Hadiyeh sprang from the slopes of the Sarmadees and away from the clutches of the jinn. Her nostrils flared in the morning air. Her tail sprang up straight, her whinny echoed off the walls of the mountains and her legs stretched out, barely touching the rocks. The sun, moon, stars, animals and trees felt her life, saw her beauty and praised the Creator.

The jinn danced around violently as the Creator returned to his throne, for they had been robbed of a creature they had worked so hard to create and who promised much harm to mankind. With their power depleted by the Creator and their hearts filled with a mix of fear and anger, the jinn had no choice but to go their own way as their "gift" to mankind flew on ivory legs down the mountainside.

REJECTION

For some time Al Hadiyeh was unseen by men, but she did not go unnoticed by the Creator. He saw that every other animal he had created had a mate and so decided to bless Al Hadiyeh with one also. The Creator was drawn to the beauty and spirit of this mare and the strange, yet clever, choices of the jinn when moulding her and decided to create a mate in her likeness. The Creator, like the jinn, gathered the strength and majesty of the Sarmadees and wove this with the ivory-like horns of the aurochs and the life of the west wind. But before the Creator brought him to life, he thought for a time to himself. He then took the regal arrogance from the lion and placed some of it into the creature's forelock. The lion may be a king, thought the Creator, but there was room in the world for another.

On a balmy, summer evening the Creator presented Al Hadiyeh with a mate named Narimah. He was a bay stallion with three white socks sitting just above his fetlocks. His mane and tail were even more luxuriant than Al Hadiyeh's and Narimah knew just how splendid he looked. He pranced up to Al Hadiyeh with eyes sparkling and on legs barely touching the ground. There was a swagger to his movement and pride in his arched neck and as he drank in the feminine fragrance of the white mare his nostrils fluttered. To gaze upon this dark, proud, sultry stallion was to be drawn into his presence and power. However, Al Hadiyeh was not made from the strength of the mountains and the aurochs to be overcome at the sight of another who seemed so intent on controlling her, especially one who was so arrogant. She trotted up to Al Hadiyeh to show she was not intimidated and with necks arched and nostrils blowing, they made their acquaintance. As Narimah's excitement grew, Al Hadiyeh spun on her haunches and raced swiftly down the valley. Narimah was caught by surprise but quickly realised he needed to chase this mare who smelled so delicious and as he was finding out wouldn't bow easily to him. Many animals saw them together and were amazed at their symmetry and beauty and creation nodded knowingly at the presence of another king on the earth.

Time passed and the love between Narimah and Al Hadiyeh grew. When the hot south wind began to blow Al Hadiyeh bore a filly who was bay like her sire but had the gossamer beauty of her dam. She was mischievous and bold. They named her Farah, as she gave such happiness. As she grew she began to wander further from her parents, as foals are led to do, looking for juicier grass. One day she wandered far away and climbed onto a hillside, unaware of the danger that was already present. As desired by the jinn, a hunter had spotted her and was won by her young beauty, and he crept closer to see more. The filly slowly made her way back down the valley to where her parents were grazing, unaware that the hunter was following.

Nimrod the hunter was wily and clever and as he followed her tracks back to the valley he was careful not to be seen or smelt. He stood in awe as he gazed upon the grey, Al Hadiyeh, and the bay stallion, Narimah. They had the maturity and elegance that the filly didn't yet have. He could already imagine the stir he would create throughout the region if he led such a prize into camp. Nimrod was well-renowned for his hunting skills, but this catch would have generations remembering him.

Nimrod crept closer and looked up at the animals before him. He thought they were probably quite slow and clumsy. So with an outstretched hand, he sprang out of the bushes towards Al Hadiyeh but with the speed of lightning she powerfully broke away, showering him with dirt and clods of grass. At the sight of Nimrod, Narimah and Farah lifted their heads and tails to the sky and flew down the valley behind her.

Unable to move, Nimrod stared after these strange creatures. He knew he would never be able to capture these horses alone, so he made his way back to camp, spreading the story of these surprising animals. And so, Al Hadiyeh the first horse, her mate Narimah and their beautiful filly Farah, came to be known among men. Their beauty and grace travelled from fireplace to fireplace and men marvelled at this new creature."

Ibrahim clasped his hands, folded his cloak around himself and sat down. His eyes twinkled, knowing he had held his people spellbound. The children stared wide-eyed into the fire, their minds overflowing with the images of horses racing down into the valley, their manes and tails streaming behind. In their hearts they gave a short laugh at the shock they imagined on Nimrod's face. Slowly, quiet talk started to fill the air. Some around the fire began to speak of the fabled Al Hadiyeh, others of seeing her qualities in their own horses. Meanwhile, the little children closed their drooping eyes and curled up in their mothers' laps. As the fire crackled on and sparks rose to the moon, the women and children moved off for the night, leaving the men to talk.

Selim breathed freely, his responsibilities far from him. He delighted that this was his home and these were his people.

CHAPTER 4

Faraj fought the bit, wanting to run and enjoy the exhilaration. Selim remained calm and held him tightly. The race they were training for was not a sprint and it would take many kilometres of steady training to build the toughness in his muscles that was needed. Ibrahim had warmed Faraj up lightly, his muscles rippling in the morning sun, and like threads of gold his coat reflected the sunlight brilliantly. The gold coat now started to darken with sweat even though Faraj's stride was long and easy.

Selim could feel the muscles, sinews and bone working together to bring smoothness and strength to the movement of Faraj. Each time he swung onto the back of Faraj and settled into the saddle he found a different world. He found himself coupled to a power which was larger than him and yet one he was able to master. With a light touch of the reins or slight pressure on Faraj's side, the power surged under him in any direction he wanted.

Selim urged Faraj to a slow canter and Faraj, always alert to the mind of Selim, collected himself, snorting and dropping his head lightly as he did so. They moved onto the river plain past the fields and followed the road the caravan had come along. The road was flat and worn, and safe for a sustained canter. Faraj started to blow with each stride but kept up the collected pace asked of him. The pace was slow and rhythmic and built up his lungs, muscles and heart. Selim rocked gently in the saddle as the tendons of Faraj's legs and shoulders stretched with the pressure of their combined weight, taking the shock of Faraj's contact with the ground.

The track snaked along the path of the river and they travelled for some miles at a canter before Selim slowed Faraj to a fast trot. Faraj had begun to sweat but his breathing was still easy and unstrained. Faraj's ears were still pricked and he was ready to go further. Selim smiled as he sensed Faraj's eagerness and it made him love Faraj even more. This was a horse who loved life, who was alert to everything around him, yet so sensitive to his rider and so eager to please. Often, Selim found Faraj could read his mind, doing what he had only just thought of himself. This showed that Faraj was not just a well-built athlete but a thinking stallion who acted not only because of instinct or fear, but also out of intelligence and love. Again, Selim's thoughts strayed to the origin and ancestors of his tribe's horses. For them to be so gentle and clever, yet marked with strength and size, amazed him. His thoughts ran quickly over Ibrahim's recent story and wondered how true it might be, for the same spark of wisdom seemed to live in Faraj as it did in Al Hadiyeh.

Darting out, a desert fox with large ears appeared on the path in front of them, before shooting off down the track. In a burst of exuberance, Selim called out, pushing Faraj into a gallop to try and run it down. Faraj quickly gathered himself and in less than two strides was galloping eagerly after the fox. Although it was a hopeless effort Selim enjoyed the competition just the same, knowing Faraj would enjoy running like the wind, whether there was fox or not. After its blind flight down the track the fox finally gathered its wits, cut off the track and disappeared amongst some rocks. Faraj kept going and Selim let him have his head. As the track turned to sand Selim slowly pulled him back and while resistant at first Faraj shortened his strides, eventually coming back to a slow trot. Selim pulled him up and turned him around to head for home.

Faraj was sweating heavily now, his neck and flanks soaked with foaming sweat, darkening the golden colour of his coat to a rich brown. Selim let Faraj walk and trot back towards the fort. As they neared it, Selim could hear shouting and the sounds of horses, and as he swept down into the river plain he met a group of riders coming up the hill. A number of them were riders from his tribe, but others were from the caravan. In a cloud of dust they came upon Selim and before anything was said they spun their horses around and urged them to a gallop. Selim and Faraj became swept up in the frenzy and before Selim knew it they were in the middle of the group, galloping along with them. Selim tried to pull Faraj to a walk but Faraj fought him. He was caught up in the excitement, and wasn't going to miss out on the fun. Dust, tails, manes and cloaks flew into the air.

Faraj easily kept up with the other horses and despite his recent work was keen to overtake them. He surged ahead as the reins slipped a little in Selim's sweaty hands. His nostrils flared and his stride increased but as he did so something triggered in Selim's mind. Out of the corner of his eye, he caught sight of the faces which had turned to look at him. While some were the faces of his own people, the ones nearest to him were those of the men and boys from the caravan. They wore a look of intent and purpose which went beyond the joy of a race. He could see them examining Faraj, looking at his stride, his movement and condition. He suddenly realised he had been tricked. How foolish of him! To show these men the quality of Faraj and to give them the ability to sum him up before the race was a mistake. He knew they would travel to the tribes of the cities and desert, carrying on their tongues about the power and endurance of Faraj, as well as what they thought were his weaknesses.

Selim pulled hard on Faraj to slow him down. He was annoyed at getting caught up in the gallop and pulled on the reins harder than he normally would. Despite this, Faraj was taken up by the mass of horses and it was difficult to slow him down. Eventually, Selim pulled him to the side and veered off toward the fields. He slapped his thigh in anger and shook his head in disappointment. Faraj neighed frantically to the other horses in response, jogging on the spot in eagerness but soon dropped his head and gave in to the voice and persistence of Selim. His eyes and ears were alert, switching between the disappearing horses and his rider. Although Faraj was pulling at the bit, Selim managed to keep him walking towards the fort. Faraj was slick and foamy with sweat and needed to be cooled. As Selim and Faraj entered the fort Ibrahim came forward to hold Faraj so Selim could dismount. Ibrahim raised his eyebrows. He could sense the excitement of Faraj as well as the angry mood of Selim. Selim loosened the girth, swept the saddle off Faraj and left him with Ibrahim. After removing Faraj's bridle and replacing it with a halter, Ibrahim walked Faraj down to the river for a wash, checking him carefully for any cuts or swelling. Ibrahim bathed his legs carefully in the cool, clear water of the river before returning him to his stable.

The milky moon was rising as Ibrahim made his way through the gardens to check the stabled horses before dinner. The scent of jasmine was heavy in the warm night air. A few voices could be heard in the distance and there was the occasional snort, as a horse cleared the dust from its nostrils and shuffled through the straw.

Ibrahim quietly waited for Selim to return. Since he was a boy, Selim had been courteous and kind but like a lot of young men needed the time and freedom to say what was on his heart.

Selim had no problems saying what he felt now and blurted out to Ibrahim, "I was so foolish. I fell into their game, their trap. I didn't think about what might be going on," as he hit the stable wall and then hung his head.

Knowing how intense Selim could be, Ibrahim said gently, "Tell me, what actually happened?"

"They caught me by surprise. They made Faraj run with them. I didn't know who some of them were and they kept looking at Faraj. They wanted to know what he was like, how fast he was," Selim answered, "And now they know," he added more slowly.

"But surely Faraj didn't go as fast as he could. He would have stayed with the other horses," Ibrahim replied.

"Yes, but he did put on some speed at one point," answered Selim. "I've let you and everyone down."

"Maybe, but I forgive you," said Ibrahim.

Selim's face rose in surprise at those words. He looked up at Ibrahim and then turned his face away, nearly spitting out his words. "I've ruined our chances and the tribe's. My stupidity. How could I have been so stupid? Faraj could have been hurt."

"Yet," said Ibrahim, "and yet I forgive you. Can you forgive yourself?"

Selim's shoulders sagged and his face relaxed.

Ibrahim reached out and laid his hand on Selim's shoulder. "Is anyone accusing you? Is anyone angry with you? Has anyone said anything to you?"

Selim shook his head.

"Then how can you be so hard on yourself? The harm you've done to the tribe or to Faraj's chances are like windblown sand, but the harm you do to yourself when you don't forgive yourself is like the poison of the rock snake. It will shrivel you up inside, until you become like a thorny cactus."

Selim hung his head low, then raised it up again to meet Ibrahim's gaze. "You're right. Thank you, Ibrahim."

"Tomorrow we will ride slowly for many miles to build up Faraj's stamina," said Ibrahim.

"Go and eat, then sleep… and be at peace," were Ibrahim's last words as Selim left him.

Ibrahim remained where he was, bathed in moonlight and the jasmine scent. He knew how much gold, silver, livestock and wares were wagered on the outcome of the race and that men from all tribes lost and won large amounts. They would need to take greater care of Faraj and his rider. If news of Faraj's ability became widespread they could become a target for those who would stop at nothing to win the race, or to make sure a bet was won.

"Be quiet!" said Selim to his growling stomach. It was nearly time for dinner with Feluj. They would all hear news from the outside world.

As dinner neared an end, the men moved out to the central square of the fort where a blazing fire had been set. The crackling of the fire and an excited chatter met the men as they made their way there. Many families from the caravan had gathered themselves around the fire, making new friends or renewing old acquaintances.

After letting his meal settle and taking his share of the rich, dark coffee, Ibrahim rose from the ground and called for quiet. After the attempt to steal Al Maksour and with so much talk going on about the sword, he thought a story about it would be fitting. He knew that the people from the caravan would spread the story of the Al Bedi's attempt throughout the desert and sea areas and increase the fame of Al Maksour. His lined and darkened face reflected the firelight as he pulled his cloak around him and began.

"In the lost ages of time, Al Maksour was not the Broken One. It was healthy and vibrant and was wielded by the strong arm of its owner, Arpaxchad. Used in battle and hunting, its balance and strength seemed to give it a life of its own. Together the two became known as formidable opponents. They were the objects of envy and jealousy throughout the land.

It was at this time that the giant bison roamed the earth. Arpaxchad regularly led his tribe in the hunting of these creatures who were large and powerful. The bison would defend themselves if attacked yet gallop for miles making huge plumes of dust across the sky if they were ever seized by panic and fear. The largest bison Arpaxchad had seen was nearly three metres tall at the shoulder. A single bison of this size was able to feed their entire tribe for a month.

There was one hunt that proved the power and ability of both Arpaxchad and Al Maksour. His group of hunters had crept up on a small band of bison which included a number of their young. Both the mothers and the males were particularly uneasy, as they knew the young calves were easy prey for hungry cats and wolves. One bull in particular was very agitated. He was snorting and throwing his head around, pawing at the dirt and turning in circles. His eyes roamed the longer grass and bushes where Arpaxchad and the other men were crouching. They were downwind so they could not be smelt, yet the bull remained nervous and agitated.

One of Arpaxchad's tribesmen pulled on his sleeve.

"Look, Arpaxchad," he whispered. "There is the tip of a spear stuck in his shoulder. It looks like it has been there some time. It must be painful."

Arpaxchad focused his eyes on the bull's shoulder and sure enough he could make out a dark patch of dried blood. On the bull's matted and shaggy coat he could see a spearhead moving around with the bull.

"Chadden, you've got eagle eyes. I didn't see it. Well done."

Chadden's heart lifted as he heard the words of this great hunter and a smile of thanks and pride touched his lips.

"Tell the others so they are aware," Arpaxchad added, and quietly Chadden moved away.

Arpaxchad motioned to three others with him who were each to lead a band of men and complete the trap. He quietly directed each man and informed them he and his group would occupy the attention of the large injured male as they made their attack. It was a familiar dance for Arpaxchad and if he was given a chance he would bring the bull to the end of its life.

As soon as he and his men heard the signal from the others they broke into the clearing. The bull immediately swung its head towards Arpaxchad and his men and began snorting and pawing the earth. The men fanned out to confuse the bull. However, it was in no mood to be put off. The pain of the infected wound and the memory of a man causing the pain blocked any restraint or fear. His small, beady eyes fell on one of the younger men and immediately the bull threw his head down, and with his long, curved horns aimed at the man he started to charge. The speed of the bull was too frightening for the inexperienced man, and at the sight of the angry bull rushing towards him he turned and bolted into the cover of the bushes and grass, hoping to hide. The bull kept after him, gouging a track through the grass and bushes. But in his anger he lost sight of the man and trotted back to the clearing.

His anger unquenched, the bull locked his gaze on Arpaxchad. Arpaxchad had pulled Al Maksour out of its scabbard and was gripping it tightly. The dance had begun. The bull launched into a powerful canter toward Arpaxchad and the ground between the two shrank rapidly.

REJECTION

Time moved slowly as Arpaxchad came face-to-face with the bull. Al Maksour seemed to move by itself and lifted his arm into the air. Arpaxchad instinctively moved his weight behind the swing and as the bull came near he stepped to the side. Faster than Arpaxchad was able, Al Maksour swung down toward the passing bull, dragging Arpaxchad's arm and body into the swing. Al Maksour bit deeply into the neck of the bull and it roared with anger and pain. Its momentum kept it going beyond Arpaxchad but it soon turned and digging its hooves into the ground it began another charge. Arpaxchad turned around to meet the bull and Al Maksour guided his arm. Again, Arpaxchad sidestepped the roaring bull and as he did Al Maksour moved swiftly past his hip, slicing smoothly into the side of the bull. Al Maksour passed through the rib cage of the beast and dug deeply into its large pumping heart, the bull's momentum ripping the sword from Arpaxchad's hand. At the last beat of its heart the bull's front feet sagged, and his nose and face dropped to the ground, grinding a yawning furrow into the dry dirt. His huge body followed and for some metres the carcass ploughed across the ground, adding to the dust of the fight.

Unaware of the cheering of his men, Arpaxchad stood there in amazement. Al Maksour had acted without him before but never against such an awesome opponent or with such precision.

Together the men gathered around the giant bull and as Arpaxchad pulled out the sword and held it up to the sky he joined the others in their victory cries. Arpaxchad and Al Maksour grew in reputation and favour within the tribe, but soon other tribes and nations came to hear of their bravery, ability and power. Some tried to buy Al Maksour and others plotted to steal it, so the sword became more precious and important, and more loved by Arpaxchad and his tribe."

Those from the caravan who had sat entranced as the story unfolded now turned to grin at the tribe's people and exclaim at the wonder of the story and the good fortune of the tribe. Ibrahim sat down slowly, a wry grin on his face. The reputation of Al Maksour, as well as that of the tribe, had just grown and would continue to in places near and far as the story was retold over and over.

CHAPTER 5

As the caravan wove its way brightly along the mountain road, Ibrahim and Selim stood on the fort wall. Pleased with the latest cloth and the exotic goods brought to them from the ports on the coast, the women there waved happily to the departing caravan. Feluj had not been as happy when he left as on his arrival. This unhappiness was due to what he considered "the stubbornness of the inland people." He had complained to Selim about the women of his tribe who he thought "could haggle a goat out of its beard." Selim had only slapped him on the back and smiled, knowing the wily Feluj hadn't lost out on his trading over the last few days. If anything, the tribe had come off second best. The two men remained on the wall for some time, making sure no-one was left behind as a spy to watch Selim and Faraj.

As they made their way to the foal paddocks, Selim excitedly described the young colt he had seen earlier. Standing tall among the other foals, the colt could easily be picked out. He swung his head toward Ibrahim and Selim, catching their movement. A few of the foals nickered to them thinking they were bringing more sweet green grass. As Selim and Ibrahim walked among the foals, they judged the young colt's conformation and his eyes. The body gave an indication of the strength and endurance of the horse, but it was the eyes which reflected their nature and spirit. Ibrahim nodded to himself as he recognised the soft, liquid eyes and the hint of wisdom Selim had mentioned. The colt was to be a deep, dark bay, very much like his dam's sire.

"He's as you described Selim," said Ibrahim. "Both refined and yet so strong." Selim was pleased Ibrahim agreed with his assessment of the colt.

"He's got balance in his body, spring in his step and he seems to do everything with ease and power," replied Selim. "I can't wait for him to grow up so I can ride him. I'm sure he'll be like Faraj. He may even have more power."

"His shoulders and pasterns have the perfect angle to them, and I can see he would be both comfortable to ride and fast. His coupling is strong, and his hip is long," replied Ibrahim.

Ibrahim managed to hold the head of the colt and felt between his jawbones. "There is room for growth but there is certainly already good width here for his windpipe," said Ibrahim.

"Yes, and look at the skin of his nostrils. It's so soft and flexible. Those nostrils will double in size when he is running," exclaimed Selim. He could hardly contain his excitement as he looked more closely at the colt.

"He has good sized hooves, a highset neck and long legs, while keeping the deep chest and barrel. His ears are alert, and his eyes are set low in his head. Yes, there's much here we have been breeding for," said Ibrahim, with growing admiration.

Ibrahim quickly moved back from the colt and signalled to a boy whom he had called to accompany them.

"Run them Seetha. They need the wind to fill their lungs," called out Ibrahim.

Picking up two dry sticks, Seetha started knocking them together and ran toward the foals. The foals' tails and heads immediately lifted, and they sprang away from the strange noise. With dust rising behind them, they flew around the paddock. Already the bay colt had reached the lead while the other foals strained behind him. Ibrahim and Selim noticed the reach of his hind legs underneath his body and the length of his stride. What struck them the most was the ease with which he could reach and maintain his speed. Every now and then as they flew around the paddock he would put on a burst of speed and leave the other foals even further behind. He was a sight to behold and both Selim and Ibrahim thought about what the colt might do given time and training and food. This was a special colt indeed! Their hearts expanded as they imagined him racing against the best of the other tribes' horses and easily beating them as he was now with the other foals.

"My hopes for Faraj have been exceeded and Bashasha has produced her finest child," cried out Ibrahim. "Blessings upon her and her womb for what she has produced. She is a mare of mares and I will tell her story to the tribe so she will not be forgotten."

The foals began to slow and a number of them were trotting with the prance of a gazelle, bouncing off each leg as though on springs. Their eyes were bright and alive, their nostrils wide and their tails flicked, pointing upward, showing their readiness to take off again at the slightest suggestion. Some came to a stop and snorted at Seetha, wondering what he was going to do next. Their dams looked over with a knowing look in their eyes, remembering their flight around the yards when they were fillies.

Ibrahim and Selim left Seetha holding out bits of lucerne to the foals trying to gain their forgiveness. Selim smiled knowing they were more curious than fearful and that Seetha would soon be stroking their necks.

"We should repeat this breeding," said Selim.

"Yes," replied Ibrahim, "but Bashasha doesn't have many foals left in her. Let's pray for a filly who is the same quality as this colt."

"What will we name this one?" asked Selim.

"Good question Selim. A colt of this ability will need a special name," replied Ibrahim.

"Do you have any ideas? You were the one that noticed this colt, so maybe you should name him. I haven't given a name any thought, but I will," Selim replied.

The men parted company as Selim needed to keep working on his own fitness. He wanted to be as fit as he could to train Faraj and for the race itself, which was known to be gruelling. Daily he worked on his swordsmanship as well as his accuracy with the bow.

Selim practiced with Sekeen, the best swordsmen of the tribe, who trained all the young men in the use of the sword. Sekeen was a nickname, meaning Dagger, as he had swift hands and threw daggers almost faster than the eye could see. He was known to have knifed rats as they ran along the bottom of the walls. The young boys of the tribe were both afraid of Sekeen as well as in awe of him.

When Selim arrived he saw Sekeen warming up. His sword swished back and forth through the air. The concentration in his face made him appear frightening to anyone who didn't know him, but Selim knew he was a humorous man who often joked and who was gentle with his wife and children. The focus on his face showed his dedication and Selim knew from his own experience how much Sekeen extended him in his swordsmanship. Sekeen took the training of the young men very seriously as he knew they were the ones who would protect the fort and the families and livestock they all treasured so much.

Selim took off his outer clothing and pulled his sword out of its sheath. The sword he used had been his father's, passed on to him when his father died some years before, one moulded and crafted by the artisans of the tribe. A lot of the metal their craftsmen worked on was mined from the Sarmadees, with only some bought from traders. The red-tinged metal from the Sarmadees was not only easier to work with, it also ended up harder and more durable. However, it was not easily found and the tribe tended to keep it for their own use. Selim's sword had a well-balanced blade and a feeling of lightness, and the handle felt just right in Selim's hand. As a child he used to hold the sword when his father was sharpening it and dreamed of the day when he could swing it easily.

Selim began to warm up, swinging his sword and stepping forward and back. As his muscles relaxed he gradually increased his speed and soon he was lost in the rhythm of his movements, his sword flashing before his eyes.

"Selim, come. Let's fight before you wear yourself out," Sekeen called.

Both Sekeen and Selim moved toward each other, standing with legs spaced out and sword in front. They bowed their heads to each other, then both bodies became rigid and supple at the same time as they moved to their highest level of alertness, gauging where each was going to attack. Selim attacked first, trying to swing and thrust the way Sekeen had taught him only recently. Sekeen called out to Selim as he parried the attack, "Selim, you've got to use your imagination. Be creative. Don't do what your enemy expects!"

Selim was both embarrassed and angered by his comments and his face tightened as he attacked again. This time he struck low and then high, then low again. It caught Sekeen by surprise and he had to hurry his strokes to block Selim's attacks. Selim was encouraged by this and pushed even harder, forcing Sekeen back as his strokes increased in speed and fluency. Sekeen regained his composure at the end of Selim's flurry of strokes and with genuine respect in his voice said, "Selim, that was some of the best stroke play I have seen in this fort. You're really putting together a strong series of strokes. But, don't fight in anger. When you do, you give control to your enemy. A mind angered is a mind narrowed, and this is dangerous, not for the enemy but for its owner."

"You're right," said Selim, nodding his head in response. He took a deep breath and cleared his mind, and again he took his stance. He and Sekeen continued and Selim called on his training and the various strokes he had learned and pieced them together in varying sequences, learning from each sequence what was effective and what wasn't.

"I don't know where some of those strokes came from, Selim," said Sekeen as they ended their sparring for the day. "It's like all the separate parts we have worked on over the years have suddenly joined up into one."

"You have taught me well, O Master," Selim replied with a grin on his face. Sekeen picked up his towel and threw it at him.

Selim walked down to the river to wash off the sweat and dust. He drank deeply from the water and its coolness made him turn his eyes to the mountains from which it came. The Sarmadees towered around the river valley and

REJECTION

Selim was reminded of just how protected, yet isolated, they were because of these impressive mountains.

The following weeks became a blur of training and riding. Selim talked often with Ibrahim about the route of the race and how he would approach it. He knew the race would be complicated by having other riders around him who were all as intent on winning as he was. Selim believed Faraj had the stamina and strength, and only hoped he would be able to cope with the distraction of the other horses and listen to his rider. This was something he discussed with Ibrahim and the other experienced riders of the tribe. He and Ibrahim also spent nights with their craftsmen, building, cleaning and preparing the saddle and bridle to be used on Faraj. They had measured Faraj carefully over the last few months to make sure the girth and saddle fitted well and wasn't going to give pain or discomfort.

Each morning as he prepared Faraj for training he could see the muscles rippling and growing. Faraj's coat began to take on the sheen of burnished bronze as the sweat of each ride soaked into it and the mountain water washed it off. The special diet he was fed worked its way into his system, filling him with vibrancy and life, right to the tip of his hairs. Ibrahim took on the job of brushing Faraj, massaging the black skin and drawing the oils from it into the coat. Ibrahim didn't miss an inch of Faraj's body, and his bony hands worked carefully and gently each morning preparing Faraj to be at his best for the race. He spoke softly to Faraj as his hands worked his body. The stallion stood perfectly still, and his eyes glazed over as the hands worked on knotted muscles. The trust the horses developed in their owners was a thing to behold. The tenderness and care the men showed to the horses from the time they were born drew these sensitive, fearful creatures into the loving hold of the tribe and with each generation the bond between man and creature developed.

For Ibrahim and the tribe, the horses had come to mean their life. They needed family and food and the strength their tribe gave, but their horses had been with them for so long they couldn't think of life without them—the warmth of their bodies, the smell of their coat, the softness of their manes, the quiet neigh of welcome and the look of total trust in their liquid eyes. Not only did they provide some sense of contentment, but they were their means for hunting, transport and prosperity. Buyers of their horses paid enormous amounts, increasing the income of the tribe and allowing them the luxuries sold by the caravan merchants. Ibrahim smiled to himself as he worked, remembering the words of his great-grandfather who had once said, "The world rests on the back of our stallions and mares." Truly, for the tribe, their world rested on these powerful, intriguing, demanding, yet giving animals.

Ibrahim gave Faraj's tail a final farewell wipe and closed the stable door quietly. The rising of the moon reminded Ibrahim that tomorrow was the day. They were to leave in the morning for the city of Al Huraydah. Ibrahim made his way up to the battlements to check the soldiers on duty. They greeted him happily and reported there was no movement as far as the eye could see. Ibrahim thanked them and nodded, knowing, so far, they were safe. He only hoped it would be true for the days to come.

Sleep did not come easily to Selim nor to Ibrahim that night. Both lay awake and pondered the days to come and all the things that could go wrong… and right. Faraj slept soundly in his straw, blissfully unaware of what the next sunrise was to bring.

CHAPTER 6

The dogs sensed the excitement and expectation and were awake early as the men and women strapped bags and utensils to the horses. Many of the tribe were making the trip to Al Huraydah to watch the race and cheer on Faraj. Families were chosen on a rotational basis and over a few years every family was able to enjoy the trip and watch the race. Carts for the women and children were loaded and horses saddled and soon the tribe was on its way. The pace was slow, but they had left plenty of time for travelling and settling in at Al Huraydah. The horses wore their brightest tack to celebrate the occasion and, like the dogs, sensed the importance and excitement of the day. Faraj pranced beside Aisha as Ibrahim led him. He looked the fittest he ever had, and the entire tribe often looked over at him, awed by his carriage, power and beauty. Many murmured prayers for him as they travelled, pleading with the gods, for health and soundness and victory, and cursing the jinn, wishing them to stay away from Faraj and Selim.

They travelled for eight days, enjoying the travel by day and the campfires and communal banter and food at night. On the eighth day they arrived at the hills which overlooked Al Huraydah. They stopped to gaze on the spectacle of the city and the mass of tents and colour which surrounded it. Many tribes and contestants had already arrived and staked out their area. Excitement rose in the group and the chatter increased as they made their way down the hills and onto the plain.

The tribe settled into a sandy area filled with palm trees. They pitched their tents with Faraj in the centre of them for protection. Men took up guard duty so no-one could enter their camp without permission. Faraj stood tethered on a mat of straw munching on stalks of lucerne and though he looked totally uninterested in anything around him, his ears gave him away. They moved constantly, taking in all the sounds of the camp. Ibrahim and Selim were quietly proud of the way Faraj behaved. They had never been sure how Faraj would respond to the crowds and unknown horses, but he was acting in a quiet and mature manner.

There was tension in the air as they sat around the campfire that night but not enough to dampen their excitement at exploring the city the next day.

The following day Selim saddled Faraj and together with a number of the tribesmen he and Ibrahim rode back down the road they had come from. Faraj had only walked the last eight days and he needed to be exercised. The walk had maintained his fitness, but he needed far more strenuous exercise to return to race fitness. More than ever they needed to protect Faraj from the eyes of their opponents. Taking him back into the hills would allow them to continue his training without prying eyes. Ibrahim had decided Faraj only needed to loosen up today and not exert himself, as they needed to build up his lungs and heart again. Ibrahim sent riders out ahead to scout out the hills and track ahead. The men galloped off on their horses, stirring up the dust. They were eager to have something productive to do, especially since they had been walking for so many days.

They made their way up the dirt to the top of the hill, and then waved to show the area was safe. Faraj was keen to run. He pulled at the bit and shook his head as Selim released the reins a fraction. His nostrils flared, ears pricked forward, and his eyes grew wide. Selim spoke calming words and settled into the saddle, then sent Faraj into a canter. Slowly, Selim called for more from Faraj and he picked up his speed, galloping down the sandy track for three kilometres. Selim then slowly tightened the reins and called Faraj back to a very fast canter. Faraj fought him all the way but he knew the softness of Selim's hands and voice and his heart responded. Feysul galloped up alongside Faraj on his bay mare and as he slowed his mare Faraj slowed as well. He brought his mare to a trot and Faraj, not wanting to be separated from the mare, slowed to a trot. They turned the horses around and trotted back to Ibrahim. Faraj had developed a sheen of sweat but was breathing lightly. Ibrahim looked him over carefully and was happy with what he saw. It was enough for the day.

Later that morning Selim and Feysul visited the city of Al Huraydah. There were many new sounds and smells as well as many things to see. Ibrahim would not leave Faraj and after washing and brushing him kept a close eye on him. He could not afford to leave the camp but was happy for Selim and Feysul to go.

They made their way through the campsites of the other tribes and up to the gates of the city. The old wooden gates were open and people flowed through easily. The city was large and the huge earthen walls loomed before them. There were many houses attached to the walls and narrow streets ran like a maze through the city. Selim and Feysul followed the main street, which they knew would eventually lead them to the centre of the city and to the bazaar. They wished to see the quality of the blades made by the city dwellers. As they came closer to the centre of the city the noise increased. The street opened on to a large square where hundreds of people were milling around. There were booths and shops and sellers out in the open calling out to passers-by that they had the best items in the city. Their senses were overloaded by the items being sold: the freshly cooked food, fresh fruit, cloth, spices, perfumes, incense, leather items, belts, saddles and tack for both horses and camels. Above the noise of the crowds the clanging of hammers on metal could be heard as bronze, iron and even gold was shaped into new forms.

Selim was keen to find the shops and stalls which sold books and parchment and Feysul to see the workers of iron and metal. At one stall Feysul eagerly picked up some shining blades lying in the sun and examined each one carefully. He held them up in the air feeling for the point of balance. Selim too cast his eye over the swords and daggers and was particularly taken by a short dagger with a carved ivory handle. It had a beautifully filigreed scabbard made of bronze and lined with the skin of a goat. The blade had a slight curve and was tapered to a sharp point. It felt strong and comfortable in his hand. He had never seen an ivory handle carved so delicately and intricately. Many of the swords and daggers were of high quality and Feysul already seemed to have decided on one in particular and was haggling with its maker. Selim decided to leave the dagger for now, leaving Feysul to haggle, while he went to look for a stall with books.

Ever since he could remember shapes on paper and vellum, the writings which told of people from long lost days, had intrigued him. He remembered sitting on his father's lap as his father read from the few parchments and books which the tribe had collected over the years. The scrolls and parchments of the stall were now spread out on a cloth on the ground. His hands ran over the soft leather cover of one book. It was worn and thin and the few pages inside were marked with dirty fingerprints and had pieces missing. He couldn't make out the meaning of the symbols on the page so he placed the book down and picked up another. As he was leafing through the pages the owner of the stall rose from where he had been shading himself from the sun and said, "You are a learned man, are you? A man of script and thought?"

"Only a little," replied Selim. "My father taught me some of the common script and their shapes."

"Ah, I see you hide your talents," said the seller with a glint in his eye. "I am Aboud, the scribe. Peace to you."

"Peace to you," said Selim.

"These parchments are from the north, from a place called Persia. The script is not easy to read, but here, I have some in our script," said Aboud.

He reached down to where he had been sitting and picked up an object covered in cloth. He removed the cloth to show a leather-bound book, which he opened cautiously.

"It is a book of love poems and songs written many years ago. It is common to think of love poems as the sayings of those who write beautiful words about those they love. But these are the struggles of warrior men to win the love and the life of the women they love. I have read them all. I see you have an interest in them too, Selim," said Aboud, eyeing the expression on Selim's face.

Aboud passed the book to Selim who looked carefully at the words and slowly turned some pages. Indeed, he was interested. However, books of this sort were worth a lot of silver.

Selim handed the book back saying, "It's a lovely book. But I am interested in other things. What other books do you have?"

"I have parchments from Egypt, writings from Babylon, stories from Saba, legends from far-off Crete, and even some from the cold, wet place the Romani called Britain. Histories, stories, myths and legends from the world. Writings to stretch your mind and beliefs. Many of the things I can't believe myself, but they are wonderful to read and, if true, well, they would make what we know now as nothing."

"Do you have any book which mentions that the world was once covered by water?" asked Selim.

"Do you mean by a flood, my lord?" asked Aboud.

"Yes, I suppose, if that is the name it goes by," Selim replied.

Aboud mused a moment. It was obvious his mind was recounting the stories of the books he had read, trying to find one which contained such an event.

"Hmmm, I can't recall any book with a story of a flood, but then I have not read every book in the world, my lord," Aboud said deprecatingly. "Is there any reason you ask?" Aboud asked carefully, afraid of prying but strangely intrigued by this stranger's question.

Selim was reluctant to reveal his knowledge of the cave and its pictures and dismissed the idea quickly. "It's of no consequence. Just a shadow of a story I once heard some time ago. I thank you for your time," said Selim and bowed to Aboud.

Aboud bowed in return and bid Selim a good day. Aboud's eyes did not leave Selim though, until he had disappeared well into the crowd.

Feysul met Selim on his way back to find the daggers and swords and together they made their way through the crowd. The day was getting hotter, the noise louder, and the dust thicker. Feysul left to get a drink of water and Selim made his way to a shaded section of the square. As he stood there, he heard a loud cackle from below him.

"Help a blind man. Help a blind man. A coin for my meal. A coin for my meal."

As Selim looked down he saw a dusty figure crouched in the dirt. At the same time a pungent smell wafted towards his nose and he quickly raised his hand to his face to protect himself from the odour. He noticed that the dusty figure was a man holding up a wooden bowl. The eyes of the man were directed at him, but they seemed to see right through him. Noticing a distinct lack of clarity in his eyes, Selim realised he was blind. The man's face was dried and wrinkled, and it showed neither despair nor hope, as though he were beyond both.

"When did you last eat, old man?" asked Selim.

"Two days have seen me go hungry," he replied, "Will you take the pain from my stomach? A simple penny will buy me a meal."

Selim reached into the pocket of his tunic and pulled out two small silver pieces and placed them into the bowl.

"This should buy you enough meals for the week," said Selim.

The man quickly snatched the coins as they made a settling clunk in his bowl, calling out, "Thank you sir, thank you, you are generous beyond your years. May the gods smile on you and bless all you do."

Selim made to leave but the man reached out with knobbly fingers and grabbed Selim's sleeve, saying in a strange distressed tone, "Beware the pale rider, beware the pale rider. The pale one will be both bitter and sweet, sweet and bitter."

The voice faded and as Selim turned back around to look at him the beggar's head drooped. It was as if he had been wrung of all energy and as Selim stooped down and lifted his head he saw that the man's eyes were closed and he seemed to have lost consciousness.

"What do you mean, old man? What do you mean? Are those words for me?" Selim demanded as he shook the limp body. He received no answer so Selim turned and called out loudly, "Feysul, Feysul! Come, and wet the end of your turban." Feysul pushed his way through the crowd and dipped his turban into a trough. Selim took the end of the turban and squeezed its water onto the man's face.

"What is it Selim? What do you want with this dirty beggar?" asked Feysul.

At first Selim did not answer. The man's eyes were beginning to open. "He told me to beware of a rider, a pale rider. I need to find out what he meant. He could be talking about a rider in the race."

"Wake up old man," Selim called out as he continued to shake him.

"Feysul, get me a cup of water. Here, take his bowl and fill it with water," said Selim as he handed the old man's bowl to him.

As Feysul ran to get water the man started to groan and show more signs of life.

"Here, drink this," said Selim as he pushed the bowl Feysul had returned onto the lips of the man. He drank greedily and the water sloshed onto his clothes.

The old man rested his head on the wall but kept his eyes shut. He managed to speak, but only in a croaky whisper. "Who are you? What happened?"

"Don't you remember?" said Selim.

"I don't remember anything," said the old man. "What's your name?"

"I'm Selim, and this is Feysul," said Selim. "Just before you passed out you said, 'Beware of the pale rider, he is both bitter and sweet.' Why did you say that?" asked Selim.

"I don't know. I…don't know. Sometimes a heaviness comes over me and I say things before I fall asleep," he replied. "Sometimes I can explain what I said, but not always."

Selim indicated to Feysul and said, "Help me with him. We will feed him and see if he can unravel the words."

Together they half carried the old man to the closest inn. They found a table in the cool interior and ordered food and wine. The aromas of boiled goat, spices, vegetables and warm milk made their way into the room from the kitchen. The old man smelt them, and his head turned toward the kitchen in anticipation. The wine arrived first, and while Selim and Feysul sipped theirs the old man drank deeply from his cup. He seemed quite refreshed after the wine and colour came back into his face. Selim was reluctant to push him for an explanation and waited patiently for the food. However, the old man asked again for the words he had spoken. He listened carefully to Selim, then looked away as if he needed time to think them over. The food arrived and Selim knew he wouldn't get an answer until the old man had finished, as he left no gap between mouthfuls for speaking. Finally, he finished and sat back with a large sigh and an even larger burp. The old man seemed to have recovered quite quickly.

"My mother had it too," he began. "She would cry out words to a person who walked by or whose name she heard, and it would affect her like it affects me. She never knew where it came from or when it was going to come. I was the only one in our family who received this curse."

"Did her words have strength? Did they come to pass?" asked Selim impatiently.

"Oh yes, every time. She was revered and feared because her words held both blessing and curse. Sometimes her words passed judgement on a person and they would become sick or die, and other times good things came into the lives of the people she spoke about," the old man replied.

"And what about your words for me?" Selim asked.

"Yes, yes. They seem to be a warning, don't they? Do they have any meaning for you?" asked the old man.

"Well, I am going to ride in the race here in Al Huraydah so the words about a rider certainly caught my attention. So, yes, they may have meaning for me. But what does 'pale rider' mean?" replied Selim.

"It must refer to the colour of his skin," said the man. "I've seen pale people before. They were slaves and not only was their skin pale, but their hair was the colour of dried barley stalks or desert sand and their eyes were the colour of the clearest sky. There was something strangely haunting about them, but they were also very beautiful."

"One of the riders must be one of these people then," said Selim. "But what about him being 'bitter and sweet'? What does that mean?"

"I feel only time will tell. I'm not able to tell you the meaning of all the words I speak. Many of them are secrets of the future and are revealed to you as events take place. Obviously though, he will cause you bitterness and bring you sweetness, though how and when, I know not," the old man replied.

Selim had heard of another with this ability, although it had appeared in other ways than it did in the old man. He was not sceptical, nor did he dismiss the words and their possible meaning immediately. Time would tell whether the old man had a true gift of declaring the future. Selim rose and thanked the old man. He in return thanked them for the meal and the wine and wished them good fortune in the race.

Selim and Feysul made their way back outside the city and the heat hit them hard as the sun neared its full strength. Selim was unsettled by the events of the morning and didn't want to linger there. Feysul was curious about what had happened and was concerned a tribe may have cursed Selim and Faraj through a jinni. He tended to talk a lot and was devising schemes to avoid the pale rider and even creating curses to return on the offending tribe. Selim let him talk as they walked, fully occupied by his own thoughts.

When they returned Selim found the camp calm and peaceful. Ibrahim was sitting outside his tent and Faraj was dozing in the sun, with his head down low and back foot cocked. He was covered in a light cloth to protect him from the dust and flies. Ibrahim listened carefully as Feysul and Selim recounted what had happened to them in the city. He pulled at his beard as he thought through what these words might mean for Selim and Faraj and ultimately for the tribe.

But age and experience had made Ibrahim practical and he said to the men, "We must continue to prepare as we have planned. We can't fight an unknown future. Selim, we will need to think about what you must do in the race if you encounter this pale rider and he attempts to injure you or Faraj in any way. We don't know if the rider or his tribe have planned to do anything to Selim or Faraj, before or during the race. There is so little to go on, but, at least, we have been warned. The key thing is for you, Selim, to never be on your own. I will make the guards aware there is a possible threat and make sure they remain alert."

The men nodded, recognising the wisdom of these words, and left to have lunch. As the sun was setting after a lazy afternoon, Selim took out his sword and started practising. It made him supple and stretched, much needed if he wanted to stay fit for his riding, and he thought that maybe, just maybe, he would need his sword and fighting skills to deal with the pale rider.

CHAPTER 7

Feluj strode into camp with an air of importance. He went straight up to Ibrahim who called Selim, Sekeen and some other men to hear what he had to say.

"I have some news, my friends, which may be of interest to you," Feluj announced. He paused theatrically, loving the attention. "On our second last visit there was a small group that joined our caravan before we arrived at your fort. One of my regular travellers told me he had noticed the leader of the small group speaking to some boys from your tribe down by the river. The trader spoke to me when he saw the small group leaving the caravan at a lonely and desolate place and he thought it quite strange. He hadn't been close enough to hear much but he did hear the words "Al Maksour" and saw the boys wave their arms back towards the fort." Feluj stopped to take a breath and then went on.

"When I heard this, I thought I needed to pass it on to you. This is the first chance I've had to do it. I don't know if it helps you at all," finished Feluj with more than just the slightest hint of satisfaction on his face.

"That's how the Al Bedi must have known where to look for Al Maksour. Those boys told them where it was," blurted out Sekeen.

"But how did these young boys come to know of its hiding place?" asked Ibrahim.

"Who knows with young boys? They are often unseen but listen in to grownup talk. They may have heard it from any one of us or even tried to find its hiding place, especially after the stories they have heard about it over the years," said Feysul.

"Yes, why not? Which of us as boys didn't dream of touching the sword?" added Selim. "Anyway, I'm glad no person of our tribe deliberately passed on any information. We can easily forgive some innocent boys."

"Hmm," said Ibrahim. "Thank you Feluj. It's good to be able to put all the pieces of the puzzle together. But this information doesn't change anything. It simply warns us to be careful with Al Maksour. Please, Feluj stay for a drink," added Ibrahim.

Feluj smiled happily, expecting the invitation considering the importance of the information he had brought. The men called for drinks and gathered themselves on the carpet inside the tent. Talk turned to the race and the horses that Faraj and Selim would race against.

"Do you know if the Al Bedi have entered the race?" Selim asked Feluj, wondering whether the pale rider might be riding for them.

"No, I haven't heard anything about the Al Bedi," Feluj answered. "But I have seen a young grey mare on a training run. She showed an excellent length of stride and powerful muscling and her rider appears to be an experienced and talented rider. When she walked her back feet landed forty centimetres in front of the imprints of her front feet. She'll cover a lot of ground with this type of overstep."

However, as he was speaking his eye turned to Faraj whom he could see through the open flap of the tent. Feluj noted Faraj was taller and stronger looking than the grey mare and he had never seen Faraj as fit as he looked now. His coat reflected the sun like the still surface of the mountain water. Feluj also noticed his noble head and the gentleness of his expression. He knew winning a race of this type took more than physical abilities; it also took willingness and mental strength. He could see Faraj had all of these qualities but was not so sure about the grey mare. In his mind he reminded himself to place a wager on Faraj winning the race.

Feluj complimented the men saying, "I have never seen a horse look so ready for this race. He looks relaxed and yet so physically fit."

Selim replied, "Thank you Feluj, we've worked hard on his fitness, but his attitude has come from years of breeding."

"Have you seen any of the other horses, Feluj?" one of the men asked.

"Yes, but none that really stood out. Some are long and lean and look like they will travel far and long, but I wonder if they have the speed. Others are small and seem not to have the appearance of either speed or endurance but... I have long dismissed size as a reason to discount these smaller horses, as their heart always seems to show itself larger than their size suggests."

"Well said. Never underestimate a smaller horse, for they seem to carry the same power as the taller ones and have many characteristics larger horses don't have. I have often found them to suffer less leg injuries and they are excellent in the hard, rocky areas of the mountains. They seem to be almost able to smell the quickest and smoothest path over the rocks," said Ibrahim.

Selim listened carefully and quietly to this. He had heard it before, but it helped him to be mindful of the qualities of certain types of horses. He was, of course, totally biased about Aisha and Faraj and their entire herd as he considered them the finest horses in all the land, and he loved them dearly. He knew the qualities they possessed, and he had ridden them, and felt their power and their love for him. In his mind, small or tall, they would always be the best.

"Thank you, gentlemen for the drink and the conversation but I must return now. May blessings be upon Faraj and you, Selim, as you race," said Feluj bowing to them. Then with a grin and a twinkle in his eye, he added, "For I will have a wager on his winning."

The men laughed, knowing Feluj would probably make a wager on a number of horses. The men rose and bid him farewell.

Selim left the men and went to check on Faraj, picking up his feet and checking his legs. His confidence for the race grew as his hands and eyes ran over the body of Faraj. Faraj instilled confidence back into Selim's nervous heart. Talking about the horses had made him realise just how close the race was and had brought with it the fears of competing in his first gruelling race against riders with far more experience and horses who were, like his tribe's, bred to run in a harsh land.

The men in the tent had lowered their talk to a low murmur once they realised how Selim must be feeling and occasionally he had felt their eyes on him. It did not bother him though, as they were men he trusted, men whom he knew cared about him and would die for him rather than accuse or belittle him. The community and love of the tribe was his strength. They would be behind him in this race as if they were racing themselves and he loved them for it. Some of the more confident men made their way out to appraise Faraj and encourage Selim, making jokes to try to lighten the atmosphere and ease the tension. As the sun began to set they gradually dispersed to feed their horses and prepare for the evening meal.

The next morning over breakfast Ibrahim spoke to some of the men saying, "I want each of you to go to the training runs of the horses entered into the race. Observe all they do, find out who the riders are, what their horses are like, and how they are training them. Look for any information that will help Selim and Faraj."

The men went off, keen to help as much as they could. Selim and Ibrahim as well as their group of protectors rode back up into the mountain range to exercise Faraj. Ibrahim had carefully prepared Faraj's legs with an oily ointment made from the leaves of several plants. It helped to warm his legs and strengthen his bones. Ibrahim did it regularly and Faraj enjoyed the morning massage after his rub down.

Selim sent Faraj into a slow trot to warm him and then picked up the pace for a number of miles along the mountain tracks. Ibrahim could see Faraj's muscles hardening into iron and his blood vessels pulsing cleanly beneath the silky skin, and he felt satisfaction rise in his heart. He knew Faraj would be ready in time for the race. After Faraj had enjoyed a cooling walk back and a long rub down, Ibrahim and Selim met with the men who had returned and they all listened carefully to their reports. Feysul was the first to speak. He had been out to visit the Kindah tribe who had entered a bay stallion in the race.

"Their horse is large, strong and well-muscled but his legs aren't long and I wonder if he will have endurance. He will be fast over the sand because of his strength but speed is not his strongest point," reported Feysul.

"Hmm" said Ibrahim, "he may take a lead in the race because of his strength, but don't be concerned by this Selim. It seems he could fade at the end, and if he doesn't and wins from the front then he is a worthy winner."

"Sekeen, what do you have to report?" asked Ibrahim.

"The Sayhads have a black stallion who looks lean and fit. He is fiery but his rider sits on him lightly and is able to control him well. Once he starts running he is like an arrow loosed from a bow. He seems to have good conformation and he is also known to have endurance. I did notice though the rider sat with shortened stirrups. His knees were up high, level with the horse's withers. It was so strange, but as I said, he sits lightly on his horse and balances very well. The shortened stirrups don't bother him at all, but I'm not sure why he does it."

Sekeen paused as if weighing up whether he should say more. "There is one other thing, which is of no importance really, but the rider of this black horse was almost white. He must be from another country."

Sekeen laughed and then added, "But it shouldn't worry Selim as the Nejd have the best riders and the best horses."

Selim and Feysul glanced at Ibrahim, who gave no response except to briefly widen his eyes. Ibrahim continued on as though nothing had happened, calling on Yusef to share what he had seen at the camp of the Jurhum tribe.

"They have a grey mare, not large but well-built, who looks like she has the will to win. She looks fit and keen to race and will persevere when others give up. I wouldn't underestimate her," said Yusef with certainty.

Nothing else of great concern was reported but the information the others shared was helpful to Selim. A final tally revealed Selim and Faraj would race against three bay stallions, two bay mares, two grey mares, two chestnut mares, three grey stallions, one chestnut stallion, and the black stallion with his pale rider.

Finally, Ibrahim raised the topic of the pale rider. "Sekeen, your report was more informative than you thought. Selim has been warned about a pale rider so it's good to know his tribe and the horse he will ride. Did you happen to get an idea of where the pale rider comes from?"

Sekeen looked up, surprised at the importance of his information. "No, I didn't talk to anyone from the tribe. I didn't want them to know how interested I was in their horse or rider. How did you know they had a pale rider?"

Selim spoke up. "It was yesterday, when I was in the city. An old man fell into a trance just after I spoke to him and he warned me about a pale rider who would be both 'bitter and sweet.' Afterwards he didn't remember anything and when I pushed him for an explanation he couldn't tell me more. At the time we didn't know of any pale rider in the race and I really want to know what 'bitterness' he might bring. It must have something to do with the race. Did you notice anything about the rider, Sekeen, that might help us?"

Sekeen sat thoughtfully for some time, reflecting on what he had seen.

"No, nothing. As I said he was a competent rider and handled Aswad well. Aswad, that's the horse's name. The rider seemed in control of him the whole time and managed to get every bit of speed and focus from his horse. I only saw him riding, nothing else."

"Hmm" said Ibrahim, "I doubt whether we will learn much from watching him, but we will do it anyway. Sekeen, I want you to watch his training every day to learn what you can. But do it carefully. We don't want to let the Sayhads think we are afraid of their horse and rider. Meanwhile, I'll need to speak to Feluj to see if his vast knowledge includes anything about a pale-skinned race of people. Now as for the shortened stirrups, what benefit do they give?"

This question started immediate discussion between the men who were intrigued and excited by the information they had heard. Each offered their own explanation.

"It must be to make the rider lighter," said Hazim.

"But how can that be," replied Haddad. "Changing your leg position doesn't change your weight."

"I agree," added Jalab. "Maybe the horse is sensitive on its sides and they raise the rider's legs to avoid touching them."

"Maybe it allows the rider to spring out of the saddle more easily… to jump on Selim," another man offered.

Most of the men chuckled at the suggestion, then as they realised what this could mean for Selim, their faces took on a look of concern. Others looked down, ashamed at laughing at such a silly thing.

Talk quickly turned to the origins of the pale rider and what "sweetness" he might have ready for Selim and Faraj. The talk slowly died down and the men went off to complete their evening jobs around the camp. Selim also left to feed Faraj and bed him down for the night. As he worked he pondered the reason for the shortened stirrups.

"It must have to do with the rider's weight," he thought, "but how does it make any difference and what benefit is it to the horse or rider?"

By the time he had finished with Faraj he had decided to try shorter stirrups on Faraj in the morning. It was the only way to work out what the real difference would be.

While eating dinner he mentioned his idea to Ibrahim who smiled at him and said, "Good thinking Selim, but I suggest we don't use Faraj as a trial horse. Why not ride Aisha? It doesn't really matter which horse we try it on but if something goes wrong and Faraj is injured then we may end up forfeiting the race."

"Yes, of course," answered Selim.

After thinking about the matter for some time, Sekeen said to them, "I wonder if this style of riding has more to do with the horse than the rider. Does it somehow allow the horse to move more freely? It's easy to think about the comfort of the rider but we don't often think of the comfort of the horse and how he might be restricted by a saddle and rider."

The men were up early, eager to have the trial over before they left to watch the other horses training. Once Aisha was saddled and Selim had mounted, Ibrahim shortened the length of the stirrups to about the length Sekeen had mentioned earlier.

"This feels awkward," commented Selim. However, as he started walking and trotting Aisha he began to develop a greater sense of balance. After some time he moved her into a canter. She felt almost the same under him, although he noticed she moved with a little more reach and was a little more flexible in her strides. As her speed increased, Selim sensed the need to put more pressure on the stirrups, rather than have his weight rest on the saddle seat. As he did this, he found himself moving slightly forward over Aisha's withers, which seemed strange, yet he seemed to find a new point of balance and harmony with her. It was starting to feel good and somehow "right." He swung Aisha around and returned to the group of men. They eagerly asked Selim how it felt.

"I need to get used to it, but it feels like I am freeing Aisha to move and run more lightly. It's exactly as you said Sekeen." Sekeen nodded in response, giving a small satisfied smile.

Ayyam, who was known for his knowledge of horse conformation said, "I think you're right Selim. When you moved forward on your legs it allowed Aisha's rear end and legs to move more freely and to increase her stride. I think over many miles this will be a great advantage as the horse will be able to cover more distance."

Ibrahim was quietly excited. His own thoughts had been right, but he wanted to go further than just to shorten the stirrups. "When Sekeen mentioned last night about restricting the movement of a horse I thought that using a lighter saddle, one without all the tassels and wood, may also help."

The men nodded, obviously mulling this over and trying to imagine what this saddle would look like.

Ayyam spoke up again. "I see your point Ibrahim and it's a good one, however while we are getting more freedom in the hindquarters aren't we in danger of overloading the shoulder and possibly restricting it?"

"Good point," replied Ibrahim.

"It is a good point," added Selim, "but as I rode I found a new place of balance which seemed just right for Aisha. It's further forward than we would normally sit."

The men agreed with Selim as they all knew how important it was to be balanced as a rider but also to be at one with the horse.

"Hazim, Karif, take the saddle from Aisha and remove anything which isn't needed. Selim will race with a lighter saddle," said Ibrahim with finality.

Selim dismounted and the men took the saddle away. The rest of the men left, satisfied that the pale rider no longer had an unknown advantage over Faraj and Selim. They were also proud of the way the mystery had been turned to their advantage through the combined thinking and skill of the men of their tribe.

"Well," said Ibrahim as he and Selim led Aisha away, "it's been an interesting morning. We've learnt from the pale rider. So far, he has only given us 'sweetness.'"

"Yes," replied Selim, "Faraj will feel like a new horse when I ride him."

"It will be interesting to see how much more freedom it gives him," replied Ibrahim. "Aisha certainly seemed to like it."

After Hazim and Karif had finished stripping down the saddle to its bare minimum, Ibrahim saddled Faraj with it, who sniffed it with disdain. Selim kept Faraj to a slow canter but all the men could see Faraj's loin was looser, that he carried his back legs further under him and that his shoulder and front legs were as loose as they had ever been. Faraj snorted and shook his head asking to go faster and though Selim could feel a new point of balance and harmony with Faraj he needed more time to feel totally comfortable with having his legs bent so much. His confidence grew because of what he could feel and even Faraj looked at him a few times, acknowledging something new had fallen into place between them.

Ibrahim sent a man to ask Feluj to dinner, knowing he would not refuse a meal. He wanted to ask him about the origins of the pale rider. Feluj soon arrived, on top of one of his horses. He rarely rode his horse but it would have seemed a little pompous to arrive on a camel when the distance was so short. The camel was his preferred form of transport as he was a sizeable man and the camel knelt on the ground, allowing him to get on easily. Over dinner he wore a look of importance, and a secretive smile on his face. He took his time, enjoying his meal and burping several times. They had talked about the horses and what they thought of their chances, but not about the change in the saddle or riding style. They knew if they told Feluj it would be all over the city before sunset the next day.

Ibrahim came straight to the point. "Feluj, in your vast travels have you heard of a people who are fair-skinned, fair-haired, with blue or blue green eyes?" He paused and Feluj shifted in his seat as if getting ready to answer, but Ibrahim went on.

"The reason we ask is that one of the tribes, the Sayhads, have a rider who fits this description. We're wondering if you can tell us anything about them, their skills or their history with horses and riding. We can't understand why the Sayhads haven't chosen a rider from among their own tribe."

"Ah," answered Feluj, "now we come to the heart of the matter as some would say. The price of a dinner." The last comment was muttered into his beard.

"Yes, yes, the Sayhads. I have heard of this rider and yes, I have heard of a people far, far to the north who are known for their riding skills. It is said they ride their horses on ground covered in grass which extends as far as the sand of our deserts. Their horses are fast and tall, and the riders are said to be born in the saddle as their women also ride. They are known as Sakas. I saw some when I travelled to the furthest cities in the north. They were all slaves taken in battle and some were sold on until they reached the south of our land, though there were not many. These Sakas certainly are an odd colour and one must wonder what the weather is like further north. I don't understand how they can survive in our deserts."

"Oh, yes," added Feluj. "I believe they also cover their bodies in blue tattoos, but I have only once before seen one on the arm of an older Saka."

Selim was intrigued to hear of this different race of people. "Do you know anything about their riding style or ability, Feluj? Do they have any special tricks or ways of doing things that we don't know about?" Selim he leaned closer to Feluj.

Feluj shook his head slowly. "No Selim, I've heard only what I have told you. Their skills and ways of riding are a mystery to me."

"Do you know what their horses are like?" asked Selim.

"Again, I can't answer that," answered Feluj. "But from what I have heard, the Saka riding the Sayhads' horse is a very skilled rider. I have heard his name is Ishkuz, which means "archer" in the Saka language. He is supposed to have some skill with the bow. He may even outshoot all of you," Feluj said, taunting the men, though he himself had no skill at all.

"I believe he won a bet to ride the Sayhads' horse in the race. He was bought as a slave but soon showed his skill with the bow and challenged some of the tribe's younger men. He beat them easily and soon others in the tribe wanted to test themselves against him, not believing someone from the north could shoot better than them. He told the men that he would only continue to challenge the best archers in the tribe if he was allowed to ride in the race. His success with the bow had dented the men's pride and many still wanted to challenge him. They agreed, but only after he showed them his riding ability. They didn't want to enter their horse with a rider who didn't know the difference between a hoof and an ear. Apparently, he showed enormous skill and so the archery challenge continued. I heard he missed only two moving targets throughout the contest and beat every man who came against him. So, he's riding in the race. The Sayhads have a grudging respect for him but they don't treat him well."

Thankful for the information they received from Feluj, they plied him with cake and wine, which he didn't refuse.

CHAPTER 8

Aisha nudged Selim's arm as he and the other riders listened to those in charge. Together they were going to ride over the track set for the race. Ibrahim and a few other men from their tribe joined Selim in order to assess the best way to ride the race, given the path and terrain. Selim kept an eye out for the pale rider, Ishkuz. He had not yet seen him and was interested in looking at the foreigner who had been prophesied about. It didn't take long to identify him. His head was uncovered and thin blond, faintly reddish hair blew in the breeze. His face was the colour of clean desert sand and his eyes sparkled brightly like a cloudless sky. He was of average height but walked with suppleness and confidence. He too, was accompanied by some men from his tribe.

Selim remembered that Ishkuz was to ride Aswad, a black stallion, and he turned his head to where they had their horses, but he couldn't see a black one. They must also have left their racehorse back at the camp. He was eager to see Aswad, as black horses were rare. Even within his own tribe only a handful of them had been bred, and he wanted to see the horses he and Faraj were racing. Selim was keen to compare his tribe's horses with those of other tribes. Were their horses more intelligent, resilient, stronger, bigger or better conformed than what his tribe was breeding?

Selim looked up at her Aisha as she neighed loudly at the other horses and he was reminded that there were no finer horses in the land than from his own tribe. Aisha's desert spirit sprang to life through her eyes and quivered at the end of every hair. Men around her turned to look, as if they too were touched by it.

Following the lead horseman, they all made their way around the track. It was well marked with flags and they made note of the changing features and different footing. Al Huraydah was fortunate it was close to both the mountains, flat lands and sand dunes that were to be part of the ten-kilometre race.

"This terrain is no different than what we cover all the time. It won't be difficult for Faraj," Selim commented.

"No, it won't," replied Feysul. "But the challenge will be to not let the other horses pressure you and Faraj into using energy at times and places when you should be conserving it. The sand part of the track, for example, isn't the place to be racing other horses. You'll need to take Faraj through the sand in a way most comfortable to him, so he has enough strength and speed to run on the flat lands."

The other men joined in with pieces of advice and Selim took it all in, though he already knew most of what they were saying. Like him, they were becoming a little tense about the race and were talking more than normal.

Tomorrow he would face the pale rider, Ishkuz. As he thought of racing against the riders with more experience than him and the horses that had been prepared as well as Faraj, he felt the tension grip his stomach. Sensing this, Ibrahim reached over and put his hand on Selim's shoulder. He turned and smiled at Ibrahim, thankful for his reassurance.

That afternoon Selim met with Sekeen to practice his swordsmanship. As his body moved and his arms swung and hit Sekeen's blade he felt the tension dissolve from his muscles, his resolve build and a steely, cold determination settle into his stomach. Over and over in his mind he repeated, "I am ready for tomorrow."

Before closing his eyes that night Selim spotted Faraj outside the tent. The light from the fire flickered on his coat and danced like horses running across the desert. Faraj lifted his head and turned toward Selim. His eyes reflected the dancing fire but beneath this was a peace which seemed to stretch down into Faraj's heart, and it followed Selim into a deep sleep.

Ibrahim was awake and busy before any of the others, even Selim. Before Selim awoke, Faraj had been brushed, watered and fed. There wasn't much time before the race as it was to be run before the heat of the day set in. Selim ate a light breakfast as the other men and women continued to wake. Excitement was beginning to brew and singing and cheering could be heard throughout the camp. Men patted Selim on the back and gave him all sorts of encouragement as they passed by.

Finally, the time came. Saddled on their horses, the men of the tribe surrounded Selim and Faraj as Ibrahim mounted on Aisha led them down to the starting point. A crowd of people poured out of Al Huraydah. Fresh and keen to race, Faraj instantly picked up on the atmosphere of excitement and expectation. Now that he was in the saddle of his strong and willing chestnut stallion, Selim actually felt calm, his confidence rising as he felt his horse beneath him.

As Selim left for the starting line, Ibrahim called out, "Trust your senses and trust Faraj. He will bring you home."

Selim trotted up to the starting line with the thirteen other horses and took his place among them. Aswad and Ishkuz were toward the other end of the line and Ishkuz took no notice of Selim or Faraj. The last three contestants joined the line. All the horses were being held tightly, tensing keenly against the reins. The noise of the crowd increased as each tribe began to cheer on their horse and rider. The horses pranced, each on their own spot, stirring up the dust in the sand. As the tension rose to breaking point the sheikh of Al Huraydah dropped the flag and the race began. Released by their riders, the horses sprung forward as one. Selim felt the power of Faraj's hindquarters catapulting him forward. In three strides he was half a body length ahead of the other horses and increasing his speed. The horses, nearing full speed, galloped down the flat dirt surface which led to the mountain section of the race. Selim tried to preserve Faraj's strength and called on him to slow down but Faraj was intent on racing. He shook his head and kept up his speed. The excitement of the race drove them on at amazing speed. The riders were keenly aware of the steep mountain paths still to climb and the deep sand ahead of them which needed strength to get through.

After a mile of racing Selim could see out of the corner of his eye that a thin grey horse and a black one were edging to the front of the group. Aswad and Ishkuz were challenging the group. The mountain track was coming into view and they wanted to gain the lead before the track narrowed and it was difficult to pass others. The group slowed as they jostled for their places. The strong bay stallion of the Kindah tribe was rushing up fast as his rider knew the mountain and sand sections were his strength.

Selim wasn't keen to push Faraj through the mountain section of the race and so allowed the three horses to overtake. Putting on a burst of speed the bay stallion took the lead, with the grey mare close behind, Aswad and Ishkuz third and then Faraj following. The thud of hooves on sandy soil turned to the slower clatter of hooves on hard stone and packed dirt as the horses made their way up the mountain track. Selim saw the bay stallion pulling away from the grey mare, his large, strong haunches pushing him quickly up the mountain. A sheen of sweat glistened on Faraj's coat and his lungs were beginning to work harder. While the ground and footing were firm, the path was steep. Selim saw Ishkuz leaning forward on his stirrups over the withers of Aswad and Selim copied him. He could see Aswad's hindquarters were able to push more powerfully and he hoped Faraj's would do the same. Behind him he could hear the breathing of the other horses and the encouragement of their riders.

The path finally levelled out and the riders slowed their mounts to a trot to allow them to catch their breath after the steep climb. The horses were blowing hard and the rocky track at the top of the mountain was slippery, so none of the riders wanted to risk passing the horse in front of them. It became even more dangerous as the path began to wind down the mountain. In some places the path was so steep that the riders pulled their horses to a walk and the horses sat on their haunches to stop themselves from gathering speed. The horses could see the sand stretching out below them and having gained some of their breath back were eager to stretch themselves again. The bay at the front hit the sand and his enormous muscles pushed his legs deeply into the sand. The grey mare found the sand difficult and lost some of her contact with the bay stallion. Aswad and Ishkuz had just reached the bottom of the mountain with only a small stretch of rocky path left when Ishkuz suddenly pulled back on Aswad's mouth and sat back hard on the saddle. Aswad's hindquarters dropped beneath him and his hind legs slid along the rock track. Taken completely by surprise, Selim and Faraj had no time to react. Faraj's chest slammed into Aswad's hindquarter and he bounced off to the right, his head and neck going high into the air as he tried to protect himself. The reins were slippery with sweat and because Selim was so high in the stirrups he lost his balance more easily than he normally would have. He flew through the air and landed heavily against the black rock. His right arm and shoulder hit the rock first, taking the weight of his body. A loud snap came from his arm and Selim cried out in pain. He grabbed his right arm and held it tightly to himself. The jagged end of a bone could be seen poking through his skin just above the elbow. He sat stunned, cradling his arm.

As his mind began to clear, Selim realised he would need to wrap his arm to keep it as clean as possible. The sleeve of his shirt was torn and with his good arm he ripped off a strip and bound up his arm as well as he could. Struggling to his feet Selim looked around. Ishkuz and the black stallion were racing away without a backward glance. Faraj was standing in the sand looking dazed. Selim called him over. He had no intention of giving up the race despite the pain. Faraj came near and Selim pulled him over to a small boulder. As he put his foot up onto the boulder a wave of nausea hit him. He wobbled off and fell hard against Faraj. The other horses and riders passed, one or two of them throwing him a glance but without any concern or compassion. Falling from a horse was one of the risks of the race and each rider was intent on winning.

Selim rested for a moment then tried to mount Faraj again. This time he managed to crawl into the saddle, but not without seeing stars and feeling clammy. He rested for a moment and then urged Faraj on. After wobbling in the saddle he gritted his teeth and sat down to ride with the reins in one hand and his other held close to his chest.

Faraj quickly moved into a gallop. Selim was glad they were running on the sand as it cushioned his ride and the jolting of his arm. The last horse was in clear view and as Faraj closed in on it Selim could see it was struggling with the sand. They passed it quickly and soon made up more ground on some other horses. Selim continued to grit his teeth and wince in pain, and though he remembered the advice to preserve Faraj through the sand and not burn up all his energy, he pushed it aside. Faraj would need to run his heart out for the rest of the race if they were to win and call on every bit of strength and courage and perseverance to pass the other horses, and time was running out.

Selim urged Faraj on between moans of pain and Faraj responded with longer and more powerful strides. They grew closer and closer to the other runners. Faraj came up beside one of the horses and he left it behind him in four strides with a wild defeated look in its eye. Selim sat as still as he could on Faraj's back but urged him on. They passed one horse, then another, and then another, till there were only two horses left ahead of them. The grey mare and the black stallion, Aswad.

The sand became dirt and the finish line lay around the side of the hill. The grey mare, compact, yet long legged raced around the hill. After making up a lot of distance in the sand, she was closing the gap on Aswad and Ishkuz. Completely focused on his running and on the horses ahead of him, Faraj was giving his all. Selim was certain he had never run this fast before. He was gaining on the grey mare and the black stallion but every jolting stride sent shots of pain through Selim's arm. His teeth clenched tighter and he had very little strength left to control Faraj with the reins. However, all Faraj needed to do now to win was to follow the other horses.

Stride by stride Faraj made up ground on the grey mare and he was soon only two horse lengths behind. Aswad was a further five lengths ahead. As Faraj came up behind her the horses broke from around the hill and the hard road into the city opened up before them. Deafening cheers came from the crowds lining the road but Selim couldn't hear anything. All he was aware of was the grey and black horse ahead of him and the thudding of the horses' feet.

"More Faraj, more!" Selim called out to Faraj.

Faraj's stride lengthened, his front and hind legs now stretching as far as they could. Very quickly he was next to the grey mare. The rider's eyes widened as he saw them coming, unsure how they had made it back into the race. He honestly thought they were out of the race and now they were passing him. His mare did not give in and to her credit fought back with all of her ancestor's endurance. However, Faraj's momentum was too great, and though she did not lose ground to Faraj she could not regain her lead. Spurring one another on they ate into Aswad's lead and when Ishkuz turned in the saddle to take a look back, Selim saw a look of fear and he felt a grim satisfaction.

Selim's resolve to win hardened even more. Anger began to boil within him, blocking out the pain from his arm. Selim pushed Faraj harder but he had no more to give. He was already giving his all. However, in front of him, Aswad was tiring as well. Beside him the grey mare was falling back, and it also seemed that in front of him Aswad was dropping back. Within the space of twenty strides Faraj's speed and Aswad's tiredness had brought them together. Both riders were hunched over their horses, urging the most out of them. As they raced along stride for stride Faraj looked straight into the eye of the black horse.

The horses continued racing at top speed, despite the fact they had been up and down mountains and through heavy sand. However, it was here that a difference emerged between the two horses. From deep within the spirit and heart of Faraj, rose the strength of the Sarmadees in which he had been born.

It surfaced as a calm confidence which overwhelmed the other horse not with raw power or arrogance but by an iron assurance and self-belief. Due to Faraj's unrelenting challenge, Aswad's confidence wavered, and his eye fixed itself on Faraj, even as his rider urged him on. He was being challenged not just in his body, but in his spirit. It was unlike any other challenge he had faced and he questioned himself like never before.

Faraj was not weakening, and his eyes filled with more fire and determination. The contest had become a battle of spirits. Both horses were sons of the sand and sun and both wrestled with themselves for a place of peace and power.

Faraj was the first to succeed and he began to pull clear of Aswad, his hooves resounding like heavy rain falling in a spring storm. He carried his tail high and it seemed to stream behind him as a signal to Ishkuz and Aswad that their race was over. They passed swiftly between two large flagpoles outside of the gates to the city, signifying the end of their gruelling race.

A cloud of dust flew up from the crowds lining the road as they closed in on Faraj. Loud cries came from among Selim's tribe as they hugged each other joyfully. Ibrahim grinned widely and in their excitement some of the younger men grabbed him around the neck and kissed him and pushed themselves through the crowd to where Faraj had stopped. His sides heaved as his lungs drank in fresh air and thick rivers of sweat and foam dripped down into the sand. The men had never seen Faraj so spent. Yusef grabbed hold of Faraj's bridle and other hands reached up to congratulate Selim. As they did, Selim slumped and slid from the saddle into their arms. One of them noticed the bloodied rag tied roughly around his arm and pointed it out to Ibrahim who carefully examined Selim's arm. They gasped as he slowly removed the wrapping, exposing the broken bone and open flesh. Under Ibrahim's instructions the men carried Selim to their tents, their excitement rapidly turning to shock. They pushed their way through the crowd, eager to have Selim tended to.

When they arrived at their tents they lay Selim down, supporting him with cushions. He began to groan and writhe in agony. Aseela, the chief herbal woman was called to mix up some herbs and wine to reduce the pain. Ibrahim and Sekeen carefully peeled off his outer clothes but found no further injuries. Apart from some grazes the broken arm was the only real problem. But the break was serious, jagged and exposed. The men and women who had seen serious breaks like this were afraid of the way that wounds could turn poisonous and begin to smell sickly. This type of infection was hard to heal and often a person became very sick and died. The treatments they knew and used weren't always able to cure the wound even if the bone could be put back into place.

Ibrahim gathered a group of women together and some of the men. "We have to move the bone back into place and then pray to the gods that the wound heals cleanly. I will need you four men to hold Selim down while I push the bone back into place. Women, I'll need you to get bandages, water and all the herbs you have with you. We need to save this arm and Selim."

The women raced off while the men went to Selim. Ibrahim rolled up his sleeves and while the men held Selim's struggling body, Ibrahim carefully pushed the bone back into place. Selim cried out in pain. Ibrahim was able to remove some small pieces of bone and lay the skin back over the opening. The women returned with clean cloths and placed some herbs over the wound before Ibrahim carefully wrapped his arm.

Selim had turned an even lighter grey, sweat and dust mixing together, but his writhing had slowed, and he seemed to be a little more peaceful. The men slowly let go of him and with a look of concern left the tent. The women then took over his care, wiping his brow, mixing herbs for fresh bandages and getting Selim to drink. He had not only lost blood, but was fatigued and dehydrated. He needed strength for his arm to heal and to fight the growth of the infection they all feared.

Feluj rode up to the tent as the men waited outside, muttering among themselves. He quickly dismounted and called out to the men, "I know what happened. I've spoken to one of the riders. It was the pale rider. He did this to Selim."

REJECTION

Hearing Feluj's voice, Ibrahim opened the tent flap and joined the men.

"I spoke to the rider of the Fezzan horse. He was behind Selim and saw the pale rider stop his horse with a sudden slide. Selim and Faraj had no choice but to run into the back of Aswad. The sudden stop unbalanced Selim and he fell to one side of Faraj and then onto the ground. It seems the pale rider had taught Aswad to fall back on his hind legs and skid to a halt, even though he was running fast. He is a very clever rider and obviously cunning as well."

"How is Selim? Is he awake?" Feluj continued.

Ibrahim answered, "He is resting and not awake but we have reset the bone as well as we could. I hope it is enough, as there were some splinters."

"Are you sure Feluj, about Ishkuz?" Ibrahim's focus had changed, and his voice took on a steely edge.

Feluj took a step back. "Yes, yes. I am sure. I spoke to the rider himself. He saw it all."

"So, the prophecy came true," said Ibrahim angrily. "At least half of it."

The other men started murmuring heatedly among themselves.

"What do you mean the 'prophecy'?" asked Feluj. "What has been going on?"

Ibrahim spoke up. "This week when Selim was in the city an old beggar fell into a trance and said, 'to beware of the pale rider as he was both bitter and sweet.' We really didn't know what it meant but we warned Selim to be cautious during the race and we took every precaution we could. Alas, to no avail. Maybe he stayed too close to Aswad trying to keep an eye on his rider, but it has led him into trouble. Curse the prophecy and the rider of Aswad and the Sayhad tribe. They had their hand in this, I have no doubt. If Selim is overcome by poison they will have blood on their hands."

Ibrahim turned quickly and returned to Selim. Feluj had never seen Ibrahim so angry and began questioning the men. "Is there a danger of this?"

He knew of the possibility of poison entering a wound, but not having seen it he wasn't sure how much danger Selim was in.

One of the men who had held Selim answered, "There is a hole in his skin where the bone broke through. He has lost a lot of blood and the wound is jagged and the bone splintered. I saw Ibrahim push the bone back, but it won't heal smoothly. There is a lot of exposed flesh which could become poisoned."

All thought of the win had left their minds and talk turned to revenge. Some even raised the idea of an attack on the Sayhads and of killing Ishkuz, but others warned against this, advising that if anything was to be done it had to happen with the agreement of the tribe.

Behind them a group of riders rode into camp, pulled up their horses and dismounted. From the pennants they carried it was obvious they were from the sheikh of Al Huraydah. Their arrival was no surprise as it was common knowledge that the winning tribe was given a special invitation to celebrate their win in the sheikh's palace.

The leader of the sheikh's men saluted the gathering and then said, "Sheikh abd al Kurasi congratulates you and your horse and rider. Your horse has shown its true heritage and proved to everyone he was worthy of the win. The sheikh also said to salute your rider especially as he showed tremendous courage and resilience in continuing the ride after his fall. The sheikh understands under the present circumstances that your tribe may not wish to celebrate with him tonight but wishes a speedy recovery and health to the rider. He has also ordered food and drink from his kitchen to be brought here for you to enjoy. He also wishes to know the condition of the rider and if there is anything he can do to bring about recovery?"

By the time he had finished delivering his message Ibrahim had returned.

"Tell your sheikh a thousand thanks are owed to him for his generosity and that we appreciate the offer of food. Tell him we fear to leave our rider and will remain in camp. Selim's life is in the hands of the gods and there is little we can do but wait to see which hand he will be dealt. Give our thanks to the sheikh."

The men bowed and promised to report this to their sheikh. Mounting their horses, they left the camp in a cloud of dust.

The visit had not lifted the atmosphere of anger and apprehension covering the camp. There was no room left for celebration. The men sat huddled in small groups, their faces grim and solemn. Those who had cooled and washed Faraj now brought him to the centre of the camp and some of the others gathered around to look at him. He had no scratches or marks but when Yusef pressed on his chest Faraj winced and it was obvious he had suffered bruising from his collision with Aswad.

Yusef spoke to the men who had cooled and washed Faraj. "Did he limp in any way when you walked him?"

"No, he didn't show any sign of soreness in his legs or feet, even after his muscles had cooled," one replied.

"Good," said Yusef, "at least there isn't ligament or bone damage. The bruising of the chest will heal. Make sure he is walked every day so that he doesn't become tight in his chest."

Inside the tent where Selim slept, there were quiet whispers between Ibrahim and Aseela, the most experienced medicine woman among the group. They would be taking turns to watch Selim throughout the night and ensuring that he took drank. The night was to be a crucial time.

Selim slept fitfully in the dim candlelight unaware of the goals and dreams he had achieved against the odds. He was oblivious to the noise the other tribes were making around their campfires as they celebrated his victory and courage and sang the praises of Faraj and his ancestors.

CHAPTER 9

The new day dawned and the thick wool of the tent had already begun heating up in the morning sun. Under the tent's cover Selim moaned as he woke slowly from his restless sleep. The sleeping draught had worn off and he could feel an intense throbbing in his arm. One of the women went to him asking, "Are you thirsty? You must drink as you have lost a lot of blood."

Selim nodded and the woman took a clay flask and poured weak wine into a beaker. She held it up to Selim's lips and he sipped carefully. Slowly some colour came to his face and with the woman's help he was able to raise himself and sit up on some cushions. She left to get food for him and Ibrahim entered through the flap of the tent.

"Selim," he said. 'It's good to see you awake. How does your arm feel?"

"It's so sore. It's throbbing badly and I feel very weak. Have I slept long?"

"We brought you here after you finished the race, so you have slept through yesterday and the night," replied Ibrahim.

"Faraj? How is he?" asked Selim.

"He's fine. He's a bit sore in the chest but he'll heal in a week or so. He ran a great race, and you rode an even greater one. I am truly proud of you," Ibrahim said.

"I was so angry after Ishkuz pulled Aswad up suddenly. I had no time to miss him. All I wanted to do was to catch up with him and beat him. After all the business with the prophecy and he tries this simple trick to get us out of the race. How foolish was I? I was sitting behind him so I would know what he was up to," answered Selim.

"Don't blame yourself Selim," said Ibrahim. "How were you to know he was going to pull up so quickly? Anyone in your place would have done the same."

"And," Ibrahim went on, "you won the race. Even with his trick Ishkuz couldn't beat you. Faraj surely has to be the best our tribe has ever bred, the horse our ancestors dreamed of breeding. Imagine how much you would have won by if you hadn't fallen. You surely have to be the bravest son of our tribe for riding with that injured arm. You truly are a descendant of the Sarmadees."

Selim's mind began to piece it all together. He had been so caught up in his anger at Ishkuz and the damage he could have caused Faraj that he hadn't thought much further. The pain he had felt in his arm as he rode had blocked everything but winning from his mind.

Pictures of the race slowly made their way into his mind and he remembered them passing horses and finally defeating the ebony Aswad and his white rider. Flashing before him were the eyes of Aswad and Ishkuz as he passed them, filled with defeat, and perhaps also fear?

Snatching him from his thoughts were some women entering the tent offering fresh fruit, cold meat, soft bread, honey and nuts, and some fresh milk and water. Selim smelled the food and immediately his stomach grumbled. He hadn't realised just how hungry he was and eagerly ate what was set before him.

Despite his mind feeling a little groggy, Selim still managed to sense a vague uneasiness and tension at the edge of his consciousness, as one of the women unwound the bandage on his arm. All eyes in the tent were on his arm and while he winced a number of times, he too was keen to see the damage the fall had caused. It was only when Ibrahim and the women exchanged glances and let out a quiet sigh, he realised why the tension had been so high. The wound looked ragged and red and there were grains of sand and some larger stones embedded in the remaining flesh, but there was no sign of poison. The women gently washed the wound, applied fresh salve and herbs and rewrapped it.

"So far so good," said Ibrahim, "but I am concerned about whether your bone will reset cleanly. There were some bone chips in the wound and it was difficult to put the bone back exactly in place." Selim lay down, a little more pale than before. Ibrahim noticed and said, "You must rest Selim. Your arm will heal well and be as useful as before. Just rest."

Ibrahim shooed all but one of the women out of the tent and then left himself after whispering instructions to Aseela. Selim's full stomach was adding to his drowsiness and he gave in to the desire to close his eyes. In the darkness which overcame him he heard Faraj neigh, but the heaviness was too great to fight and Selim slipped away. While he slept through the rest of the day, food was prepared, Faraj was walked and stretched, and the men talked angrily about the Sayhads and about Selim and Faraj in heroic terms. At various times, men from other tribes ventured into the camp to examine Faraj and talk about his breeding. They also spoke in awe of Selim's ride and wished their blessings on Selim and his recovery. Faraj stood quietly during the visits. While he sniffed and eyed the men who came to look and touch him, his mind and ears were focused on Selim's tent. He hadn't seen Selim for two days and he knew something wasn't right.

In the evening the women changed Selim's bandage again. As the bandage came off the air began to fill with a sickly, sweetness which overpowered the pungent herbal smell. There was a visible sag in the shoulders of the women, Ibrahim and Yusef, who had come to see Selim. Without looking they all knew the wound had become poisoned.

With a firm voice Aseela took control. "We must clean the wound again. Surely there is some way to rid the wound of this poison!"

"Yes, there must be," said Yusef. "I'll ask around the camp. Maybe one of the other tribes knows of a herb or ointment which can help."

He left through the flap of the tent and Selim and the others could hear him giving out commands to the men to go to the tribes and ask about their ways of treating poison in a wound. His voice faded as he moved away but Selim managed to pick out the word Sayhad. He wondered what Yusef had said about them, but the thought soon left as Aseela began to wash the wound, stirring up pain in his elbow.

His thoughts began to focus on what the poison might mean for him. "Was he going to die?" "How sick would he become?" "Was there no way out, after all he had achieved?"

He felt the hatred rising within him. He didn't know Ishkuz but he had affected his life beyond the winning or losing of a horse race. One reckless act and he was in danger of suffering a painful death, yet Ishkuz continued to live without punishment or judgement.

Selim wanted revenge!

Selim had never had feelings this strong before. Most of his life had been carefree and uncomplicated, except when his father had died when he was eleven. But that was different. The pain inside had disappeared over time, but here he was faced at worst, with his own possible death and at best, a painful healing of bone and flesh. He hadn't done anything to Ishkuz or to the Sayhad tribe. His mind wavered between his anger at Ishkuz and the aching in his arm. Aseela gave Selim another drink of mixed herbs and his mind slowed, and he became drowsy. He drifted off with his elbow pounding, murmuring the name Ishkuz.

The cool night air had settled over the camps and the fires had died down when a cloaked figure moved quietly over the sand and rocks toward the tent where Selim slept. Slipping through the ring of guards, the figure was so quiet that even the horses didn't sense him. He crept slowly to the side of Selim's tent and pulled a wooden handled dagger from his belt. Pushing it into the side of the tent and carefully pulling downward, a large enough rip was made in the woven fabric for him to fit through. Inside the tent it was even darker than outside and he sat quietly on his haunches just for a moment to let his eyes adjust to the light. Slowly he stood up and as he put his hand into his cloak a hand with an iron-like grip attached itself to his arm and pulled him to the ground. He felt the weight of a man on him, holding down his arms, calling for help. Confused guards entered, and some women in their nightwear appeared with lamps. The bright light blinded the intruder who was held firmly on either side by the guards.

Ibrahim stood up slowly from his bed. "I'm too old for this," he muttered. The other men who had been woken now rushed into the tent and Selim fought through his grogginess to understand what was going on.

"We have a visitor," remarked Ibrahim wryly.

"A late-night visitor who came uninvited and is unwelcome," added Yusef grumpily.

"Who is it and what does he want?" asked Selim.

Ibrahim pulled the hood covering the head of the downcast figure off his head and everyone in the tent recognised the blond hair, pale skin and blue eyes underneath.

Angry murmuring erupted and some men raised their swords, ready to injure Ishkuz, there and then. Even Selim gave a low curse while moving to a more comfortable position in his bed. The women cowered back and huddled together at the sight of Ishkuz as if they had seen a jinni.

"I see you've come to finish off the job you started," quipped Yusef. "Isn't it enough you've injured Selim and cursed his life with the wretched infection? So now you want to speed it all up with a dagger, do you? Answer us, you pale snake!" he added with derision.

Ibrahim held up his hand to silence Yusef. "Why have you come here at this time of night?" he asked Ishkuz.

The intruder lifted his head and looked straight at Selim. Selim was struck by the clearness of the blue in his eyes and couldn't break his gaze from him.

"I came in the night because I feared for my life. I was too afraid to turn up in daylight, even if I could. I know how angry you are at me. The sheikh of the Sayhads forbade me to visit. I heard Selim's wound had become infected and that's what has brought me here. I have some dried herbs, only a small amount, which I brought with me from my homeland. It can rid your wound of the poison. I wished to leave it here for Selim," answered Ishkuz.

"Why didn't you pass the herbs onto your sheikh to give to us? Why come skulking at night?" questioned Ibrahim.

"If you knew Sheikh Absalom you would know he would quickly trample the herbs under his foot and curse Selim to a deep, dark grave," replied Ishkuz. "He is a cruel man. His name means 'Father of Peace' but he's anything but that. He's the one who made me pull Aswad up and cause Selim to fall. He saw me teaching other horses the sliding stop and ordered me to teach Aswad. He threatened me so that I would do it. He has already beaten me for losing the race," Ishkuz added dolefully.

He pulled his robe off his shoulder to reveal some large red and purple welts. The men winced at the sight of them. A sudden change rippled among those present. Their judgements, their anger and their curses melted away. All they saw now was a beaten and bullied slave.

Pity for the young man began to wash over Selim and suddenly he realised why Ishkuz had looked fearful as he was passed in the race. He had been afraid of what the punishment would be for losing.

"Curse the Sayhads," said Yusef. "They have been a scourge on the sands since I have known them."

"Yes, yes," said Ibrahim to Yusef. "But the herbs, Ishkuz, what are they and will they work? What do you know of them?"

"Many years ago, a friend of mine injured himself in a similar way and the women used these herbs on him when the infection appeared. They have an earthy odour and when you breathe them in you think of strength. Not the strength of a horse or an auroch, but the strength of an immovable mountain or an ancient tree no wind can blow down."

With the words Ishkuz spoke, a new respect rose up in the hearts of the men and women listening.

"The herb must be placed on the wound and left for three days. It will remove the infection and clean the wound. I have never seen it fail. The herb is rare, even in our lands. What I have left is old. I was saving it in case I needed it for myself…" he trailed off, "but it keeps its strength for many years."

Ishkuz reached into his cloak and brought out a small leather bag. He handed it to Ibrahim who opened it and smelled the aroma. His eyes widened slightly and he nodded at Ishkuz and then handed it to the women to examine. The intensity on their faces as they passed the bag around proved to Ibrahim that this was a life-giving herb.

Aseela spoke up. "We smell the strength in this herb as the man has said and its aroma is vaguely familiar. Perhaps it is related to some of the herbs we know. We are happy to use it, Ibrahim, if you and Selim agree."

"Everyone return to your beds," Ibrahim said, addressing the men. "We need to speak further about this. It appears Ishkuz is no harm to Selim or to us and may be more of a friend to us than to the Sayhads. Good night to you all. Yusef and Sekeen, can you please stay with us," said Ibrahim.

The men left, some doubtfully, but all were willing to leave the matter to the leaders of their tribe. Ibrahim indicated to Ishkuz that he should sit. Ibrahim, Yusef, Sekeen and Aseela found positions next to him on the carpet while Selim carefully lifted himself up to a sitting position.

Ishkuz spoke before the others could begin. "Selim, I am truly sorry for your accident and pray to my gods there will be no lasting effect on your bones. I'm sure the herb will save you from the infection. I never wished any harm to you or Faraj and wish none now. I already know Faraj was not harmed for he ran the last part of the race with speed and power, like a desert wind, and your ride with a broken arm is worthy of joining the stories of your ancestors."

Selim was a little overwhelmed and murmured his thanks.

Ishkuz continued. "I haven't seen a horse like Faraj in all my time and travels. He truly is a horse worthy of the mountains and sand. Aswad is a good horse and the best of the Sayhads, but for Faraj to win like he did shows what a heart and spirit and body he has. He would be welcome in my tent," Ishkuz ended, with a smile.

Enjoying the compliment Ibrahim replied with half a smile, "You are a fair judge of horseflesh it would seem. I hope your knowledge of herbs is as good."

He added, "Have your welts been attended to?"

"Yes, thank you. I have had ointment put on. They will heal quickly," answered Ishkuz.

"Have you been beaten like this before?" asked Selim.

"Yes, quite a number of times. It all depends on Sheikh Absalom's mood. Sometimes he will overlook a major thing and then beat you for something small. I have always tried to do my best so I stay out of trouble but sometimes I can't avoid it," answered Ishkuz.

Ibrahim and Selim looked at each other thoughtfully and knew the other was feeling some pity for this pale-skinned young man but were not willing to say it.

Ibrahim spoke first. "Selim, what do you think? Do you trust Ishkuz and the herb?"

Selim took a moment to answer. He was beginning to feel more awake and able to think things through. "It's hard to deny what he says. We know a little of his background and we know that the Sayhads are a harsh tribe. The welts and bruising may have come from losing the race, or for another reason. However, if he wished me dead, he needn't have come and risked himself, as he knew that the infection had begun. There is more reason to believe him than not," answered Selim carefully.

After a moment he added, "the herb won't hurt me more than the infection and in the end it might save me. It's a risk I think is worth taking."

Ibrahim let out a sigh. He had come to the same conclusion but wanted Selim to willingly accept the herb.

"Very well," he said. "Aseela, take the herbs and apply them to the wound."

Aseela came and took the bag of herbs and said to Ishkuz, "What is the best way to prepare and apply them?"

"You'll need to break them more than they are already, "he replied, "then spread them over the wound, and wrap it to hold the herbs in place. Leave them there for three days. Don't put fresh bandages on each day. When you remove them the wound will be clean and healthy."

Aseela nodded and called one of the women to help her.

There was silence for a time, then Ishkuz asked, "What will you do with me?"

"Nothing. You are free to leave," replied Ibrahim. He then continued, "It may seem strange to you but before the race we knew you would cause trouble for Selim, but we also knew you would bring some sort of relief or goodness to him."

"How could you have known?" stammered Ishkuz in surprise.

"Selim was given a prophecy from an old man in the city before the race and was warned that a pale rider would be both bitter and sweet toward him. We didn't know of you at the time but soon found out a pale-skinned rider was to race for the Sayhads. We weren't sure if you would attempt to harm Selim or Faraj in the race. The prophecy didn't say either way, but we warned Selim to stay close to you and Aswad so he could see what you were doing. As it turns out he stayed too close." He paused. "However, it's time to rest. You may go, but please go through the front opening of the tent. The men will not harm you."

Ishkuz had many questions for Ibrahim but restrained himself from asking for fear of upsetting him and also Selim, who looked in pain. He simply asked, "May I call again to see how Selim is doing?"

"That's up to Selim. Selim, do you want another visit from Ishkuz?" asked Ibrahim.

"Yes," he answered. "Come tomorrow, but make it in the afternoon."

Ishkuz bowed to the two men before leaving. Selim settled down to sleep after the women had dressed his wound with the herb, though he found it hard after the excitement and with the pain in his arm. Ibrahim lay down on his bed too, which just happened to be right next to the cut in the tent.

CHAPTER 10

Selim slept fitfully but late into the morning. His body was still recovering from the shock of the fall and his broken bones, and though he felt stronger, he was fearful of what was under the bandage, even with the herb Ishkuz had given. After he had eaten, he felt strong enough to visit the horses. When Faraj and Aisha saw him they both neighed. As he walked closer to Faraj, Selim could see he showed no signs of stress or injury. His appetite seemed unharmed. He had eaten all his food and was looking for more.

Knowing Selim's concern for the horses, Sekeen came up to him and said, "The only thing we've needed to tend to was some tightness in his muscles. We have already walked him today and will keep doing so every day to loosen them. Otherwise, he could run the race again. He is such a fine horse."

"During the race he showed more heart and stamina than I have ever seen in him," answered Selim. "When I asked for more he gave it. He stared into Aswad's eye as we passed him and I saw the fear in him, as if he had never lost before and didn't know how to deal with it."

"Hmm," said Sekeen, "in every physical part of life there is also spirit. Aswad may be strong and fast, and bred to run, but he needs more than the physical to deal with the difficulties of a race. It's the spirit which must overcome the inner obstacles so that he can run at his best. His spirit was challenged, maybe for the first time in his life, and will need to be developed if he is to overcome his fear and this setback and go on to win."

"I have never thought of racing in this way," Selim replied. "I know in all of us there is a spirit separate from the body and yet it's so much a part of it. It seems horses are no different to humans in this way. I always seem to struggle with problems and issues inside and it seems once they have settled they no longer affect what I do or how I feel."

"That's how life goes Selim. It's not so much about what we achieve in our life but what we overcome in ourselves. Your spirit will be stronger for the fall and the determination you showed in getting back on Faraj, as well as overcoming your injury and the poison. Your spirit has already been shaped by these things and your courage sharpened beyond those who haven't experienced these things."

Selim nodded thoughtfully at Sekeen's words. "But," he thought, "to benefit from this I have to live." It struck him deeply how much his life depended on the herbs Ishkuz had given. He desperately hoped they would work. If they did, then there truly was sweetness to Ishkuz as the prophecy had said, for he would have saved him from death.

Sekeen left Selim to pat Aisha, who was waiting impatiently. She nuzzled him affectionately and her large deep black eyes gave Selim a sense of peace.

"Peace to you Selim, how are you doing?" called out Feluj as he arrived at the camp.

"I'm stronger Feluj, thank you. But the wound is infected, and I don't hold out much hope," replied Selim. At this stage he didn't want Feluj to know about Ishkuz's visit or the herbs he had been given.

"Oh, come my lad," said Feluj. "You are young and strong and if the way you rode in the race is any indication, you are spirited and courageous as well. The whole city is talking about you. Don't worry. You will come through. Don't give up hope. As I told my third wife one time…"

Ibrahim walked up to greet Feluj and winked at Selim. "Peace to you, Feluj. Selim, Aseela wants to see you in the tent."

Ibrahim took Feluj's elbow and directed him away. Selim went back to the tent, thankful that Ibrahim had rescued him from Feluj's story and from his shallowness. Aseela didn't actually want him, so he lay on his bed and dozed.

An hour or so after Ishkuz came into camp, calling quietly to Selim. Selim beckoned him into the tent and Ishkuz seated himself on the ground. He offered Ishkuz some wine and dates and then said to him, "We have heard a little about your country and people from Feluj the merchant but tell me more about your land and people and your horses. Where did you learn to ride? Was it with your people or among the Sayhads?"

"No, not among the Sayhads. My own tribe are people of the horse and grasslands. As a child I was put on the back of a horse and have been riding ever since. We are a roaming people with no fixed home. We travel in wagons and herd our horses and flocks to places with the best grass. My lands are far to the north where grass is as plentiful as the sand is here." Ishkuz paused. "I was taken captive in a raid and sold a number of times, each time further south until I ended up with the Sayhads."

Selim had many questions but the one he needed an answer to first was whether all his people had blonde hair, blue eyes and pale skin.

Ishkuz smiled, as it was a question he was asked often.

"No," he replied, "many have dark hair and dark eyes. Only some have blonde hair, and there are even some with red hair!"

"Red hair!" blurted out Selim. "I can't even imagine that. Do you mean red like our chestnut horses?"

"Yes" said Ishkuz and then he went on. "My mother had blonde hair and blue eyes and came from the north west. She told me almost all of her people are some shade of blonde and most have blue eyes."

Again Selim found it hard to imagine. All of his people were dark haired, dark eyed and had various shades of dark skin. Selim sat thoughtfully for a moment. "Are your horses as fast as Faraj?" he added.

"We have fast horses," answered Ishkuz, "but none as fast as Faraj. He is a prince among all horses. Our horses are taller and longer but also narrower.

They will travel day after day, with little food or water and their hooves are as hard as rock."

Selim realised again that his image of Ishkuz needed to change. Here he sat with as much skill as Selim had and he openly and honestly stated Faraj to be one of the fastest of all horses he had seen. There was no boasting or exaggeration. He hadn't expected this from Ishkuz. His image of him had been shaped by his fear of the first half of the prophecy, "he will be bitter."

Selim went on, "Tell me who came up with the idea of the shortened stirrups."

"Yes, I saw you shortened your stirrups for the race. The idea came about by accident and we don't ride with them like that all the time. You would know from riding with short stirrups just how easily you can become unbalanced."

Ishkuz's face coloured with embarrassment and he bowed his head.

Selim waved his hand, dismissing the comment and said, "Go on Ishkuz. How did the short stirrups come about?"

After a moment Ishkuz went on, "Short stirrups are no good for herding cattle or hunting but really help with racing, which our tribes do all the time. It was actually a woman of our tribe who started riding this way. She found it was more comfortable for her being a number of months pregnant. She didn't have the stirrups as short as they could be, but we noticed the horse moved more freely when she rode this way. We experimented with different lengths and found that when short stirrups are used and the rider's weight is carried forward it helps the horse to run more freely. Is that what you found?"

"Yes," answered Selim, "we tested the shorter stirrups on Aisha, a mare of ours, and it felt really strange. I needed to find a new centre of balance and use different muscles to hold myself on. I know in the race it helped Faraj a lot, especially up the hills when I could lean forward a lot more than with long stirrups. It really freed up his hind legs. I think we will be riding this way more often."

Ishkuz smiled proudly. He was glad his tribe's idea would be copied so far from his homeland.

"What is the name of your tribe and country?" asked Selim.

"We call ourselves Scythians but others know us as Sakas. We don't own any land," replied Ishkuz.

"I haven't heard the name Scythian before but I like the sound of it. I only heard the name Saka recently. Our tribe tries to learn as much as we can from travellers, especially from traders, for we are quite limited in our contact with others. We live many days from here but to the southwest, so a visit to the city to see other tribes is a big event for us. And to win the race gives our tribe much honour, and much pleasure," said Selim.

Ishkuz nodded to Selim in respect. Selim then lowered his voice and asked in a serious tone, "Will these herbs really work? There are only two nights and a day to go and…" His voice trailed off.

Ishkuz looked concerned knowing what Selim was unable to say. "I know they have worked before and pray they will work for you."

Selim nodded in return. Ishkuz had said the same the day before but it helped to hear this again to push back the fear which kept eating up his hope. They sat in silence for a time, both of them aware of the seriousness of Selim's situation.

"Just another two nights and a day and I will know," Selim thought.

Feeling awkward, Ishkuz decided it was time to leave. On the one hand he enjoyed talking to someone his age with the same interests in horses and riding, but on the other hand he felt responsible for Selim's situation.

"The bandages will be taken off the day after tomorrow. Is that right, Selim? Ishkuz asked. Selim nodded.

"May I visit again tomorrow?" asked Ishkuz.

"Yes, of course," answered Selim. "You may come."

"Until tomorrow then, Selim. Be at peace," said Ishkuz.

"Peace to you," answered Selim.

Ishkuz left the tent and made his way carefully back to his camp as he was still forbidden to visit Selim.

Selim felt no extra pain in his arm. He couldn't tell whether the herbs were working or not. He wished he could, and the men noticed him looking often at his bandaged arm that night around the fire. They purposely did not ask him how it felt, as they knew he needed to keep his mind off it.

From the talk around the campfire it appeared that Al Maksour was being given credit for Selim's win in the race. Ibrahim had heard this type of thing before. When things went well Al Maksour was the cause of all blessings and when things didn't go so well, the jinn or the gods were blamed for turning against them. Even the Creator who played little part in the lives and thinking of the tribe was blamed for all sorts of things when life did not go so well.

Talk of remaking Al Maksour had also begun. This discussion resurfaced in the tribe from time to time and some thought the sword should be honoured by being made whole again. They said it may even increase its power for good and this would make the tribe even stronger. Ibrahim was sceptical. He had seen too many years change from good to bad and from bad to good to believe a sword had any power over life, especially a broken one. He was convinced the world was far more complex and intricate than many thought. No sword or jinni or even the Creator could control or direct all the happenings of even an hour without being completely overwhelmed.

Selim excused himself from the campfire and went to his bed. He tried to sleep but he did little more than toss and turn thinking of the third day approaching and trying not to lie on his arm.

The sun had been up for some hours before he stirred after his restless night. He got up and lifted the flap of the tent. Shielding his eyes against the sun, he saw one of the men leading Faraj around in circles. The sun shimmered on his coat and glistened like gold on his swaying mane and tail. When Faraj was turned in the direction of the tent Selim called out to him and he whinnied in response.

It was already heating up so Selim moved back into the tent. He was restless and impatient. He knew the bone would take weeks to heal but it meant nothing if the infection remained. He wandered down to the horses and chatted with the men feeding and cleaning them.

After lunch Ishkuz slipped into camp, watching his back to check he wasn't being followed. Despite this he greeted Selim happily. "Selim," he said, "how are you?"

Selim replied honestly. "I just want the bandage off and I want to know whether the herbs have worked."

Ishkuz thought Selim might appreciate being distracted for a while so he decided to ask Selim about his tribe's horse breeding in an effort to pass the time more quickly and keep his mind off waiting.

"Selim, I have been wanting to ask you about Faraj's breeding. What are his sire and dam like, and how about Aisha? I saw her the other day and asked one of your men her name. I think she is magnificent. What a character she has! Do all your horses have her spirit?" Ishkuz blurted out.

The questions took Selim by surprise. He suddenly realised how eager he was to think about something else.

"Aisha is everything you would want in a mare. She is fast, safe and her ancestors trace to the first horses my tribe captured in the Sarmadee mountains. She knows the mountains and its tracks and while she is high-spirited, she is fiercely jealous and loyal. Her dam was a chestnut who was also fast. Her sire was a flea bitten grey like Aisha, a strong, masculine stallion. He could run all day and be fresh and ready for another day's running the next morning. Ibrahim will be able to tell you more, as I only knew him as an old stallion. Faraj is one of the best my tribe has ever bred, and we have his first colt at our fort who is just as good or better than him."

Ishkuz's mouth and eyes opened at the possibility of there being a horse better than Faraj and said, "I would really love to see that colt. What is his dam like?"

"The colt is bay and his dam is an old bay mare named Bashasha. She's produced a lot of excellent horses for us. She is a tough, hardy mare with a deep body and powerful movement which makes her glide over the ground. We are going to repeat the same mating and are hoping to get a filly next as she has not many years left to breed," Selim replied. He then added, "I wish you could see the colt and our other horses. I would love to show them to you. Any one of them is more than equal to the horses of the other tribes. Although, your Aswad has many qualities our tribe likes to see in their horses."

"Yes," answered Ishkuz, "he is a fine horse and I have grown fond of him since training him for the race."

Ishkuz paused to consider and then said, "It seems to me the horses here in Arabia seem to understand me more than those at home. I find it hard to explain but they seem to know what I am thinking… and they're interested in what I am doing. They seem more human. I know it sounds strange but it's the feeling I get. I haven't told anyone this as it sounds so strange."

Selim responded, "I haven't been around any other horses to compare, but most of us in the tribe know the feeling and have experienced horses becoming very attached to one person. It doesn't mean others can't handle them or ride them but there seems to be a connection on a level beyond the physical, it's sort of spiritual."

Selim immediately thought of Sekeen and what he had said about there being a spirit in living creatures. He had never thought of his relationship with his horses in quite that way. He wasn't sure if it was a good description. He would have to think about it.

Selim changed the subject, realising he hadn't offered Ishkuz refreshments.

"Would you like a drink and some fruit?" he asked.

"Yes, yes," answered Ishkuz. "Thank you."

They both seated themselves on the ground in the shade of the tent and Selim called one of the women to see if she could serve some milk, dates and oranges. They continued to talk about horses and breeding and riding. Selim was keen to see what he could learn from Ishkuz, as he did seem to have some clever ideas. Ishkuz was impressed when Selim told him they had stripped Faraj's saddle in an effort to reduce the overall weight Faraj had to carry. He confessed they had always expected the horses to carry whatever weight was on them and didn't think that a few extra kilograms here or there would matter very much. Selim agreed they had thought the same way but that the shortened stirrups had made them think more about the horse's movement and what might stop it.

Some of the men of the tribe joined them in the tent, thirsty after working and cleaning the horses. Most were still wary of Ishkuz, but they knew they might have to change their minds about him if his herbs healed Selim's wound. It would show he had not wanted to hurt Selim in the race and had been threatened by Absalom as he said. However, time would tell, so they held onto their prejudice.

The afternoon passed and as the sun began to descend Ishkuz took his leave. Selim thanked him for the visit. It had certainly made the day go much faster. He had just one more night and day to go. Selim slept fitfully that night, his body filled with anxiety.

Late the next day Ishkuz again came but he and Selim didn't speak much as the tension of waiting was weighing on everyone. Finally, Ibrahim came to them and said, "Let's not wait any longer. Let's see if these herbs have destroyed the poison. The waiting is killing me."

Selim and the others jumped up and Ibrahim called for Aseela. She and the other women and the tribesmen gathered around, eager to see what the herbs had done. Aseela carefully unwrapped the bandages to reveal the wound. Her eyes widened as she looked at it.

"The infection has gone," she declared. "The wound is clean and healing well."

The onlookers cheered and clapped and some of the men slapped Ishkuz on the back and smiled. Inside Ishkuz felt greatly relieved. He didn't know what they would have done if the poison had remained. Selim lifted his head and smiled broadly at Ishkuz. The smell of death had gone and parts of the wound were looking pink and healthy. The herbs had disappeared as if they had lost their existence while destroying the infection, but the job had been done.

Selim let out a huge sigh, as if he had been holding his breath for the whole three days. All he could think of was that he was going to live. He was going to live. The prophecy about Ishkuz entered his mind—"bitter and sweet." He knew he owed Ishkuz his life, but he also realised how sweet it was to be given his life back. All this went through his mind as Aseela carefully rebandaged his arm and put it back into the sling across his shoulder.

Ibrahim called out loudly, "Tonight we celebrate. Selim is back from the dead and Ishkuz has become one of our closest friends. He has helped return Selim to us. Send the good news to the sheikh of Al Huraydah. Our tribe will celebrate its victory in the race and we will salute our rider and his horse."

There was a roar from the men and women and Selim couldn't keep the grin off his face. He was finally able to think about how he and Faraj had won the race and what it meant. He rose and went over to Ishkuz, embracing him with his one good arm.

"Ishkuz," he said. "I thank you. And my tribe thanks you for your honesty and courage in coming to help me, offering the last of your special herbs. You are welcome at our fire and fort any time."

Ishkuz nodded and looked down, somewhat embarrassed by the attention.

Selim went on, "You must join us tonight in our celebrations. You are part of the reason we celebrate."

Ishkuz looked fearful. "But what about Sheikh Absalom? He won't let me come. I don't know if I can sneak away again. He is bound to notice."

"I don't think you have to worry about Sheikh Absalom again," Selim replied. "Ibrahim and I will take care of him. Stay here with me in our camp. Ibrahim and I will go and see him this afternoon. Our men will protect you if anyone comes looking for you."

Ishkuz was taken back by Selim's words. He was surprised Selim wanted to help and protect him. It was unusual for a slave to be protected from their masters. Slaves were the property of their owners and usually did to them as they wished.

Selim had moved over quickly to Ibrahim and led him aside to speak to him. Ishkuz could see Ibrahim nodding and looking at him as Selim spoke. Sekeen was also called over to them and he too listened to Selim and nodded in agreement. Then Ishkuz saw Selim and Ibrahim leave the camp. Feeling unsure of what to do he went over to Faraj and smoothed his mane and forelock.

As Ishkuz watched on, the men and women began preparing for the celebration dinner. Fires were stoked and men went for more firewood and fresh water while the women busied themselves preparing breads and meat. It felt strange not to be involved in the preparations. He felt apprehensive about Selim and Ibrahim meeting Absalom. Absalom would not easily give permission for Ishkuz to be in the camp and to celebrate with the winners of the race, even if the leaders of this tribe asked him.

"This is so odd," he thought. "I'm a slave and here I am in another tribe's camp patting the best stallion in the world, all by myself. And the leaders of a tribe I met this week are speaking on my behalf to my owner so I can join in their celebration." Ishkuz's head spun.

It didn't quite seem real. It was as if he had been transformed in the blink of an eye into a person of importance and respect when before he had been nothing. He knew Selim and the tribe appreciated his help in giving of the herbs but he didn't expect to be rewarded in any way. He just felt he needed to make up for the pain and injury he had been forced to cause Selim.

The hearty smell of cooking meat began to fill the camp and men gathered around the fire readying themselves for the festivities. On their return, Ibrahim and Selim made their way to Ishkuz.

"It is all organised. Come, join the men, eat your fill and celebrate my double win. A horse race and my life back," said Selim with great pleasure in his voice.

Ishkuz felt somewhat confused and simply followed Selim to a spot on the carpets laid out around the fire. He couldn't begin to think what they had said to make Absalom agree. He only hoped when he returned to camp tomorrow that Absalom would not punish him.

Visitors from other tribes joined in the celebration and musicians played as men and women danced and sang the praises of Faraj and Selim. Spirits were high, as the tribe no longer lived under the shadow of Selim's death. Fear and worry no longer mingled with the joy of winning the race. Tonight was a night of joy alone.

After the meal Ibrahim stood and asked for quiet. He looked at the faces gathered around.

"Tonight, we do not just celebrate a victory in the horse race, a race run with tremendous courage and determination by both horse and rider. We also celebrate the health of Selim. For this we owe a debt of gratitude to Ishkuz. It is a debt we cannot pay. However, we will attempt to."

Then directing his comments to Ishkuz, he said, "Ishkuz please stand." Ishkuz rose awkwardly and stood with his eyes facing the ground.

"I want to welcome you not only as a free man but as a member of this tribe, if that is what you wish. You showed great courage to come to us and offer help to Selim. We have negotiated your freedom with Sheikh Absalom for your act of kindness, for returning Selim to us."

Ishkuz looked around, dazed. The crowd shouted wildly and then continued with their singing and dancing. They had yet another thing to celebrate. Ishkuz turned to Selim and mouthed, "How?"

Selim shrugged his shoulders suggesting he wasn't prepared to share it with Ishkuz but had a knowing smile on his face. Ishkuz bent down and Selim said to him, "Absalom drives a hard bargain."

Then with a bigger smile he said, "We hope you're worth it." With this he jabbed him in the ribs with his good arm and both of them laughed.

CHAPTER 11

The return to the fort was a joyful trip. Selim felt stronger every day and he enjoyed riding with Ishkuz, his new friend. It was strange how the man he had hated and wanted revenge on was now part of his tribe and they were travelling home together. Ishkuz was talkative and full of laughter, grateful to have received his life back too. He was no longer a slave and was free to go back to his own people. For the time being he wanted to stay with Selim's tribe and experience their life and see their horses.

Ishkuz and Selim had become firm friends. They seemed to have a lot in common and actually liked being in each other's company. Each young man had found in the other a desire for understanding and knowledge about life and horses and the wider world, and each had been able to learn from the other because of their different experiences and origins. Ishkuz could hardly contain his interest when Selim told him about the cave with the painting of the large boat and the animals on the walls. And when Selim told him of the grass painted on the wall which seemed as vast as the desert, Ishkuz nearly fell off his horse, as this was what the grass was like in Scythia.

As they rode their talk turned to the prophecy Selim had received. Ishkuz still had many questions he wanted answered.

"Is this telling of the future common among your tribe? I didn't ever hear of it among the Sayhads. I only remember a strange long-haired woman from my childhood who at times said things to our tribe, which either seemed to scare them or make them very happy. I got the feeling she could tell the future, but I'm not sure."

Selim replied, "I don't know much about this type of thing. The old man's prophecy is the first I've heard. He did say that a strange feeling comes over him and his mind blanks out and then he says things he has no control over. It wasn't something he tried to do or wanted to do, it just happened to him."

"Are there others in your tribe who might know more about this?" asked Ishkuz.

"Yes, I think Sekeen might be the best. Let's ride up to him and ask," replied Selim.

Earlier they had seen Sekeen ride up to the front of their tribe's caravan, so they spurred their horses on. They found him there and rode up beside him.

"Sekeen, we have some questions for you," said Selim. "What do you know about prophecy? It seems so strange for a person to tell the future. How do they do it? Where does it come from?" he continued quickly.

"You have asked some deep questions," replied Sekeen. "And I certainly don't have all the answers. Do they relate to what the old man said to you in Al Huraydah?"

"Well, yes and no," Selim replied. "I think we are trying to understand... understand what world... the words come from? What power is out there that can bring the future into the present?"

"Hmmm," said Sekeen, "you've chosen a mystery no-one I know can give a satisfying answer to. The traditions and stories Ibrahim tell us show there is a world beyond what we see. A world of the Creator and jinn and spirits with which we have little contact. Maybe, somehow, some people are chosen to be a channel, a doorway, for a time between the two worlds. How and why this happens is beyond me. We haven't had anyone in our tribe I know of who could speak about the future like the man in Al Huraydah."

"I haven't really thought of the jinn and spirits and the Creator belonging to another real world before. I've heard of them through Ibrahim's stories but never really thought of them as existing somewhere and actually affecting us," reflected Selim.

Ishkuz chimed in, "Me either. All I see is the sky and grass and sand, the things of this world. It's hard to believe there is a world somewhere beyond this one, but the old man did somehow know about the future. It's hard to argue with what he said."

Selim went on, "I have to say I have thought a lot about how I responded to the words. At first, I thought you knew about these words and were going to bring some bitterness to me because you were evil. But then I found out you were a slave and that Absalom had threatened you. The prophecy was right about what happened, but said nothing about what made you do it. I was angry with you and judged you, and I wanted to kill you after the race. But when you came to us, I had to change my thinking about you. The prophecy made me think you were evil, but you were reacting to evil in your life. It was all very confusing, until we learned why you acted the way you did," ended Selim.

Then he added, "It seems prophecy needs to be understood carefully."

"I think you're right, Selim," said Sekeen. "While prophecy may give us a glimpse of the future, it doesn't give us a full picture which is why it can be so misunderstood."

Selim and Ishkuz spent the rest of the day riding with Sekeen who asked a lot of questions about the horses belonging to the Sakas. Ishkuz was eager to answer and talked like he had been part of the tribe for a long time and Selim couldn't help but smile at his eagerness and confidence.

After some days of riding, they finally made their way down the mountain road which overlooked the river valley and the fort. Some of the men whose families hadn't been able to make the trip raced ahead to meet them and then they all made their way through the wooden gates and into the fort. Eager hands helped to unload horses and remove saddles. Many congratulated Selim on his win, while others gathered around Faraj and looked at him with new respect and pride. Faraj pranced proudly as he was unsaddled and led away to be washed. The story of Selim's victory had spread quickly through the fort and many wide eyes cast themselves toward Ishkuz, who was a little uncomfortable with all the attention.

Selim's mother and sister were waiting to greet Selim. He hugged both of them and his mother, Almas, questioned him about his bandaged arm. Selim explained to them what had happened and then pulled Ishkuz over to introduce him. Selim's mother held out her hand and grasped the hand of Ishkuz. With deep emotion she said, "Thank you Ishkuz. Thank you for giving your herbs to him. Thank you for letting him come back to us, to me. I lost his father in a riding accident when Selim was seven. I couldn't bear to have lost him in the same way. Thank you. Selim has told me about you, and you are welcome to stay as long as you like."

She pulled a reluctant Ansim forward and, presenting her to Ishkuz said, "This is my daughter, Ansim."

Ansim's eyes were wide with hesitation and yet showed amazement and interest. She had never seen a pale-skinned person before. She lowered her head and eyes and nodded to Ishkuz and then said, "Welcome."

Normally Ansim was a lively character, full of life and joy, and she loved playing practical jokes on her family and friends. She was seventeen years old and her beauty was clearly evident. Her hair was dark and thick and her eyes were also large and dark, made darker by the soft, smooth, brown skin which surrounded them and the black makeup common to the women. She had full lips and straight, white teeth which contrasted with her complexion when she smiled. Ishkuz was overwhelmed by her beauty and couldn't take his gaze from her. At the same time, he was embarrassed to be looking at her so intently in the presence of Selim and his mother. He suddenly felt hot and cold all over, a sensation he hadn't experienced before. He managed to stammer out a "Thank you."

Selim took Ishkuz into the fort and showed him to his room. Once alone, Ishkuz wandered around the room, looked through the window at the mountains in the distance and pondered how much his life had changed in the past few weeks. It all felt like a dream. Freedom certainly felt good. Inside he had a new energy, and was eager to see the horses which had produced Faraj and Aisha. Somehow, he knew that here in this valley lived horses which riders the world over would want underneath them. They were horses of character and strength. Horses toughened on the slope of the Sarmadees and the furnaces of the desert. Horses whose thirst was slaked by the melted snow of the mountains and whose stomachs were satisfied by the grain and lucerne of the fertile plain. Horses whose blood and life seemed to spring from the mountains themselves.

He moved to the door, intent on finding Selim so they could go to the paddocks and stables and see the herds. He made his way through to the main rooms and found Selim speaking with his mother and sister. He felt awkward intruding on their private conversation and before he could leave unseen, Selim called to him. Ishkuz came over but seemed to have lost the confidence he showed on their trip back from Al Huraydah. He tried to keep his eyes on Selim but twice his eyes diverted to Ansim.

He said rather haltingly, "I was wondering, if you have time, of course, whether you could show me the horses you have here."

Selim responded by slapping Ishkuz on the back saying, "Of course. We always have time to look at horses. It's one of my favourite jobs, and it looks like you could do with some air. It gets stuffy in here. Let's go."

As they made their way out of the rooms deep in the fort Selim couldn't keep the smile off his face as he realised Ishkuz was attracted to Ansim. As a slave he had probably never learned how to interact with beautiful young women.

Selim said to Ishkuz, "There is a saying in our tribe: 'Beware of the beautiful colours of the lizard which lies under the rocks, for the lizard bites those drawn to its colours.'"

Ishkuz turned his head quickly toward Selim as the meaning of the saying became clear to him. He blushed and dropped his head again. Selim laughed as he realised he had guessed correctly. Ishkuz just wanted to disappear, be taken by a jinni, or dropped into a hole.

As the paddocks came into view the feeling passed and his attention turned to the mares and foals grazing. They climbed to the top of the fence and some of the grazing foals lifted their heads to look at the two men.

"These are the mares with foals," said Selim. "They will be weaned soon."

He pointed to Bashasha's bay colt and said to Ishkuz, "This bay colt is one of the finest horses we have bred. He's already tall, strong and fast. He is one of the first sons of Faraj. His mother is an older mare, the bay over there." Selim pointed her out to Ishkuz.

Ishkuz was deeply impressed by the colt. He still had the shaggy coat of a foal but Ishkuz could see the colt's quality, height and confidence. Some of the fillies also took Ishkuz's eye. One of them was a chestnut who looked similar to Faraj.

He asked Selim, "Is that filly one of Faraj's?"

"Yes," Selim replied. "She has the longest legs of any horse we have bred and she looks a lot like Faraj when he was young. Her dam is the chestnut one in the corner. She was very fast when she was younger, so we expect the filly to be even faster knowing Faraj is her father. The mare's dam was a grey mare who was known for her endurance and strength even with little to eat. She once saved my grandfather from a group of men from another tribe while he was out looking for metal rocks. They tried to chase her, but even though their horses were fresh and my grandfather and his horse were at the end of a long day, they couldn't make up any ground on her. That's where Aisha gets her endurance from, though she's not as fast as Faraj or the filly's mother."

The chestnut filly flicked its tail in the air as Selim finished speaking as if she was aware he was talking about her. She lifted her head and danced a number of steps with her eyes and nostrils wide. The sound of children playing on the other side of the paddock spooked her and she snorted at them.

Selim and Ishkuz walked through the herd, rubbing the heads and necks of those interested enough or willing to have it done. Ishkuz said to Selim, "I don't think I have ever seen a group of foals as excellent as these. Our horses are a little longer in the back and probably longer in the body overall and our horses also have the glint of gold and silver to the coats. But there is a quality and shape about your horses which makes them distinct. Your tribe certainly knows how to breed horses."

Selim smiled and thanked him. "Come on Ishkuz. Let's go and see the horses in the stables."

Ishkuz was already familiar with some of the horses, but there were some older stallions and two-and three-year-old colts and fillies he had not seen. The men of the tribe nodded to the Selim and Ishkuz as they made their way to the stables and the young men who were tending the horses called out to them. Selim asked them to put a halter on the horses they were brushing and to bring them out for Ishkuz to see.

The first horse was a two-year-old filly, a bay who pranced and snorted as her handler proudly brought her out of the stable. Ishkuz noticed her black, velvety nostrils stretching widely and her alert, playful eyes. She was keen to explore, excited and energetic, but her handler skilfully brought her to a standstill. As she stood there in the late sun, Ishkuz could see the shape of her skeleton and the angles of her bones. She had a lovely angled, long shoulder with a well-set neck and straight front tendons, which looked like they would take a lot of work. Her back was short and strong, while her hindquarter was a little high due to her growth.

"She's a little rump high at the moment, but she is only two, so she is still growing," mentioned Selim.

Ishkuz murmured his agreement as his eyes kept going over the glistening bay.

"So many good things about her. So many things that are just right," he thought to himself. While he would have liked to see a slightly longer forearm and more hind leg muscling, he knew he had to remember there was still a lot of growing in the filly and that these things could change.

"She is wonderful, Selim. A true riding horse of the desert," Ishkuz said.

"Thank you Ishkuz, we are very proud of her. She is from a different line to Faraj. I'll show you her father and mother shortly. She is a solid horse with a strong frame which is important out here in the desert and mountains," replied Selim.

"Thank you Tafsul, she is looking wonderful. You're doing a great job looking after her," Selim said.

He then turned to a boy waiting outside the next stable. "Raaqim, can you bring your horse out for us to see?"

Raaqim quickly unbolted the stable door and was soon leading out another filly just as proudly as Tafsul had done. She was a chestnut with three white socks and a thin blaze.

"This filly is nearly three years old and has the same sire as Faraj but sadly he died not long after this filly was conceived. I think she is similar to Faraj in many ways but may not have the width of his body," explained Selim.

The filly was quite placid and Ishkuz stroked her nose and ran his hand over her neck and body. She didn't move at all, trusting Ishkuz would not hurt her. He bent down and picked up one of her feet and saw the hoof was round and large and the frog was well developed and wide.

"This is a good foot. One of the better ones I have seen," he thought to himself. Then to Selim he said, "She has very good feet and a large frog to pump the blood back up the leg. I would think Faraj would have the same for him to run so far and fast."

"Yes," agreed Selim, "it came from their sire. He passed on large hooves and a wide deep frog to most of his foals. He also gave them a long, wide hindquarter which gives our horses the power to go through the sand and up the mountain trails. He was a great breeder. He was grey and not overly tall but very well balanced in both length and height. He had a neck which came high out of his withers and when he was ridden it would rise up in front of you in a beautiful arc."

"I would love to have seen him," said Ishkuz. "He would have made quite a sight."

"Yes, we miss him deeply," Selim replied to Ishkuz.

Then to Raaqim he said, "Thank you for showing us Zaynab. She is looking so healthy and she is so quiet in your hands."

Raaqim grinned happily and returned Zaynab back to her stable.

The next horse was the mother of the bay filly and she too was a bay. She showed signs of age but there was a dignity and quality which still shone through in her bearing and eyes. Ishkuz noticed how slender her throat latch was and how this made her neck seem quite long. Her legs were somewhat lumpy and scarred but Ishkuz had seen the same on other horses who were older and had worked hard over their lifetime. She nickered to the other horses but seemed quite content with her own company and the gentle hands of the ones who cared for her.

"Ishkuz, we'll go around the other side to the stallion stables," said Selim.

They made their way around and Selim took a halter from its hook outside a stable, went in and brought a magnificent mahogany bay stallion into the sunlight. He had the largest liquid eyes Ishkuz had ever seen, even larger than Aisha's. Ishkuz was shocked by the structure and shape of this stallion. His head was small with short ears which highlighted his large luminous eyes and his luxuriously thick black mane. He was a powerful and muscular horse. Ishkuz decided he looked different to Faraj, though he had the same quality and iridescent sheen to his coat. In comparison, Faraj had more height and seemed stretchier. This bay stallion was wide, solid and had more muscling, giving him the impression of strength.

"This is Kadin. Can you see how the first filly we saw has taken the best of her dam and sire?" asked Selim of Ishkuz.

"It's very obvious. She has the spirit of her father and the elegance of her mother," replied Ishkuz. "Selim, this stallion is one in a thousand. I have never seen anything like him. You have a mine of gold hidden away here in the desert with all these horses. They would be worth a fortune in the cities," said Ishkuz with awe in his voice.

"We rarely visit any cities, Ishkuz, except to race and then we have never gone any further. Feluj, the trader, has told us about some of the cities and countries beyond our travels, but we have no need to leave the valley and mountains. We have everything we need here," replied Selim.

"You sure do. It's like a paradise here with the river and your well-protected fort. But you would be the envy of every horseman beyond the desert if they knew the type of horses you have here. It's good you are so far away from others or they would be knocking on your gate to buy some or knocking it down to steal them," said Ishkuz.

"I do have one question," Ishkuz continued. "How have you been able to keep breeding your horses for so long without them becoming too closely related?"

"There have been times throughout the generations when the tribe has felt we needed new blood. This is where the races between the tribes are more than just a race. They are a way of finding out which tribes are breeding the best horses. At times, we have negotiated a sale or swapped mares for a stallion, but it isn't easy to find exactly what we want for our herd and sometimes the price is too high," replied Selim.

Just then Kadin swung his head and pricked his ears at the neighs coming from the mares' paddock. His nostrils dilated and let out a loud neigh. His eyes were focused and bright and his tail lifted just a little.

"I would love to see him run. Is it possible?" asked Ishkuz.

"Of course," answered Selim. "We'll take him to the stallion yards. There's plenty of room there and he needs a stretch anyway."

Kadin was keen to go and tossed his head and neck and pranced his way down the track with his tail arched beautifully. Selim led him into a paddock ringed by a fence made of thin, dried trees, stripped of their bark. He loosened the lead rope and Kadin immediately cantered off, neighing and tossing his head. As he made his way to the corner of the paddock he broke into a trot. It was a powerful, driving trot which brought his hind legs deeply underneath him and allowed his front legs to extend fully with lightness and ease.

Ishkuz admired the movement of this dark bay stallion. "I would love to ride him one day, Selim. He is so powerful and graceful."

Some of the men had joined Selim and Ishkuz and smiled at the words of Ishkuz, proud that Kadin belonged to them and that a pale-skinned stranger appreciated their horses.

One of the men spoke up and said to Ishkuz, "You can ride him if you beat Nabeel, our tribe's best bowman, at archery."

The men laughed loudly as they knew Nabeel was a superb bowman. However, their laughter was a little forced as they had heard around the fort of Ishkuz's reputation for being an excellent bowman. This seemed to be a good excuse to show Ishkuz that their tribe not only had the best horses in the world but the best bowman as well.

Ishkuz was a little embarrassed by the men. He looked down at the ground but regaining his composure said to them, "I'd be honoured to challenge Nabeel."

The group of men let out a cheer and slapped Nabeel on the back, for he was among them, and raised their hands at the prospect of the duel. Then they slowly made their way back to their houses as the light was beginning to fade, with Ishkuz and Selim following them.

"You know you don't have to beat Nabeel to ride Kadin," Selim said to Ishkuz.

"No, I didn't think so. But I didn't want to deny the men the challenge or the fun, and anyway I need the practise," replied Ishkuz.

"Come on," said Selim. "Let's go and have some dinner."

"By the way, Ansim is cooking tonight. I hope you like lamb," Selim said with a grin.

Ishkuz closed his eyes and lifted his head to the sky.

II.
Renewal

CHAPTER 12

The fort was ablaze with fires, music, dancing, singing and eating. The families had joined together to celebrate their victory with those who had gone to see the race. Victories like the one Selim and Faraj had achieved didn't often come along and they held up cups of congratulations not just for the win but for the way the race was won. There were already exaggerated stories beginning to spread about the injuries Selim had suffered and how the pale rider really was a jinni from the north who had cast a spell on him. His black horse was given red eyes and sharp teeth to scare the children and then they gloried in the fact that a horse and a rider from their tribe and breeding had not just beaten the pale jinni and his evil black horse but had passed them in a canter and left them in their dust.

As the night wore on and the stories became more exaggerated, Al Maksour began to be woven into the victory and the battle against the evil jinn. Some said Selim had secretly taken Al Maksour with him in the race and it had weakened the jinn's spell on him. Others said Selim had used the shards left on the pommel of the sword to fight the pale jinni when he attacked Selim, but the jinni had fled from Selim on his black horse only to be passed and beaten in the race. Others thought the spirit of Al Maksour who blessed their tribe and protected them had been present with Selim and Faraj and had given them the power to win, no matter what confronted them. As the talk went on there were calls from the people for a story of Al Maksour.

Ishkuz asked Selim and Ibrahim, "What is this 'Al Maksour'?"

"Al Maksour is a sword, or at least the parts of a sword which have belonged to our tribe for generations. We only know it as 'the broken one,' Al Maksour. We don't know where it came from. All we have are stories about it. There are stories about people who have used it and how it possesses power, as if it has a mind of its own. We have the pieces that have broken off over the years and the pommel with the top part of the sword still attached. It's very old and worn and hasn't been used since, well, we don't know when. A lot of tribes are jealous of us for owning it. They think it has magic, a protective power over and around those who have it. Just before we left for the race a tribe sent two men up to the steepest and highest side of the fort to steal it while the rest of the tribe attacked the gate. That's how important and powerful they think it is. But we have never seen any of its power or had anyone use Al Maksour. If anyone from our tribe has used it we haven't heard about it. Sometimes, when I think of how good our life is and how rich we are with our crops and horses, I wonder whether it has something to do with Al Maksour and the power people say it has," answered Selim.

"Wow," said Ishkuz. "An old sword of legend here in this fort. I'd love to hear some of the stories about the sword one day."

Ibrahim spoke up. "I must admit I've told stories about Al Maksour which show its power and lots of those stories have been passed down from person to person and tribe to tribe. Yet, Selim, it seems what you have thought about Al Maksour isn't new. The stories of Al Maksour show it has had an influence on those who own it. There is an ancient story of Nimrod the great hunter having the sword and with his army he defeated eight nations with ease, one after the other. The story tells of men who were wounded in battle who healed in two to three days instead of dying, as they should have from their wounds. Nimrod himself was said to have shrugged off spears and arrows as if his skin was made of armour.

But there is another side to Al Maksour's life. As time went on Al Maksour was revered but not wielded, honoured but not used, wrapped and remembered, but in reality, it was a shadow of its former glory. Sometimes, the stories tell us, men preferred to rely on their own skill and Al Maksour was left at home. Some became afraid of its power, not knowing quite how to use it, while others didn't know exactly what they should do with it. They wondered if it was a talisman they should carry into battle but not use. Others didn't want to take the risk of using it in battle or hunting, so left it wrapped in a secret place. This great sword found its way into their family and tribe and yet, wasn't used.

However, even when Al Maksour was not used in any way and the leaders had no use for it, the tribe prospered and strange occurrences happened among them. Men and women lived far longer than average, and many women had twins and even triplets. As a result, some tribes became jealous of Al Maksour's power. But many came to believe the stories of Al Maksour were just that, stories which had no truth behind them. It has even been said Al Maksour's blade became thinner and more frail as it was used less and that it eventually splintered into the pieces which we have in our possession today."

Selim sat stunned at this revelation by Ibrahim. He had never heard this part of the sword's story before. Ishkuz seemed even more intrigued than before. Ishkuz found his voice first and said, "Then it wasn't always called Al Maksour, the broken one, because it wasn't always broken? What could its real name have been then? Do you know Ibrahim?"

"It's strange but in all of the stories I know of Al Maksour none of them speak of it in any other way. Even when the stories are about it being used and it is whole, they always call it Al Maksour," Ibrahim replied.

"Maybe it didn't have a name because Al Maksour only tells us what it had become, not what it was. It's more of a description than a name," said Selim who was only just beginning to put his thoughts together. "I have always thought Al Maksour was its name but now I see it's a name we have given it, to describe it."

"You're right Selim," answered Ishkuz. "I wonder whether it ever had a name," he added.

As their minds processed this new information one question built upon another and finally Ishkuz blurted out, "Who made it then? Where did it come from? And how could it have so much power… and where did its power come from?"

"It was made before the breaking of the world," said Ibrahim quietly, as though he were afraid to speak about such things. "But I don't know who formed it. One story mentions Nimrod visiting a man, one of only four who came from the other side of the breaking of the world. It says that he came through the breaking, not only with gold and silver but also with knowledge and wisdom from a greater age. An age of giants and men who never seemed to die. It was he who gave Al Maksour to Nimrod. Al Maksour was not broken then, of course, but there is no mention of a name and no mention of where he got the sword."

Ishkuz, a little overawed by what Ibrahim said and the way he said it, was almost afraid to ask a question but his curiosity was too great and only just managed to whisper the question on his mind. "Can I see Al Maksour?"

Selim and Ishkuz both looked at him and then at each other.

Ibrahim finally said, "Yes of course you can. There is no harm in that. Selim will show you, but do it later tonight as there is already a lot of talk and excitement about it."

Both the young men nodded.

The night wore on. Talk died down with the campfires and soon Ishkuz and Selim were able to talk alone.

"I've never known Ibrahim to be so secretive," said Selim to Ishkuz as they made their way to Selim's reading room. "It's like he's afraid of us knowing the history of Al Maksour or of people thinking and talking too much about it. I hadn't heard most of what he mentioned tonight. It certainly has made me think about the sword in a different way. Like Ibrahim said, many think of his stories as stories and I'm one of them. I've never thought of Al Maksour as anything more than an old, broken sword."

Selim led Ishkuz into a darkened room deep inside his house, the lamp he carried throwing wavering shadows across the rough rock walls. Selim gave the lamp to Ishkuz and then bent down to a box against the wall. The wood was pitted and marked with a dark tinge as though stained. Its corners were bound in metal and a finely engraved clasp held the lid closed. Selim opened the box and lifted the sword out of its wrappings.

"We moved Al Maksour here after the robbery attempt. This room is the deepest cut room within the mountain and the fort, and we hope it is the safest," said Selim.

Selim carefully unwrapped the sword and laid its pieces on the small desk in the room. Ishkuz moved over and placed the lamp over the sword to get a good look at it. He was both excited and intrigued, as well as a little disappointed, by what he saw.

"It looks so old," he said. "It doesn't look like the kind of sword that could do what Ibrahim has told of in the stories. It looks well-made but lifeless. It's just so interesting. May I hold it?"

Selim passed him the handle and Ishkuz gripped it tightly imagining a balanced length of steel running from it.

"It feels comfortable," he said.

"Yes, very balanced and somehow like it was made to live in your hand," added Selim.

"It would have been beautiful when it was whole. There is a lightness about it even though it is broken," said Ishkuz. "Imagine what it would be like if it was remade?"

"Remade? You mean reforged? All the pieces melded back together? I haven't ever thought of that," replied Selim. "I don't even know if it's possible. But, yes, you're right. Maybe the power would come back to the sword if it was whole again."

Selim's eyes widened as he began to realise the possibilities that might come from a reforged Al Maksour and excitement began to fill his voice. "Imagine what that would mean for the tribe," he added.

He paused and then said thoughtfully, "I wonder why our craftsmen haven't suggested it before? Maybe they're afraid to do it or don't know how. But why would reforging Al Maksour be any different than any other sword? I couldn't imagine there being any great difference."

"Maybe we can ask them in the morning," offered Ishkuz. "I would love to hold the new Al Maksour. We may be able to have it done elsewhere. Perhaps there are others who have more knowledge of different metals and the reforging of old weapons."

The minds of the young men were racing with the possibilities that a new Al Maksour could bring. They picked up the shards of the sword and looked carefully at their edges. They laid them out together on the cloth and tried to fit the pieces together to make a full blade but time had worn the edges.

"If Al Maksour is to be reforged then it will have to be added to," said Selim.

"I wonder if the metal is the same as we have today?" said Ishkuz.

"I'm not sure. I know very little about metal craft," answered Selim. "Come on, let's put it back now. You need your sleep for the archery competition tomorrow."

"You're right, it's been a long night. I don't know if I'll be able to sleep after this excitement," said Ishkuz, shaking his head.

"Well, it's my first night in a proper bed for weeks. I'll sleep very well, even if you don't," said Selim with a laugh.

"I suppose a proper bed will be better than the sand and dirt. Goodnight Selim. Oh, and thanks for showing me the sword. It's been a good night," said Ishkuz.

Selim smiled at his new friend. "Goodnight. Sleep well."

CHAPTER 13

The men were up early despite the celebrations of the previous night. They were eager to see Ishkuz's skills, or his lack of them. Targets had been set up on the plain outside the fort and some of the men were checking Nabeel's arrows for trueness and his bowstrings for strength and suppleness.

Ishkuz also rose early to prepare himself and to ready his bow and check his arrows. Once he was satisfied, he made his way into the kitchen to find food for his aching stomach. Selim was at the stables checking the horses so only Almas and Ansim were there.

"Good morning," said Almas. "Did you sleep well?"

"Yes, thank you, I slept very well. The bed was very comfortable," Ishkuz answered.

Ansim looked at him and smiled, showing her even, white teeth and Ishkuz smiled briefly in return, colour rising to his fair cheeks. He couldn't help but notice the sheen and softness of her dark hair and the sparkle in her eyes. He quickly averted his own eyes to a mark on the table, which all of a sudden looked quite interesting.

Selim breezed through the door, smiling widely. Slapping Ishkuz on the back with his good hand he said, "I hope your aim is good today, Ishkuz. The men are excited about challenging you. I'm looking forward to this so much."

Ishkuz only nodded, not really knowing how to respond to Selim. Inside he was confident of his own ability as he had proved it many times, however he was not one to boast, especially with Ansim there. He would let his actions speak for themselves.

Almas and Ansim filled the table with breads, cereals, fruit and porridge and Selim and Ishkuz ate their fill. Ansim did not like to let a guest go hungry and kept encouraging Ishkuz to eat. Ishkuz appealed to Selim to get Ansim to stop but he only grinned. Ishkuz found this so frustrating. Finally, Ishkuz managed to excuse himself and Selim called out to him as he left, "I'll meet you at the stables and take you down to the targets. I have some things to do, and the competition isn't till midmorning. Yusef, my brother, will show where you can practise without anyone seeing you. He's outside waiting for you."

Ishkuz went to his room to collect his bow, strings, quiver and arrows. He also carefully placed a protective leather cover over his forearm to prevent the string of the bow tearing at his arm. As he stepped down the stairs into the courtyard, he saw Yusef come running towards him. "Ishkuz, Selim told me to take you behind the fort where you can have some privacy for your practise. Follow me."

Ishkuz was led outside the fort to a dusty and barren area, well away from the normal activities of the fort. Yusef had set up a small target and Ishkuz now fitted his string to the bow and chose his arrows carefully. He spent the next hour getting the feel of his bow and sighting his eye to the target and the conditions. His first shots landed short of the target, as he wanted to work his muscles up slowly to the tension needed to stretch the bow to its maximum. Yusef was dumbfounded at seeing this as he had heard of Ishkuz's mastery of the bow and wondered what Ishkuz was doing. As he watched and ran up and down retrieving arrows, he saw Ishkuz's arrows begin to land on the target, each shot moving closer to the middle. Yusef soon became amazed at the accuracy and consistency of Ishkuz's shooting. He watched as Ishkuz finished by stretching his shoulders and arms, then made his way to the stables to meet Selim.

Horses hung their heads out of the stable doors as Ishkuz arrived, wondering whether he was a bearer of food. Framed in the stable doorways was one beautiful head after another. There was no doubt that these were Arabian horses. Their skin was thin, hair soft and silky, and their nostrils were large and flexible. Ishkuz saw Faraj's snaking neck and fine head reaching out to sniff him. Ishkuz scratched his forehead and straightened his forelock. Faraj had already taken a special place in his heart. He was the ideal stallion, not only because of his build and nature, but also in the way he had proved himself in the race and with his first foals. Ishkuz's mind wandered back to the bay colt and the chestnut filly in the foal yards. A good stallion often produced very good fillies, but an ideal stallion produced both quality fillies and colts.

Just then Selim arrived. "How did your practise go? Was the place alright for you?"

"Yes, it was fine, Selim, thank you," replied Ishkuz.

Selim was keen to see Ishkuz shoot so he said, "It's nearing time. Let's go out to the targets."

They made their way out of the fort onto the river flats where a crowd was gathering. A target had been set up and they could see Nabeel surrounded by a number of men, no doubt giving him last minute instructions that he didn't need. The sun was warm and the sky clear.

As Ishkuz and Selim approached, Sekeen came toward them. "Good morning. I will be running the contest this morning. Ishkuz, you will be given every right that Nabeel has in this match. To beat him, you must shoot two of your arrows closer to the middle of the target than two of Nabeel's. You will each fire an arrow until you have both fired five arrows. Do you understand?"

Ishkuz nodded as though he was only half interested in what Sekeen had to say. Sekeen called the crowd to stand back and asked Nabeel and Ishkuz over to the line marked in the sand. Nabeel grinned at Ishkuz, then laid his quiver on the ground. Ishkuz took five arrows from his quiver and pushed them into the sand point down.

"As Ishkuz is our guest I invite him to shoot the first arrow," Nabeel called out forthrightly.

Ishkuz nodded and pulled an arrow from the sand. He had already checked the flights and the shaft of the arrow and so without delay put the arrow onto the bow of the string and took aim. There was silence in the crowd as Ishkuz lined up his arrow. Before him was a straw-filled bag hanging from a pole with a circle roughly drawn on it. He aimed for the centre of the circle and then made a slight adjustment to the right. His right hand let go of the arrow and with a whoosh it shot out of the bow and cut deeply into the straw on the right-hand side of the circle. Cheers erupted from the crowd. Smiling, Nabeel took his place on the line, took aim and loosed his arrow. It flew just inside of Ishkuz's arrow and again the crowd cheered.

Ishkuz stood at the line for his next turn and his arrow flew just inside Nabeel's. The crowd let out excited sighs as they knew pressure was back on Nabeel to produce a better shot. He took aim again, though this time he took longer and his arrow landed above Ishkuz's arrow but the same distance from the centre.

Ishkuz now had three shots left. He needed to put two of them in the centre or very close to it to win. He let his third arrow go and this time it flew to the left-hand side of the circle. The crowd called out loudly to Nabeel, encouraged by Ishkuz's last shot. He too seemed to have gained some confidence from Ishkuz's last shot. He knew he had to make this shot count.

Nabeel steadied himself, pausing for a long time while he aimed his arrow. Finally, it flew, hitting just to the right of the centre of the circle. The crowd started to yell and jump around and Nabeel grinned, looking quite relieved. Ishkuz let out a sigh, then took another arrow out of the sand. Taking aim in an almost nonchalant way, he landed his arrow directly in the centre of the circle. The crowd was quiet, knowing Ishkuz had done it with ease.

Feeling the tension, Nabeel began to sweat heavily. He rubbed his palms on his leg and notched his second last arrow. Both men had an arrow closest to the centre so Nabeel's last shots needed to be better than he had done so far.

Nabeel took his time to aim and then let his arrow fly. As it sailed through the warm air the crowd held its breath. It landed a thumb's length above Ishkuz's last arrow inside the circle. There was a mix of cries from the crowd, some thinking it was a great shot while others felt that it might not be enough to win. Disappointed, Nabeel prepared himself for one last shot.

For the last time, Ishkuz stepped up to the line and took aim. His arrow cut through the air, landing closer to his last shot than Nabeel's previous one. A hush fell over the crowd. Stunned, Nabeel knew he had to get as close to the arrow in the centre as he could, just to be even with Ishkuz. The crowd yelled their encouragement, knowing how much rested on one arrow. Taking a deep breath, he put his last arrow onto the bow's string. Nabeel wiped wet hair off his forehead with the back of his hand, then steeling himself, he drew back the string. He held his breath as the arrow flew through the air. A scream came up from the crowd as the arrow landed right next to Ishkuz's arrow in the centre of the target. Nabeel had done it. He jumped up into the air and threw his fist toward the sky. The crowd ran over to embrace him as though he had won.

Selim went up to Ishkuz, slapped him on the back and said, "Wow Ishkuz, that was some shooting. You really pushed Nabeel."

"Thanks, but aren't we even?" Ishkuz replied. "We both have two arrows in the middle of the circle."

Sekeen came over to speak with Ishkuz. "Fantastic shooting, Ishkuz. It was a very close contest."

Ishkuz replied, "I would like to suggest we have another contest to break the deadlock. Is that possible?"

Sekeen nodded. "Yes, there isn't any problem except that Nabeel would have to agree. We haven't had such a close contest that required a rematch. How about we ask him?"

Sekeen brought Nabeel over. "You shoot extremely well, Ishkuz. Congratulations."

"And to you, Nabeel. You showed great composure. But I would like to suggest that we have another contest to settle the matter. In our country we challenge each other by shooting at moving targets," replied Ishkuz.

Ishkuz noticed that the men all seemed a little puzzled by his suggestion. Ishkuz continued after seeing the confusion in their faces.

"All we need to do is have something thrown into the air as high as possible and then we take turns trying to hit it," he said. "A piece of wood or a stone would do, about the size that would fit into a hand."

Nabeel looked a little shocked. He had been thinking about a large goat or a gazelle, not a small rock moving through the sky. Sekeen had caught on quickly and was already looking for a suitable object. Selim smiled as he realised that Ishkuz was taking the challenge to a much more difficult level. "He must be confident. Hitting a flying object is very hard," he thought to himself.

Recovering, Nabeel asked Ishkuz, "How many times do we do this? How does it work?"

Ishkuz replied, "We each get three turns at shooting at the rock. The one who hits it the most is the winner."

Nabeel nodded. "Okay, let's do it."

Holding a stone that covered his palm and part of his fingers, Sekeen came up and asked, "Will this do?"

"Yes, that's perfect," said Ishkuz. "It's snug in your hand so you can throw it high."

"Good," replied Sekeen. "I'll be the thrower. It's probably only fair that Nabeel goes first as Ishkuz went first earlier. I'll stand over there and throw the rock straight up. Let me know when you are ready Nabeel."

Sekeen moved to a clear stretch of sand away from the crowd and the bowmen. Nabeel attached an arrow to his bow and drew back the string, aiming the arrow skyward.

"I'm ready," he said.

"After three, then. One, two, three," called out Sekeen.

He heaved the stone up into the air and Nabeel tried to follow the stone's movement. He loosed his arrow and it flew toward the stone and glanced off the side of it. A shout went up from the crowd and Nabeel could hardly believe that he had hit it. He jumped up and down hollering while the crowd yelled their encouragement.

Sekeen went to pick up the stone and then called out to Ishkuz, "On the count of three. One, two, three!"

Sekeen hurled the rock into the air again. Ishkuz pulled back on the bow and loosed his arrow with what appeared to be little effort. His arrow made a clunk as it hit the middle of one side of the rock. Both arrow and rock fell back to the sand. The crowd were stunned that Ishkuz hit the rock face straight on with so little effort. The excitement of Nabeel's first successful shot was now waning and again he looked serious, knowing he had a real contest on his hands. He hadn't shot into the air before and certainly never at such a small target but his first shot had given him confidence. He prepared his arrow and called out to Sekeen that he was ready. Sekeen called out "One, two, three," and threw the rock into the air. Once more Nabeel followed the rock's movement to the top of its arc and loosed his arrow. This time his arrow flew too high and missed the rock. The crowd let out a sigh. "Only one out of two," Nabeel thought to himself.

Ishkuz put his arrow onto the string and prepared himself. Sekeen saw that he was ready and repeated the throwing of the rock. Ishkuz's arrow whizzed through the air and again hit the rock squarely. The crowd was quiet, as they had never seen this type of accuracy before. Selim patted Ishkuz's back to congratulate him.

Nabeel readied himself, though he felt deflated. He fired his arrow as the rock climbed into the clear, blue sky. This time the arrow went wide of the rock and the crowd let out a loud "Oooohhh." Nabeel was gracious in defeat. He smiled at Ishkuz and said, "You have proved your skill with the bow. Well done, and congratulations. Kadin will gladly carry a man with such skill."

Ishkuz smiled back and thanked Nabeel.

Selim chimed in and said to Ishkuz, "You have one more shot. Won't you take it? Make it three out of three."

Ishkuz nodded and took his stance and notched his arrow to the string. He nodded and Sekeen threw the rock into the air for the last time. Ishkuz appeared to be even more languid in his movement than before and yet his arrow flew straight at the rock and again met it at the top of its flight. The arrow hit the target with a clunk.

The crowd erupted into cheers as they willingly acknowledged this type of skill. They gathered around both Nabeel and Ishkuz as they had appreciated the contest between them. As they made their way back to the fort some of the men laughingly reminded Ishkuz that he could now ride Kadin.

Nabeel laughed with his friends, satisfied with the outcome, as he knew there was no-one in the tribe who could have beaten Ishkuz. Aside from Ishkuz, his reputation as the tribe's best archer was intact. Meanwhile, Ishkuz explained to Selim that in his country there were many wild birds that made excellent eating and he had spent hours shooting at birds as they flew off, scared by the dogs that accompanied him. He whispered to Selim, "Hitting a rock that goes up and then down is easier than hitting a bird who darts and changes direction, but don't tell anyone that."

"I was impressed," said Selim. "You're not just a talented horse rider but one of the best archers we've seen. I wonder what other talents you have yet to reveal, pale face?"

Ishkuz raised his eyebrow as if to say, "You may like to know but I am not about to tell you."

"How about a ride? You could take Kadin and I'll take Aisha. You've won that right. I need to think and riding always helps me do that," Selim said. "We'll get changed and you can put your bow and quiver back in your room. I'll meet you at the stables. If you get there before me, ask the boys to saddle the horses."

They went their separate ways. Ishkuz was careful not to run into Ansim, although a part of him hoped that he would. He changed into riding clothes and made his way back to the stables. Selim wasn't there yet so he found one of the boys and asked him to get Kadin and Aisha saddled. The boy ran off and was soon back with a taller lad about the same age. They chattered together as they went into the tack room and came out holding halters for the horses. Ishkuz asked if he could get Kadin and the boy happily agreed, handing him Kadin's halter and Ishkuz made his way to Kadin's stable. He was greeted by Kadin who had his head out of the stable ready to sniff him as he approached. Ishkuz moved into his stable and easily placed Kadin's nose into the halter and tied the rope. He led him out of the stable and Kadin went quietly to the saddling post. Ishkuz grabbed a brush and began to smooth Kadin's soft, even coat. The coat was short and grew shinier as the dust from the stable was flicked into the air and blown away on the breeze. Kadin turned his head to him as Ishkuz ran his fingers through his thick, black mane and looked at him with his large, dark eyes.

Selim turned up just as the two boys had joined together to brush Aisha down who, like the princess she was, stood there enjoying the attention as if she thoroughly deserved it. Selim saw this and called out, "Look at Aisha. She has those two boys under her hoof, so to speak."

Ishkuz laughed and then asked, "Where is the saddle for Kadin?"

One of the boys immediately spoke up and said, "I will get it for you, and his bridle."

Ishkuz picked up Kadin's front foreleg to check his hooves and to feel his cannon and tendons. They were cool and the hoof was clean, well-shaped and neatly trimmed.

"They certainly know how to look after horses here," he thought to himself.

Soon both horses were saddled and warmed up, so they made their way out of the fort. Ishkuz liked the feel of Kadin. He strode out well at the walk and was behaving sensibly with Aisha close by him. If his action in the paddock the day before showed anything it was that he was in for a smooth and enjoyable ride in whatever gait they chose.

Selim echoed his thoughts. "You have chosen a good horse. He comes from a family of sure-footed horses who are very comfortable to ride. I thought we would ride to the top of the hill so that you can enjoy the view of the valley and the fort. You'll be able to see why this place was chosen to build our fort."

Selim pushed Aisha into a canter and Kadin immediately followed her lead. He was not about to have this beautiful but feisty mare get away from him. Ishkuz could feel the power beneath him but also the rhythmic swing of Kadin's body, which was fluid and smooth. "I could ride this horse all day," he thought to himself.

They wound their way up the mountain road that took them to a spur that jutted out into the valley, giving them a clear view of the fort and the river's flow. The horses stopped at the top and snorted. Ishkuz could immediately see that the position of the fort was naturally defensive, made more so by the way they had built the fort and the road leading into it. He could see the large wooden gates of the fort that he knew were thick and heavy, yet from where he was they seemed so small. The fort looked over the fields that lay along the river, which were naturally rich with flood sediment. The colours of the crops and soil contrasted strongly with each other in the bright light. High above them, a large bird of prey circled in the warm draughts and let out an occasional shriek.

"It's truly beautiful," said Ishkuz. "It's so easy to see why this place was chosen. It has everything you need, a constant water supply, fertile plains and protection," he added.

"Yes, my ancestors chose well all those years ago," said Selim.

"How long has your tribe had horses?" asked Ishkuz.

"Many generations. We've lost count exactly, but I'm sure that Ibrahim has some stories about how we came to have horses. They were wild, roaming the plateaus and mountains, and drinking at the streams and rivers. From what I remember, one was captured and tamed and soon others were captured as well. The grass and rain was far more plentiful back then. A lot of animals have gone from this region due to lack of food," replied Selim.

Changing the topic, Selim said, "Let's head back and get ready for dinner."
"I'll race you back," he cried in a spurt of enthusiasm. With that he spurred Aisha back down the road at a gallop.

Ishkuz responded with lightning reflexes and was only a fraction behind Selim and Aisha in turning Kadin and urging him into a gallop down the road toward the river and fort. The dust flew up from underneath the flying hooves and the ears of both horses were pricked, their eyes wide as they raced side by side. The wind whistled through their manes and tails and the rhythmic thud of their hooves increased as they picked up speed. Both men and horses were totally focused but Aisha managed to gain some ground on Kadin around a bend in the road. Kadin was now a length and a half behind Aisha, riding in her dust and with encouragement from Ishkuz he gave even more of himself. His stride lengthened and he edged closer and closer to Aisha. Both horses flew down the last part of the road where it made its way along the river. Ahead of them, the road ahead swung around and crossed a shallow offshoot of the river. Both horses were going to have to gallop through the water. Kadin actually loved water but Ishkuz wasn't aware of this. Both horses took the bend down to the river, neck and neck. Selim looked over at Ishkuz and smiled. Ishkuz looked back enquiringly and as they arrived at the edge of the river Ishkuz felt Kadin gather himself and jump into the air as if he wanted to cross the whole width of the river. He landed many feet into the river and after three strides came to a complete stop. Aisha, meanwhile, had not broken stride and pushed her way across the river at a fast canter, up onto the road on the other side. Selim reined her in and trotted back to the river's edge, grinning from ear to ear, while Ishkuz sat on Kadin somewhat dumbfounded.

"You knew this would happen, didn't you?" Ishkuz asked.

"Well," said Selim, "he has been known to do this from time to time, but then I thought that with your reputation and riding skill something like this wasn't going to stop you. But then again," he added casually.

Kadin was splashing the water with his hoof and enjoying himself immensely. Ishkuz pushed him to a walk and said to Selim, "Okay, you win. Did you plan that from the start, taking me up the hill and racing us down?"

"No," said Selim with a degree of satisfaction, "it only came to me as we were going up the mountain."

"Come on, let's go and get cleaned up. And don't worry, I won't tell anyone that Ishkuz the archer and rider had his horse stop dead in two feet of water during a race. That's safe with me. At least until I need it," he said with a sly grin.

Ishkuz shook his head and laughed. Together they made their way back to the fort. As they did, Ishkuz realised just how much fun he had been having, even though he hardly dared to let himself believe it. Apart from returning home and seeing his family again, he had, at this very time, everything that he had only ever dreamed about: freedom, a friend who treated him as an equal, horses who seemed to be the world's best, and a growing ability to enjoy them all without fear. Ishkuz had a good feeling about life here in the fort and everything the future would hold.

CHAPTER 14

Over the next few weeks Selim and Ishkuz spoke a lot about horses and Al Maksour.

"Ishkuz, I've called the elders of our tribe together for a meeting tonight to discuss Al Maksour. I've got a plan. I want to take Al Maksour to be reforged somewhere, to a place where they have the same metal or something similar. I've got this urge to see Al Maksour remade. I can't explain it. It's just been growing in me and taking up more and more of my thought."

Selim paused, then went on. "I want you to come with me."

The passion that Selim spoke with took Ishkuz off guard. He had never seen it before.

"Yes, yes, of course I'll come. As long as I can come back here afterward. I love this place and its horses… and your people are already growing on me," he said hurriedly. As he said this he began to blush and Ansim's face suddenly appeared in his mind. He looked at Selim but thankfully he hadn't noticed.

"Good, good, I really want you to come and of course we'll all come back. You can stay as long as you like. Ibrahim has already decided he will come too. The leaders may also want others to go but I wanted to make sure I had your support," said Selim.

"But what about your smithies? Can't they do the work on Al Maksour?"

"I've already spoken to them and they aren't familiar with the metal in the sword and don't know how to work it. They suggested we go elsewhere," answered Selim.

"Where were you thinking of going?" asked Ishkuz.

"Yathrib. It's a major city to the north. If they don't know about the metal then they may be able to tell us who does," answered Selim.

Ishkuz nodded his agreement.

It was night and many had gathered for the meeting to discuss Al Maksour's reforging. Yusef put another piece of wood on the fire and sparks jumped into the darkened sky as if drawn there by magic. The last of the tribe's leaders were settling themselves into place on the ground. Selim sat next to Ibrahim with Ishkuz on his left. It was not a closed meeting so Ishkuz was allowed to be present, but he wasn't allowed to contribute to the discussion, unless asked a direct question. Some of the younger men had joined as well, wanting to hear the discussion and learn about the processes of judgement.

It was Rasin who spoke first. Ibrahim had informed him of Selim's desires and thoughts on Al Maksour. Rasin was a grey-haired man who had showed great diplomatic skills early in life and had come to be a natural leader of tribal discussions. He was calm and composed even when discussions became heated and passionate and everyone relied on him to steer things in the most peaceful and successful way.

Rasin began, "It's come to our notice that Selim wishes this council to discuss whether it is in favour of having Al Maksour reforged."

There was some murmuring as Rasin finished and he put up his hand to call for quiet.

"You all know that Al Maksour has been part of our tribe and history for more generations than we can tell. We have always known it to be in shards, hence the name Al Maksour. Selim feels it is time for Al Maksour to be restored to some of its former glory. He wishes to seek out men who know the metal of Al Maksour and who have the skill to bring it back to life."

Rasin turned to Selim and asked, "Is this correct Selim?"

"Yes Rasin, it is. I have been thinking a lot about Al Maksour, even before the Al Bedi's attempt to steal it. Part of me says that it needs to be honoured because it's been part of our tribe and existence for so long. Also, if it is left any longer in the state it is in now it may well deteriorate to a point beyond any real repair," said Selim.

He hesitated before beginning again.

"I feel a growing connection with the sword that I can't explain. The more I learn and hear about it the more my fascination grows. It's similar to the feeling we have with our horses. They have been part of our tribe for many, many years and are like family to us. We love them and care for them and know what they give back to us in affection and trust. Some even die for us in battle. Al Maksour is as much a part of who we are as our horses. I know that some of you have thought little about Al Maksour over the years and feel it has no power. I make no judgement on that. Let Al Maksour be remade, if not because you believe in its power, then because it is a treasured tribal heirloom that must be preserved."

Selim stopped. All the men were looking at him intently as they recognised the passion with which he spoke. Many had grown in their respect of Selim since his courageous win on Faraj and were hesitant to contradict him. Many too were convinced by his argument to have Al Maksour restored regardless of whether it had any power or not.

One of the oldest men of the tribe, Ya'qub, spoke up.

"It is good to see your passion, Selim. Passion for Al Maksour is something that has been lost for many years among our tribe, even though other tribes see its value and try to steal it. Take the sword, have it remade by the finest craftsman you can find and keep your passion. May it increase as Al Maksour shows you its power."

Some of the men in the group nodded in agreement, while others looked down at the patterns in the carpet, a little embarrassed at Ya'qub's belief that an old sword could hold any power.

"I have a question," said another man. "Have you spoken to our metalsmiths to see if they can reforge it?"

Selim spoke up. "Yes, I have spoken to Aberdan, our head metalsmith and he doesn't recognise the type of metal that makes up Al Maksour. He says it is different to any metal that he has used. It needs to be reforged by someone who knows how to handle this type of metal. It is more likely that a smith from a larger city will know of it."

A number of men nodded their heads, seeing the logic of what Selim had said.

Sekeen, sitting in the circle, listened intently. He was a man unswayed by the thoughts of others and had an interest in seeing that his tribe was able to defend itself well. The stories of Al Maksour had always been a part of his life and he too had a strong attraction to Al Maksour and what it stood for.

"Selim, I too wish to see Al Maksour come to life again. To see a weapon of Al Maksour's stature and renown fall into disrepair is a sad thing to me and the honour you spoke about is long overdue. It's refreshing and gratifying to see one of our young men, especially our sheikh, take up the sword's cause."

He paused and then added, "If it pleases you and the council, allow me the honour of accompanying you on your journey."

Selim was taken aback by Sekeen's words and by the obvious strength of his feeling. He didn't know that Sekeen felt this way, nor that Ya'qub held Al Maksour so close to his heart. Before he could reply Rasin spoke.

"Thank you Sekeen for your offer, but the journey has not yet been decided. Is there anyone else that wishes to speak?"

Suhayb, a balding, middle-aged man was wringing his hands, at obvious pains to speak. Rasin nodded to him and he began. He spoke with a slight slur as the left side of his mouth was droopy.

"I respect your opinions and feelings about Al Maksour, but I feel that we may be sending many men out on a journey from which they may not return. Not only will we lose men but good horses, and most likely Al Maksour, the very thing we are trying to preserve. I admit no great faith in Al Maksour. It's simply an ancient trinket that happened to fall into our ancestor's hands and we are left with it. To put our men and horses into danger is not a wise thing. I think we should ponder this longer and consider the cost."

Some men nodded in agreement, but not as many as had agreed with Ya'qub. Others turned their heads from Suhayb and scowled, as Suhayb was known as a surly, greedy man who wouldn't risk anything if he knew he might lose something of value. He rarely helped even his wider family, unless he saw a possible gain in it.

In his usual diplomatic way, Rasin thanked Suhayb for his input. Usari was the next to speak. Known as a wise man, the men gave him their full attention.

"There is some truth to what Suhayb says. It would be unwise to announce our intentions and alert the tribes that Al Maksour is being carried around by some from our tribe. However, a small inconspicuous group would be the safest way of achieving our goal without endangering Al Maksour or ourselves. I'm in favour of seeing Al Maksour reforged, otherwise it will fade out of existence. We also have some, Selim and Sekeen and maybe more, who are willing to see this happen. We haven't had such interest in a long, long time. I suggest that those who go on the journey pretend they have another purpose. This will help to protect them and the small size of the group will also draw less attention."

"Thank you Usari. Your suggestions are noted. Is there anyone else who wishes to speak?" asked Rasin.

A number of men spoke up briefly stating they agreed with Usari and his ideas. One of them asked which horses they were thinking of taking.

Ibrahim spoke up and answered this question.

"We will need to take horses that we can totally rely on and that are proven in their ability. No journey is easy and to ensure it is as uneventful as possible we will need to take some of our best horses."

Rasin then interrupted, turning to Ibrahim.

"Ibrahim, it would be good to finalise the decision about whether the journey should take place."

Then turning to the circle of men he said, "I gather that the majority feel that the reforging of Al Maksour is something most wish to see happen, though for varying reasons. Do I have your approval?"

Many of the group nodded or murmured in agreement and the few that disagreed knew that a decision had been made.

Rasin continued, "Now that we are sure a journey will take place it needs to be decided who will go. If we take into account Usari's suggestions that the group stays small and Sekeen has offered to go, then there will not be many more needed. I suggest we leave it up to Ibrahim and Selim as to how many more go along and who they are to be."

The men nodded again, as they trusted them both.

"Before we finish," said Rasin as he looked across at Selim and Ibrahim, "has any thought been given as to where you will go?"

Selim decided to answer this question. "I thought that the best place to begin would be Yathrib. If the men there can't help us they may know of someone who can."

"Good, good," said Rasin slowly, nodding his head. "We wish all blessing and safety for you, your horses and Al Maksour. May it come back with a new name."

Rasin then stood and the rest of the group followed his lead. They bowed to each other as a sign of honour for each man's part in the discussions. Some men left while others gathered in groups of two or three to discuss the trip and to say the things they weren't confident enough to say in the larger group.

Sekeen made his way over to Selim, Ibrahim and Ishkuz. He slapped Selim on the back and said, "I am honoured to travel with you and Ibrahim. How many do you think we need to take with us?"

"No more than four or five. More than that looks suspicious and we can easily attach ourselves to some of the caravans that will be travelling our way," Ibrahim answered.

"That sounds good," said Sekeen. "Have you thought of who the other one or two might be?"

Selim looked at Ishkuz and then said, "I really want Ishkuz to come with us. I have already asked him and he has agreed, but I want your agreement as well."

Sekeen offered his thoughts first. "Well, if he shoots the way I saw him shoot this morning then I am more than happy to have him join us. He could be a handy man to have along if we get into trouble."

Ibrahim echoed these thoughts and Selim smiled at Ishkuz saying, "It looks like you're coming with us."

At breakfast the next morning Selim's mother, Almas, spoke to Selim about his trip to Yathrib. She was bustling about the kitchen readying breakfast and Ansim was quietly helping her, her head held down. As Ishkuz entered he could feel tension in the air and immediately became wary. He wasn't sure what had caused the tension and he desperately hoped it wasn't him.

Ansim turned her face to him and smiled and he gave a quick smile back but didn't say anything. He couldn't help noticing her large dark eyes and her white sparkling teeth. Both seemed even brighter than they had when he first met her. Selim greeted him breezily. It seemed that Selim wasn't tense, but Almas's body language suggested she was.

Selim went on. "It seems Ishkuz that my mother wants Ansim and a friend of hers to come with us to Yathrib. There seems to be a distant relative she wants Ansim to meet. I have said no as I think it would be too dangerous for her and we don't know if we are going to stay in Yathrib or move on. What do you think, Ishkuz?"

Ishkuz was taken aback. He didn't quite know what to say. He felt it wasn't fair for Selim to include him in a family squabble. It wasn't his place to have an opinion on this. He felt the eyes of everyone in the room on him, especially Almas and Ansim's large liquid pair.

Before he could speak, Selim added, "It seems that this distant cousin has a son who is of a marriageable age and is not yet married."

Ishkuz thought to himself, "This doesn't really help me, Selim." Ishkuz noticed that Selim's mouth turned up just slightly at one corner and he knew that Selim was enjoying himself.

"Well, the journey shouldn't be too dangerous...especially when there are strong, young men to protect her," he managed to stammer out as the pressure of their eyes got to him and his mind raced to find an extra comment.

As soon as he spoke he realised what he had said. He saw Selim grinning and giving Ansim a wide smile. In the background, Selim's younger brothers snickered, while Almas turned away to hide her pleasure. As the colour rose in Ishkuz's face Almas spoke up. "You see, Selim. Ishkuz has more confidence in himself than you do to protect the girls. It's only a week's ride. And it could be very important for Ansim's future."

"I just don't want it to distract us from our purpose. We don't know if we will be staying in Yathrib or if we'll have to move on to another city. What if we can't bring her back because we need to go in a different direction? I'm sure we can protect her...it's just an added complication."

Everyone in the kitchen looked at him, as if they couldn't quite follow his reasoning. No-one spoke. Their eyes said it all.

"Alright, alright," Selim finally said. "I'll speak to Ibrahim and Sekeen and see what they say."

Almas smiled and gave Selim a kiss and went on happily preparing breakfast and fussing over everyone. The younger boys went back to eating and Ishkuz sighed deeply, happy that he wouldn't have to comment on the issue again and get himself into more trouble. He kept his head down and concentrated on peeling his orange.

After breakfast Ishkuz found himself alone and decided to wander down to the stables, as there was something he needed for their trip. He also wanted to look at some of the other mares that were there. As he made his way along the dusty streets and paths, he noticed how secure and firm and "earthy" the whole place was. All around him were bare timbers and dried mud brick walls rising out of the dirt. It was so different from his own home, which was a moving wagon that sloshed through mud and endless rolling green plains. As he walked along, he could feel that there was something satisfying and protective about the fort and he knew the tribe must be very happy to live here.

He reached the stable area and found some of the mares in the stables with their very young foals. They were to go out to the yards in a day or so and those due to foal would take their place. He saw mares of many different colours but all of similar structure and strength. The foals with their clean and shiny new coats lay stretched out in the straw, flicking flies with their ears and tails, and their mothers dozed with their heads above them. The boys who cared for them were sitting in the shade but jumped up on seeing Ishkuz. They were full of questions for him as they had watched the archery competition and heard of his skill as a rider from a faraway land.

After he had answered their questions and explained his shooting techniques, he asked them, "Do you have any coils of rope that I can have?"

In a chorus the boys called out, "Yes!" Some grabbed his hands and pulled him excitedly to the storeroom, while others ran ahead to find some they could give him. They led him into the cool, dark tack room and he was shown a number of coils of rope. All the boys were eager to please and each hoped that Ishkuz would choose the rope they each had. Ishkuz found one that was light and thin, yet strong and easily handled. The boy he had taken it from grinned from ear to ear and he was sure to boast about it for the next month.

Before he could leave one of the more perceptive boys asked Ishkuz, "What are you going to use it for? Will you make a halter or use it as a lead rope?"

Ishkuz answered, "From where I come from a rope can be used for more than these things. We use them as a weapon."

The boys were mystified as they tried to imagine how a rope could be used as a weapon and before any of the boys could ask him about it he thanked them for their help and left. He met up with Selim on the way back to the house.

"I've just spoken to Sekeen and Ibrahim about Ansim and Warda joining us on the trip. They see no problems with the girls coming with us and so I have agreed for them to come. I suppose I've been so focused on reforging Al Maksour that I've found it hard to think of other things. Sometimes it's hard to think of the needs of my own family amongst everything else that I have to think of. One thing my father said before he died was that 'a leader must think of the needs of those he leads, not just his own.' Hopefully being a leader will grow easier over time."

Ishkuz nodded as he had little experience leading people and he was distracted by thoughts of how he was going to act around Ansim. What was he going to say to her? He couldn't avoid her for a whole week while they were riding and living together.

Selim guessed his thoughts and smiled. He turned to Ishkuz who was fidgeting with the rope.

"Ibrahim suggested that we leave in a week so that my arm is properly healed. It's already feeling better and much stronger, and if we are riding for a week then it will have extra time to heal," said Selim.

"Great," replied Ishkuz.

He then paused and Selim could see that he wanted to ask him something.

"Selim, can I join you in your sword training? I would love to learn from Sekeen and find out what sort of strategies you use. I was taught to fight by my father when I was very young but that is all the training I have had. Since I was captured I haven't been allowed to hold a sword, but I would really like to learn again."

"Well, not if your sword handling is anything like the way you use a bow, but then when it comes to the use of the sword, I'm sure there's something that Sekeen can teach you. He's a true master," replied Selim.

"Thanks. Maybe he could train us while we travel," Ishkuz replied excitedly.

"That's a good idea. I'm sure Sekeen would be more than happy to do that. He is passionate about his swords and moves. And I am really glad he is coming with us. He is worth four or five men in a fight," said Selim.

"Anyway," Selim added, "there will be plenty of time to practise when we make camp at the end of the day, before it gets dark."

Selim slapped Ishkuz on the back with his good arm and said, "Come on, let's go down to the foal paddock and see how the young ones are doing."

The sun was high in the sky as they made their way down to the foal paddocks and they chatted excitedly about the foals and the matings the tribe had tried. Selim also spoke about the horses they planned to breed in the coming year.

"I suggested to Usari and some of the others that we should breed Bashasha's sister to Faraj. Bashasha's colt is so good that we want to keep crossing this blood," said Selim.

"Oh yeah, I nearly forgot, I have to name her colt," added Selim excitedly. "He needs a name that suits his character and his ability. He is light and fast, yet strong. It's not easy to come up with names every year for the foals. We like to name them after stars. We still have Altair left as a name. It's short for An-Nasr Altair, which means "the flying eagle." I will show you the star tonight. It's a very bright one. Or maybe I could name him As-Saif, or Saif, which means "sword." I'll have to give it some thought."

They climbed under the top rail of the fence and stood looking at the foals and their mothers. Some of the foals turned their heads toward them but others kept on grazing and some nodded their heads as they slept. One particular foal, a filly, caught the eye of Ishkuz. He noticed the refinement of her bones, the softness of her skin and the length of her legs. Her nostrils were like flower petals and she was very broad between her two bulging eyes. She showed real quality and potential and seemed to have an air about her, a presence similar to Aisha. He couldn't wait to see her grow up into the graceful yet demanding princess she was going to become. He pointed her out to Selim.

"She is a beauty, isn't she?" he replied. "We bought her mother last year from another tribe. As you can see, she is a solid mare with excellent conformation and a wide, deep body. We bought her in foal to a stallion owned by this tribe who won the tribal race about twelve years ago. The stallion has superb legs and hooves and moves with so much ease when he is galloping that it seems he is hardly trying. When you see this filly trot and canter, you'll see what I mean. Some horses seem to move just their legs when they trot or run, without any connection to their body, but this filly and her grandsire's whole body works with the legs to produce big strides and rhythm with little effort. We really thought we should have some of this stallion's blood in our herd."

"And imagine the cross with Faraj. What a horse that will be!" exclaimed Ishkuz.

"Yes, I know. I can't wait till she grows up and can be bred to Faraj," replied Selim.

"Let's have a closer look at her mother," said Selim as he began walking toward her. "She is a good size and as you can see, quite broad through the body. Her sire was grey, taller and slightly more narrow, but well-muscled, especially in the gaskins and this is probably why he was able to move freely and powerfully."

"She's a lovely mare," said Ishkuz. "Does the filly have a name yet?" he added.

"No, we haven't named her either," answered Selim. "More things to do," he added with a sigh.

"Faraj's colt is just superb," Ishkuz said. "He will be an athlete and a fighter, I think. I might have a name for him, Selim. I know you like to name your horses after their qualities so maybe this one will interest you. In our culture we have a weapon that we use in war, a battle-axe that is light but effective. We call it a 'Sagaris.'"

"Sagaris, Sa…gar…is," said Selim, giving the letters of the name their full effect. "It has a smoothness to it. A light axe, easy to swing, fast and agile, yet strong. I think that name would suit him and it would honour our tribe to have you name him after what you did for me. I'll let Ibrahim know."

"Sagaris…Sagaris," he repeated, getting used to the name.

"Yes, I like it," he said. "A fitting name."

"Good," said Ishkuz. "That's settled then. One name off the list."

They made their way inside for lunch and as they walked Selim asked, "Do you have any other female names in your language we could use that might suit the fillies?"

"Yes, I'm sure we do. But I'll have to think about it as it's been some time since I have used our language. I would only want to give you nice sounding names with meaning. Your horses are worth it," replied Ishkuz.

"Thanks, Ishkuz" said Selim.

Then with a twinkle in his eye and some rather animated hand gestures he asked Ishkuz, "What do you think of the name Ansim? Is it a pretty name for a filly?"

While Selim's grin broke into a laugh, Ishkuz rolled his eyes and lifted his head to the sky. "Will I ever be free of your teasing, Selim?" he thought to himself.

Adding fuel to the fire, Selim said, "Well, you'll have at least a week to think about it."

Ishkuz just shook his head and said nothing.

CHAPTER 15

It was two days later that the small group rode through the gates of the fort and began their journey to Yathrib. They carried what they needed, cooking utensils, tents, food and clothing, and put it onto their packhorses. The two girls, Ansim and Warda, were chatting and laughing, excited to be going on a journey to see a large city. However, their eyes often darted quickly towards Ishkuz and then they would whisper and laugh. Ishkuz couldn't quite understand what was going on and hoped that no-one else noticed. Sekeen and Ibrahim appeared to be occupied with their own thoughts, while Selim happily chatted to Ishkuz. His thoughts were on the sword, which he had packed carefully in his own saddlebag.

They were to travel north-west over the Sarmadees and down onto the plain on which Yathrib lay. Yathrib was along the main trade route to the northern countries and had become a major meeting place for traders and the desert tribes. The men were also excited to stay in Yathrib as they would have the chance to hear the latest news and ideas from traders and philosophers. Despite their excitement, Ibrahim and Sekeen had both their ears and eyes alert for any dangers. Not only were there tribes that could threaten them but also unknown bands of men who spent their days living off travellers. Rather than preying on the large trading groups who hired men to protect themselves, they attacked smaller groups and it was these bandits that Ibrahim and Sekeen were most concerned about. The nights were the most dangerous times, but over the years camping areas for travellers had developed so they could provide each other with protection. The group was aiming to be at one of these campsites before night fell, hoping that others would be there as well.

Selim rode Faraj, Ibrahim was on Aisha and Ishkuz rode Kadin. Secretly, Ishkuz would have loved to ride Aisha but he knew that Ibrahim would, so when Selim asked him to choose a horse to take on the trip, he had no hesitation in choosing Kadin. He knew he would give him a comfortable ride and have speed when it might be needed. He had been well trained for battle so he was easy to manoeuvre and at eight years old was well past any immaturity. Already his heart was warming to the dark bay stallion and his friendly character. Sekeen rode a chestnut mare that was leggy and who had a long, relaxed walk. The girls rode mares that were safe and reliable, yet distinctly desert horses.

Not long into the ride both Ansim and Warda edged their horses nearer to Ishkuz and Selim. At first, they pretended not to be interested in their talk but then it became obvious that they were listening in.

Eventually Ansim asked, "Ishkuz, what are the girls from your country like?"

Ishkuz was taken aback by Ansim's words and when he turned to her he was struck at how beautiful her face looked, even though the sun was causing her to squint and there was a light covering of dust on her face. The white hood she was wearing framed her face and made her even more beautiful. Ansim's face held the hint of a grin on it that was very similar to Selim's when he was making fun of him. Ishkuz wondered what sort of trouble this question was going to get him into.

"Well," he began, "they are strong, confident riders and very good cooks," adding quickly, "though I don't remember a lot about them."

"Is it true they have white hair like yours and even red hair?" blurted out Warda.

Ansim shot a quick look at Warda. Ishkuz noticed this and wasn't quite sure if it indicated she wasn't totally happy with her butting in or with the question. However, he answered her.

"Yes, it's true," he said. "Many have white hair, or blonde, as we tend to call it, and some have a deep red colour while others have a brighter red. But a lot also have black and brown shades as well."

"And how do they wear it? Is it tied up or braided or left out?" asked Ansim.

"A lot of them braid their hair and wrap the braids around their heads. They also braid strips of cloth into them to give them a more colourful look. Well, I suppose that's the reason," he replied with a slight shrug of the shoulders.

Ansim had a thoughtful look on her face and then asked, "What do your women wear?"

"Mostly they wear tunics and trousers made of cannabis, which is a plant that can be turned into cloth. It's soft and can be made into very fine thread. Often they dye the thread and weave it into patterns so that their clothing is very colourful. They make a wonderful picture on the backs of different coloured horses when they ride."

Ishkuz had a faraway look in his eyes as he spoke and half a smile appeared on Ansim's face.

"Do they ride all the time then, the women?" Ansim asked.

"Yes, all the time. They even hunt with the men and fight in battles. Many of them are very brave," replied Ishkuz.

Ansim, Warda and Selim looked rather shocked at what they had just heard.

"What, they shoot arrows and fight with swords, in real battles?" asked Selim a little incredulously.

"Yes, they're very skilled, but they tend to use a weapon that has a short, rounded blade which is sharpened on the inside. It's not so heavy for them and very effective in close fighting. I think you call it a 'sickle' but we know it as a 'sica.' I haven't fought with my tribe as I was too young to but I remember the women when they rode out for battle. They looked terrifying."

"We would never be allowed to go hunting, let alone join in fighting battles," said Ansim with an offended look on her face. Warda immediately followed her friend's lead and nodded vigorously as if fighting against men was something she had always dreamed of. Selim's mouth broadened into a grin and he said, "I suppose they shoot and ride as well you, hey Ishkuz?"

"Well, they are pretty good from what I remember of them practising. Some of the women were better than the men."

"How did the men handle that?" asked Ansim. "Were they jealous or did they mistreat them because of it?"

"No, not at all," said Ishkuz. "Women are treated equally and are highly regarded among our tribes and are expected to do what the men do. It's even quite normal for some women to have leadership roles in the army and to train men."

"Well, that's very different to our tribe," said Ansim.

Ishkuz decided he wouldn't comment as Ansim had an offended look on her face again, but he wasn't sure if it was because of him or not.

They rode in silence for a time and then Ansim asked, "Do the women of your tribe wear jewellery?"

Ishkuz thought that this question was safe to answer.

"Yes, a lot of gold, even though it's very expensive to buy. Our tribe has taken what gold there is in the rivers, but we don't have time to mine for gold, so we trade for it. Our tribe use a lot of bone and ivory when we can get it, and I have seen some wonderful craftsmen shaping and polishing bone and ivory into delicate and beautiful pieces of jewellery."

Ansim plied Ishkuz with more questions about his tribe and background as they made their way north along the hard mountain roads. As time went on, Ansim intimidated Ishkuz less. He sensed that she was probably more full of threats than action, although he saw that her frustration about her role in the tribe was real.

The whole morning and into the early afternoon they travelled along the side of the mountain until they began to descend to the desert floor. There was going to be another three full days of travel through the desert before they came to Yathrib. Ansim was beginning to complain about the journey and the heat but no-one paid her much attention. Selim finally reminded her that the days spent travelling along the desert floor were going to be hotter than what they had experienced so far and she didn't complain again.

That night they camped on the edge of the desert where the mountain road flowed into the dry, hard landscape of the desert. The road they travelled on joined another road from the east and it was at this junction, at the bottom of the Sarmadee mountain range, that they found the camping ground. It was well worn and had the protection of the mountain range to the south and east. There was no water but by mid-afternoon the next day they would reach an oasis where they could camp and refresh their water supplies.

"There's no-one else here," said Ansim, sounding somewhat surprised.

"There may be a caravan arriving tonight or there may not," said Ibrahim casually. Yet, even as he said this his eyes scanned the low hills and the interior of the desert that spread out before them.

"So, do we have to wait another night and day to find some women to talk to," complained Ansim.

"Yes," said Sekeen. "And another day and night till we are safe from bandits."

Ansim and Warda widened their eyes at each other while Ibrahim gave Sekeen a disapproving look as if to say, "Did you really have to say that?"

The two girls chose to ignore Sekeen and any possible danger, either because they trusted the men or because they were ignorant of the real threats present in the desert. They went about making sure that their beds were going to be comfortable, moving rocks and sticks that might poke them during the night and keep them awake, then set about building a small fire to prepare a meal. The men set up a tent for the women and unpacked the horses, rubbing them down with brushes and watering them from the water skins they carried. They had brought food for the horses and once tethered they would feed them.

Ibrahim and Sekeen seemed to be more quiet than usual that night and they were not relaxed. While the fire cast a ring of light around the camp and reached out to glisten in the eyes of the horses, their attention was not on those in the ring of light or on the talk that was going on, but on the darkness and sounds outside the light. Both Ishkuz and Selim were also aware of how vulnerable their little group was and wished that a caravan had camped with them for the night.

On cushions just inside their tent the girls chatted and giggled, occasionally looking at Ishkuz as the flames flickered on his face. The talk among the men around the campfire was mostly on horses and hunting, although Sekeen tried his best to turn the conversation to weapons and hand-to-hand combat. Eager to learn from others, he questioned Ishkuz about the weapons and tactics of the Saka people. Ishkuz, predominantly a bowman, brought up the subject of archery and the shape of the bows he had seen.

"The bows we use in Scythia are quite different to the ones you have here," said Ishkuz. Sekeen, Ibrahim and Selim looked at him quizzically as he started to explain.

"Your bows have one curve and it's not sharp. I remember the bows from my father had a number of sharp curves to them. The curves were set so that you had to pull against them and this gave a lot more tension. It took some strength to pull the string right back but when you did the arrows went a long way. They were also shorter and easier to carry, especially when riding."

Sekeen listened intently and when Ishkuz had finished he said, "Can you draw the bow on the ground for me. I want to see the shape of the curves."

Taking a stick from the woodpile, Ishkuz cleared an area of sandy ground that was covered with small stones. He then began to draw the shape of the Scythian bow.

"I hope I've got it right, as it's a long time since I saw one," Ishkuz said as he drew.

He started with the top of the bow, which Sekeen saw was a tight curl. Sekeen was already intrigued as he realised that it faced away from the shooter.

The curve then shallowed out but kept going in the opposite direction of the bows that Sekeen had seen. As Ishkuz continued to draw, Sekeen could see that the bow curved away from the shooter, then toward the shooter and then away again. Sekeen's quick mind saw how the middle of the bow gave it strength, as well as the necessary resistance for the curves at the ends of the bow.

"That is a great bow with clever use of tension. I can see how it would have much more of a spring to it than the bows we use," said Sekeen with obvious admiration.

"Why haven't you made one of these, Ishkuz?" Selim said with intensity.

"I don't know how," he replied. "I've never seen them made and don't know how they make the curves or what type of wood they use."

"I would love one of them," said Sekeen, his eyes glistening with intensity. "We could hit our enemies way before they came anywhere near us." He paused then added, "And you have no idea what type of wood was used? It would have to be very strong but very flexible."

"Yes, that's right. But I was young when I was taken and don't remember the trees from home," replied Ishkuz.

"Well, I'm going to look into this. Maybe some men in Yathrib know more about this type of bow or maybe the best wood to use," said Sekeen.

The girls chattering slowed as the night wore on and eventually they slept soundly in their tent. The men also started to make moves to bed down for the night and while the fire was dying down Sekeen threw some more wood on it saying, "I'll take the first watch."

"I'll take the next watch," said Selim as he unrolled his blankets and yawned. The night turned silent and while Sekeen prodded the fire, he looked up at the sky. Above him was a vast canopy of deep purple, black and blue hues with brilliant sparks scattered across it. Sekeen was impressed with its awesome size and beauty like many others before him. It prompted questions in his mind such as "where it all came from?", "who made it?", and "if some spirit or God made it, then how big and powerful must he be to create something so vast and beautiful?" As he sat and thought about it, he realised that generally a person makes things that reflect their own character and desires. If the night sky was big and beautiful and artistic and awe-inspiring then maybe its Creator was the same? He admitted to himself he hadn't thought of the Creator like that before, even though he had heard many stories of him over the years. Maybe the Creator was better than he had thought or maybe he was just beginning to see different sides to the Creator that he didn't realise were a part of him. Maybe the Creator was more complex than he thought.

As he mulled these thoughts over, his ears caught the sound of a twig breaking somewhere to the south of the camp. It was too sharp to be an animal and it wasn't the horses as they were to the east. Sekeen quickly threw some larger sticks onto the fire for more light and quietly drew his sword. He sat still and silent so that he could listen carefully. Ishkuz lay not far from Sekeen's feet and carefully Sekeen stretched out and nudged him awake. His eyes were instantly alert and from the intent look on Sekeen's face he knew that something serious was happening. Sekeen nodded in the direction of the noise. Ishkuz slowly and carefully reached for his sword.

Ibrahim was already on his knees, sensing something was happening. He reached over, shook Selim and whispered to him, "Look to the south."

As Selim's eyes adjusted he was just in time to see five shadows rise up from various tufts of long grass just outside of the camp area and run towards them. Three of them stopped, knelt down and drew back their bows. In the shadowy light the arrows quickly flew into the camp. One flew just wide of Sekeen while the other two thudded into the chest of Ishkuz. His arms flung up and he fell backward onto the ground. As his body thudded to the ground his head hit a thick piece of firewood and he lay still. With two arrows sticking out of his chest and a grey look to his still face, Ishkuz seemed dead. The attackers were upon them in a matter of seconds and Sekeen charged them. It was three against six but both Ibrahim and Sekeen were veteran fighters and Selim was beginning to excel in his swordsmanship.

Metal clashed against metal as swords came up against each other. The three attackers who had shot arrows were a number of metres behind the others. Ibrahim, Selim and Sekeen took on the first three. One of them was large, yet swift on his feet, and his sword moved quickly. Ibrahim was wily and agile and evaded his efforts while his own sword snuck in quickly between the big attacker's blows. He struck the big man on the fleshy part of the top of his arm and a cry of pain came from his lips. Along with the pain came a mixture of fear and anger and the man attacked even more ferociously. The strokes pushed Ibrahim back as he defended this new onslaught. But he wasn't going to be outdone. Ibrahim knew that an angry enemy made mistakes so he was waiting for him to make one. In his eagerness the man stumbled on a small rise of sand. Rather than attack him, Ibrahim used the weight and thrust of the man and stepped quickly to the side and hit him on his neck as he came past. The big man fell to the sand and Ibrahim sprang on him and hit the back of his skull with the hilt of his sword, knocking him out.

It was just in time, as another attacker moved on Ibrahim. He was more cautious, circling Ibrahim with his sword up. This gave Ibrahim enough time to scan around him to see how Selim and Sekeen were faring. Sekeen was fighting two of the attackers while another was fighting with Selim. A body lay face down on the ground near Sekeen and Ibrahim could see a dark stain on the back.

Ibrahim's attacker lunged at him as his focus waned. Ibrahim brought his sword down on his attacker's sword, but the man pulled back quickly and swung again, this time at Ibrahim's head. Ibrahim quickly ducked and he heard the sound of air being cut above his head. Ibrahim stabbed at the man's stomach but already his enemy had stepped back. Ibrahim realised that there was a desperation in his opponent that made him quick, but he also felt that it was not going to last. He stepped toward his opponent and following the moves he had been taught for many years, sent his enemy staggering backward, so quickly that he stumbled and dropped his sword. With panic written on his face he looked at the sword, then to Ibrahim, then climbed to his feet and ran off.

Ibrahim turned immediately to Selim and Sekeen. He was concerned for Selim, as his arm had only just mended from the break. Ibrahim had nothing to worry about. Sekeen and Selim were flowing in the yellow light of the fire. They seemed mirrors of each other in terms of their grace and movement. Each one used only the effort that was needed and neither of them seemed in any danger of being wounded, let alone beaten. Sekeen had already dealt with another of his attackers who was holding his arm and trying to stop the flow of blood that was running from the wound on his arm. He was grimacing and staggering back into the darkness but fell to the ground and lay there. He was losing blood quickly. As Ibrahim went to help Selim the two remaining attackers looked at each other in fear and they turned around and ran. Sekeen began to chase them but Ibrahim called him back.

"It's dark. Let them go. They could hide anywhere out there. Let's fix the wounded and then tie them up."

Sekeen turned and went to the man he had injured. While Sekeen checked him for weapons, gathered his sword and secured him with rope, Selim and Ibrahim quickly made their way over to Ishkuz. The girls had just arrived at his body. Woken by the noise of fighting, they had scrambled to the entrance to their tent and screamed when they saw Ishkuz lying so still on the ground with two arrows in his chest. Ansim sat on her knees next to Ishkuz whimpering.

"You can't die now. You can't die now. I need you!" Ansim said in between sobs. Ibrahim knelt down and put his ear to Ishkuz's mouth.

"He's still breathing, but it's shallow. I don't hear anything to suggest that his lungs have been pierced. That's very strange with two arrows in his chest."

Selim put his hand behind Ishkuz's head and felt wet, sticky blood.

"He has a cut on the back of his head," he added.

Ishkuz murmured and opened his eyes.

"Lie still Ishkuz," said Selim. "Girls, go and get some water and some cloths."

Ishkuz pushed himself up onto his elbows while both Ibrahim and Selim half supported and half prevented him, not sure of what he was doing or whether he was able to do it.

"Ishkuz," said Ibrahim, "you have two arrows in your chest and your head is split open at the back. You need to stay still so we can close the wounds."

Ishkuz's eyes rolled up and he lay back down. Ibrahim undid Ishkuz's tunic and shirt and pulled them back to expose his chest. As he did the eyes of all those around him opened wide and Sekeen and Selim let out a heavy breath. All could see that the two arrows were wedged tightly into what seemed like a breastplate, but neither arrow had reached his chest!

"The gods be praised," said Ibrahim. "Another wonder of this pale face. Whatever it is has saved his life. It looks like he'll come out of this with some bruises and a sore head."

Ansim allowed herself a nervous smile and her eyes opened wide in hope. Ibrahim soaked a cloth in water and gently cleaned the back of Ishkuz's head. After asking Ansim to get some ointment from his bag, Ibrahim smeared it on the wound and then wrapped Ishkuz's head in a bandage. By this time, Ishkuz had recovered some colour and strength and was able to sit up. Ansim brought him some watered-down wine and after a little while he was able to stand. He made his way to the fire and sat down on one of the logs.

"How do you feel?" Ansim asked him.

Ishkuz replied, "My head hurts but other than being tender where the arrows struck, I feel well. I'll be fine, I'm sure. The wine helped. Thank you Ansim."

Ansim nodded her head as Selim added, "You'll have a sore head for a few days, I think."

"That may be, but I am still able to ride and do what is needed," replied Ishkuz with a slight tinge of indignation in his voice.

Selim broke in and asked, "Can you tell us what it is that you're wearing? I've never seen anything like it. You didn't look like you were wearing any type of protection and yet it saved your life."

"It's chest protection made from the hooves of horses. When a horse dies the Saka take the shells of the hooves after they have separated from the inside of the hoof and clean them. Then we join them together with leather, overlapping the hooves and then attach it to ourselves with straps. It's cheaper than metal but very effective. My tribe has made these for generations. I made this one over the years I was captive and tonight I am very glad I did," said Ishkuz.

"So am I," said both Ansim and Selim at the same time. Selim had a questioning look on his face as he turned to Ansim, but she simply bowed her head to avoid the eyes of the others.

"It must also be light," added Sekeen.

"Yes, it is," replied Ishkuz. "You hardly know you're wearing it."

"Well, you have certainly exposed us to some new ideas in a short space of time," said Selim. "Your bag of tricks hasn't emptied yet, has it?"

" How about we wait and see?" Ishkuz replied with the hint of a twinkle in his eye.

Ansim smiled and stole a glance at Ishkuz, who just managed to see it and smile back.

Ibrahim said, "You have surprised us again Ishkuz and it is good to see you well, but we have a body to bury and sleep to catch up on. Selim, you stay on watch while Sekeen and I bury this man and tie up the other. Ansim and Warda, keep your eye on Ishkuz in case he gets faint."

The night passed without further incident. A small dose of sleeping draught allowed Ishkuz to rest well but the others only dozed fitfully as their minds were still very active. Ansim and Warda asked Selim to move his bedding to the entrance of their tent, which he did without complaint. He remained awake and alert, as did Ibrahim who stayed on watch. Sekeen was the only one, apart from Ishkuz, who slept soundly. None of them liked death or the killing of other humans, but of all of them, Sekeen was the most practical and he saw no need to stay awake when someone trustworthy was on watch.

CHAPTER 16

*S*elim woke early and roused the others. It was to their advantage to arrive quickly to the next night's camping area where there was bound to be a caravan or more stopping for the night and where they would be much safer than they had been the previous night. The girls cooked some millet with goat's milk and boiled some eggs they had brought along, while the men pulled down the tent, saddled the riding horses and packed the luggage bags with their sleeping rolls and utensils.

"Sekeen," said Selim, "could you make sure there is a horse to carry our prisoner? You'll need to divide the luggage between the other pack horses."

Sekeen nodded and left to do that. The horses were alert and rested and were enjoying their morning lucerne. Ibrahim had already brushed them down and they glistened in the morning sun.

The group travelled quickly that morning, eager to put the night's attack behind them. The shock of thinking that Ishkuz had been killed kept the girls relatively quiet and Ansim's eyes never strayed far away from him. Ibrahim and Sekeen talked over the attack as they rode to see whether there was anything they could do to improve their protection. As the day wore on, the heat of the sun forced them all to reserve their strength and they rode without speaking. The horses hung their heads in the heat, snorting through their nostrils to get rid of the dust. The landscape was flat, dry and unchanging and it lacked vegetation, apart from some harsh grasses and straggly saplings. Through the haze they could just make out a yellow smudge to the east, far beyond the flat desert which Ibrahim explained was the first of the giant sand dunes that were part of the great, inland desert.

The road became more worn as it went on and as the late afternoon approached their excitement and chatter increased as they neared their goal for the day, the large campground. As they came closer they could hear the noise of sheep, goats, camels and horses and the cries and laughter of their owners. Selim pushed Faraj into a canter and the others followed along, the horses just as eager to see company as their human riders and to drink the sweet water they could already smell.

The camping area circled a large pool of water, which was fed by an underground spring. The edges of the pool was muddied with hoof prints but at its source, close to where the water bubbled from the earth, sweet, crystal clear water was there for the taking.

Selim and Sekeen took on the task of finding a suitable camping site, one that was both close to the water and yet provided protection. The others took the horses straight down to the pool. They all slaked their thirst with long draughts of the cool water, which washed the dust of the road out of their mouths. Aisha shook herself, starting with her head and neck, and then her whole body. The saddle shook along with her, but she was satisfied and let out a long sigh. The other horses turned their heads and scratched places they couldn't reach while saddled. Selim and Sekeen soon returned and they followed them back to a sandy area surrounded by palms and low brush. It was cool and shady and protected from the bustling caravanners.

They all set about making camp. Each horse was allowed a roll in the sand before being tethered and fed some lucerne. Kadin loved it so much he rolled three times before he would let himself be led to the picket and his food. Ishkuz was happy to let him enjoy himself as he had carried him well and had behaved perfectly on the trip so far. He was growing quite fond of the bay stallion. Ishkuz pulled his forelock straight and rubbed around his big black eyes. Kadin then rubbed his face against Ishkuz's arm and back, pushing him forward and nearly lifting him from the ground. Kadin tried this three or four times before he shook his head as if to put everything back into place and then nudged Ishkuz as if to say "Get me to my food."

Ishkuz laughed. "I've been on your back all day and you've carried me well. I'll get you your food." He rubbed Kadin's forehead and noticed how small his ears were, especially compared to the ears of the horses back at home.

"Home," he thought. "That's something I have been saying for so many years and now I've spent more years away from home than I did living there. I might have to adjust to the fact that my home has changed forever." A smile flicked his mouth as the thought ran through his mind.

He noticed that Kadin's ears were quite full of soft hair, even though he had a short summer coat. Yet, of course, the desert sand could so easily get into horses' ears and the hair kept it out. Ishkuz loved Kadin's eyes. They were lustrous and dark and against the thin, black skin of his face were set like large diamonds in a king's crown. His forehead was flat and as he swept the forelock to the side, he saw a white marking, not a large one, but one just big enough to break the black colour of the skin and dark brown hair. Between his eyes and down to his nose ran two ridges that turned in and gave a concave appearance to his head. Selim rubbed Kadin's muzzle and nostrils and while his muzzle was plump and firm, the skin of his nostrils was soft and loose. He had seen how this skin had stretched when Kadin's nostrils dilated.

"Quality," he thought. "He has been designed with so much balance and beauty."

He rubbed Kadin on the forehead and smoothed down his forelock, then got the barley seeds that Kadin was so anxious to have and which he probably thought he deserved after the day's ride.

While dinner was being prepared Ibrahim left to find out who the leaders of the caravan were and to catch up on any news. He also planned to hand over their prisoner to the leader's guards. Selim and Ishkuz went in search of some sticks and kindling for the fire and as they came back they overheard Ansim and Warda arguing in loud whispers. They stopped as soon as they saw Selim and Ishkuz but not quickly enough to avoid overhearing Warda say, "Why then did you say, 'You can't die now'?"

Ishkuz paid no attention to it, though he did notice that Ansim looked both angry and wary and that she walked off with her head held high.

That evening as Ansim and Warda were preparing their beds, the men sat around the fire and talked. Sekeen said to Ishkuz, "It's time that we began your training with the sword. I would like to see your style. Come, let's practice."

Before Ishkuz could answer Ibrahim spoke up, concerned about the lump on the back of Ishkuz's head he had received the night before. "You mustn't exert yourself too much yet, Ishkuz. Don't let Sekeen bully you."

Ishkuz didn't refuse as his head was feeling better, but he also knew that it would be thumping at the end of the practice.

"I can't pass this up," he thought to himself.

Both of them took off their long coats and rolled up the sleeves of their shirts. Each grabbed their swords and Selim could see that they were already thinking of the stance they would take and what their first move would be. They edged over to a vacant, sandy area and Ishkuz took his stance. He stood with his legs quite close together and both hands held his sword to the right of his body. Sekeen was about to take his stance, but when he saw the way Ishkuz stood he put his sword tip into the sand and lent on it. "Hmm," he said, "interesting."

"What?" said Ishkuz. "Am I doing something wrong?"

"No, it's just interesting. You stand like a man that I fought against many years ago and I would say that he was one of the top five men that I have ever fought. I wonder if you will have the same style and skill," replied Sekeen almost wistfully.

"Well, I've had no formal training, although we fought with wooden sticks when I was young," said Ishkuz.

Sekeen laughed and said, "As we all did Ishkuz."

REJECTION

Sekeen took up his sword and unlike Ishkuz he held it in his right hand and spread his legs to gain better balance. This different stance didn't affect Ishkuz and he advanced on Sekeen. Ishkuz proved to be no match for Sekeen and his lack of training showed as he blundered into moves that left him terribly exposed and vulnerable. Yet, this was what the training was all about, to learn from mistakes and to build form for both defence and offence.

Selim watched from his seat next to the fire and heard Sekeen start to instruct Ishkuz in his usually brusque style, one that he had experienced now for many years. Yet, he felt just a little satisfaction that there was something that Ishkuz wasn't good at, well maybe two things if he counted relating to girls. He had been keen to learn and asked to be taught and that was typical of Ishkuz. He was willing to learn and he was humble, which made him likeable, and Selim realised this made him someone you wanted to be friends with. Their friendship had developed quickly and he had enjoyed the last months, despite the terrible scare he'd had with his arm. It was good to relate to someone different, yet who also had so much in common.

Ibrahim interrupted his thoughts and called over to him.

"Selim, I was told that there was a man travelling with the caravan who is a scholar. He reads and writes and even has some manuscripts and books with him. He's on his way to Jerusalem then will travel on to Damascus. Maybe we can arrange for you to speak with him one night or even as we travel during the day."

At this Selim's interest peaked. "I'd love to do that."

"I'll speak to one of the men from the caravan tomorrow and see what we can do," replied Ibrahim with a smile.

Sekeen and Ishkuz practised until it became too dark to continue. As they came over to the fire and sat down Ishkuz was breathing heavily. Sekeen noticed this and used it to push home the point of fitness and true swordsmanship. Selim had heard this many times and though it was a little tiresome to hear, he certainly knew it as truth, as his own skills had increased dramatically when his body was fit.

Ansim brought Ishkuz a drink without saying a word and he managed to say thank you and smile. Sekeen made a face and held out his hands to Selim as if to say, "And where is mine?"

Ishkuz gave him a grin and shook his head.

That night Ishkuz slept well but they all woke early to get a good start on their travel before the heat of the day hit. The horses were fed and groomed, manes unknotted and their eyes wiped. The caravan was setting off and they joined it as it snaked its way along the road northward. Ibrahim, true to his word, cantered off on Aisha to find the scholar. He soon came back and motioned to Selim to follow him, who then called Ishkuz to join him. Together they cantered along the side of the road past the colourful wagons and loaded animals. They noticed that many eyes turned their way to admire the white mare and the chestnut and bay stallions, all gleaming in the sun with manes and tails flying high in the air.

They came to a group of camels and Ibrahim slowed down. He walked Aisha up to one of the camels whose rider was a wizened old man. The old man waved at them and called to one of the men riding with him. He handed his reins to another rider, jumped off his camel and ran back down the line. The old man called out to them and said, "I have sent him to fetch a horse so that I am not so far above you."

The man soon returned with a saddled and bridled horse. She was a thin chestnut with a dry coat, yet despite this she had bright eyes. Ignoring his old age, the man swung his leg over the camel's saddle and slid down onto the mare next to it and then brought her over to Ibrahim, Selim and Ishkuz.

"This is far better for talking, and a horse smells far better than a camel," he added with a laugh.

Selim got the impression that the old man carried life lightly despite what Ibrahim had said about his learning.

"I am Feysul, Feysul ibn Gharoub. I heard from the caravan master that you wished to speak to me."

"Yes," replied Ibrahim. "We heard that you were travelling with the caravan and we have only just joined it today. I am Ibrahim and this is Selim and Ishkuz."

Feysul's eyes met Selim's, then moved onto Ishkuz's. Their eyes remained locked as Feysul took in the unusual colour of his skin, eyes and hair.

"It is my honour to meet you all. If you will forgive me, Ishkuz, are you a Gomerian?"

Ishkuz showed his surprise at being spoken to so quickly and by one so eminent. He had never been treated as anything but a slave. He replied, "I believe that we may be distantly related, but I am a Scythian. We are also known as Sakas, which is my tribe's preferred name."

"Ah yes, that makes sense. I have had more to do with Gomerians but am familiar with Scythians," answered Feysul. "And where are you all travelling to?" he added.

"We are heading to Yathrib," answered Ibrahim.

"Ah, I will travel to Yathrib but am going on further to Damascus," replied Feysul.

Selim was intrigued by this as he had heard of Damascus from traders and there was something about the name that made him want to explore every corner of the city, every hidden alleyway and every garden.

Selim asked Feysul, "Are you from Damascus or are you just on your way there?"

"I am from Damascus, but I have been travelling through some of the cities and towns of this area looking for old manuscripts and writings of the various tribes and people who lived here before. I love finding out about the history of our lands but in particular I want to learn about the ancient languages of the people of these regions," answered Feysul.

"You need to talk to Ibrahim. He knows all the stories of old, although he hasn't written them down," said Selim.

Feysul looked at Ibrahim with some admiration and then narrowed his eyes and said, "My friend, we may need to sit together one night so that I can hear some of these stories. I would like to know if there are any that are new to me, as I have collected local legends and tribal histories for many years now. You may be able to extend my collection. Ibrahim, would you do me the honour of eating with me tonight?"

Ibrahim swelled a little with pride. "It would honour me to share your fire and food. Thank you."

Selim chuckled inside at the way Ibrahim responded and the effect that the offer had on him. Yet, Selim was also glad that Ibrahim was recognised for his stories and that someone of Feysul's reputation was interested in them.

Selim spoke up. "Feysul, have you come across any stories that mention a large boat with lots of animals? We have a cave in the Sarmadee mountains, near to our home that has a picture on the wall. It shows a large boat in the middle of dry ground with animals running around on what looks like a desert full of spring grass. It doesn't make sense."

"Ah, I think I can help you out there, Selim. It is Selim, isn't it?"

Selim nodded and Feysul went on. "There is a people called the Jews who have in their writings a story about a man who built a large boat for animals so they could be saved from a great flood. I have read the story but don't remember all the details. The Jews have many books and I must admit I haven't read them all. Maybe one day I will get around to it."

Feysul then stopped and looked as though he was reading a part of his brain. He added, "I think his Jewish name was Noah, but he was also known as Ziasudra. He lived for many years and it is believed that he and his family were the only ones to have survived the rising of the waters. It's interesting that you have a picture of this story in your region, as Ziasudra is associated with the north, far north of Damascus. But more than that I cannot say."

Selim answered, "In the picture there are horses that look like our horses and I was wondering if that's where our horses come from. The picture is either very old and either our land has changed or someone travelling to the Sarmadees carried the picture from another place. I love finding out about the

REJECTION

history of our horses and why our tribe has had them from time beyond our memories."

"Yes, your horses truly are quality horses," Feysul answered as his eyes glanced over the horses they were riding. "And you say that the horses in the picture are the same as yours?"

"Yes, very similar in looks and colour," answered Selim.

"That's very interesting. I don't have much experience in the history of animals or their breeding as I travel so much and am occupied by so many other things, but what you tell me is very interesting, very interesting indeed," replied Feysul as he rubbed his chin.

"Do you have any idea how old the drawing might be?" asked Feysul.

"None at all, except that our tribe only knows our region as being desert, not with the deep green grass that the picture shows. We also don't know many of the animals that are in the picture. Many have never been seen by our people and some we know are either very rare or stories tell us they no longer exist. It must have been drawn many, many years ago for the land to become so dry and for those animals to disappear," answered Selim.

The men chatted and shared stories as the caravan moved along and Selim's heart swelled as he heard of faraway places and the lives of others. His mind was stirred to hear of manuscripts and of bound pieces of paper called books that could hold so much more writing than vellum or thick manuscripts. His mind travelled ahead to Yathrib where he hoped he could find some books and old manuscripts to look at.

They finally left Feysul to rejoin the girls and Sekeen. Ansim questioned Ishkuz repeatedly about his head until he became quite embarrassed, and he was glad when they stopped for the night.

Once more Ishkuz practiced his swordsmanship with Sekeen. His head was feeling better and the bruising on his chest wasn't enough to stop him from fighting. Ansim felt concerned and watched him spar with Sekeen, but she did so discreetly. Ishkuz was fully focused on doing his best and on learning as much as he could. He was in awe of Sekeen and the fluid way he moved, the skill with which he wielded his sword, and the strength he could bring to each and every stroke. Ishkuz hoped that he wasn't making a fool of himself with his limited ability and training. However, Sekeen was encouraging and instructive and Ishkuz's confidence was growing.

They all slept well that night and after a solid breakfast they saddled the horses and joined the caravan on the road. They expected to reach Yathrib later that day, so they rode with an air of expectation and excitement. Ansim was both excited and somewhat nervous and this made her quite talkative. She whispered frequently to Warda and every so often Ishkuz would see her looking at him and then whisper to Warda, and it was unnerving. Once he caught her smiling widely at him and surprisingly, he found himself very much attracted to the openness of her face and the honesty she showed.

He realised that Ansim was a sensitive young lady who might well struggle to hide her feelings, but he also felt that those around her shouldn't treat them lightly. He decided that he would have to be very careful about how he responded to her feelings.

Ishkuz knew he was attracted to the warmth that Ansim showed, not just to him, but to others as well. She was definitely passionate, especially about what females could and couldn't do, but surrounding that was an openness that allowed you to see right into her soul. He immediately pictured Aisha and the way her eyes let him do that, but he suddenly realised that Ansim would never accept being compared to a horse, even a magnificent mare like Aisha. He swung his head to look at her and she caught his movement and smiled again. He gave a quick smile back and then turned away. "If she knew what I was thinking, I don't think she would be smiling," he thought.

It was strange though, as he had never had the feeling that her attention and smiles gave him. His chest and stomach filled with warmth and he liked how it felt soft and nice and somehow made him feel important and alive. It was as though Ansim had reached into his chest with her hands and left the warmth of her body there.

As predicted by Ibrahim they saw the walls of Yathrib late in the afternoon and as they approached various boys and women made their way out of the city offering fruit and trinkets for them to buy. The noise of the city began to fill their ears and their eyes darted around to gather in the sights and people of the city. There were guards patrolling the streets as well as on the city walls. Men and women sat outside their houses, often at small stalls where they sold food or carvings, boxes and sometimes silver and gold items. Selim took note of the metalwork but it didn't seem to be of great quality. He hoped that somewhere in the city there would be an experienced craftsman who was qualified enough to reforge Al Maksour.

Ibrahim slowed the group after they reached a square where a number of streets fed away deeper into the city. He leant over the neck of Aisha to speak with a young man behind a stall. The young man listened then pointed toward one of the streets. Ibrahim motioned to the others and they followed after him down the street as it snaked its way through the city. Ibrahim scanned the houses at the end of some narrower lanes and finally pulled up at an old wooden gate, set in a mud brick wall, just a little higher than their horses' heads.

"I'm fairly certain this is the house of your relative, Selim. Sekeen, Warda and I will take the horses to the stables. I will send word of how to find us," said Ibrahim.

Sekeen and Ibrahim took the reins of the horses as the others dismounted. They made their way to the gate and rang a bell that was hanging on the wall. Within a minute a middle-aged woman opened the gate and Ishkuz was surprised to see how much she looked like Ansim's mother.

"Yes, can I help you?" she said without any sign of recognising Selim or Sekeen.

"Auntie Rana, I am Selim, the son of Almas, and this is my sister, Ansim."

"Selim? Son of Almas? How can this be? But wait, Ansim? I haven't seen you since your father died. It's been such a long time."

Her expression went from shock to joy and excitement.

"Come in, come in! It is so good to see you!"

In her excitement she moved from one thought to the next and asked about their trip and the health of their mother without even giving them any time to answer. She hadn't even begun to register Ishkuz and how he might fit in. She led them through a paved section of the garden and into the coolness of the interior of the house, alternating between questions and comments about the house and her relationship with their family. They were taken into one of the sitting rooms with thick carpets and numerous pillows of various bright colours, some with tapestry, some with tassels and there they sat down.

"Let me get some food and drink, you must be quite tired and hungry," she said and left to organise them.

Very soon they were drinking some sweet, watery wine and eating sesame cakes drizzled with light fruity oil and a range of fresh fruit. It all tasted far better than the food they had eaten over the last few days. "Well, this is a surprise. I haven't had contact with your side of the family in many years," said Rana.

Ishkuz was only half listening as Rana spoke with Selim and Ansim. His eyes turned toward a finely made cage hanging just outside the door, inside of which came a trilling whistle. Through the bars he could see a bright yellow bird stretching toward the sky and singing as though its heart would burst. His thoughts were interrupted when he heard Selim mention his horse hoof chest shield and realised that Selim was telling Rana about the attack on them. Rana looked horrified and incredulous.

"Well, you are safe in the city. We don't hear much of that sort of thing here, but I suppose there are wild men out in the desert who are uncivilised and bloodthirsty," said Rana, wrapping up the story of their attack. Ishkuz couldn't help wondering if somehow she was including them in that group but Rana quickly went on.

"Come, enough talk now. Go out into the garden and refresh yourselves and I will see about getting a meal together. Here, take your food and drink, there are tables out there to put them on," she added.

The three of them moved out of the room through a door that led directly outside. The sun was low but still hot and they shaded their eyes. As their eyes adjusted, Ansim gasped and both Selim and Ishkuz were taken aback at the beauty and serenity of the garden before them. Trees of different shapes and sizes ringed the mud brick fence and they could hear the soft cooing of birds. Shrubs with delicate flowers lined the garden beds and almost every colour available appeared in some type of flower or another. Luxurious green grass covered the ground where the terracotta paving stopped and Ansim let out a squeal and pushed her feet and toes into its coolness, sighing deeply as she did. In the centre of the garden was a pool and in the middle was a fountain where water trickled gently down. Selim and Ishkuz both sat on the low wall and scooped some water up in their hands and rubbed it on their faces.

"This is truly a paradise," said Ishkuz.

"Yes," replied Selim. "I've never seen a garden so beautiful and so peaceful. It is so refreshing, especially after the heat and sand and rocks of the desert."

"I could live here forever," said Ansim as she lowered herself down to the grass to run her hands over the blades of grass.

"That may just happen," said Selim with a tone that Ishkuz couldn't quite work out.

Ansim looked quickly at Selim and said, "I will not marry him, however beautiful his garden is, and I am not staying here." She turned away from Selim with finality and looked at a distant part of the garden.

Ishkuz sensed the tension between them and didn't want to be drawn into it. He had already picked up that there might be a potential husband here, but more than that he didn't know. Strangely, he didn't like the idea of not having Ansim around. She certainly added something to their conversations and like Aisha had a spirit about her that reached out to those around her, drawing them in. "Oh no," he thought, "I have to stop comparing her to a horse." He too turned his attention to a distant part of the garden, the opposite part to where Ansim was looking.

Selim shook his head. "I will speak to Auntie tonight after the meal. I promised Mother I would do this."

Ishkuz thought that he recognised regret in Selim's tone now. Ansim did not reply.

CHAPTER 17

It wasn't long before Rana's son came home. She was sitting with her visitors on some cushions in a paved area of the garden, under a large tree that offered them great shade from the hot but weakening afternoon sun. Rana heard him enter and went in to get him so she could introduce him to them. He came through the door and with one glance Ansim became even more convinced that she would not marry him. His stride was short and his small, round eyes were set in a face that was both pudgy and greasy. This did not appeal to Ansim in any way. Part of her felt a pang of guilt for judging him, but it was quickly pushed aside by her determination not to live with him for the rest of her life. Although she had always been quick to judge, she felt a certain amount of satisfaction that in the past her judgements had often proved right.

Muhair was introduced first to the men. His eyes lingered on Ishkuz, as many eyes in this part of the world did. However, Muhair was polite and courteous to them all in his greetings and expressions of welcome and care.

"It is a privilege to meet you all. It has been a long time since we have met up with your side of the family and it is an honour to have you here. You are from the deep south, the Nejd?"

"Yes," answered Selim. "A number of weeks travel. We live in a fort by a river in the Sarmadee mountains. It is very different from a city."

"I imagine it would be," replied Muhair, "but I am not one for the harsh living of the desert."

Rana added quickly, "Muhair is a clerk in the city and loves working with writing and numbers. He is very good at what he does and much appreciated by those he works for. They even said that he will progress quickly into other more responsible areas if he keeps up his level of work." Her words faded a little at the end as she realised what she was saying, and she began to lower her eyes. All of them could see that she was proud of her son, but Ishkuz suspected from the way Muhair looked at his mother that he held a certain degree of disdain for her.

"My mother and our extended family send their greetings to you both. They are all in good health and my mother thanks you for taking us in as your guests," Selim said, respectfully diverting attention away from what Rana had said.

"What brings you to Yathrib if it is so far from your home?" Muhair asked.

Both Selim and Ishkuz suddenly felt nervous, as they didn't want to reveal anything about Al Maksour, however they had all agreed that the journey would have a number of purposes that would hide their real one, the reforging of Al Maksour. One was to find more manuscripts or books, so that Selim and others in the tribe could read more widely and better understand the world outside of their desert. The other was for them all to gain an education in life beyond the desert and their own limited existence. As Selim explained this in the most convincing tone he could muster, Muhair glanced over at Ansim and Warda. Muhair's look left Selim in no doubt that he questioned Selim's story and knew that the girls had some part to play in the journey, but he did not ask outright why they were with them.

When Selim had finished speaking Muhair replied with pride, "There is no finer place for manuscripts and books than Yathrib. I would be happy to show you some of the best shops. I know some of the owners as well."

Selim answered, "Thank you Muhair, that would be terrific. Do you have time?"

"Yes, that is not a problem. Would tomorrow suit you or do you need some time to rest?" asked Muhair.

"Tomorrow would be fine, if that is alright with you," replied Selim, casting a look at his auntie.

"Of course, you do what you like, enjoy the city and learn as much as you can," she replied. "But come, let us eat."

They sat and chatted together over their food. After the table had been cleared, Selim followed Rana into the kitchen area.

"Thank you so much for the meal and your hospitality. We are indebted to you," said Selim. He continued, "My mother has asked me to talk to you about Ansim. She was wondering whether your son, Muhair, might be interested in marrying her."

Rana was a little taken aback. "Selim, this is a surprise. I have wanted Muhair to find a nice girl and settle down, but he doesn't seem interested. And to marry in the family, that is a good thing, a very good thing. Yes, I'll speak to him. I'll do it tonight and encourage him. Your mother was very clever to think of this. Thank you, Selim, thank you."

She then added, "How old is Ansim?"

Selim replied, "Eighteen."

"Good, good, a perfect age and there's a family connection. Let me clean up and I will talk to Muhair about it."

"Thank you, Rana."

In his heart Selim was greatly relieved as he had done his job and was not responsible for the outcome. However, he had a strange feeling about Muhair. He seemed polite, yet arrogant, and some of the comments he had made during the evening had been condescending. He also didn't have a great deal of respect for his mother and Selim wondered if she knew as much about him as she thought. His greatest concern was that Muhair seemed to have a very sharp mind and might suspect more than he let on. Selim's only hope was that in Muhair's arrogance he might not give any more thought to his desert relatives or seek to find out more about their motives for visiting.

After sleeping well in comfortable beds with fresh linen, Selim and Ishkuz left early the next morning to find Ibrahim and Sekeen. Ibrahim had sent word to them the night before on how to find the stables. Muhair was going to meet them there as he knew the place and planned to take them to the shops and bazaar from there. They found Ibrahim and Sekeen in a large stable complex with a high roof that kept the stables and horses cool.

Ishkuz was quite taken by it. "This is a great place. And look at all these horses. I could live here myself!"

Sekeen turned up his nose and said, "Well, you can have the smell. I'm just glad we don't have to sleep with the horses."

"Where did you sleep?" asked Ishkuz.

"There are rooms off the stable where you can close the door and keep the smell out," answered Sekeen.

Ibrahim added, "A lot of traders and travellers keep their horses here. It has a good reputation and the horses are well fed."

Aisha lifted her head up from the straw on the floor and called out to them. Selim and Ishkuz looked at her and walked over to pat her. She looked refreshed and was certainly no worse off from the trip. Aisha was freshly washed and her white coat shone. As Ishkuz removed some straw from her mane, he was struck by the fineness of the hairs and their quality.

Selim moved over to Faraj, while Ishkuz went to see Kadin who was shuffling about in his stable. A solid wooden door that looked a hundred years old was attached to the rendered brick walls and Ishkuz opened the gate. Kadin's coat had been polished to a reflective shine and as Ishkuz ran his hand down his neck it felt like the skin of a newborn deer, so soft and thin. Kadin nuzzled his shoulder and Ishkuz rubbed him between the eyes. Looking over Kadin he could see that Ibrahim had taken care of every aspect of Kadin. His tail and mane were straight and untangled and even his hooves had been rubbed clean of the dust and dirt from the days of travel. Instinctively, Ishkuz picked up Kadin's near front leg and checked the sole of the hoof, which was clean and dry and free of manure.

He noticed that Selim had gone back to Ibrahim and Sekeen and that they were busy talking to another man. After a moment, Selim gestured for Ishkuz to come.

"That was a message from Rana. It seems that business of some type means that Muhair can't take us to the shops. We'll go on our own as he has given us instructions on how to get there."

"That's great, Selim, but what about…" and then Ishkuz lowered his voice to a whisper, "the sword?" asked Ishkuz.

Ibrahim answered for Selim. "It's probably best if Sekeen and I look for the ironworkers and ask around for the best ones. Selim's family doesn't know us and it will prevent any unnecessary questions. Then you and Selim can go straight to the best one and speak to him."

"Sounds good, thanks Ibrahim," said Ishkuz.

Selim and Ishkuz followed the instructions that they had been given and soon found themselves in a large marketplace. They breathed in the tangy fragrance of oranges and mandarins and the thick, mesmerising waft of spices, as well as the sizzling scent of frying fat and meat. Their excitement rose as their eyes darted from stall to stall to take in the displays and the wares that were offered before them.

"What will we look at first?" asked Ishkuz.

"I am going to head towards the manuscripts," replied Selim. "I want to find out more about the man Feysul told us about. What was his name? It was something to do with the Jews."

"Yes, the Jews" said Ishkuz, "but I think he was in the Jewish writings. Feysul didn't say he was a Jew, although he could be. He gave him two names. One was Nochah or Nonah or something like that. The other one was much harder to pronounce, but I know it started with a 'Z.'"

"It was something like that. I'll ask the stall owner. He'll probably know," said Selim. "Feysul must have a memory like a trap. He pulled both of those names out just like that when we mentioned the big wooden boat from the painting."

Just then Selim spotted a small nondescript building on the outskirts of the open market that sat back from the temporary stalls, as if it was shy about being noticed. There was a wooden sign on the wall that said, "Manuscripts and historical artefacts." Selim motioned to Ishkuz and pointed to it. They made their way toward it and entered the door which was set in the thick mud brick walls.

As they went inside and the coolness of the room engulfed them it felt like they were stepping into another world. Filling their nostrils was a combination of leather, liniment and old things, and a hint of smoke and incense. As their eyes adjusted, they saw shelves of scrolls and books of parchment that were covered in thick protective pieces of leather. Some were studded with metal decorations and looked like they had once belonged to someone important, a rich and powerful sheikh perhaps. A small man emerged from the depths of the room to greet them.

"Peace to you both and my greetings. Can I be of service to you?" he said.

"Peace to you too," replied Selim. "Maybe you can be of help. I am searching for manuscripts or books ..." and motioned to a large shelved area with books, "that have a story of a large boat that carried animals on it. Have you heard of one such as this?"

"May I introduce myself first? I am Walid ibn Turaq. Yes, I have heard of that story. While there are a number of sources for it from different traditions the most comprehensive account appears in the Jewish writings," he replied.

Selim and Ishkuz turned to look at each other.

Walid saw them and said, "I suspect that you have heard that before."

"Yes, we have," replied Selim. "But only very recently. There is a man in the story named Nonach or something like that. Have you heard of him?"

Walid nodded and said, "Noah was his name and his boat was known as the ark."

"Ark," repeated Selim, "So that is its name. Do you have a copy of the Jewish writings or the story?" he asked.

As Walid moved toward the rear of the shop and beckoned them to follow, Ishkuz asked him, "Do you know of another name for this Noah that starts with a 'Z'? A scholar we met on our travels mentioned it, but we have forgotten."

Walid turned his head back toward them as he walked and said, "This scholar is a true scholar if he knows the Sumerian name, Ziasudra. This name is used in another tradition of the story of the great flood and the ark. They are very different names but definitely the same man."

Walid arrived at a box on a shelf and lifted it down onto a bench. Inside were a number of scrolls made of thick parchment. Walid sorted through them and then pulled one out. "This is the first of the writings of the Jews. It is called 'Beginnings.' It speaks of the creation of the world but also has the story of Noah and the ark," stated Walid.

"May I look at it?" Selim asked. Walid handed it to him and carefully Selim opened the scroll. It was in Arabic so he was able to read it and he read the first lines out loud. "In the beginning God created the heavens and the earth."

Selim looked at Ishkuz whose face reflected what Selim felt, a look of astonishment and awe. It seemed that they had just opened a door to something they knew nothing about and both of them at that moment felt very small. It wasn't that Selim hadn't heard creation stories before, but there was a weight to the words he read out that his tribe's stories didn't have. Despite the astonishment that Selim felt, his interest in the scroll had increased. He rolled it back up and said to Walid, "How much for this scroll?"

"It takes many hours to copy them out, so it is not cheap. Five silver pieces," answered Walid. The price was no surprise, but Selim was not going to be forced into paying that much.

"Three silver pieces," he replied confidently.

"Four," answered Walid.

"Deal," replied Selim.

Selim took his money bag from his top pocket, drew out four silver pieces and handed them to Walid.

Walid smiled, a little too much like a wily fox, and bowed as he said, "Thank you, and peace be on you both."

"Peace be yours," replied both Selim and Ishkuz.

"Can we spend some time looking around? You have some very interesting things here and no doubt a lot of interesting books and scrolls," asked Selim.

"Of course, go ahead and take your time," replied Walid.

Selim and Ishkuz spent time opening some of the big books and looking at the titles of some of the scrolls. Some were in different languages and their script was strange, yet beautiful and symmetrical, and to Selim rather mysterious, as though he was being denied some of the secrets of the world. Ishkuz was taken by the various assortment of strange items that Walid had for sale. Not only was there an array of writing materials, large feathers, curiously carved wooden sticks with sharpened ends and ink, but also clay tablets with strange pictures and what he supposed was writing on them, as well as bronze and metal objects. Some seemed decorative but others like knives with ivory handles were much more useful looking.

After some time, they made their way out of the shop and as they entered the brightness of the sunlight Ishkuz asked Selim, "Why did you pay that much for the scroll? You could have got it for less surely?"

"Maybe for one coin less, but I had to have it. I feel there are things in here that are, well, important. And the story of the boat and … Noah," replied Selim, taking his time to pronounce Noah the way Walid had.

"Well, maybe you could read it to me," said Ishkuz a little sheepishly.

"Sure," said Selim, but then seeing the expression on Ishkuz's face he added, "You can't read, can you?"

"No, I've never been taught," Ishkuz replied.

"Well then, we may have to teach you," said Selim with certainty.

"Wow, thanks," is all Ishkuz could say.

They browsed the stalls and shops for two hours and it began to get hot. They weren't hungry as they had bought honey-glazed pastries and some wine. They really wanted to find out if Ibrahim had found out anything from the metalsmith, so made up their minds to leave even though there were stalls they hadn't looked at. They headed back to the stables and as they entered Ibrahim and Sekeen came walking around the corner.

"Not good news I'm afraid Selim. Many of them have little experience beyond the common metals and of course they wished to view Al Maksour so they could see what sort of metal it was made of," said Ibrahim.

"Well, we knew that at some stage we would have to show someone. Was there one that seemed more experienced than the others?" said Selim inquisitively.

"There was one that talked quite freely with us and he seemed to be more interested than the others but whether he was more experienced I don't really know," replied Ibrahim.

"I'll take Al Maksour to him and see what he says. We've come all this way. I think we need to do what we can. Ishkuz and I will go and get the sword and meet you back here."

Selim and Ishkuz returned to Rana's and Selim found the leather bag that had Al Maksour wrapped up inside. They made their way back to the stables and together with Ibrahim they went to find the metalworker. It took them some time to weave through the narrow alleyways towards the outskirts of the city. Finally, the city opened up to a dirtier, more makeshift area that smelt of acrid smoke. Ibrahim took them to a lean-to on the side of a bigger building. Selim could see a large man gleaming with sweat who was stoking a fire. As they entered the lean-to they were overcome by an intense metallic smell, one mixed with smoke and sweat. The man turned as he heard them approach and said "Ah, you've brought some friends with you."

"Yes," replied Ibrahim, "we wanted to hear more from you and show you some shards from the sword we would like remade."

"Hmm," he replied, "I don't know how much help I can be, but I will have a look."

Carefully, Selim unwrapped a large piece of sword blade from the cloth and handed it to the smithy. He took it from Selim and brought it close up to his face. Looking at it intensely he held the shard to his nose and sniffed the metal.

"Unusual," he said. "It is similar to some metals that I've used and yet it isn't the same. May I hammer it to see how it reacts?"

Ibrahim and Ishkuz looked at Selim, but Selim wasn't sure what to say, as he hadn't expected anyone to ask that. However, he quickly realised that it would have to be beaten or even melted one day if it was to be put back together.

"Yes, yes, of course," he finally answered.

The smithy picked up a medium-sized hammer, took the shard to the anvil, placed it on the anvil and swung the hammer. There was a loud thud and he picked up the shard to examine it.

"Nothing," he said.

He picked up the hammer again and swung with more force. Again, there was a thud and a ringing sound. The smithy once again examined the shard.

"No impact at all. This seems like a very strong metal, stronger than I have ever used. Unless you have enough shards to melt and remake the entire sword, I cannot help you. I have no metal to add to what you have. Whatever I use will be weaker than this," he said, holding up the shard.

"I'm sorry, I can't help you," he said as he handed it back to Selim.

Selim packed the shard in with the rest of the sword in his bag and replied, "Thanks for your help, we appreciate it very much."

"Anytime," the smithy said, turning away to stoke his fire. Before Ishkuz could express his disappointment, the smithy called out to them, "You could try Cairo."

The three men stopped and turned as one. Caught off guard, Selim called back, "What did you say?"

The smithy stood and repeated his words, "You could try Cairo," and pointed in the direction of Egypt. "I know from travellers they have some very different types of metals there. If you find the metalsmiths and ask for Ibn Tubal, he may be able to help you."

Selim managed to thank the smithy who just waved his hand to them, his back already turned.

"Cairo," said Ishkuz, "I have heard that name before and people speak of it with awe. It must be a city like no other."

"It's a long way from here, however great it is," said Ibrahim.

"Yes, a long way," repeated Selim, not all that heartened by the smithy's suggestion and already disappointed that he couldn't help. They were silent as they walked, each absorbed with their own thoughts and disappointment. Ishkuz's thoughts were quite positive and he was buoyed by the possibility that Al Maksour could be reforged there. Ibrahim's practical mind was thinking about what would be needed for a return trip home and a possible trip to Cairo. Selim was rather annoyed and he couldn't yet process what this might all mean.

They found their way back to the stables and met Sekeen who was brushing Faraj outside the stables. Faraj's coat glistened like gold and his mane and tail were clean, straight and untangled. Sekeen had obviously started on those first. Faraj turned his head from side to side as Sekeen's brushstrokes flowed from wither to rump and massaged his muscles.

"What a horse! He looks so good," thought Ishkuz.

The heat of the day was upon them so Selim, Ishkuz and Ibrahim moved to a cool, dark and secluded corner of the stable so they could talk. Ishkuz could see the frustration on Selim's face.

"We came all this way, and no-one can help us," he blurted out, flinging his arms into the air.

"But Selim, the metalworker said someone in Cairo could help," said Ishkuz.

"And maybe they can't," said Selim with obvious anger. "What if we go all the way there and no-one can help us?"

Ishkuz bowed his head, finding it difficult to cope with the strength of emotion that Selim was revealing.

Ibrahim saw this and spoke up. "I don't want to travel further, Selim, but if it is truly your desire to see the sword remade then you must go on to Cairo.

You spoke with such passion at the meeting of men believing Al Maksour was more than just a relic of the past and wanting to see it remade, yet now you seem to have given up. Even if those in Cairo cannot help then you know that you have done everything you could to remake Al Maksour and have not let yourself down. Be true to yourself and don't give up on what you think is right and good."

Both Selim and Ishkuz looked at Ibrahim, knowing that his words had opened a pathway through Selim's cloud of frustration and had given his mind another perspective. They all sat quietly, letting the full meaning of Ibrahim's words take their effect. Ishkuz was hoping that Selim would see the sense of Ibrahim's words and decide to go to Cairo.

"What about Ansim and Warda? Do we take them with us?" asked Selim.

Neither Ibrahim nor Ishkuz replied as they thought through what Selim was asking. Finally, Ibrahim responded. "We could leave them here and pick them up on our homeward trip, if your auntie is willing to have them."

The idea seemed to satisfy Selim, as he didn't reply. Ishkuz's thoughts, on the other hand, were suddenly thrown into confusion. He hadn't thought about Ansim, only about seeing the great city of Cairo. He was suddenly a little confused, unsure he wanted to leave her here in Yathrib. Just a minute ago he had wanted to go to Cairo as though there was nothing else in the world and as soon as he had thought of Ansim he no longer felt he could go. What was happening to him? He'd never been this confused in his life. Her dark hair and eyes appeared in his mind, and his heart caught mid-beat, his breath mid-breath. She was so beautiful! How could he leave her?

Selim suddenly stood up and it appeared that he had made some sort of decision. Ibrahim looked down a little and smiled, but Selim noticed and said to him, "Why are you smiling?"

"You've just reminded me of your father," Ibrahim replied. "It gives me great joy to see that your father still lives in some way."

With no reason to be offended, Selim fiddled with the front of his jacket as he struggled to let go of his anger and disappointment. "Alright," he said, "let's go to Cairo. I will speak to my aunt and arrange to have the girls stay while we are away."

As Selim headed for the stable doors, Ishkuz saw Ibrahim give a brief nod and he immediately realised that something deeper was happening here. Ibrahim had spoken to Selim the way he did, as he knew he would want to act in a thoughtful and mature way, just like his father. Ishkuz looked over at Ibrahim and with a twinkle in his eye he winked back at Ishkuz.

At that moment, Ishkuz felt he just didn't know Ibrahim at all. With a smile and a word Ibrahim had nudged Selim out of his self-pity and helped him to think about how his father would act at a time like this. Ishkuz shook his head. Ibrahim was certainly one to watch.

Both of them followed Selim into the street and then Ibrahim said to Ishkuz, "You'd better run and catch up with him. Sekeen and I will prepare the horses and the supplies for the trip." Ishkuz looked quickly at Sekeen and back to Ibrahim and then set off running. Sekeen was left looking at Ibrahim quizzically, while Faraj had turned to look at both of them wondering why Sekeen had stopped brushing him.

When Ishkuz caught up with Selim he could sense that Selim had lost most of the anger and disappointment he had shown in the stable.

"The artisans must be more skilful in Cairo. What was the name the smithy called out? Ibn Tulal, Ibn Tugal? Do you remember, Ishkuz?"

"I think it was Ibn Tubal because the name reminded me of one of the few names that I remember from my family, Bubal, my grandfather's name."

"Excellent, we won't forget the name then as we need to find this Ibn Tubal." They walked for a few minutes in silence and then Ishkuz spoke.

"Selim, have you thought about Ansim and how she might react to us leaving her here?"

Selim stopped walking and turned to Ishkuz, his eyes narrowing.

"Or do you mean how you might react to Ansim not coming with us?"

"No, no, not that," said Ishkuz, with just the slightest hint of annoyance in his voice. "I was thinking of her being with strangers, even if they are family. It won't be easy for her," replied Ishkuz.

Selim didn't answer straight away as he wondered which train of thought he should follow.

"I don't know that it would be wise to take both girls further, and they are safe here. It will allow us to move more quickly and cut some time off our travels. Ansim might not like it but I'm sure she will see the sense in it eventually."

Ishkuz realised he didn't want to leave Ansim here in Yathrib. He almost felt that he could fight with Selim to have her come along, but the sudden strength of his feelings left him feeling rather shocked that he could be so affected by this young lady. He needed to think more about it.

Later, while dusk was sneaking in and small bats flew through the mystical half-light, the fountain tinkled with coolness and the scent of orange blossom filled the air. Ishkuz found himself a bench seat near the edge of the garden. It was peaceful and Ishkuz's mind strayed to a faraway place where he had heard a name for somewhere like this. It was a Persian name, "Paradise," and it meant a walled garden.

A dove cooed in a neighbouring garden and the warmth of the day still wrapped around him. He found himself thinking how it was that he was now in a world so different to the one that he had been in only a few months ago. Life for him was becoming better all the time, but he couldn't quite understand how or why. It dawned on him that while his world and his relationships had changed, he hadn't. In his mind he was still the slave, the pale-faced outsider, unable to make decisions, and not worthy of another glance except to confirm how pale he was. Yet this new world didn't treat him that way. He was an equal, someone expected to contribute, and who others thought had something to give. Somehow his mind and perspective still hadn't caught up with this new world.

As he came to that conclusion a door slammed and Ansim came out into the garden. She scanned it as though looking for something, or someone, and then made her way straight to him. Ishkuz stood up, rather alarmed at the determination in her walk.

"Are you alright, Ansim?" he asked as she got closer and saw the fire in her dark eyes.

"How can I be, Ishkuz? Selim has just told me that I am to stay here while you go to Cairo and that it will give me time to get to know Muhair. I don't want to get to know Muhair," said Ansim vehemently.

Then more quietly she said, "I know my mother wants me to marry Muhair, but I only came along so that I could be with you."

Ishkuz stammered back, "You want to be with me?"

"Of course. Haven't you seen that?" said Ansim.

"Well, yes I have. But why would you want to be with a slave and a pale-faced slave at that? You should be looking for a man from your people," replied Ishkuz.

"You are not a slave, Ishkuz. I have never seen you as a slave. Why would you still think that?" she said with some strength. "And as for your skin colour, I don't care," she added.

Then she whispered, "I love the sandy colour of your hair and the blueness of your eyes."

Ishkuz blushed and stepped back from Ansim.

"I have never had anyone say anything like that before," he answered. "It's hard to think that anyone could love things about me. I've never thought of myself as being able to be loved by someone or able to love a girl…a woman. I still think like a slave even though I'm free. It's like my body is free but my mind isn't. I can travel miles to go to Cairo with no-one to stop me, but I can't let myself think that you could like me."

"You'll need to change your thinking, Ishkuz, and make your mind catch up with reality. You are a man free to make decisions and with every right to do so," answered Ansim.

"I was thinking about that just before you came. I know, I need to do that," stammered Ishkuz. "It's just so hard. I have always been in a place, in a position where I thought I would never escape from. Now I am out of there, I still act the same way, even though I don't really want to. I want to be different. I want to get to know you better and talk with you and be around you. My heart bursts whenever I see you." Ansim looked down and smiled.

He went on a little terrified, "I can't believe I just said that. I would be beaten by my old tribe if I had ever said that to a woman."

Ansim reached out and took hold of his arm, struck by his admission and his struggle.

"Ishkuz, you're safe now. No-one is allowed to harm you. You're free."

She moved closer to him and pushed herself against him, letting her head nestle onto his chest. Ishkuz's eyes widened and his body stiffened slightly. He could smell her hair and feel the softness of it against his chin. Slowly, very slowly, he wrapped his arms around her shoulders and his body relaxed. Somehow it felt like the best thing in the world and yet there was the nagging thought of what Selim would say if he saw them.

"Don't even think of him, Ishkuz," said Ansim. "I will deal with him."

Ishkuz pulled his head back. "How in the realms of the world did you know?" asked Ishkuz incredulously. "Are you a mind-reader?"

"Only of certain people." Then she added, "Only those I choose to know very well."

He settled his chin lightly on her head, amazed at her insight. He realised he would have to be very careful of his thoughts around her. He tried hard not to remember the times he had compared her to the horses but the more he tried, the more he thought of them. He took a deep breath and the scent of nard and cinnamon from her hair mixed with the orange blossom fragrance from the garden filled his senses, relaxing him.

"Truly, this is Paradise" he said.

"Hmm, yes, it is," murmured Ansim.

Ishkuz finally pulled free. "What will you say to Selim?" and then added, somewhat doubtfully, "Or should I speak to him?"

"No, I will talk to him. I will tell him I have no need of this Muhair because I have you now. And I'll warn him not to make fun of you as he does," she replied.

When Ishkuz gave her a questioning look she added, "I can see it in his eyes."

"Won't your mother be upset if you come back with…with me?" asked Ishkuz.

"I'll let you into a little secret, Ishkuz. My mother never wanted me to travel here to marry Muhair. She wanted me to be close to you, but Selim would never have agreed that I should come if he didn't think we were being serious. We wanted him to feel that he was doing the right thing for our family," she replied.

Ishkuz realised that a whole new, complex world had just opened up to him and that it would take years to fully understand, something which left him feeling quite overwhelmed.

Keen to change the subject, Ishkuz raised the question of whether Ansim was going to stay in Yathrib or travel with them. "So are you going to come with us to Cairo?" he asked.

"Me? No Ishkuz, I won't travel any further. I'll wait here for you to return. This garden and city are enough for me now that we are together."

Ishkuz felt a little confused. "But you just complained about having to stay here. Don't you want to come with us, with me?" he asked.

"Ishkuz, I know that you will travel faster and be back sooner if you don't take Warda and I along with you. Besides, mother wants a number of things from the markets here and I need time to get them all. I will miss you but to know you are mine is all I ask for now," she replied.

Ishkuz was quiet, his head spinning. He was exuberant, yet he was also straining to understand everything that Ansim had said and what it meant. So much about Ansim had been turned upside down in such a short space of time. Maybe he needed the trip to Cairo to take everything in.

"I can't believe that you are sitting here, Ansim," Ishkuz said shakily. "You're so beautiful and my heart is bursting with excitement. I don't feel worthy of your love."

Ansim smiled at him and her eyes sparkled even more brightly at him. He couldn't take his eyes off her. The dove cooed again from the neighbouring garden and suddenly the orange blossom smelled stronger, the moon shone more brightly, and the evening became warmer. They all seemed to weave into an atmosphere of gold and richness, the like of which he had never seen or felt before.

CHAPTER 18

That night as Ishkuz was getting ready for bed Selim came to him. His face was serious and Ishkuz wasn't sure what to think.

Selim said, "I've just spoken to Ansim. It seems I have been used and abused, pulled this way and that." Ishkuz's face lost any colour it had.

"And you, my friend, are the winner of all the intrigues and wiles of the women," added Selim as his face broke into a grin. He grabbed Ishkuz and slapped him on the back.

"Somehow, I think now you will love the smell of roast lamb cooked by Ansim, if you didn't already. What has been going on that I don't know about Ishkuz?" Selim asked.

Ishkuz felt weak, but relieved. "So you approve?" he asked.

"Approve! Of course I approve. You are as crafty with the women as you are with that bow of yours and your horses," Selim replied. "I have been teasing you all this time about liking Ansim and now she tells me she doesn't want Muhair, but you. And you, do you have love for her?"

"Love," said Ishkuz. "I know little of love, but I know that my heart is bursting and I long to see Ansim all day and every day."

"You know little of love, hey?" replied Selim. "If that's all you know, then that's enough. I must say I was shocked, not because Ansim is taken with you, but with the suddenness of it all. But I'm happy. You are a humble and talented man and I enjoy your friendship, and I know that Ansim will as well. Sleep well then, if you can, for tomorrow we will land on Egyptian soil. Ibrahim has sent me a note saying we can ride to the coast and catch one of the boats there to cross the strait. It will cut our riding time by a great deal."

"Thank you. Thank you, Selim. Thank you for everything. You are a true friend," replied Ishkuz. Selim smiled and as he left he shook his head and muttered under his breath.

Ishkuz sighed deeply and stood in the middle of the room, somewhat overcome by the events of that evening. He slipped into bed, but he didn't sleep for many hours as he replayed the time in the garden with Ansim over and over in his mind, relishing every detail. He could remember the smell of her hair, the glint in her eye and the timbre of her voice. He was amazed that someone so beautiful could love him.

The next morning they were all up early packing and saying their goodbyes. Selim and Ishkuz needed to get Faraj and Kadin and then they were to meet up with Ibrahim and Sekeen. Selim kept his eye on Ishkuz as they said their goodbyes, noticing how awkward he seemed around Ansim. Yet he also saw that when the two of them were close they seemed to reflect a great sense of peace and contentment.

They walked their way to the stables through the slightly chilly morning air and found Ibrahim and Sekeen ready with all the horses saddled. They greeted each other and climbed onto their horses. The horses snorted and tossed their heads as they sensed a new purpose in their riders. In her typical style Aisha began to prance, pulling her neck in and arching her tail as her legs moved up and down. As Ibrahim climbed into the saddle he gently squeezed his legs together and Aisha dropped her head and relaxed her body. Ibrahim led the way on Aisha and they clattered their way through the streets of Yathrib. They came to the outer walls of the city and as they headed out of the western gate the land spread out before them angling downward. It was dry and dusty but still cool for both horses and riders.

"It will take us about three hours of solid riding before we reach the coast. There is a town there that has a good harbour where we can find a boat. The traders I spoke with said that they leave quite frequently for Egypt and back again as there is a lot of trade that happens," said Ibrahim.

They rode in silence as they trotted and cantered, eager to reach the coast. All at once they reached a cliff and found the deep blue sea filling their gaze. White caps on the waves contrasted with the deep blue and the men couldn't restrain themselves from commenting. Even Ibrahim was suitably impressed by the vastness of the sea.

"How can there be so much water in the world?" said Sekeen. "It's unbelievable," he added. All Selim could say was "Wow," over and over again.

After they had taken in the power and majesty of the sea some more practical thoughts entered Selim's mind. "So we have to cross that in a boat, with the horses?" he said. "I honestly didn't think the water would be that big. Is it really safe?"

"Ships cross all the time, so it can't be that dangerous," answered Ibrahim.

They headed down the rocky road that hugged the cliff and saw a ramshackle assortment of buildings, some more sturdy than others. They were spread out along the shoreline and a number of jetties poked themselves somewhat fearfully into the deepening sea and oncoming waves. Next to them a number of ships lay in the water, some dancing a little more than others on the swells as these were unloaded and ready to be filled for the return trip. The horses navigated the rather steep road easily as they were used to the angles of the Sarmadees and as they descended into the town people turned to look at them. Ishkuz could tell that they were looking at their horses who made such a display with their varying colours, tail carriage and expressions. He also noticed that their eyes lingered a little longer on his face compared to the time they spent looking at the others, but overall, it was the horses they were looking at. He felt a certain pride grow in him just from being associated with these horses. He was immensely proud of Kadin and the other horses and knew their quality showed through even to those who knew little about them.

"Let's go south," said Ibrahim. "The ship at the last jetty is the next to sail, or at least that is what I was told."

They made their way down to the jetty and Ibrahim and Sekeen dismounted. They gave the reins of their horses to Ishkuz and Selim and went to talk to the sailors on board the ship.

They came back and Ibrahim said, "They leave within the hour as the winds are blowing in the right direction. We should load the horses now so they have some time to get used to the sway of the ship."

They dismounted and took the saddles off the horses. They allowed them a short drink and then moved them to the boarding area.

"It's much bigger than I thought," said Selim. "It seems that there will be plenty of room for the horses. I don't want them too close to each other in case they slip," he added.

"Sekeen, you take your horse up first so the others can see that it's safe for them to follow," ordered Ibrahim.

Selim turned to Ishkuz and added, "Sekeen's mare is fairly old and usually very quiet so she should do this easily."

Sekeen's horse moved up easily but not without a snort or two as she carefully eyed the boarding planks. Seeing this, the other horses followed her up. As usual it was Aisha who made the most fuss, but none of the men became impatient as they knew her temperamental nature so well. Ishkuz was impressed with the way Ibrahim worked with her and the gentle but firm way he encouraged her up the boarding planks. It was obvious to him that the horses had developed a lot of trust in their carers.

Soon they were all on board. As Selim had said the ship seemed to have more room than he first thought and there was plenty of support for the horses if the seas became rough.

They were surprised at how quickly the ship cut through the water after they cast off and while the flapping of the sail gave the horses quite a fright, they were able to settle them with an encouraging word and some pats on the neck. They headed in a north-westerly direction and chatted to the captain as he came to inspect the horses.

"They are fine looking horses. Where have you come from?" he asked them.

"We have come from Yathrib," replied Selim, "but before that we came from the Sarmadee Ranges, a week's ride south of there."

"Yes, I have heard of the Sarmadees," the captain replied. "A dry and harsh place, I fear."

"Yes, a hard place but not without its oases and the odd river or two that gives us enough water to live," replied Selim.

"As you can imagine I have had traders on this ship from almost everywhere and some of them have spoken to me of their travels through the Sarmadees and surrounding areas. What brings you to visit Egypt? You don't look like traders," said the captain.

Ishkuz got a bit fidgety at the question but Selim continued easily with the conversation. He replied, "We are on a journey of discovery and learning on behalf of the tribe. We wish to see what is beyond the sands of the desert, not just hear from traders about the magnificent things of the world. Our hope is to find some books and manuscripts that we can take back to our tribe."

"Well spoken, young man," said the captain. "You're eloquent for one from the desert. Well, I won't hinder any male or female that wishes to learn and see the world. Part of my love for the sea is the way it allows me to travel to other places. No, I can't begrudge you."

Sekeen spoke up then, seeking to direct attention away from their trip. "Have you been to Cairo, Captain?"

The captain swung his head to look at Sekeen and replied, "Oh yes, many times. Cairo is alluring. It has a magic and mystery to it and it's always alive. Even the nights are lit up and trade and talk go on and on. The Nile River brings so many people into the city from different places and the things they bring are beyond imagination. I think you will love it. Maybe you won't even want to leave."

"We have much to go back to Captain, both things and people," said Ishkuz with a degree of enthusiasm.

The captain looked at him thoughtfully and then at the horses. "Yes, well with horses like these there must be some good herd for you to go back to. I would be careful in Cairo with your horses," he said. "There are many there who would gladly see a knife in your back to get horses like these."

A man called out to the captain and he left them looking at each other in bewilderment. The day wore on as they sailed through the sparkling blue water. It was just as Ishkuz was feeling that he'd had enough of this sea travel that they sighted the shore. The wind was still blowing briskly and very soon the thin shoreline grew into boats and buildings and jetties. As they drew close the wind died down and what looked like a straight shoreline was actually a deep cove nestled in low hills with protective bluffs on both sides of it. The sea settled and the ship slid easily into its place next to the jetty. The horses went easily across from ship to jetty, prancing down with snorts and lifted tails. Both young and old looked and pointed at the spectacle they made, and a small crowd gathered on the beach to see them as they came ashore. One old man came up to them excitedly, pointing and calling out "Asil? Asil?" They all nodded at him.

The horses were still excited and some of the crowd followed them as they came to what looked like a road between the rows of buildings set just behind the beach. As they made their way along it the crowd gradually dwindled.

Earlier, Ibrahim had spoken to the captain and he had given them directions through the town to the road that would take them to Cairo.

As they rode Ibrahim said, "We can spend the night here or we can camp out in the desert."

"I'm not keen on staying here," said Selim. "The horses are too exposed. I would rather be in the desert where we can see people coming than caught here in a corner," he added.

"I'm of the same mind," said Sekeen.

"Ok then, let's keep riding. We'll still have a few hours of daylight to find a good camping place," said Ibrahim.

They made their way through the town in a canter, scattering chickens and scaring the odd person to the side of the road. They quickly made their way to the edge of the town that hugged the coast and was much longer than it was wide. The landscape beyond them was flat and bleak and radiated heat. The sea breeze died off as they rode along and the horses began to drip with sweat. As all of them were fit they were able to keep up a solid pace.

Ishkuz watched Faraj as he rode behind him. His tail was held up in a gentle arc, but it was the hind legs and their movement that he watched most closely. He noticed that in both a trot and canter that the hind legs were almost always vertical, even at the hock, the most likely place for a hind leg to move off vertical and lose the power being directed through it. He also noticed just how much power Faraj generated because his hocks bent so much and seemed to have great spring in them. It dawned on Ishkuz that Faraj had the agility and lightness of a cat and was able to transfer every bit of power he generated from his back hooves forward and could shoot his body off the ground with every stride. No wonder he was so fast and so easily kept his speed on sand and rocky surfaces as well as on hard ground. Ishkuz shook his head at just how good these horses were.

Selim turned back to Ishkuz and noticed the concentration on his face. "What are you doing Ishkuz?"

"I'm looking at how Faraj moves his legs. He has a lot of power moving through those back legs. Even at a walk he brings them through with a real swagger and reaches way over where the front hooves land. It's no wonder he is so fast and covers so much ground."

Ibrahim spoke up and said, "You have a keen eye for conformation, Ishkuz. Our tribe believes that the way a horse is put together will often determine how it moves and for how long. We've spent many generations maintaining the excellence of the horses of the desert as that excellence keeps producing sound, healthy and enduring horses. The Creator knew what he was doing when he created the desert horse."

"That reminds me, Ishkuz," said Selim butting in, "Ibrahim knows a great story on how the desert horse was created." He called to Ibrahim, "Can you tell it to him some night? I'm sure he will love it."

"Yes, of course," replied Ibrahim.

Selim then sat a little straighter in the saddle, drew in a breath and with a dramatic expression quoted part of the story with the voice of Ibrahim. "The jinn were terrified as the Creator swept down onto the Sarmadees and saw the first mare creation had ever known."

Ishkuz was a little shocked but Ibrahim and Sekeen both broke into laughter. Eventually Sekeen stopped laughing and said to Selim, "You can take over Ibrahim's storytelling at my fire any night, Selim."

Ishkuz had expected Ibrahim to react very angrily but he didn't. He remembered that when he was a slave among the Sayhads, anyone who had made fun of the sheikh could be beaten. There was so much openness and acceptance among these men and their tribe. There was also so much that had to change in his own mind as he experienced a larger world than the one he had been in.

Very shortly they passed a rocky outcrop and Ibrahim pointed to it. They could all see the rocks would protect their back and they would easily be able to defend themselves if the need arose. That night as they were sitting around the campfire drinking sweet coffee, Ibrahim spoke up.

"I'm uneasy," he said. The others all turned to him for if Ibrahim was uneasy then there was reason for them to listen. "I'll be honest. I am afraid for our horses. Not that they'll be injured in Cairo but rather that someone might try to steal them."

Selim and Sekeen both made movements as though they were going to speak and disagree with him, but Ibrahim held out his hand to them.

"Please hear me out. I don't doubt your courage, Selim, or your skill, Sekeen. I have the utmost respect for you both. But we'll be in a large, unknown city that I am afraid may not have seen the quality and type of horses we have.

When we left the town this morning you saw how the crowds reacted and how they questioned whether our horses were asil or not. Even this small town was taken in by our horses and there was no way that we could have overcome them, not without a lot of bloodshed."

Selim and Sekeen were no longer keen to talk but listened quietly.

"What if the horses that we have grown up with and are familiar with are beyond the quality of the horses here and people compare our horses with theirs? Surely there will be some who will want our horses for themselves. What if it is a great lord with a guard who doesn't care and he sends his soldiers to take our horses?"

"I will die defending them, Ibrahim. They are our life and history, our honour and livelihood," said Selim with passion.

"Yes, I understand, Selim. I just think it's wise to avoid any danger to the horses or to us. A battle avoided is better than a battle fought, but if you must fight a battle, prepare well and fight hard."

Selim had joined in the second half of the proverb with a somewhat mocking tone, as he had heard it many times from the lips of Ibrahim. However, this time, with his emotions somewhat stirred up, he didn't really wish to be taught.

"Alright," said Ibrahim. "I need not have quoted that. But you do understand what I am saying, don't you?"

Sekeen spoke up now and said, "I understand and I'm sure that you have thought about how to avoid this battle. What's the plan?"

"I think we should cover the horses in mud and make them look as plain as we can to try to cover up their quality and looks. We can keep them covered with cloaks as much as possible so that people have little chance of seeing what they are really like."

Ishkuz nodded in agreement and then said, "You're right Ibrahim. I've never seen horses like these in my life, so many with so much quality and breeding. If I could steal one, I would," he said boldly. He then turned a little red in the face as he felt the eyes of the other three on him and he realised what he had said.

He added slowly, "Ahmm, I didn't mean it like that. I would never actually do that. I just meant that they are worth stealing."

As their faces didn't change he appealed to them, "I'm part of your tribe, aren't I?"

Ibrahim and Sekeen remained quiet. They stared into Ishkuz's eyes and then they nodded, seemingly convinced. When he looked at Selim, Ishkuz saw that he had a smirk on his face. Selim then swung his head toward Ibrahim and spoke up. As he did Ishkuz rolled his eyes and let out a long, slow sigh.

"I do understand you, Ibrahim, but rubbing dirt into their coat and manes and tails goes against everything we do."

"I know, I know. I don't like it myself but if it means protecting them, then I think we need to do it. It will only be for a short time," replied Ibrahim.

"I agree," said Sekeen. "We shouldn't be in Cairo long, whether or not the sword is recast. It's best to keep the horses hidden."

"I know it's for the sake of the horses and I will do it, but I don't have to like it," said Selim.

"So when should we do it?" he added.

"I was thinking we should as soon as we can. Perhaps when we find some water along the way," replied Ibrahim.

They slept easily that night and for three days travelled along the road to Cairo. The road swung gently away from the coast and was well worn due to the frequency of traders, camels and horses using it. They saw little of interest as the land was similar to their own: bleak, lifeless and hot.

On the fourth morning, villages started to appear and the road began to get busier. They knew they were nearing Cairo. Both Ishkuz and Selim were excited and even Sekeen seemed to show a keen interest in the things they passed. It wasn't long before they crested a hill and an amazing scene opened up before their eyes. Before them lay a large blue river. It was flanked by green fields and dotted with small boats with triangle shaped sails. Beyond the river and the green fields, a large and sprawling city arose from the ground.

"That has to be the largest city I've ever seen," said Selim. "It's so much larger than Yathrib or Al Huraydah," he added.

"It's spectacular," added Ishkuz. "There are so many different buildings."

"But what are those pointy things over there?" asked Sekeen, gesturing beyond the city.

"Wow, they're massive," cried out Ishkuz. "Look how they shine in the sun."

"I've never seen anything like them," said Selim. "What are they?" he added.

Even Ibrahim shrugged his shoulders, then said, "Whatever they are, there is a lot of water in the river down there and I think we can find enough mud to cover our horses. Let's go before too many people see us."

They followed him down to the bank and onto a flat piece of land. The dirt there was thick and black and the horses weren't keen to go near it. The men grabbed handfuls of black mud and rubbed it into the horses' manes and tails and over every exposed area, even their heads.

"They look horrible," said Ishkuz. "It's going to make everything dirty, especially when they flick their tails," he added quickly.

As Ishkuz threw up his arms Kadin flicked his tail at some flies and blobs of black dirt came flying toward him. He tried to scrape them off, but he couldn't remove the stain they left.

"The only good thing about this heat is that the mud will dry quickly and hopefully not get on anything else," said Selim.

"The horses look half their quality," Ishkuz commented when they had finished. "At least we know what they are really like."

With the horses looking like they had never been looked after, they made their way down the main road, toward the strange yet enticing city of Cairo.

"We need to find stables for the horses and somewhere for us to stay. So keep your eyes open for an inn or guest house," said Ibrahim.

Selim and Ishkuz found it hard to keep their eyes off the different people and the shops and wares that surrounded them, and the combination of aromas was so great it would take them days to identify them all. However, Ibrahim was sensible and followed some camels that seemed to be part of a trading party, hoping they would know the best places to find lodgings and stables. They followed the camels along and soaked in the atmosphere and sights of the city. No-one had glanced at them or their horses, which was good, although they were still on the edge of the city, which tended to house the poorer people whose interest in horses was probably minimal.

Ibrahim pulled Aisha to a stop as the caravan ahead had paused and he said to the others, "Wait here and I'll go and ask the traders where we can stay."

There was much activity as the camels were made to sit and as men came out from the surrounding buildings and began to unload them. Ibrahim was soon back and he pointed to an alleyway on the other side of the road. They followed him down, then took a turn to the left. The road, which had been quite narrow, opened up to at least the width of six horses. On the right a little further down from where they were was a large and cavernous stable complex that would easily take their four horses. A large man came to greet them and wiped his greasy hand on the front of his tunic before he stretched it out to shake their hands.

"Welcome, weary travellers. Are you looking for a place to keep your horses and yourselves while in Cairo?" he said as his eyes twinkled and his smile widened to reveal white meat stuck between his teeth.

"Yes, we are," replied Ibrahim, "for four horses and four men. Do you have room for us all?"

"Yes of course. Lots of room. Come, come," he replied as he held out his arm and indicated for them to move into the stables.

They dismounted and led their horses into the stables. The lodgings and stables were similar to the ones at Yathrib. That night they ate with the owner, whose name turned out to be Absat. He was very helpful when it came to finding out about the city, however the more they questioned him, the more he questioned them. It was all done courteously and with ease and grace, nevertheless they all began to feel uneasy about sharing anything with him. Behind the eager smile and feigned humility, they could feel that he was carefully putting together every little bit of information they gave him. He just seemed to want to know too much.

They didn't want to ask him anything about the whereabouts of the metalworkers and that night as they were preparing for bed Ibrahim said to them quietly, "I will talk to a stall owner tomorrow morning about the whereabouts of the metalworkers. At least we will avoid Absat's beady eyes and pointed questions."

The others smiled, as they knew exactly what he was talking about. The quicker they were on their way home the better. The next morning while Sekeen, Selim and Ishkuz cleaned up the stables and fed the horses, Ibrahim left for the market, some streets away, to casually enquire about the city and where the metalworkers might be found. He had seen some stalls on the way in which sold metal items and thought they would be the best to ask.

Naturally, the men did not brush the horses as it would quicken the removal of the mud and so far no-one had looked twice at the horses except for Absat who had commented on the length of Faraj's legs, but had said no more. They had also covered them with cloaks after stabling them so at least their bodies weren't seen.

Ibrahim soon returned. Rather than speaking openly, he simply nodded to them and they knew he had found what they were looking for. Ishkuz felt excitement grow in him as once again the possibility of having the sword remade grew closer.

They decided that Sekeen would stay behind with the horses and the other three would leave the stables one at a time and meet further down the street so that Absat would have nothing to be suspicious about.

When it was his turn to leave Selim made his way down a street. He heard the clip clop sound of a horse's hooves and turned around to find that there was a man leading a horse around the corner of the street. The man and horse came closer. Selim was keen to see what type of horses were in Cairo and he stopped to let the man and horse pass by. Ibrahim and his father had trained him since childhood to look at a horse and assess it, looking for the qualities their tribe so valued in a horse. He could immediately see that this was a quality horse. In fact, as he looked more closely, he could see that she was a magnificent creature. It came as a shock to him as he didn't expect to find any horses here in Cairo that rivalled Faraj and Aisha. But here she was, a dark, mahogany bay with bright, liquid eyes, a slender high-set neck and long legs that carried her lightly down the street. She was well muscled through the shoulder and over the hindquarters and her coat shone brilliantly in the sun. Selim noticed her fine but well-shaped legs and wide, open hooves as well as the large overstep in her walk. He was so surprised at her quality that he simply stood there, staring. Before he knew what he was doing, he ran down the street and called out to the man leading the horse.

"Hello, excuse me. Is this your horse?" he said quite quickly.

The man turned to him and shook his head. He pulled the horse to a stop as he could see that Selim wanted to ask more questions.

"She is magnificent," said Selim. "Who owns her?"

"She belongs to the King of Egypt and I am taking her back to the stables of the king. They are only a few streets away," he answered. He looked at Selim as if waiting for more questions and Selim definitely had some.

"Are there more like her?" he said.

"Some, but the others are not as good quality. The king has collected his horses from all over the world, wanting to breed the best," answered the man with growing pride in his voice. "Nariman," he said, indicating to the bay mare, "is one of the finest the king has bred and she has been bred to run. But many are not like her. There are some with her qualities but few have all of them."

His eyes turned to look at the mare and there was both pride and love in the look. "I think others would say there are better horses in the stable, but I would differ with them."

A thought entered Selim's mind and he spoke it out loud. "May I come and bring my friends to see the horses sometime? Is that possible?"

"Well, it's not a common thing. The king brings people in to view the horses …" he began, then trailed off and reached up to straighten Nariman's forelock.

"But, if you come late in the afternoon at the side entrance on the eastern side of the stables I may be able to show you some of the horses, but only in their stables. I can't get them out for you to look at."

"Certainly, I understand. I am grateful for being able to have a look at them," said Selim. "I, my friends and I, we have horses at home, in the Nejd." He held out his hand to the man. "I am Selim."

"I'm Wajdan," he said, and took Selim's arm in greeting. "But I must keep going," he added as he started to walk off.

"Yes, of course. Thank you," said Selim. "Late this afternoon then. Thank you."

Selim stood there for a moment longer and then suddenly remembered that he had to meet Ishkuz and Ibrahim. He swung his head around to get his bearings, then took off at a run down the street. He met Ibrahim and Ishkuz at the corner of another street and they looked at him with questioning faces.

"What have you been doing?" asked Ibrahim.

"I saw a horse and had to find out about her," said Selim between heavy breaths.

Both Ibrahim and Ishkuz looked at him strangely and then Ibrahim said with a tone of mock surprise, "You saw a horse? What do you mean? There are horses all around us."

"Yes, yes, I know. But this wasn't any horse. This was a horse like ours. I didn't expect to see horses like ours, like this, here in Cairo. I spoke to the man leading her and he was willing for us to come and look at her and the other horses. They belong to the King of Egypt. We can go later this afternoon. He will meet us at the stables and show us around."

"Wow," said Ishkuz, "I would love that. But she wasn't better than your horses, was she? As good as Faraj and Kadin and Aisha?"

"No, there were some differences, but she was certainly a high-quality mare. The man leading her said that not all of them were as good as her, but it would be worth having a look at them all, wouldn't it?"

"Yes, it certainly would," said Ibrahim. "I would really like to see what the King of Egypt's horses look like."

III.
Revelation

CHAPTER 19

They set off to find the metalworkers and as they walked Selim described the features and weaknesses of the beautiful bay mare he had seen. They headed to the outskirts of the city and passed by a number of small shops selling spices and fruit of varying colours. Other shops they could smell before they arrived as the owners were cooking delicious meats and vegetables in oil and sweetened pastries with honey. Some were selling clothes or furniture but Selim couldn't yet see any that sold books or manuscripts.

Ibrahim led them on and eventually they began to breathe in the smoke of furnaces and hear the banging of hammers on metal. They came to a stretch of the street that backed onto the desert. In between was a long row of open shop fronts, each with a fire and various metal implements hanging from the roof beams and men stoking fires or swinging hammers. They stopped at the first one and watched as a man took up a long piece of metal he had been hammering and plunged it into a tub of cold water. It hissed and spat, and steam rose from the water. He pulled the metal out and then turned towards them.

"Can I help you?" he said.

"Yes, we hope you can. We are in search of a metalsmith called Ibn Tubal. Do you know of him?" asked Ibrahim.

The man replied, "Yes, I know of him, but he no longer works here. He is old and has finished his days of metal shaping."

Selim's and Ishkuz's hearts sank at hearing these words as they had so much hope resting on him.

However, Ibrahim did not give up. "Do you think he would be willing to speak to us?"

"I don't know. But his son works two shops down, so you could ask him," he replied.

"Thank you. We will do that. Good day," said Ibrahim.

They headed down to the shop and the hearts of Selim and Ishkuz lifted a little at the possibility of speaking to Ibn Tubal. A large man was working the anvil, beating out a sheet of copper. He looked up at them as their shadow fell across his anvil.

"We were told that you are the son of Ibn Tubal," said Ibrahim. "Is it possible to speak to him on a matter of metalwork?"

The man replied, "Yes, I'm his son. Is there anything I can help you with?"

"Ibn Tubal was recommended to us by a metalworker in Yathrib. He is obviously known for his skill with metal," said Ibrahim, attempting to show the man they were no threat and that they respected his father.

The man seemed convinced. "He doesn't live far from here," he said and pointed in the direction of his father's house. He gave them directions and they thanked him and left.

It didn't take long to find the house and they knocked loudly on the door. The door opened and they were greeted by an old lady. After enquiring about Ibn Tubal she led them into a sitting area and there on the rich carpets surrounded by pillows sat an old man.

"Welcome friends," he said with enthusiasm.

"Thank you and peace to you and your household," said Ibrahim. The old man nodded in recognition of the blessing. "My wife says that you wish to speak to me about metal.

"Yes," said Ibrahim. "You were recommended to us by a metalworker in Yathrib and we have come here to Cairo to seek your help."

The old man laughed a little and leant back. "So my reputation has reached that far, has it?" he said with a gleam in his eye. "What is it I can do for you?"

"We have an old sword that is in pieces and have asked our own metalworkers as well as those in Yathrib whether it can be remade. None of them can identify the metal and we are unsure how to go about remaking it, or even if it is possible," said Ibrahim.

The old man's eyes narrowed, his interest aroused. "Can I see the sword?" he asked.

Selim took the bag off his shoulder and opened it to get the sword out. He unwrapped the cloth and laid the remnants of the sword before the old man. Ibn Tubal carefully grasped the pommel and looked closely at the sword. He then reached for a piece of glass that lay on a pillow next to him and held it up to his eyes, moving it backward and forward as he looked through it at the pommel and blade. The glass was rounded, not flat, and as Ishkuz looked at the old man's eye in the glass he saw that it was twice its normal size.

"How on earth has his eye grown like that?" he asked himself.

The old man examined all the pieces and after seeking permission carefully scratched one of the shards with a thin pointed object.

Eventually he said to them, "An interesting piece. I have to admit that in all my years of working metal I have never seen anything like this. Well, some like it, but not identical. I don't think it is beyond repair. And you say you have had it for a long time?"

"It's been in our tribe and family for generations," replied Selim.

"And you have no idea where it came from?" asked the old man.

"No, we only have old stories but none of them talk about where it came from," replied Selim.

The old man was silent for a time. Finally he said, "I remember some of the different metals that I've worked with and to work with them properly and maintain their quality I had to do the opposite of what was normal practice. Instead of heating them to a great temperature they needed less heat.

Somehow the metal was workable and kept its quality despite the lower temperature. I have a feeling this metal is going to be like that."

Selim spoke out eagerly, "So you will remake it?"

The old man looked at Selim and seeing his youthful passion and remembering his own he said, "Yes young man. It is time that the anvil saw my hammer again. Come, we will go to my son's shop and see what is possible."

Selim wrapped up the pieces and the four of them made their way to the metalworkers' shops. Along the way the old man introduced himself as Zaad ibn Tubal.

"My family have been metalworkers probably as long as you have had this sword. We have passed on what we know to our sons without a thought of doing anything differently. Already my grandson is learning the trade. But then there is always the need for new items for the house and for weapons," he said.

They reached the shop where his son worked, and he looked up with surprise at seeing his father walk in and start to take off his outer robe.

"Father," he said, "what are you doing?"

"Move over Naaim. Your father has a job to do," Ibn Tubal replied.

Naaim looked over at Ibrahim, Selim and Ishkuz, and Selim shrugged his shoulders.

"Stoke the fire Naaim, but not too much. I don't want it too hot," Ibn Tubal told his son.

Ibn Tubal chose some tools and then went to Selim. Selim handed over the cloth and Ibn Tubal laid it on the table and carefully unwrapped it. He took the shards and laid them to one side. He then took the pommel that had a large part of the sword still attached to it. The men watched on as his mind worked out what needed doing and in what order. Selim knew that the pommel was in reasonable shape but needed recovering. He saw Ibn Tubal push the blade to see how secure it was in the pommel and saw him nod, satisfied that it didn't need attention.

"Naaim, go down to the tanner and get me some thick leather and some strong leather strands. I'll need them to re-cover the handle," said Ibn Tubal.

Naaim left and Ibn Tubal said to the three men, "The handle and the blade attached to it are strong. I'll clean it and join it to the shards. I'm sure it will work."

Ibn Tubal gathered up the shards and placed them into the hot coals. In a very short space of time they started to glow and Ibn Tubal took them out with a long set of grips. He took the longest and placed it onto the anvil. He lifted the hammer and let it fall onto the metal. It bounced off, leaving it with a slight dent. He did it again and again.

Ibn Tubal stopped. "It is extremely hard metal. My instinct tells me to heat it more to soften it, but my experience tells me to let it cool to reach just the right temperature," he said to the men. He picked up the shard with the tongs and looked at it closely, then put it down and wandered around the workshop. He examined the handle and then came back to the anvil. Again he hit the shard, and the men could see that it had spread out just where the hammer hit it.

"That is better," said Ibn Tubal.

He went on shaping the metal, which seemed to bend and flow easily under his skill. He took the other pieces, heating them and then began hammering them and joining them together.

Selim said to the others, "It looks so easy. The metal seems to flow together and take shape more quickly than his hammering."

Finally, Ibn Tubal took the long part attached to the handle and carefully heated the end. He had crafted one long piece out of the separate shards and began to join that to the rest. It didn't take long at all for the two pieces to be joined, far quicker than Ibn Tubal expected, and he said as much.

"This metal has a mind of its own. One hit of the hammer seems to achieve three times more than with other metals. It's strange, very strange. And all this when the metal is cooler than most other metals. I admit again I have never seen any metal like this or one that joins so easily."

He held the sword up and looked at it. All of them noticed that there seemed to be a dull, golden glow to it despite the darkness of the metal due to the heat.

Ibn Tubal plunged the sword into a bucket of water and strangely it gave off no steam. They looked at each other, puzzled by what they were seeing.

Selim couldn't hold back his excitement. "This is a special sword. Maybe all the stories about it are true. It's amazing!"

Ibn Tubal looked closely at the sword and felt the edge of it. Solemnly he said, "It is more amazing than you think, young man. I have not sharpened this sword, as you have seen, and yet it has the keenest of edges on it. Here, feel it."

He took the sword over to them and they all ran their finger over it, amazed at the fine sharp edge they were feeling. Ishkuz exclaimed, "I feel goose bumps all over me. I've never seen anything like this before."

Meanwhile Naaim had returned with the leather and Ibn Tubal began to cut a piece to fit snugly around the handpiece. He took some glue from a pot on the shelf and glued it on, and then wound the thongs of leather around the hand piece for added grip and support.

"There is one more thing to do," he said. "The sword needs to be polished."

With that said, he took a cloth and a tin of abrasive polish and seated himself. He lay the sword across his knees and began to polish, checking and feeling the metal after each spot. The top of the sword joining the pommel had not been heated and still wore years of grime and corrosion. He had to work hard to remove what the heat had cleaned from the other part of the blade. Selim, Ishkuz and Ibrahim sat in the shade of the shop waiting for him to finish. Ibn Tubal was thorough and worked hard to bring the top of the blade to the shine and finish of the rest of the sword. When he came to the section just below the crosspiece of the handle he began to look very closely at one side of the blade. He polished it some more and looked closely again. The three onlookers sensed something wasn't quite right and sat up a little with interest.

"Young man," he said motioning to Selim. "Can you make out what is here at the top of the sword?"

Selim got up and took the sword from Ibn Tubal. Even though he was thinking about what could possibly be on the sword, his mind still alerted him to the lightness and harmony of the sword. It was effortless to hold. He put this aside and moved out into the light to get the best view. He turned the sword this way and that to catch the sun at the right spot and then looked very closely. "It looks like some sort of writing, but it is very fine and detailed," he said. "It's in a strange language. I don't recognise it," he added.

"I will polish it some more to see if we can bring it out more clearly, but I fear it is faint and the polishing will not help all that much," said Ibn Tubal as he took the sword back. He sat and began to polish it again and then said to Naaim, "Go to my house and bring my looking glass. That may help."

Naaim left immediately and returned quickly. Ibn Tubal took the glass and held it up to the sword and looked closely. "Have a look," he said to Selim. Selim took the glass and held it up to read the script.

"Whoa!" he said as he pulled his head back. "It makes it so big!"

"It's called a magnifying glass," said Ibn Tubal with a large smile.

Selim looked again and said, "I can't read it, but I can see the shapes clearly."

"Why don't you make a copy. Maybe we can find someone who knows this script and can translate it for us," said Ibrahim.

"Good idea," said Ibn Tubal as he went in search of some writing things.

"I bet you that Feysul would know what it says," said Ishkuz with some passion.

Selim copied the script down carefully, checking over and over that he had it exactly right. He knew that each mark or scratch might mean something and help to give the right translation. He gave the sword back to Ibn Feysul.

"Well, this has certainly been an interesting morning. You are never too old to see new things," said Ibn Feysul, shaking his head. "Let me finish polishing it and then we will be done."

He sat again and polished the areas that he hadn't finished and then held it up with his arm outstretched. As they looked at it Ishkuz said, "Am I seeing things or is there a blue tinge on the edges?"

"No, you're not seeing things. I see it too. It's like a haze around the edges," answered Selim. "Like it has come alive now that it has been remade."

Selim felt both awe and pride rise in him as he looked at the sword. This was his sword, the sword of his tribe, and it was not a trinket or broken-down relic. It was reborn in all its glory. They all felt drawn to the sword and couldn't take their eyes off it. Finally, Ibn Tubal lowered the sword, breaking the spell, and handed it to Selim.

"It was an honour to be a part of the re-forming of this sword. It is unique. May it bless you and you it." "I don't want any payment for the work," he continued. "My old muscles have not felt so good in years and to see this sword regain life due to your passion and desire gladdens my heart and spirit," said Ibn Tubal.

The three of them bowed and Ibrahim replied to him, "It was a pleasure to see a true craftsman at work. Your reputation will be carried beyond Yathrib. The sword will forever be evidence of your ability and craftsmanship. Many, many thanks."

Selim and Ishkuz repeatedly added their own thanks as they turned and left.

"It's strange, but I feel like the sword has always been a part of me. That's how good it feels in my hand. It's a weird feeling," he said to the others. They looked at him without fully understanding what he was saying but said nothing.

"We can't call it Al Maksour anymore, can we?" said Ishkuz. "It's no longer broken," he added.

"No, we can't, but I don't know what to call it," replied Selim.

"I think that the sword will give us its name over time," said Ibrahim. "It's shown that it wanted to be repaired and gave itself sharp edges without any grinding. It may well reveal its own name."

Selim and Ishkuz nodded as they realised this was entirely possible after what they had just seen the sword do.

"I think we should buy a scabbard to hold the sword," said Ibrahim.

"Why don't we go to the marketplace and see what we can find?" said Selim.

They made their way there and found the stall of a leather worker. There were some beautifully crafted scabbards that would all do honour to the sword, so they chose one for it. Selim tied the scabbard to his waist and slid the sword into it. It felt good to carry the sword on his side.

They made their way back to Sekeen and the horses. Sekeen was busy cleaning halters and saddles as the horses could not be brushed down. Some of their mud had begun to come off from lying down in the straw and where they had rubbed themselves, but they still looked half of what they should have.

Sekeen was eager to hear what had happened. He looked at the new scabbard on Selim's waist and the handle sticking out from the top.

"Did you get it done?" he asked.

"We sure did," said Selim. He drew the sword from the scabbard and held it up. "Look at this!"

Sekeen's eyes locked onto the sword and his mouth opened.

"Wow, that's fantastic! I never expected it to look like that when it had just been old, broken pieces," he exclaimed. "It looks so good, so regal, so useful!" he added.

"Can I hold it?"

"Yes of course," said Selim and he handed the sword over to him.

"Amazing balance and lightness," he observed. "It's like holding fire in your hands," he said swinging the sword around in arcs.

"I know. It's so light, yet so strong. The metalsmith had trouble even marking the metal until he had it at exactly the right temperature. And he said it was a lower temperature than what he would normally use. He's never seen metal like this," Selim responded.

Ishkuz then added to the story. "Do you know what else happened? When he had put all the pieces together and joined them, the sword came up with sharpened edges on both sides and he hadn't sharpened it at all. It's like the sword has a mind of its own."

"Well, that's what the stories tell us," said Ibrahim. "The sword seems to know what to do in any situation. I thought these were just stories but having seen what the sword did this morning I am starting to think that there is more to these stories, or rather more to this sword."

They continued talking as they sat and ate lunch and Selim also told Sekeen about the mare that he seen and how they were to visit the stud that afternoon. All of them became excited at seeing these horses and they had a long discussion about where the king's horses might have come from and whether their horses were better or not.

Later Selim took out the scroll he had bought in Yathrib, and he and Ishkuz found a spot in the stable near to the horses and began to read it. Selim read it slowly out loud, as the words seem to demand this. Ishkuz listened intently. He had never heard a story like this before and they read chapter after chapter. Their minds were opened to new things with each sentence, as they learnt of the creation of humans by God, a man created from mud and a woman created from a bone. There were many things they didn't understand, as the book dealt with things far beyond their thoughts and experiences.

"So, this man and woman lived in a garden and then ate a piece of fruit God told them not to and then they died, but didn't really. Does that mean that they might have lived forever?" asked Ishku, realising it all sounded so confusing.

"I suppose so," answered Selim.

"But listen to this," he said with excitement in his voice. "After he drove the two out of the garden, he placed cherubim, whatever they are, and a flaming sword flashing back and forth to guard the way to the tree of life. A flaming sword. I don't know what cherubim are but there was a sword, and it was flaming. It must have been on fire but it didn't get burned up."

"Did you just read that God put the sword there?" asked Ishkuz.

"Yes, God sent them from the Garden of Eden and didn't want them to come back in, so he put the sword there and these cherubim things," answered Selim.

They sat in silence as they took this in. Finally, Ishkuz spoke up. "But that means that God was the first one to make a sword. I mean so far swords aren't mentioned at all in the story and now all of a sudden one appears from heaven."

"Yeah, you're right," said Selim. "And it was on fire and obviously didn't melt."

"But that means humans copied God. I mean he made a sword and then we must have copied the shape. But how did we find out what swords are made of and how to make them?" asked Ishkuz.

"I really don't know," answered Selim. "I wonder what happened to that sword?" Selim added.

Just then Sekeen called out to them, "It's time to go if you want to meet this man of yours at the stables."

They both got up quickly and Selim rolled up the scroll and put it away.

CHAPTER 20

In no time at all they were making their way through the streets of Cairo toward the stables of the king. They were able to find their way, only stopping once to ask for directions. They were a little early but found the door that Wajdan had spoken about, which was set in a high wall made of bricks. Long branches of wisteria and honeysuckle reached over the top and spread their scent. While they waited the afternoon sun was kept at bay by the large peppercorn trees shading the street. Soon they heard the sound of a lock being loosened and a handle being turned. The door swung out towards them and Wajdan came through.

"So good to see you. Welcome. Ah, I see you have brought some friends. Good, good," he said to them.

"Thank you for meeting us and letting us see the horses," said Selim.

Wajdan led them past the larger yards, some with low walls and others with wooden fences. There were some weanlings in the yards but not many. They came to several large buildings with thick brick walls and high roofs. As they entered into one through the large iron and wooden gates the temperature dropped by about ten degrees. There was a breeze coming through some of the high windows and as their eyes adjusted to the light, they feasted on close to fifty Arabian mares tied up to the walls.

"Oh wow!" Ishkuz let out as he saw the silhouettes of many beautiful mares, outlining curvy necks, long legs, strong straight backs and powerful hindquarters. The mares turned their heads to the men and as they passed by they could see the delicate skin of their nostrils flare as some of them let out a soft nicker. Their eyes were bright and large and though some were small and others taller in height they all displayed not just quality but a peaceful confidence about themselves. Their coats shone brightly and they were in excellent condition.

"These are the mares and the mare stable," Wajdan said matter-of-factly.

"They are all magnificent," said Selim.

"Look, there is the bay mare I was telling you about," he said to the others. He went over and the others followed. She turned her head to them, and they could all see her neck lengthen beautifully as she stretched to smell them.

"This is Nariman," said Wajdan. "One of the better mares the king has bred. She is six years old and after she has finished racing she will become a mother."

"She has long, clean legs," remarked Ibrahim, "and remarkably short coupling with a long hip and croup. No wonder you race her. Has she done well?"

"She has improved with each race and in her last one she was second by only a short distance. She has only raced seven times. But she is from a very strong line of racers. However, they are slow to mature, so we expect improvement from her to continue with every race and when she is seven she will most likely be at her best."

He then added as if as an afterthought, "She'll be racing in the king's new year race in four days' time. The king himself attends with the most respected and important people of Egypt."

Ishkuz had moved over to a grey mare who had not yet turned white but who also showed great strength and depth of body. "This one is a beauty too," he said. "Look at her eyes, and her eyelashes. They are so long." The others agreed and Wajdan came over and stroked her head and straightened her forelock.

"She has a great broodmare body and of course a beautiful, beautiful head, but she lacks a little in muscling in her gaskins and her front tendons are tied in a little. Her sire is probably the best stallion we have, a beautiful, white stallion. Her dam had similar legs, though this mare's sire has improved them," said Wajdan.

"Does the king make all the breeding decisions?" asked Ibrahim.

"Well, he has the final say, but he does discuss the planned breedings with the stable managers," replied Wajdan.

"He certainly seems to know what he is doing," said Ibrahim, "and he must have started with some very good stock. Do you know where the original horses came from?"

"The king's father and grandfather were all horse breeders, and I am told the grandfather in particular loved the Arabian breed and tried to find the best he could to start his breeding program. He bought horses from Syria, around Damascus, in the Sinai and of course on the Arabian Peninsula. I have heard it said that some of the best came from the peninsula," answered Wajdan.

He then added, "Yasmin here has a number of lines on both sides of her pedigree that trace to horses from the peninsula. This grey mare mainly has lines from Syria. They are hardy horses but different to the peninsula horses. Let's walk through the stables and I will show you another mare by the white stallion."

They walked past many beautiful and different coloured horses and then came to a milky white mare who turned her neck and head to them as they approached. Her neck swung around easily as her large, dark eyes with long, long eyelashes focused on them. None of them could deny the beauty of her head and slender neck.

"This mare has the same sire as the grey we saw earlier. Isn't she a beauty?" asked Wajdan.

"Absolutely," said Selim as his eyes swept over her body and legs. "She is so pretty and so well put together. She has the most fascinating face and her hindquarters are so smooth and strong. She is muscled beautifully all the way to the dock of her tail and her tail is set so high. She is truly a lovely mare."

Wajdan smiled and rubbed her neck lovingly. "One of the king's favourites," he said, and then added, "one of mine too. Come, I will show you the stallions."

They walked through the rest of the stable and looked at all the mares as they passed. There was a black mare that Ishkuz really liked, who had a beautifully chiselled head with large eyes. Her legs were long too, and she was deep through the girth area.

They came to the end of the stable and went out into the sun again. The stallions were further down and on the way they passed carefully manicured green grass with large peacocks parading under the palm trees. Large white pigeons flew above them as they went from scouring the ground for spilled oat seeds to the safety of the roof. As they turned a corner, they saw the row of stables and the heads of the stallions reaching out beyond the doors of the stables. They neighed as the men came into view. With the stallion heads in profile, Selim, Ishkuz and Ibrahim could easily see there were all sorts of colours and a range of shapes. Some had long heads and some were much shorter, some were more concave and others more straight in profile, and others were wider between the eyes. But nearly all of them had large, lowset eyes and soft skin making up expansive nostrils.

Wajdan took a halter from the wall of one of the stables and opened the stable door.

"I said I may not be able to bring any of the horses out for you to see but I have the time to do it."

He put the halter on the shiny chestnut stallion and led him out. As soon as he came through the stable door, they could see that this was a large and powerful stallion. He had a strong, lengthy shoulder that had a lovely slope to it which carried deep into his back. He had a short back and a deeply muscled hindquarter. Selim noticed that his croup was a little short, leaving less room for muscle. He also noticed his neck was a little thick which made it look short and lacking in elegance, though he didn't say this to Wajdan. Overall the stallion was smooth and well-built with excellent legs and hooves.

"Ishkuz, notice how his leg bones are straight and in line with each other and the tendons are placed evenly from the bones along their length," said Selim.

Ishkuz moved from the front of the stallion to his side to see what Selim was saying.

"You're right, and he has such good muscling on the forearms as well," replied Ishkuz.

"He is very powerful," added Ibrahim.

"Thank you for your compliments. You obviously know about horse conformation," said Wajdan.

The men smiled in return, for little did Wajdan know of their horse knowledge, or the breeding and quality of their horses. Nor were they going to let him know, lest he pass on that three desert-bred horses superior to the kings were in a stable in the city.

"Let me show you what I think is our best stallion," Wajdan said.

He put the chestnut stallion back in his stable and went across the lane to a stall a little further down. Inside was a grey stallion and as they went closer they could all see the quality of the stallion. His head was exquisite with large dark eyes, large nostrils and small ears.

Ishku commented, "He has eyelashes as long as a camel!"

"Yes," replied Wajdan. "He is a true beauty and has produced some of the most beautiful fillies and mares for us, all with a similar head and eyes. Remember the two grey mares I showed you? This is their sire."

"Wow, what a lovely shaped neck," said Selim as the grey stallion stretched his head out to them. "It's like a desert snake, so long but with good muscling."

Wajdan grabbed the stallion's forelock and pulled it down straight between his eyes. "This is Nurai, named after the milk white of the full moon."

He entered the stable, placed a halter on Nurai and brought him out. Nurai danced lightly on his legs as he came out of the stall, and his neck curled and his eyes grew bigger as he called out to the other stallions. He raised his tail in a gentle curve and continued to dance in the lane at the end of the lead. He was a sight to behold and even Ibrahim who had seen many excellent horses was taken in by this dancing, glistening white-haired stallion who seemed to dance on air and announce to all around him that he was the king of the stables.

"Nurai is the king's favourite," said Wajdan, "and he rides him often. With his red and gold saddle and bridle on he is like an animal from another time and place. Everyone stops and stares at him and he knows he is being looked at."

"He is absolutely beautiful," said Ishkuz.

"Yes, he is," said Selim as he moved into various positions to look at his conformation and legs. He added after a little while, "He is almost perfect, not just in looks but build as well."

Even Ibrahim added his agreement. "He is a horse from the imagination and a wonderful stallion. It would be truly interesting to see what he and Aisha would produce together."

Selim looked at Ibrahim, a little shocked to hear him speak so openly about their horses. "He really must be impressed to want to use this stallion, and over Aisha of all the mares we have," he thought to himself.

They continued to look carefully at Nurai and marvel at the spring in his legs and the way his whole body flowed from one end to the other, in harmony and balance. For a few minutes no-one spoke as they soaked in this creature, knowing that he had been blessed with many excellent parts that combined to one magnificent whole.

The spell was broken when Wajdan led Nurai back into the stable and let him go. They all gravitated to the stable door as Wajdan slipped out and Nurai, finished sniffing around for food, stuck his head out above the door.

"Does Nurai have any sons?" asked Ibrahim.

"Yes," replied Wajdan, "but they were sold when very young. We will get some more in the spring, no doubt. There is a demand for them, but I don't think any of them were as good as him," he replied, pointing to Nurai. "He is still young and I'm sure he will produce many like himself, if not better."

Just then three women and a man appeared from around the corner of the stables. All four men moved closer to the stable walls, giving them room to pass. As they approached all of the men were drawn to look at the woman in front. Her eyes were piercing and yet large and liquid. Her skin was smooth and her face perfectly shaped. She wore a thin golden veil over her head that wafted in the breeze behind her and only lightly covered her glistening, dark hair. She walked with purpose and authority and a gentle sway to her hips.

Wajdan fidgeted slightly and then said with some surprise, "Your highness ... I did not expect you here ... now. Is there anything I can help you with?"

The woman stopped and turned to him, looking at each of their faces in turn.

"Wajdan," she said, ignoring his question. "I see you have company."

"Yes, your highness. These men are from the Nejd region. They are looking at your father's horses as they too are horse breeders."

"And you're showing them Nurai?" she asked.

"Yes, your highness," answered Wajdan.

"And what then do you think of our white stallion?" she asked, indicating to Nurai.

Selim couldn't help himself and answered with some enthusiasm, "He is magnificent, your highness. Congratulations to your father for breeding such an excellent example of a horse."

The lady smiled at him and was silent for a short time, looking at him carefully. Then she replied rather cryptically, "Hmm, thank you, but my father is not the only horse breeder in this palace."

She went on with a wave of her hand, "And does he match the horses from your desert?"

Selim answered with a wisdom he didn't know he had, and which surprised him.

"My lady, a spring may start in the mountain, but it doesn't become a river till its water travels far from the mountain and joins with other waters. Your Nurai is the river and our horses the spring. He is a jewel."

The lady looked at him and smiled as though knowing how carefully he had maintained the reputation of his horses, and the king's. She nodded her head and then reached out to Nurai.

"Yes, he is a jewel. A diamond, I think. Perfectly shaped and cut to do what he was made for. Have you seen his daughters?"

"Yes, we have seen them. Wajdan showed us. They are gems, your highness," answered Selim.

"Yes, yes they are. Well, I must go. Enjoy your visit," replied the lady.

She walked off but not before her eyes lingered briefly on Selim, an glimpse that Ishkuz did not miss. After she had left the stallion lane, Wajdan let out a sigh.

"That was the princess, daughter of the king, and she knows her horses too. She advises the king a lot about breeding, but I don't know if he always listens to her or just follows some of her ideas to keep her happy," said Wajdan.

"Come, let me show you to the gate," he added.

They made their way out and said their farewells to Wajdan, thanking him profusely for allowing them to see the royal horses.

As they were walking back to the stables Ishkuz said, "I wish we could show Wajdan and the king our horses. Faraj is at least Nurai's equal and I would love to see him face Faraj in a race. Then we'd see who the diamond is."

"It's for that very reason that we can't show them," said Ibrahim. "Nurai is a magnificent stallion, but I believe that Faraj, Aisha and even Kadin are better horses."

Then he added with less strength and just the hint of teasing, "However, I would love to see what he and Aisha could produce. A little of his blood in our horses would not harm them at all."

Selim looked at him and saw the sparkle in his eyes. "So, you are open to bringing blood from outside the desert into our herd, Ibrahim. This is new. Nurai really must have affected you."

"Maybe I'm getting old," said Ibrahim, "and sentimental. I don't know. But can you imagine the foal? A combination of Aisha's strength, resilience and beauty with Nurai's smoothness, structure and beauty. What a horse that would be!"

"You really have a soft spot for Aisha, don't you Ibrahim?" asked Ishkuz.

"You might say that," replied Ibrahim with a slightly defensive look on his face.

They made their way back to the stables and shared with Sekeen all they had seen.

CHAPTER 21

That evening as they were sitting together Ibrahim raised the question of how they were to find out the meaning of the markings on the sword.

"Where do we go for that?" he asked. "I am no scholar so I have no idea."

"Maybe some of the book merchants can help us or at least tell us who can," replied Ishkuz.

"Well," said Selim, "I'm keen to look at some of the booksellers here in Cairo. I mean while we're here we may as well make the most of it. Everything has gone so well up till now and there must be lots of scrolls and parchments and very interesting scrolls and books to find."

He looked thoughtful and then said, "I wonder if there is a book recording the other tradition of this Noah. Remember that Feysul the scholar mentioned Noah's Sumerian name was Ziasudra and that he had read that tradition, or at least heard of it."

"Yes, I remember him saying that," said Ishkuz.

"Tomorrow we will ask around for help to decipher the sword's writing," said Selim.

Ibrahim nodded. "Yes, you need time for that. It would be a pity not to know about the secret the sword carries. Knowing the sword's secrets will make our story much more interesting when I tell it around the fire after we get back."

Having decided about the next day's activity, Ishkuz began to talk about the king's race that Wajdan had mentioned.

"It's in only four days. Couldn't we wait around to see it? I would love to see what horses are entered and how they race here in Egypt," he said enthusiastically.

Sekeen spoke up and said, "All the talk around the stables has been of the race. People come from all over to race and Absat told me that the prize is a breeding to one of the king's stallions. That is, if it isn't one of the king's horses that wins."

The other three all stopped what they were doing and looked at Sekeen with astonishment.

"What did I say?" he said, spreading his hands out to appeal to them.

"What?" said Selim. "A breeding to one of the king's stallions? Why didn't you tell us that was the prize?" Selim demanded of Sekeen.

"I didn't know that it was important. We were supposed to leave, not breed our horses here," said Sekeen in a slightly pained way.

Ishkuz whistled and then said, "A breeding to Nurai? Amazing."

For a time no-one spoke but it seemed Ibrahim, Selim and Ishkuz were thinking the same thing.

Selim and Ishkuz both spoke up. Ishkuz indicated for Selim to go on, then he said with a slow, soft voice, "What if we enter the race?"

Ibrahim responded with a shake of the head and said, "We can't risk it. However much we may want to add Nurai's blood to our herd, we cannot risk harm coming to our horses, or to us for that matter."

Ishkuz was deflated and dropped his head. However, Selim was not so easily swayed.

"I know you want to protect the horses, but I think that if we enter and do just enough to win and we keep the horses covered and looking unkempt, no-one is going to take notice of us. Surely there have been lots of horses to win the race that didn't belong to the king. If we are out in public and there are people all around, how can anyone deny us our victory?"

Ibrahim sighed and some of the fight went out of him, but he wasn't convinced.

"I don't know. It all just seems too dangerous. It's not worth it," said Ibrahim.

"We could all be on our horses and be ready to ride away if anything bad was to happen," added Ishkuz enthusiastically. The others ignored him.

"You know that you want to see Faraj race," said Selim passionately. "You want to see our desert horses, the horses of our tribe, of the Nejd, win against the others that race. You want that, don't you Ibrahim?"

Ibrahim didn't answer but the tightening of his jaw muscles showed he was struggling with what Selim had said.

Finally he replied, "Yes, there is a part of me that wants to let our horses run as fast as the fire and win and show everyone how good they are. I am tempted, but it is a risk, a big risk."

For a time there was silence. Then Ibrahim shook himself and said with both reluctance and finality, "I can only allow it if the horses remain covered and stay coated in mud, and if Faraj is in the front at the end, he is not to win by a lot. We must do all that we can to protect them."

Selim sat and all of them remained quiet as the meaning of this decision sank in.

Sekeen spoke up. "It's one thing to plan a breeding to this stallion but you still have to win the race, and all sorts of things can happen in a race, no matter how fast our horses are. There are also a lot of things that need to be done. We don't even know how to enter the race or how long it is, or where it begins for that matter."

"You're right Sekeen. There are a lot of things to think about and organise. We'll make a list and divide it between us," said Selim.

Just then Ishkuz spoke, but in a quiet, careful way, knowing how difficult this was for Ibrahim. "Will Faraj and Aisha race?"

"You mean enter two horses?" asked Selim.

Ibrahim then spoke softly and slowly to decide the issue. "If one horse races it won't matter if two do. We'll be known as having the best horses either way. I also know how much you want to ride Aisha. I've seen you look at her and like us have been drawn into her web. She will give everything she has of her feisty character, and I know you will ride her with all the skill you have."

Ishkuz bowed his head, all of a sudden feeling quite humbled but also quite surprised at Ibrahim's change of heart.

Ishkuz replied, "It will be an honour to ride her, Ibrahim. Thank you."

He then turned to Selim with his eyes sparkling and a slight grin on his face. Selim met his gaze with a wily look as they were going to be racing against each other again.

"Alright," said Selim taking charge. "Ibrahim and Sekeen, tomorrow you will find out the course of the race and how to enter our horses. Ishkuz and I will prepare the saddles and take off anything we don't need. We'll need to exercise the horses and find a quiet area to do it. We only have four days, but the horses are fit already from the long trip here."

"They will be ready," said Ibrahim. "They're probably fitter than all the other racers now, without more training."

They could all hear the pride in Ibrahim's voice and both Ishkuz and Selim felt more confident hearing Ibrahim say this.

Selim and Ishkuz were too excited to sleep and sat up talking about the race, strategising and imagining what the other horses looked like and how they were going to race with each other. They went back through their memory of Nariman, the bay mare the king was going to race, and discussed how good she might be. Then quiet and dark ended their talking and they lay down and slept.

The next morning all of them were up early, cleaning stables, stripping saddles and making enquiries about the race. By lunch Ibrahim and Sekeen had returned from following up enquiries.

Sekeen was excited and as he spoke he held up a roll in his hands. "We're in! You're racing and we have a map of the course! There are over thirty entrants and we've confirmed what Absat said about the prize. It's a breeding to one of the king's stallions but the winner also gets a large bag of gold." As he finished he rubbed his hands together, just a little too eagerly.

"That's great!" said Selim. "This is getting better all the time. Can we see the map?"

Sekeen handed over the map to Selim and going over to a table they all looked closely at it.

Ibrahim pointed to three triangle shapes and said, "These are called pyramids and they are the three large objects we saw on the first day. I was told that they are the burial places of the kings."

Ibrahim lifted his hairy eyebrow and Ishkuz and Selim looked at him with a degree of disbelief. "That's what I thought when I heard it, but it seems to be true," he said.

"Just a bit extravagant," said Sekeen sarcastically.

Ibrahim went on. "Most of the race takes place on the outskirts of the city and at one stage you race around the pyramids. We have asked around and it looks as though the race is either on sand or on the packed earth around the city. There is a short section in the hills, just here," he said, pointing to an area on the map, "but it is nowhere near as steep or rocky as the courses you have raced on."

Sekeen added, "It seems to be a straightforward course that simply focuses on speed. There really aren't any areas that might favour certain types of horses."

"Well, that suits us. Faraj and Aisha have plenty of speed and they can keep it up for a long time. This should be a very interesting race," said Selim.

"You will have to watch both Faraj and Aisha at the beginning of the race as they will be very eager to go all out, but you'll need to save them for the end no matter how good we think they are," said Ibrahim.

"Hmm, I was wondering about that," said Ishkuz. "Do you know what the distance of the race is? From the map it looks to be close to eight or nine kilometres."

"Wow," said Sekeen. "That's nearly spot on. They told us the race was nine and a half kilometres. It's a fair amount shorter than the race at Al Huraydah and that just shows they are most interested in speed."

"Tomorrow we'll look at the course and see if there is anything else we need to be aware of," said Selim.

Over lunch they continued to examine the map to get an idea of where the main features of the course were. It was a simple course that they could easily memorise, once they had walked it and worked out their bearings.

After rubbing more mud on the horses and trying to be as discrete as possible about it, Selim and Ishkuz made their way down to the market to find the booksellers. Despite the excitement of the race, in the back of their minds were the markings on the sword that needed interpreting. They were still intrigued by what the sword had hidden about itself, and what was now in plain view. Having discussed it, they all felt that a bookseller might have some knowledge of the writing or know someone who would. They were also aware that they had limited time to find both the meaning of the marks on the sword and the story of Ziasudra.

They found a manuscript shop quickly and were thankful to move into its cool shelter, as it was a particularly hot afternoon. The attendant was a thin, dry skinned man with narrow features and sharp eyes. He eyed the two young men and ended his evaluation with a slight upward turn of the nose. Despite this, his years of experience with customers caused him to hold tightly to his opinion of them and he spoke with politeness.

"Good afternoon, young men. Can I help you?" the attendant asked them.

"Well, yes, we hope so," said Selim. "We are searching for a copy of the life of Ziasudra. Have you heard of him?"

"Yes, I have heard of him, but I don't have a copy of his writings," answered the attendant.

"Oh," said Selim with obvious disappointment in his voice. "Maybe then you can help us with this script."

He pulled the paper out of his pocket with the script on it and gave it to the attendant. He looked at it closely but then shook his head and frowned.

"I'm not familiar with this writing. I suggest you go to the Cairo library. It may have a copy of Ziasudra's work and there may be some scholars there to help you with the script," he said.

Selim's face brightened.

"Can you give us directions to the library? We will go straight there," Selim said.

The attendant gave them directions and they thanked him for his help. They made their way toward the library, only stopping to buy a drink at a stall. The streets were bare of people, as the heat had driven them into cooler places. Finally, they came to the centre of the city, and they noticed how the buildings grew in size and beauty as they drew closer. They found the library among some noble buildings and were surprised at its size and elegance. There was some large writing at the top of its front entrance that they couldn't read. The first thing that struck them as they entered the large doors underneath them was the smell. As the aroma of old leather hit Selim's nostrils, it immediate brought back memories of the tack room at home.

To their surprise there were a number of floors to the library and each one of them was stacked with scrolls, large parchments and leather-bound books, though the books were far less in number than the others. A neat-looking man introduced himself as the keeper of the library.

"Good afternoon. I am Selim and this is Ishkuz. We are wondering if we can speak to someone about some words that we need translated. Is there anyone here who could help us?" Selim asked.

"You have come to the right place," the keeper said. "I suggest that you speak to one of our scholars and translators. I think that Nizar al Tayyib would be the best to talk to. Follow me."

The keeper led them through a number of corridors and down a flight of steps and then stopped and knocked at a door. He opened it and led them inside the room. The keeper introduced Selim and Ishkuz to Nizar al Tayyib who was a short and rather rotund man with a greying goatee, reddish cheeks and brilliant, sparkling blue eyes. He moved quickly toward them with his hand outstretched in welcome.

"Please sit down," he said, pointing to some chairs near the back of the room. "It is always good to speak to those interested in history and writing. The past is stimulating but speaking to others about it gives it much more depth and meaning. Now, how can I help you?"

"Thank you for your time Nizar. We really do appreciate it. We are wondering whether you would be able to recognise and possibly translate some script that we found recently," said Selim.

"Yes, of course, how interesting. Do you have the script with you?" asked Nizar.

Selim reached into the pocket of his gown, pulled out the parchment on which he had written the markings and handed it to Nizar. Nizar looked closely at it and made some noises that indicated he was thinking deeply.

"Hmm, it looks like Sumerian to me, but I will have to check," he said.

He got up and went over to a shelf that contained a number of scrolls and scraps of paper. He rifled his way through them and opened up a number of them until he found the one he was after. He laid it open on the desk, eagerly pushing a number of scrolls and books off the desk to make room. Selim and Ishkuz looked at each other and raised their eyebrows at his rather enthusiastic behaviour.

"Look, look," he said to them, motioning them to come over. Selim and Ishkuz got up and went to look at the open scroll. They couldn't make anything out. It just looked like a lot of lines to them.

"This writing is the same as your script. It is Sumerian, of that I am sure. But, now to translate it. That is the challenge. You see Sumerian has words or symbols that can mean many different things depending on the context in which is used."

Nizar stared off into the distance and again Selim and Ishkuz looked at each other wondering what he was doing.

"How can I explain this?" Nizar said. "Take the symbol for bull. It may appear as a picture or a series of strokes, like these," he said pointing to the scroll. "But it can be interpreted as strength, or sacrifice, or even just bull, depending on what is being talked about. But I am getting sidetracked. Let me see what I can make out."

He looked closely at the script on the parchment and went back and forth between it and the scroll. He then searched for a quill and ink and a piece of parchment to write on and began to make a series of marks.

"Sumerian is an ancient language and may well be one of the first to be written. But from what I know of it these marks mean 'star' and these mean 'fire,'" said Nizar, pointing to Selim's parchment.

He went on, "Now remember what I said about the context. The symbols may represent something different to what they actually are so while it may mean 'star fire' it may mean something else, just as 'bull' may mean 'sacrifice.'"

With excitement in their eyes, Selim and Ishkuz looked at each other for a third time, knowing they were near to finding out the secret of "Al Maksour."

In his enthusiasm Selim blurted out, "So, what could it mean then?"

"Well, from what I remember the symbol for 'star' can mean star or it can represent the heavens. It could also mean, though this translation is more rare, heavenly beings, or gods or just god. The symbol 'fire' can mean fire, but I have also seen it in a number of places as breath or spirit. With all of those combinations you can have a number of meanings" he replied.

He then looked more intently at Selim and asked, "Do these words have a context, some story that might give us an idea of what they stand for?"

"No," said Selim, "we found them just as they are written, totally alone."

"And what were they on?" asked Nizar. "No, no, don't answer that. I can see on your face you don't wish to tell me. It doesn't matter anyway. Very strange, though. Very strange indeed."

"May we copy the possible meanings onto the other side of our parchment so that we don't forget them?" asked Selim.

"Yes, of course. Use this quill and ink," said Nizar, pushing the bottle of ink over to Selim.

While Selim copied down the possible translations, Ishkuz couldn't restrain himself and asked Nizar, "What do the words on top of the front of the building mean?"

Nizar replied, "Ah, I see you don't know Greek. Many years ago a Greek king called Alexander conquered Egypt, but he was not just a warrior or a destroyer of culture. He actually paid to have this building built so that the knowledge of his empire could be collected and protected for future generations. The words on the building say 'Alexander's library.'"

For some reason Ishkuz needed to talk more, despite feeling overwhelmed at Nizar's knowledge and the wealth of information in the library. The next thing that popped into his mind was Feysul ibn Gharoub.

"Do you know Feysul ibn Gharoub?" he asked.

Nizar laughed heartily and then said, "I haven't heard that name in years. We studied together in Damascus. How do you know him?"

"We met him in a caravan travelling to Yathrib. We spoke briefly to him about some ancient drawings that Selim has seen about Noah or Ziasudra, as some know him," answered Ishkuz. "We are actually looking for a copy of the annals of Ziasudra. We already have the Hebrew book that tells his story but Ibn Gharoub told us there might be another version. We have looked for it but can't find it, even here in Cairo."

Selim looked at Ishkuz sharply, but totally unaware of his warning look Ishkuz happily carried on, trying hard to fit into the new and exciting place.

"Ziasudra, Ziasudra's annals. I think I have a copy somewhere here. Let me look," said Nizar. Off he went in his determined manner and rummaged again through scrolls and parchments, then came back with a rather old looking scroll.

"This is a copy that I had made many years ago. We have another in the library, but I like to have my own," he said.

"Wow, is this really the story of Ziasudra?" asked Ishkuz.

"Yes, every word," replied Nizar.

"May we look at it?" asked Selim.

"No," said Nizar.

Selim and Ishkuz looked a little startled and hoped that they had not offended him. After a moment Nizar smiled and said, "You may keep it. I can easily have another copy made."

Selim and Ishkuz couldn't thank him enough.

"You have helped us so much Nizar and given us a lot to think about and read," said Selim holding up the scroll. "We really appreciate your help and your generosity."

"You have certainly intrigued me with your questions and brightened up a slow afternoon," replied Nizar.

"We don't want to take up any more of your time. Thank you again and goodbye," said Selim.

"Yes, thank you and goodbye," added Ishkuz.

"May you travel safely and well on your trip. Do you know how to return to the entrance?" asked Nizar.

"Yes, I believe we can manage to get back, thank you," replied Selim.

They left Nizar's room and made their way back to the entrance. The heat was heavy as they moved outside and they made their way back to the stables, sticking to the shade as much as possible.

They sat down with Ibrahim and Sekeen who had prepared spiced wine and fruit and shared their story.

"So," said Sekeen. "From what you have said the writing may mean 'star fire' or 'star spirit' or 'star breath'; or 'heaven's fire' or 'spirit/breath'; or 'god's fire' or 'spirit/breath.'"

"They are the options," said Selim. "I just wish it was clearer, but as Nizar said, the older the writing the less precise it is."

"It's not really enough for a name but I suppose we can at least say that the two main ideas are something to do with the heavens and with spirit or fire," added Ishkuz.

"Well, putting it that way makes it sound like the sword isn't from this world," said Sekeen jokingly.

"Yeah, you're right. It's almost spooky, isn't it?" said Ishkuz.

"Well, it certainly has a history to it that we haven't yet found and Al Maksour isn't making it easy for us to find it either," said Ibrahim.

That night Selim began to read the annals of Ziasudra and found that it was quite different from the book of "Beginnings." It was not as wide ranging and began with the life of Ziasudra before the flood. He fell asleep that night with the scroll lying across his chest.

They saddled the horses the next morning and rode out quietly through the city to an area that Selim and Ishkuz had found the day before. It was a flat area leading into some low-lying hills that made Faraj and Aisha work hard and increase their heart rate. It was also deserted which was necessary so that no-one would see the horses as they exercised. Both horses enjoyed the work and chance to really stretch their legs, despite the inclines.

"I love this mare more than ever," said Ishkuz enthusiastically. "She is so smooth to ride and covers ground so easily and just wants to keep going. What more could you ask of a horse?"

"Well," said Selim. "You could ask for a smoother rider than hers on a horse that is faster than her," he said, teasing Ishkuz.

"Faster you think? Let's race to that bush on the far side of that low hill," he said.

He spurred Aisha into a gallop, and she sprung deeply from her haunches, her eyes wide and her tail lifted in excitement. No sooner did he do this than Selim sent Faraj into a gallop after her. Faraj was keen for the challenge, and he dug deeply into the ground to send himself and Selim into full speed within a few strides. His legs moved more quickly than Aisha's from the first stride and within fifty metres he was beside Aisha and beginning to slow as Selim pulled him up just enough to stay with Aisha. Ishkuz and Selim looked at each other from their flying horses and grinned, feeling the joy of the race, the wind blowing against them and the power of the horse on which they were seated.

Both of them asked for more from their horses and they gave it. Aisha put her head down and the staccato rhythm of her feet increased in speed. Despite this burst of speed, Faraj jumped out of the ground as though catapulted and his long legs ate up the ground, putting two, then three, then five lengths between them and then swept past the gnarly bush.

Later that night they discussed the course of the upcoming race that they had walked that morning. As Ibrahim and Sekeen had suggested the course was straightforward and the footing firm. They discussed two key points in the course where they thought things could get difficult, especially if there was a group of horses all trying to get through at one time. Ibrahim urged caution and suggested they move to the back of the group and let the others go through first as they could always catch up later. Both Selim and Ishkuz took this advice quietly and nodded. However, both knew in a race that decisions had to be made in a split second and plans made before a race may have to change during the race.

The next couple of days followed much the same routine. The horses were worked and final changes made on the saddles. They kept the mud on the horses despite their sweat and few took notice of them as they made their way through the city each day.

On the night before the race Selim decided to read more of the annals of Ziasudra, partly out of interest but also to take his mind off the race. All of them sat in a cozy section of the stables to keep an eye on Faraj and Aisha. Neither horse showed any signs of stress, in fact Aisha was dozing with her head resting on the mud brick wall and Faraj was twisting his neck and head around to get a piece of lucerne that was half in his mouth but which he couldn't quite get between his teeth. Ibrahim sat plaiting some rope and Sekeen was busy cleaning a sword, but all wanted to hear some of Ziasudra's story. Selim picked up from where he had last finished. He had moved along from the flood story and Ziasudra, as an older man, was reflecting on some of the things that had happened during his life.

"It is many years since I passed the sword on to Gilgamesh. I have heard it told that he has achieved great things with it, but it was with regret that I handed it on. Not many know of its origin, as I have not wanted to draw too much attention to it.

"Gilgamesh came to me many years after the flood, intrigued by my long life and intimacy with God. He had travelled far and was desperate for some direction, some help for his life. It seemed he was fearful of death and wished to avoid it like he thought I had. I had nothing to offer him for this. All I could do was to remind him of God's love for him. I gave him the sword as he was in great distress and I thought it would comfort him. Before I gave it to him I marked the blade, just under the handpiece to identify it, if that was ever necessary to do. But I have run ahead of myself. How did the sword come to me?

"It was a day I will never forget, as it was the day the rain began. The animals and birds were on the ark, except for the male and female pair of golden eagles. God was about to shut the door of the ark when a shadow darkened the doorway and the golden eagles flew down to enter. They were huge birds with powerful wings and the wind of their wings knocked me back. As they flew in I saw that the male eagle had something in its claws. It came over to me and dropped a long, thin object on the floor of the ark, which clunked heavily on the timber floor. I saw that it was a sword. It had no scabbard or covering, and its blade gleamed red and orange. I picked it up and as I moved it around the edges of the blade gave off a light blue haze, giving me the impression of purity and strength. As I looked more closely, I realised that I had seen the handle of this sword before. At first I couldn't remember where, but then it came to me. The handle belonged to the sword of God, the guardian of Eden, the blazing, fiery sword that God had placed at the entrance of the garden. Many before the flood knew of it and had seen it and I had also journeyed to Eden to see it. I remembered I couldn't see the blade as it was engulfed in fire, but I could see the handle. It was the same as this sword's and now I was holding it. It had been named 'Fire of Heaven' or 'Anizi' in the Sumerian tongue by those who saw it. I marked the blade with this name."

Selim stopped reading, looked at Ishkuz with wide, open eyes and then jumped to his feet with excitement, saying, "The words are 'fire of Heaven.' This sword is Al Maksour. We have the sword from heaven. The sword from the garden. It has the marks of Ziasudra on it. Can you believe it?"

"Are you sure?" asked Ibrahim.

"Everything fits. The stories, the markings. Their meaning fits with the ones Nizar gave us," replied Selim excitedly.

All Ishkuz could say was "Wow," over and over. Sekeen just stood there with his mouth hanging open.

Selim reached down and grabbed the sword and pulled it from its scabbard. He held it up and they all looked at it with new respect and awe.

"The stories are about the power of the sword," Selim continued. "It has its own personality because it's not a sword made by humans. It came from heaven and was covered in fire and didn't burn up. That's what the book of Beginnings told us too. Ibrahim, you told us stories about its power. Don't you believe them?"

Ibrahim looked shocked and yet was processing all of this as quickly as he could. Like the others he was trying to bring all that he knew about the sword and all the stories he had told and heard about the sword from fantasy to reality.

"If it's true and it seems to be," said Ibrahim, "then we have something truly special with us. And to think that it has been in the tribe for so long and no-one knew."

"I think our tribe knew they had something special but forgot about it. No-one that we know of made an effort to find out where it came from and what it really represented," said Selim.

"You're right, Selim. It belonged to us, and its story was being told, but it didn't really mean much to us," said Ibrahim. He paused and then added, "To be truthful, I thought many of the stories of the sword had been made up over the years. This is really quite extraordinary. We have a sword made in heaven. A sword of power."

"The 'fire of heaven.' So now we have a name for the sword. Just as Ibrahim said it would, the sword has revealed its name to us," said Sekeen.

Selim looked again in awe at the sword.

"'Anizi', the 'fire of Heaven,'" he whispered as they stood and stared at it.

Ishkuz broke their silence.

"Keep reading, Selim. He might say more about it."

Selim went to put 'Anizi' down but decided against laying it on the ground.

"Here Sekeen, you hold it. I don't want to put it on the ground now, knowing what it really is," said Selim.

He bent down to pick up the scroll and continued to read.

"I had little use for the sword as the years went by, but I often wondered why God wanted the sword to survive the flood and stay on earth. Why didn't it return to heaven? All of Eden was engulfed with water and destroyed. We never again saw the cherubim that God placed near the sword and we assumed they had returned to heaven. But not the sword. The only conclusion I could come to was that Anizi had been made for life on earth and not for heaven. It had a purpose beyond its role at the gateway to Eden. As I pondered on these things it came to me that 'Anizi' was designed to protect. But it wasn't protecting the garden. It was protecting us. Its job was to keep us from harming ourselves by eating from the tree of life in the garden. Somehow it was going to continue that job. I knew that it would be a protector. It would bring good things to us."

Selim kept reading quietly for a minute and the others waited.

"It seems that's all he has to say about the sword. He goes on about other things. I'll keep going through the scroll to see if he comes back to it at all," said Selim as his eyes scanned the scroll.

"Wow," said Ishkuz. "That's amazing. Made in heaven and brought to earth, and not just for a little time but for all time. And we have it. Your tribe has had it just about forever."

Ishkuz stopped for a moment then went on. "I wonder how your tribe got hold of it? Maybe you're descended from this guy Ziasudra gave it to. What was his name again?"

"Gilgamesh," answered Selim.

"Maybe he passed it down through your ancestors," Ishkuz added.

"It's possible," said Ibrahim slowly. Then with far more enthusiasm he said, "In fact, anything is possible after this."

"This is a lot to take in," said Sekeen as he put his hand on his forehead and sighed.

CHAPTER 22

The next day was overcast and definitely cooler than the day before and there was a northerly wind that made its way up the river from the sea that was keeping the heat of the desert at bay. All four men were up early preparing breakfast for the horses and for themselves and getting things together for the race. Sensing the tension in Selim and Ishkuz the horses became fidgety and restless. Ibrahim and Sekeen had decided to ride out to the race as being on horseback would give them a better view as well as allow them to move quickly if they needed to help either Selim or Ishkuz. They all took with them their weapons.

The race was to take place in the morning when it wasn't as hot and soon the four of them made their way out to the start of the track. They snaked their way through the streets of Cairo amidst the chatter and noise of the city. Occasionally they glimpsed the top of the pyramids above the rooftops. Soon they met other horses and riders making their way to the starting line. As they left the city they could see people and horses flowing from every direction. The colours from the horses and the people's clothing mingled into a giant patchwork of color that shimmered as they moved.

As they approached the starting line, they passed a raised section of land on which stood a wooden shelter. Inside it were some chairs and a number of richly dressed people. On one of the chairs was a man who appeared relaxed, yet when Selim saw his eyes he thought of a spring, coiled and ready to be released at any moment. Selim decided that this must be the king of Egypt. His thoughts were confirmed when he saw, next to the king, the lady that he had met at the king's stables, his daughter. As he looked at her she caught his eye and after a moment gave him a slight nod of recognition along with the briefest of smiles. Selim returned the nod and the smile. Selim wasn't sure if she was acting in her official role or whether there was something more to it. Just then her father leaned across and spoke her name as he pointed to a group of approaching horses.

"Afari, so that is her name," Selim mused. Deep within he decided he liked it.

They made their way to a tent where they needed to confirm their entry. Sekeen and Ibrahim had already left to find themselves a good vantage point. Selim and Ishkuz noticed that some of the other riders were looking at them and Selim became anxious that they were looking at Faraj and Aisha and weighing up how much of a threat they might be, but then he saw a rider point at their stirrups and he let out a sigh. All of the other riders had long stirrups and so seeing two horses ridden with very short stirrups was certainly something of interest. Some of the men gave a short laugh after seeing them and that relieved Selim even more as now they were being dismissed as strange and of no real threat.

Very soon, all of the racers were gathered at the starting area and the tension was beginning to build. There were many racers, all eager to claim the prize. Some of the riders wore expensive clothes and the horses had beautiful, richly coloured bridles and saddles, the type only the very rich could afford. Other riders and horses wore plain, even tattered clothing, saddles and bridles. It was obvious men from every part of Egypt were entering the race. Ishkuz noticed a milky white horse with red and gold livery and pointed him out Selim.

"One of the king's horses? Maybe even a son of Nurai. What do you think?"

"Most likely," he answered. "I also saw Nariman, the bay mare we saw at the stables. She looks very fit."

"No-one is riding with their stirrups up," said Ishkuz.

"Yes, I noticed that. Let's hope we stay on!" said Selim.

Ishkuz turned quickly to him as the memory of Selim's fall in the race at Al Huraydah came back.

"If you fall off this time, it won't be my fault," said Ishkuz defensively.

Selim gave him a big grin and waved him off.

A man with a large flag made his way to the side of the track to signal the beginning of the race. The riders lined up the horses as straight as they could as the horses pranced and flicked their tails, eager to be off. The flag dropped and the horses went back onto their haunches as all their pent-up tension, excitement and training poured into the moment. Four horses sprang to the front and claimed two to three lengths on the others as their riders gave them their heads and gave into their excitement.

Strangely, a thought flicked through Selim's mind as Faraj powered forward. "Will Anizi help me?"

The thought dropped away quickly as horses and dust mingled together and riders jostled for room and a clear pathway. One rider cut across in front of Faraj as his horse had been jolted to the right and Selim had to pull Faraj up hard so that he wouldn't hit himself on the back legs of the other horse. Faraj fought the pull of the bit on his mouth but slowed enough to make room. He soon settled into his stride and Selim looked around for Aisha and Ishkuz. They were a number of lengths ahead of them and Ishkuz looked intent, his head close to Aisha's neck and her mane covering part of his face.

"So far so good," Selim thought.

The first part of the race was along a wide stretch of dirt that swung slightly to the left and the horses flew along, much more spread out now as some wanted to get a good lead and others were holding back for the end part of the race. Selim looked around for the milky white horse but in the dust he couldn't see it. He wasn't sure who was going to be the greatest threat in the race as he knew nothing of the horses but knew that the king's horses were some of the best and were worth being concerned about.

The pack swung into an area where the desert met the road and their footing became sandy and soft, the sand taking them to the low hills west of the city. The dust from the earthen road was left in their wake and Selim could see more clearly where he and Faraj were in relation to the others. Aisha was still ahead of them, ploughing through the sand with a determination typical of her. He noticed the milky white horse was ahead of her, as were a group of ten or so frontrunners. Like the other horses, Faraj called on his strength and endurance to get through the sand, though it was not as deep as further out in the desert. Sweat and foam were mixing with the dried mud on Faraj's neck and flanks and some of it began to run off his coat as it was carried away with the rivulets of sweat that ran off him. Faraj was breathing hard as it always took an effort to get through the sand, but Selim knew that due to his training he would recover quickly once they got back to firmer footing.

Only one or two horses made any ground during the sandy part of the race. The majority held their positions, preserving their horses and waiting for better ground. They swept over the low hills, and it was here that Aisha dropped back just enough for Selim and Ishkuz to talk to each other.

"We'll be out of the sand soon," said Selim. "We can make our move then, but only gradually. There's still a lot of the race left to run."

Suddenly a loud crack sounded from the sky and some of the horses flinched. The riders looked up to see a thick, dark cloud hanging above them. Another crack rang out from the cloud and then large drops of rain began to fall. The drops stung the faces and hands of the riders and then the rain grew heavier. The air seemed to be filled with water and the horses blinked hurriedly trying to keep it out of their eyes. The horses each slowed instinctively, hoping that this would lessen the force of the rain, and both horses and riders became drenched.

Ishkuz called out to Selim, "This is going to wash the mud off."

"There's nothing we can do about it," Selim yelled back, trying to be heard over the rain and thunder.

The rain soaked the manes and tails of the horses, and thick, black mud slid off Faraj and Aisha, staining the sand below them. The rain continued for another couple of minutes and then eased off before finally stopping. Within two kilometres the dark cloud had passed. Here and there the sun shone once more through the clouds, and the horses and riders shook themselves where they could and focused again on the race. They were now heading down out of the low hills and the pyramids were coming into view, which meant the sandy section of the race was over. Some of the riders spurred their horses down the hills, excited to be through the slowest section. Both Selim and Ishkuz urged Faraj and Aisha on and they lengthened their strides, somewhat refreshed by the rain.

There were still a number of horses in front of them but they were beginning to slow a little, having gone out hard from the start. They galloped out onto the road and Faraj fought the bit, tired of being behind the other horses. Selim let out the reins a little, which were hard to hold onto because of the rain, and Faraj's strides increased. Aisha was not to be outdone and she fought to keep up with him. They made some ground on the horses ahead and began to overtake them. They swept past the pyramids but paid little attention to them. However, it was here that they needed to take the lead and then hold it, as they were now three quarters of the way through the race. Both Ishkuz and Selim knew that from here they would ask everything from their horses and both of them, supremely fit, relished the speed and the fight before them.

The horses put their heads down and the wind in the faces of Ishkuz and Selim grew faster and faster. Faraj's stride was longer than Aisha's and while Aisha kept up her fast hoof beat Faraj's beat was just as fast but covered more ground in his stride. He slowly began to leave her behind but Aisha's determination made her dig deep for more speed and the gap between her and Faraj stopped lengthening. They passed a grey horse and his surprised rider and then came up to the back of the group of frontrunners. They were all straining. In the middle of the pack was Nariman, the bay mare, and the milky white horse. Both seemed to be running well, although like the other horses their nostrils were stretched to their maximum and their ears were pinned back. As the horses' tails dried in the wind they crept back up and began again to point to the sky, hair streaming out behind.

A number of riders looked around to see if there was anyone threatening to overtake. Some of them saw Faraj and Aisha and swiftly turned their faces and called their horses to greater speed, desperate to hold their position. Despite this, some horses forged to the front and passed them. A pack of five including the milky white horse, Nariman, the bay, Faraj and Aisha, and a long-legged, rangy brown horse, who seemed ungainly but who was obviously fast, claimed the lead. They headed down the last part of the road, which was straight and firm.

In the crowd Ibrahim and Sekeen could see that a chestnut, a bay and two white horses were part of those in the lead. They hoped that Faraj and Aisha were amongst them. The crowd were on their feet chanting and urging the horses on. The king and Afari were also trying to make out who was in the lead. Slowly the rangy brown horse fell a length, then three, then four lengths behind. Nariman showed great spirit, staying with the others and the white horse. However, both the white horse and Nariman were at the peak of their speed and it was only their endurance and spirit that kept them at that pace. Aisha had only a little more to give, and she began to push her head and neck out beyond them. But it was Faraj, who seemed to grow in size who took the lead and began to leave the others behind. The other riders, though urging their horses on, couldn't help but notice this golden horse, ridden by a rider who sat over his withers, stride out before them at a speed none of them had seen before. They were awed as Faraj moved five then ten lengths in front of them, seemingly going faster all the time. The crowd couldn't believe what they were seeing as they knew the horses in the race and the reputation of the king's horses. To see one win by so much was enough for many of them to stop yelling and chanting, just to watch. Ibrahim and Sekeen urged the horses on, half yelling, half crying at what they were seeing and they knew that the crowd could not deny the speed and power of these horses bred in the Sarmadees.

Meanwhile, the king's eyes grew small as he saw this raw display of speed and endurance. He knew that none of his horses could run as the chestnut had run, or even as the flea-bitten mare had. He wondered where these horses could have come from and asked those around him, but no-one could answer him.

The crowd regained its voice as Faraj and then Aisha raced past the finish line. Despite their exhaustion there was a pride in the way they carried themselves with ears pricked and eyes on fire. They held their necks and heads high as the crowd closed in on them, all wanting to see the winners. The king was quick to act and he sent his men in to keep the crowd back. Ishkuz and Selim reached out to each other and clasped hands, huge smiles on their faces. Sekeen and Ibrahim rode up and shouted out their congratulations.

When the other horses had made it over the finish line the king had a servant call Selim and Ishkuz over to receive their prize. The crowd quieted as they made their way over and the king addressed them. His eyes swept over both Faraj and Aisha and Selim knew he was looking carefully at their conformation.

"I have never seen horses as fine as these. Congratulations on both their looks and your excellent performance," said the king, with what seemed like honesty, but with just a hint of pretense.

"Where are you from, if I may ask?" he said.

Selim replied, "We are from the Sarmadees in the Arabian Peninsula, your highness."

"And you have travelled from there just for this race?" asked the king.

Selim nodded, as agreeing to this avoided a lot of unnecessary interest in the real reason for them being in Cairo.

The king then addressed Ishkuz. "And you, young man. Where do you come from with such a delightful mare?"

Ishkuz looked at Selim briefly as though hoping for some direction from him. He then said, "Your highness, Selim and I are from the same tribe and so are our horses."

"Are these all the horses you have brought with you from your tribe?" asked the king.

"No, there are four of us altogether and four horses," answered Selim and he indicated to where Ibrahim and Sekeen were sitting on their horses.

"Congratulations to you all and to your tribe. You have shown us here in Cairo what the desert can breed and achieve. As the winner you have earned this bag of gold," said the king to Selim. Afari walked out to Selim and handed him a brightly coloured bag tied with a thin leather strap.

"Congratulations. You have done well, very well. It seems as though the spring is stronger and faster than the river," she said with a knowing smile.

"Your horses are magnificent," she added, patting both Faraj and then Aisha on their necks. She smiled widely at Selim and then returned to her father.

The king spoke again but said somewhat dismissively, "You have also won a breeding to one of my stallions, but knowing the quality of your horses you may not want it."

"Your highness, we would be grateful if we could use one of your stallions with our mare, Aisha," replied Selim pointing to the flea-bitten grey.

"Well, that will be arranged as promised, but the foal may not be yours," said the king.

All those around wondered what he might mean by this and even Afari looked questioningly at her father.

His meaning became a little clearer when he called out to his soldiers, "Seize them! Seize all four and their horses and take them to the palace!"

Pandemonium broke out as soldiers both mounted and on foot moved toward Selim and his men. The crowds ran from the riders, seeking safety, while the other riders and the horses of the race weren't sure where to go and at first blocked the soldiers from Selim and Ishkuz. It gave Selim and Ishkuz just enough time to talk about what they were to do.

"We need to fight our way out of this. We can't let the horses be taken," Selim cried out to Ishkuz. Sekeen and Ibrahim spurred their horses up to the other two, swords already drawn.

"Stay together," called Sekeen. "It will make it harder to get to us and we can protect each other."

In the chaos Selim had a brief glance towards Afari. She seemed shocked and was pulling at her father's arm, but he couldn't tell what she was saying. Selim pulled Anizi from its sheath without thinking and a slight tingling ran up his arm. Ishkuz had already placed an arrow in his bow but wasn't sure whether to shoot or to wait. Two soldiers on horseback were the first to get close and they had drawn their swords. Sekeen met them with fluid ease and his sword baffled their wielders with his strokes and snake-like speed. Though his horse was not young he was an experienced fighter and Sekeen was able to move him into position easily with his knees and weight. He managed to wound one of them on the upper arm and as the soldier grabbed at it, his sword dropped to the ground. However, by this time other soldiers had made their way to them and all four had to fight for themselves. The weight of the soldiers' horses pressed in on them. Faraj took the brunt of the weight and was pushed away from the others until Selim and Faraj were separated and surrounded by four soldiers and their horses. He had managed to fend off two of them, but now there were four. His sword strokes were confident and quick, and his natural skill kept the four at a distance.

As the fight went on, however, he began to feel he was losing control of his sword arm. It wasn't that he was weakening or that his strokes were less fluid, in fact, it was the opposite. Anizi seemed to be guiding his arm, rather than the other way around. The sword was beginning to act on its own. The strokes that he had been making were mainly defensive, but now with great ease he was actually attacking four swordsmen at once. With a flick of his wrist Anizi cut into the arm of one of the soldiers. It then parried two attacking sword strokes and turned on the third swordsman, and with a quick twist pulled his sword from his grip and flung it onto the ground behind the soldier. He retreated out of the reach of Selim while the wounded soldier reined his horse back to let the other two move in closer.

Suddenly, Selim saw the arms of one the soldiers get pulled tightly to his side and stay there. Ishkuz, who had knocked one of his attackers off his horse with an arrow in his shoulder, had just enough time to loosen the rope he had brought and throw a carefully made loop of it over the body of the horseman and pull it tight. He then quickly turned Aisha, who with her strength and weight pulled the horseman from his saddle. While that left only one of the first four attackers that had battled Selim, another two joined him. Selim's anger started to boil at the injustice of what was going on and he threw Faraj at the three soldiers. Unknown to him at the time, the edges of Anizi began to glow blue and his attackers fell back in fear. All three of them later swore that when Selim was coming toward them it appeared that not just one sword, but three swords were swinging through the air and coming for them. They didn't retreat, but even together all three of them couldn't overcome the speed and accuracy of Anizi. It seemed to hit them on the arms and body after slipping easily through their defenses and yet didn't cut them. They were pushed back by the onslaught and each of them knew that Selim could have killed them a number of times over. The fury of Selim and the sheer brilliance of Anizi caused the king's soldiers who were still fighting to stop their attack and watch Selim and his skill. They had never seen such swordsmanship. Ibrahim, Sekeen and Ishkuz were taken by surprise at the sudden withdrawal of their attackers and turned to see what they were looking at. Silence, except for the clanging of four swords fell on the whole area.

Then the king's voice rang out loudly, "Enough! Stop! It is enough."

The words slowly sank into Selim's mind as he saw his enemies pull away from him. He swung Faraj around to see what had happened to the others. Everyone and everything was still, and all eyes were on him and his sword.

The king called out to him. "I see not only that your horses are superior but so are your fighting skills and weapons. I don't want to see you harmed or any more of my soldiers hurt. I would speak with you."

The king came down from the shelter and Afari followed him. They came and stood in front of the four of them.

Afari spoke up before her father could and addressed them all but looked at Selim with both concern and shock at what had happened.

"Are any of you hurt?" she asked.

"No, I'm not," answered Selim curtly.

"Ibrahim has a cut on his arm," said Sekeen pointing to Ibrahim's arm.

"It's nothing. It's not deep. It will be fine," added Ibrahim.

Selim looked at Ishkuz and he returned his look with a shake of his head. He had not been harmed.

"Thankfully Ibrahim's cut is the only injury to us. It could have been worse," said Selim angrily. "Why did you have your men attack us? We won the race fairly" he demanded of the king.

"I confess, I was overcome by your horses. Their speed, endurance, power and beauty are amazing. I have no excuse for what I did and I sincerely apologise. I'm very happy that none of you were seriously injured. I only wanted you captured but you made it more difficult than I thought. I didn't want anyone to be hurt," the king said and then he paused.

"I want to make this up to you. Will you stay in the palace with us, until your mare is ready to leave? You will have the finest of care and food, and your horses will stay in my stables," said the king with intensity and eagerness.

"How will we know that you won't try to harm us or take our horses again?" asked Selim with anger and scepticism.

Afari answered his question with her own anger and finality.

"I will guarantee your safety and not let my father do anything this foolish again," she said, as she directed her words to both Selim and her father.

"He has discredited the royal name with his actions and we'll do all we can to make up for this embarrassing shambles," she added.

Selim and the others exchanged looks. None of them wanted to go through what they had just experienced, yet the apology from the king and the assurance of Afari were convincing.

The king then added, "It's obvious that you are able to take care of yourselves, even against twenty of my men. You have skills that we haven't seen.

You will be under royal protection. No-one will attack you while you are in Egypt." With a hard look from Afari, he added, "On my word as king."

Sekeen, Ibrahim and Ishkuz then nodded to Selim, agreeing to stay in the palace.

"We'll take up your offer but leave when our mare, Aisha, is confirmed to be in foal," said Selim.

Both Afari and her father bowed their head slightly, showing their agreement.

The king then said to the commander of the guards, "Lead these men and their horses to the royal stables and see that their horses are provided for. Every help is to be given to these men and they are to be treated as though they are one of the royal family."

"And do not fail in the smallest detail," added Afari in a threatening tone.

"I will have someone meet you at the stables to take you to your rooms and you will dine at my table tonight," the king said to the four of them. He then raised his hands as they left and the crowd cheered and sang a victory song to the men and horses of the desert, honouring them for their win.

After washing Aisha and Faraj and seeing to their feed and bedding, Selim, Ishkuz and Ibrahim made their way to the palace. Afari was present as were many of the royal family and courtesans. Sekeen had agreed to remain at the stables, as they still were not confident that the horses were safe. The king allowed them to take any precautions they wanted as he wished them to feel safe in the palace.

Afari sat next to Selim and on the other side was her father. On the king's other side sat Ibrahim. Afari had come down to the stables later in the afternoon as she wished to look at Faraj and Aisha after they had been washed and cleaned from both sweat and any remaining mud. She was in awe of the balance they showed in every area. Refinement, strength, wisdom and beauty were also what she saw and commented on. Now, over the meal she asked question after question about the horses, their breeding, the tribe's breeding decisions, their feeding and everything else that could be imagined. There were questions on muscle placement, the angles of particular bones, neck and back length, and the spirit of their horses. Selim could see that many there kept their ears tuned in to his answers, as they were all interested in what they could learn.

During the meal the king stood and toasted Selim and Faraj as that year's winners of the race. Then he did the same for Ishkuz and Aisha for coming second. The whole table stood and saluted them as both Selim and Ishkuz remained seated. Afari did not hold back and held her golden cup up high and smiled at Selim as they toasted him. However, Ishkuz felt like an intruder. Just some months ago he had been a slave and now he was sitting at the king of Egypt's table, eating his food and being toasted by the king himself.

Late into the night they partied. As guests began to go home and Selim was to take his leave Afari took his hand and looked into his eyes.

"Thank you. Thank you for trusting me. My father can do some impulsive and strange things at times and I apologise for him. Yet you stayed. I know that you don't fully trust him and I can understand that. You want to protect yourselves and your horses. But you have given us time to learn from you and time to look carefully at your horses, if you are happy for that of course. They are 'the first streams of the mountains' as you have said and they have not been affected by other streams. To see them, to have them here in our stables is an honour."

Her hand lingered on his and Selim looked down at it. Her skin was so clear and smooth. Her fingers were slender and her nails perfectly polished and shiny. A number of rings sat on her fingers and glistened in the lamplight. Selim looked into her eyes. They were large and dark and in them was both strength and vulnerability. He looked down to her lips. They were soft and unblemished, their texture like the velvet of a rose petal. For just a moment he wanted to reach down with his lips and feel that velvety softness. He caught himself and saw that Afari was looking at him with the hint of a smile and a knowing look on her face.

He cleared his throat and then replied, "I confess I only trust you and not your father. I can see in your eyes and in your manner that you can be trusted to act honourably."

Afari pulled her hand from his and turned her eyes away. She wasn't quite comfortable with the scrutinising way he had assessed her, but she was glad for the positive outcome.

"May I talk with you more tomorrow? About the horses I mean?" she said.

"Of course. Any time would be suitable. We love nothing more than talking about horses and learning from others about them," he replied.

"Good night, then," she said.

"Good night, Afari. Sleep well."

Later that night Ibrahim, Ishkuz and Selim sat on lavish cushions in a large lounge area outside their rooms. The night breeze made its way through the white lattice of the large arches that opened onto the gardens. The smell of roses and exotic new fragrances were carried into the room as they sipped cool wine and discussed the day's events. A servant lingered in the background ready to do whatever they wanted.

"Have we done the right thing in staying?" asked Selim. "Are we really safe here?"

"I think we have little choice, Selim," replied Ibrahim. "If the king had wanted he could have called his army out against us. We couldn't have escaped from them even if we all had our own 'Anizi.' But his daughter is different. I think there is compassion and wisdom in her. Maybe you should try to talk more with her, Selim, and gain her confidence. She may well be able to stop the king from trying other ways to take our horses, and knowing you, us better, she may want to stop him for our sake as well."

"I don't think Selim will have any trouble getting to know Afari better, especially after the way he was talking to her tonight," said Ishkuz.

Selim shot him a look, but he had to admit he wasn't that upset Ishkuz had noticed the attention of Afari.

"Well, she does want to talk more about our horses with me, which I'm going to do. She had so many questions tonight," said Selim.

"She was very thankful that we stayed and seemed genuinely apologetic about what her father did," he added.

Changing the subject he added, "How did 'Anizi' look to you when I was fighting with it?"

"One time I looked at you it was glowing blue," said Ishkuz.

"I didn't see that but from the moment I took it out of the scabbard I felt some tingling in my arm, but it wasn't until later in the fight that it took over and my arm just followed where it went, without any difficulty or pain. It's so strange, it just seemed to want to fight to protect us," said Selim. "And it did it with perfect precision and timing. Every move was right and every swing not too long or short. Each stroke had the right amount of power behind it. It was amazing!" replied Selim.

"Sekeen said to me this afternoon that he had never seen a sword wielded with such skill, speed and precision. He actually described it as "heavenly" if I remember," said Ibrahim, with a slight grin on his face.

He then went on a little more seriously. "Many have been interested in Al Maksour, sorry, in Anizi, for its power only. I'm glad that the king didn't question me on the sword at dinner. I think he thought that you were a very skilled swordsman, and he was probably too far away to see the blue tinge on Anizi."

"Talking about skills, what about you, Ishkuz, with the rope? What was that all about? I've never seen anything like it," encouraged Selim.

"It's called a lasso. You make a knot around the rope that doesn't tighten but rather slips along the rope until it is tight around whatever you put it on. My tribe used it all the time for catching young horses or cattle or just for pulling things. It takes some time to learn how to throw it accurately, but it usually doesn't hurt the thing you throw it over," answered Ishkuz.

"Another trick from your bag, hey Ishkuz? Will there be an end to them?" said Selim.

"Whether there is or isn't," said Ibrahim before Ishkuz could reply, "it's a valuable trick that you will have to teach the whole tribe."

"By the way, both of you rode beautifully today. I am proud of you and know the tribe will be as well. The horses were allowed to do what they were bred to do and they didn't disappoint us in any way. If the rain had held off the horses may not have been exposed as they were but somehow I think that there was little that could hide their quality and spirit," said Ibrahim. "Seeing you come in first and second was an experience that will live with me for a long time and will make a great ending for the story of our travels."

Both Selim and Ishkuz nodded at him with thanks and respect.

"The king asked about your shortened stirrups tonight. He seemed quite intrigued by them. I didn't give much away about it. He can think it through for himself like we did," continued Ibrahim.

The other two nodded and then Ishkuz yawned and said, "I suppose the day could have ended worse, if you think about it."

"Yes, much worse," agreed Selim. "You might have won the race."

He laughed and threw a thick cushion at Ishkuz.

CHAPTER 23

Afari was true to her word and the next morning she turned up at the stables. It was already warm so Selim was working with his shirt off. Faraj was tied up outside and Selim was rubbing his coat with a soft cloth. It glistened in the morning sun, none the worse for the mud on it over the last few weeks. As Afari came around the corner to the stallion lane and saw Selim, her immediate reaction was to turn around, but she found it difficult to take her eyes off the tightening of his back and shoulder muscles as he groomed Faraj. She noticed there was no body fat on him and that his taut muscles rippled under his dark but clear skin. She felt frozen on the spot, unable to go forward or back. The spell was broken when Ishkuz came out of another stable and saw her standing there. She had to go on, so with courage she walked down to them.

"Good morning to you both. I hope you slept well," she said, trying to avoid looking at Selim as much as she could.

"Very well," they both said at the same time.

Ishkuz coughed nervously and then left them, muttering something about Aisha.

"He looks relaxed," Afari said, nodding her head toward Faraj. "Does he have any swelling or heat?"

Selim's eyes had been fixed on Afari from the moment he saw her and now he jumped a little as what she said registered with him. He turned quickly to Faraj, throwing the cloth from one hand to the other.

"No. Nothing. He's relaxed and fit and could probably run the race again," he replied. He sighed inside as he realised the arrogance of his last comment. For some reason he felt so much more confident with her yesterday than he did today. He felt relieved that she didn't seem to notice.

"Well, he has the conformation to stay sound and strong. There shouldn't be any reason he couldn't do it again today," she said.

They talked for some time and Selim realised that Afari was finding it difficult to look at him. He began to feel self-conscious and decided to put his shirt on. He managed to get around to where he had it and casually put it back on. She seemed to relax after that. They talked about hoof shape and the frog of the hoof, ear size and many other parts of the horse. Time swept by and each of them became more relaxed until they were speaking easily and freely. It felt good to talk this way with a female, thought Selim. Afari was so eager to learn, but she was also knowledgeable, and his respect for her continued to grow as they spoke.

"Is Aisha ready to be bred?" Afari asked him.

"Not quite, but she is getting close," he replied.

"Have you chosen the stallion?" she asked.

"Ibrahim thinks that Nurai would be a very good cross with her and is a fantastic stallion. He is a little different from our horses in some ways but also very similar," Selim replied.

"What do you mean?" asked Afari in her normally inquisitive way.

"Well, in length and line he is very similar. His shape is what we want to see in our horses. Your horses by him did really well in the race so they must have good overall conformation and spirit. But he is lighter in bone than ours and could do with a little more height and depth in the body," answered Selim.

"Okay. So we would do well to have some of Faraj's blood crossing with our horses," she said with a grin.

"Have you been talking to your father, Afari? It sure sounds like it," he said.

"Well, just like you want some of Nurai's blood in your herd, we naturally want the blood of the best horses in ours," she replied defensively. Then she added, "But not in the way that my father had in mind."

"I would love you to see our mares and foals. We have one colt by Faraj that is so fast already, way faster than the other foals. He seems to float across the ground. He may even be faster than his father, but we will have to wait and see. I mean I can't really remember Faraj running the way this colt does at his age. Ishkuz wants to name him 'Sagaris.' It means a light but fast axe in his language," said Selim with some passion.

Afari replied softly, "I would love to see them, Selim. The name sounds perfect too."

"Do you think you could come one day? I mean, make the trip to our mountains?" he asked.

"I don't see why not. Especially if it has to do with horses. My father could send some men to see whether we could buy some of them," she said eagerly.

Selim wasn't surprised at her eagerness to visit but he wasn't sure if it was because she wanted to be with him or if it was just related to seeing the horses. She had been understandably cool toward him at their first meeting. However, since winning the race her smile seemed to come more freely. Yet, the horses always seemed to be the main topic of conversation. He couldn't work out how interested she was in him. He knew that he was growing in respect for her and not only enjoyed her company but her mannerisms, looks and movements were all becoming familiar, and he found he really liked them. Was it possible for her to like him, even love him? They were obviously friends, but would she even be allowed to love a man like him, a man from the desert who lived so far from the cities and far away from Cairo?

All this flashed through his mind in a second as he looked upon her open face and large eyes. He was tempted to tell her how much he was beginning to really like her but just couldn't bring himself to do it. Instead, he went on with their conversation.

"When do you think he could organise that?" he asked.

"I'll have to talk to him and find out," she replied.

Just then Wajdan came around the corner.

"Your highness. It's good to see you here. Is there anything I can do for you?" he asked.

"No, Wajdan, nothing. I am trying to learn more about these desert horses from Selim. It's all very interesting," she replied.

"Faraj is a stunning animal, isn't he?" Wajdan said.

"He is near perfection and yet Aisha is one of the most beautiful mares that I have seen," she replied. "Kadin is a proud, sultry stallion as well."

"And they have speed. Speed enough to win by some lengths yesterday," said Wajdan.

"Yes, we are aware of that," said Afari, a little frostily.

Wajdan's eyes opened a little wider as he realised what he had said and he quickly agreed with her. "Yes, your highness. I had better check on the mares."

He bowed and left them. "Well?" she said to Selim who had a questioning look on his face. "I don't have to like you winning, do I?"

Selim gave a short laugh and rubbed Faraj on the neck, who turned his head and looked at them, wondering what was going on.

"Oh, by the way, you are invited to eat with my father and I tonight. My father wants to make up for his, what I call stupidity, as much as he can," said Afari, changing the topic.

"Thank you, I look forward to it," said Selim.

* * *

Aisha's time to be bred to Nurai came and Wajdan led Nurai to her while Selim and Ibrahim held Aisha. His screams echoed on the walls and the whole stable complex knew what was happening. It would be a wait of a couple of weeks to find out if she was pregnant. The four men spent their days looking over the king's horses, talking to the grooms, reading both "Beginnings" and Ziasudra's story, and Ishkuz began lessons in reading. When Afari heard that he could not read and that Selim was to give him lessons, she became very excited and wanted to help. It impressed her that Selim was willing to teach him to read. She thought perhaps that he was more sophisticated than she had given him credit for. Afari came to them every day or invited Ishkuz and Selim to the palace library to have lessons there. Selim saw how gifted she was at teaching Ishkuz. She was patient, yet persistent, and she was humorous as well. This was a side Selim hadn't seen much of at all. She became more relaxed as the days wore on and occasionally he saw her looking at him while Ishkuz was focused on his work. He smiled at her when he saw her do this and she smiled back, making her face soft and warm.

One day as Selim and Ishkuz were walking back to the stables after a lesson Selim said with a sigh, "I think I'm falling in love."

"Well, if I didn't love your sister, I would be too. Afari is amazing," said Ishkuz openly. "And I think she is falling in love with you."

Selim turned his head quickly to look at Ishkuz. "What? You really think so?"

"I don't always have my head in the book, you know. I can see what you two do," he replied. "Besides I don't see her talking to any young Egyptian men, do you?"

"No, I suppose not," said Selim thoughtfully. "I used to think there was a soft side to her but that it got lost in her 'royalty.' But since the race I haven't seen anything but kindness, interest and friendliness."

"Well, she has asked me about you when you weren't around," admitted Ishkuz.

"Really!" exclaimed Selim. "What did she say? I want to hear every word. And what did you say?"

"Well, it started off with her asking why I was with you. You know, being your friend and part of your tribe when I am clearly from another place. So I told her about my background, about the race and your arm, and how you gave me my freedom and so on. What you had done for me really intrigued her, and so she asked about the sort of person you were. I told her you were a sheikh of a large tribe, that you were a skilled rider and swordsman, but that you were also interested in reading about the past. I didn't mention 'Anizi' in case you are worried. I told her you liked to think about things and that we've talked for hours on all sorts of topics," said Ishkuz.

"She seemed impressed, or at least she didn't say much after I told her those things. Sort of like she was thinking it over. I think the sheikh thing got her as now she can sort of think of you as royalty. That's good, isn't it?" he added.

"I'm not sure that being the leader of a distant desert tribe is very impressive," answered Selim.

"I wouldn't look down on your position, Selim. It's a very important one and you have a lot of people relying on you. And from what I've seen you are a very good sheikh. You've come to Cairo to get the sword remade and you will be taking home the greatest sword on earth. Who knows what it will bring to the tribe?" said Ishkuz with growing passion. "Just think too, what woman, princess or not, wouldn't want to be with the man who carries 'Anizi'?"

"Well now that you put it like that …" Selim trailed off, but then went on more passionately. "I don't want her to love me because I have the sword. I want her to love me and like being with me. You know."

"I don't think that will be a problem from what I can see," said Ishkuz.

Selim was left with a lot to think about before he and Afari were to meet again.

Every night they ate at the king's table. The king was not always present, but Afari was. Sometimes others joined them, dignitaries, ambassadors, and high-ranking officials of Egypt. Afari often needed to entertain them and Selim watched carefully at how she related to these people. It was obvious that she had learnt diplomacy well. He noticed too that when a guest crossed the line physically or verbally she acted with discretion and dealt with their gestures and words with wisdom and without offence.

One night after dinner he asked her to walk with him in the garden. A large male peacock stood there puffing out his chest, parading his tail feathers to two females, who weren't paying him much attention. While Afari and Selim enjoyed the spectacle, he hoped that it wasn't a sign of the way their relationship was at the moment or was going to be in the future.

"We'll be leaving shortly," said Selim.

"Yes, I know. If Aisha refuses Nurai tomorrow then she is almost certainly pregnant," Afari said. "So, you come here out of nowhere, take the king's gold, breed to his best stallion and then disappear back into the desert. You have it all, don't you?" she added with a laugh.

She turned then and ran her finger through the silvery water in the garden fountain. Selim though had seen the disappointment in her eyes before she turned away. Again, he wasn't sure if the pain was related to his leaving or because they had taken the race, the gold and maybe a foal from her father.

Selim licked his lips nervously and then said softly to her, "You know that all of these things can be yours. The gold, our horses, the foals. You could disappear into the desert with me, Afari."

Afari turned and looked at him with soft eyes and was quiet as she thought about what he meant.

"Afari, I love you. I love the way we talk, your love for life, your passion and compassion, your wisdom and your beauty. I want you to come to the mountains with us," said Selim with increasing passion and a little desperation.

Afari moved her head toward Selim's and kissed him. He returned the kiss and then she leant into his chest and hugged him tightly.

"I have never really known love. My mother died early on and my father is not the easiest person to be around. But being with you makes me feel whole somehow," said Afari.

"Do you miss me when I'm not around?" asked Selim.

"Yes, yes I do. I wonder where you are and what you are doing and when we will be together again," she replied.

"And isn't that love?" asked Selim.

"Yes, I suppose it is," answered Afari. "You know that I asked Ishkuz about you?" she asked. Selim nodded.

"There is a lot more to you than you let on and I like that about you. When Ishkuz told me some of the things about you and what you do, it made me more intrigued."

"Does that mean that you will ... will you marry me, Afari?" asked Selim.

"Yes Selim, I will marry you," she answered.

As Afari moved closer Selim searched for her warm lips. He took her by the shoulders and kissed her long and gently.

"You have made me the happiest man in the world, Afari!" said Selim.

Afari smiled at him, content to see him so happy and elated to feel the warmth of love flow through her body.

"We need to talk to your father," said Selim.

"Yes, but let's leave it till tomorrow. I just want to hold you now and enjoy this time," replied Afari.

They found a bench in the garden and sat there together.

"I'd never have thought that I would marry a man from the Arabian Desert," said Afari. "An ambassador or a high-ranking courtesan I could believe, as that is the usual arrangement. You're like a breath of fresh air in Cairo. Thank you for coming," she said as she turned her face to his.

They continued to talk into the night and to share the thoughts that had built up over the last months and simply enjoyed the security of belonging to each other.

Later that night when Selim had returned to his rooms, he shared what had happened with Ibrahim and Ishkuz. They were very surprised but happy for Selim and warmly congratulated him.

"This trip to Cairo has been incredible. We've had Anizi remade, and found out where it came from, won the race, we will have a foal from the king's best stallion, and now you have won the heart of the king's daughter. What could be better?" said Ishkuz.

"Maybe Anizi has the power to bring some of these good things, as the stories tell us," answered Ibrahim.

"I hadn't thought of that," said Ishkuz.

"I've had that in the back of my mind for a long time, but I haven't mentioned it as it all seemed so unreal. But now that Anizi has shown us that its power in a fight is real, maybe it can affect things around it or influence things for those who have it," said Selim.

"That's awesome," said Ishkuz. "Selim, you said that it seems to have a mind of its own when fighting. Maybe it's really alive and knows what's going on around it," he added enthusiastically.

"But how can a thing that was dead come alive? I mean you saw what it was before it was remade. It was rusted and broken, and parts of it were missing. 'Dead' might not be the right word but it has been lifeless for so long," said Selim.

"You're right, but it certainly came 'alive' in your hands when you were fighting. You've never seen that before, have you? So in one way it has come alive again," Ishkuz responded.

"Yes, I suppose you're right. Something has changed, whatever it is," said Selim.

"Have you told Afari about 'Anizi'?" Ibrahim asked Selim.

"No, I haven't mentioned him at all. I will though," replied Selim.

"You just called 'Anizi' *him*," said Ishkuz.

Selim looked at Ishkuz a moment, reflecting on what he had said.

"It's strange, and I don't understand everything about the sword and its power and origins and everything like that, but somehow I get the feeling that it is a person rather than an object. I mean for it to, and I don't know how to say this, but for the sword to fight for itself, to fight as though it could see everything around makes it feel like a person, not a thing," Selim responded.

The others nodded as though it followed some sort of logic, though it was difficult to make sense of.

"Well, I'm going to bed. Tomorrow we will find out if we are heading home or staying here for another few weeks," said Ibrahim. "Good night."

Selim and Ishkuz said their "good nights" as well and headed off to bed.

Before Ishkuz opened the door to his chamber he called out, "Selim, are you sure she didn't agree to marry you because she wants your horses?"

Selim didn't take the bait and answered dryly, "Good night Ishkuz."

Ishkuz smiled to himself as he closed the door.

The next morning a crowd gathered around Aisha who had been brought out of her stable. She had been washed regularly and her coat and mane glistened in the sunlight. Her mane and tail were milky white and the dark brown spots on her coat stood out clearly. She looked regal and everyone there admired her. Her dark eyes were bright, and her dark nostrils flared as she stretched out her neck and called out to the stallions. Afari shook her head and said, more to herself than anyone, "She is so beautiful and so fast at the same time. What a mare."

She turned to Selim who stood next to her. "I can't wait to see the foal from this mating." He smiled widely at her and whispered back, "You will see it being born my darling, in the mountains of the Nejd."

A scream came from around the corner and then Nurai appeared, tail swishing, eyes wide and expectant, jumping rather than walking. He was pure moonlight white with a neck reaching up and out, and at the end of it sat a small, sharply chiseled head at an exquisite angle. His ears were small and pointed and he was fluid and easy in every movement he made. Aisha's ears went back and she began swishing her tail frantically. They knew already that she was not going to accept him in any way and that she had probably conceived.

Wajdan led Nurai closer but slowed him down as he saw Aisha's reaction. He then pulled him up and Nurai stood squarely and still with his neck reaching out as far as it could go, nostrils dilated to full capacity to catch Aisha's scent. His back and hindquarter flattened and his tail cascaded behind him as he lifted it in his excitement. Aisha was not impressed by Nurai's display and would not change her mind, no matter how grand and powerful Nurai looked. She squealed again, warning him not to come any closer. Nurai screamed in his frustration and lashed out with a front foot.

Wajdan turned him and as he led Nurai back to stallion row he said to them, "I think you have a foal on the way. May the gods bless it and may it be a filly."

They celebrated briefly and then led Aisha back to her stable, after which Selim and Afari left to speak to her father.

They were not seen for the rest of the day and Ishkuz and Ibrahim were not invited to the king's table that night. A message came to them that they would have food brought to their rooms. They didn't know if this was a good or bad thing. That night Afari and Selim joined Sekeen, Ishkuz and Ibrahim at the stable as they were doing the last feeds and checks of the night. It was balmy and pleasant, and pigeons cooed from the rooftops.

Ibrahim was concerned for them and asked, "How did it go? Did your father give his consent?"

"Oh yes," replied Afari. "That was the easy part. The hard part was getting the wedding organised."

Selim rolled his eyes a little and sighed. "We spent nearly the whole day talking about it. The wedding will take place two weeks from today."

Ishkuz groaned.

"I know you are missing Ansim, but it was the earliest we could hold it without rushing the preparations and we needed to give enough time for some of the guests to travel here," Selim responded. "We have also decided to have a wedding when we get home, for the tribe. Maybe a double wedding?" he said, winking at Ishkuz.

"That's a great idea," said Ishkuz enthusiastically.

"There was one thing the king wanted," said Selim. "He wants to be able to buy some of our horses. He's sending Wajdan and a large guard with us and Wajdan will take the horses back. Mind you, he was insistent on having relatives of Aisha and Faraj."

Then he said with a grin, "I think Afari is worth all the horses her father gets and more."

"Hmm, desert sheikh. We might have to discuss my worth to you in some more detail later on, I think," Afari said to Selim as she pulled him close and looked sharply into his eyes.

Sekeen, Ibrahim and Ishkuz were behind Afari, and they stifled a laugh as Selim's eyes grew wide with fear.

Selim and Afari left and the other three headed back into the stables. Ishkuz waited until Afari and Selim were out of earshot and then said, "Last night I said that Afari agreed to marry Selim because she wanted his horses. But I think the truth is that the king agreed to the marriage because he wants Selim's horses."

All three of them laughed their way into the stables, as they all knew how much the king wanted horses like theirs.

They didn't see Selim much over the next two weeks and even less of Afari, as they were so busy with the wedding. Ishkuz kept working on his reading, which was developing nicely. He enjoyed it and would pick up the "Beginnings" scroll to try and find words he knew. Cairo received news of the coming wedding and began to celebrate and decorate various public areas. Selim noticed more and more people coming and going into the palace. Some were delivering various things, but others were obviously important guests.

The days passed, but not quickly enough for Selim. The clothes, the details and the rehearsals were beginning to stifle him. Sometimes he would escape to the stables and join the others just to survive.

Finally, the day arrived, one of colour, richness, ceremony and joy. Sadly, Afari's mother had died three years before so she could not be part of it. Even without her mother overlooking the event everything was done in a timely and competent way. Afari had made sure of every detail and everything had someone responsible for it.

After the marriage ceremony they emerged onto some wide steps so that the public could see and congratulate them. Afari had asked for them to ride Aisha and Faraj around the city so that the people could join in the celebrations. Both horses wore rich costumes that complemented their coat colours and when they mounted the horses a new roar arose from the crowd at the spectacle. Afari looked magical in her wedding clothes. Her dark hair shone, and her eyes were large and bright, and everything she wore from her jewelry to her nail colour and veil complimented her and let her joy shine on her special day. Selim was immaculate in carefully designed and fitted clothes and he looked regal and handsome seated on Faraj. He was not just a desert sheikh, but also a prince of Egypt.

Ishkuz, Sekeen and Ibrahim were proud to be part of the entourage for Selim, and Ibrahim and Ishkuz led Aisha and Faraj as the newly married couple rode. The festivities went on for days and each night the city was brightly lit and entertainment and food from the palace was provided for all.

CHAPTER 24

A week after the wedding the party of four that had entered Cairo some months before now left Cairo with a party of over forty. Most were amongst the best Egyptian cavalry belonging to the king but some were servants and cooks to provide for the princess and her new husband. It was a quiet farewell and they made their way out of Cairo with little attention. The trip to Yathrib was uneventful and they made good progress over their days of travel.

Ishkuz became more talkative the closer they came to Yathrib. His mind had been engulfed with many things while in Cairo but he had still thought of Ansim daily. He was to see her again soon and each day saw him more excited.

Sekeen leaned over and whispered to Ibrahim, "What has happened to him? Did he eat something in Cairo that makes you talk more?"

"It's not what he ate in Cairo. It's what is ahead in Yathrib," replied Ibrahim.

Sekeen thought about it and then said, "Ah, I understand," touching his nose and winking at Ibrahim.

They arrived at Yathrib and stayed the night with Rana, their auntie. Ishkuz and Ansim couldn't be separated and spent all the time talking about what had happened to them over the time they were apart. Selim introduced Afari to Ansim, Rana and Muhair. Meeting Afari, the princess of Egypt, overawed both Rana and Muhair and neither dared to speak. Ansim and Afari, however, immediately became firm friends and found they had things in common, Selim not being the least of these. The next morning they left for the Nejd region.

Late one afternoon they made their way around the top of the mountains and looked down on the river valley, the green crops in the fields and the brown rambling fort with its large wooden doors and various watchtowers. It was a hive of activity and in the horse paddocks dust flew up now and again as horses swatted flies or wandered over to the drinking troughs.

"Oh Selim, it's beautiful," exclaimed Afari.

"Yes, I thought you would love it," replied Selim. "I can't wait to show you around."

They had obviously been seen by the lookouts as they rode down toward the fort as riders began to come out of the fort at full gallop to welcome them. News of their return would be spreading quickly throughout the fort. They entered the gates of the fort with a fanfare and inside people were gathering. It was always a time of celebration when tribe members returned from trips as they all knew the dangers that faced travellers.

Selim's mother, Almas, was waiting in the crowd eager to see if her plans with Ansim had been productive. Almas easily spotted her riding next to Ishkuz who stood out clearly from the others with his pale skin.

"This is positive," she thought to herself. Ansim raised her arm and waved at her and then grabbed Ishkuz's arm and lifted it high as though in victory. Ansim's smile was as wide as it could be and her mother lifted her hands to her face, tears building in her eyes.

The group began to dismount and Ansim and Ishkuz made their way over. Ansim hugged her mother and to the questioning look on her mother's face she said, "Yes mother, yes, it has all worked out. I love him and he loves me."

Her mother then reached out her arms to Ishkuz who hesitantly moved toward her for a hug. He felt uneasy. A woman had not hugged him for many years and now in the space of months he had hugged two. Tears rose in his eyes as he felt the love and acceptance of Ansim's mother.

Meanwhile, Selim had given out some orders to take care of the soldiers and their horses and had helped Afari to dismount. He made his way to his mother, holding Afari's hand. Ansim turned her mother toward them. A confused look came over her and she raised her hands to her face in shock.

"Mother," said Selim, "this is Afari, the princess of Egypt, daughter of the king of Cairo and Egypt, and my wife."

His mother looked at him in disbelief and wasn't sure how to respond. Questions whirled through her head and though at first she hesitated, she finally reached out and hugged Afari as she had Ishkuz.

"It's not just women who can have secret plans," Selim said as he eyed Ansim.

"Yes, my son, you're right. We deceived you and for that I am sorry, but all has turned out well. In fact, much better than well," replied his mother.

"Come on," she said, "we can't leave the princess out here. All of you come inside."

"Please, call me Afari, mother," said Afari.

"Oh, well, yes, of course, Afari. Come, the trip has been so long. Did you go all the way to Cairo?" she asked Selim.

"We'll tell you all about it, mother," said Selim, as they made their way inside.

After refreshing themselves they gathered in the main sitting room and began the story of their travels. Selim told most of the story while Ansim and Ishkuz and even Afari added bits and pieces to it. Their mother sat quietly, trying to take it all in and commenting at some important points. When they had finished, she picked up on the thing that excited her the most and said, "So we are to have two weddings! One for a couple not married and one for one couple that is." The others laughed.

The weddings were organised under the watchful and competent eye of Almas, and in time the tribe celebrated the weddings of the two couples. It was a unique time as this was not just a marriage, but the marriage of the sheikh and his wife, a woman who was not from their tribe but a princess of Egypt. Not only that, but the wedding of the sheikh's sister was to a man from a tribe from the faraway north, a pale-skinned man whom the whole tribe had come to respect and accept for his friendship with Selim and his skill with the bow and horse. No-one had any trouble with him marrying into the tribe.

Afari and Wajdan looked over the tribe's horses and marvelled at their uniform structure, strength and beauty. They were in awe of Faraj's bay colt by Bashasha, whom Selim had named Sagaris, as Ishkuz had suggested. He was one that Wajdan wanted to take back with him. He was, however, not yet weaned but both Afari and Wajdan were content as Selim had not denied them the colt outright. They did manage to find a number of mares and fillies that they were allowed to purchase, as well as two colts that Wajdan believed showed great promise and would breed on well.

"Wajdan, my father will be very happy when you return. These are excellent horses with the blood of Faraj's and Aisha's family in them. If he complains, just remind him of that," she said to Wajdan.

In due time, Wajdan and the soldiers left the fort with their treasures.

Life seemed to have reached a higher level of satisfaction for Selim. So much had happened over the last year. Some of it was not so good, like his broken, poisonous arm, but there was much that was. Afari fitted into tribal life like she had grown up in it and the more Selim got to know her the more he loved her.

He had not yet spoken to the tribal council about Anizi. A couple of men had mentioned Al Maksour, but Selim put them off saying he would explain later. He was a little concerned at the reaction of some of them, once they were told the full story. He knew though that it had to be done, as Al Maksour was the reason they had left in the first place.

Once all the wedding celebrations had finished and things had become more settled, Selim organised a meeting to discuss the sword. Many men of the tribe and even some of the older women turned up to hear about Al Maksour. Selim laid Anizi on the carpet in front of him, still in its scabbard, all eyes watching as he did. Selim could feel the expectation rise in the room and it became quiet. He went on and told them their story. He told them that no-one in Yathrib was able to help but that it was possible a man in Cairo could. He told them of the reshaping of Al Maksour by Ibn Tubal, its strange metal, the blue tinge and the way it sharpened itself. As he told them of finding the markings on the sword the group became very quiet. Selim was revealing a history they had never heard before. No-one asked him any questions, they simply soaked up the story.

"The markings we found on the sword made no sense, but I copied them down to show someone who might know what they meant. We went to the library of Alexander and there a scholar identified them as Sumerian. He knew Sumerian and told us that the markings meant the 'fire of heaven,' Anizi," he said.

A few of them gasped. All of them looked bewildered as they had never heard that name before.

Selim went on, "The name didn't mean anything to us. But you all know that I have been interested in the drawings on the cave wall in the mountains that show a large boat. I asked another scholar, whom we met on our trip, about the large wooden boat and he said there was a story in the Jewish writings about one like this. The owner's name is Noah but the scholar said there was another version of the story written in Sumerian where the boat owner is known as Ziasudra. Ishkuz and I looked for a copy of those stories and found them both. The Sumerian story tells of Ziasudra getting the sword that guarded the gateway to the Garden of Eden. Before the great flood an eagle brought the sword to Ziasudra. He named it Anizi, fire of heaven, as he and others had seen it burning and blazing in front of the garden after it had come down from heaven. He tells us that he marked the sword just below the hilt with the Sumerian words 'fire of heaven,' Anizi."

Some people called out, thinking that the story was finished. Selim waved his arms for quiet and then continued.

"Ziasudra marked it because he gave it to Nimrod and he didn't want it to be confused with any other sword.

REVELATION

"When we had finished the race in Cairo, the king wanted to take our horses from us as he had never seen any horse the equal of Aisha or Faraj."

A few people cheered but Selim went on, "All four of us were on horseback and we fought back. I took Anizi out and then, as in the stories that Ibrahim has told us, it began to move by itself. My arm followed the sword and it moved with a precision and speed that even Sekeen couldn't match. It gave off a blue glow and fought off four soldiers as though fighting one."

He stopped and there was silence. He then stated quietly what everyone there was beginning to comprehend.

"The rusted and broken pieces of Al Maksour that our tribe has owned since before memory are Noah's and Nimrod's Anizi. It was designed and created in heaven of heavenly metal with a heavenly power."

Selim then reached down and picked Anizi up. He stood and carefully pulled the sword from its scabbard and held it out for all to see. As it glimmered dully in the light some pulled back a little as though it might do something magical. Slowly, some voices called out and questions were asked. Some whispered to their neighbour of what they thought, fearful of being overheard.

Selim held up his hands for quiet and then went on.

"I wanted Al Maksour to be reforged to honour it and to prevent it from decaying even more. I had no idea that it was Anizi. I may have had a boyish wish that it was a famous sword or was once owned by a famous person, but what we have before us is beyond our imagination. No tribe has what we have. No tribe has the heritage we have in Anizi. The Al Bedi tried to take it from us many months ago not even realising what they were really after."

"You have just given a new shape to an old trinket, Selim" called out Suhayb with derision in his voice. The whispering and talk stopped and there was a tense silence.

"What has it ever given us, or me, over the years? Nothing beyond what anyone else has, if not less?" he added with a scowl on his face. "You and the others have too much imagination to think this sword has any power," he said, waving his arm loosely at Selim and the others.

Ya'qub then spoke up. "I have nothing but admiration for what Selim and the others have done. Al Maksour, or Anizi as we know it now, has always been part of my life and I won't reject it, even if I don't know everything about it. It's always been special, and Selim and the others have brought a much deeper understanding of its worth and history. They've done the tribe a great service and should be honoured as we honour the sword."

Selim and the others nodded their heads at Ya'qub in thanks for his words.

Others also raised doubts about it all. "We can't deny the remaking of the sword but this doesn't mean it's got power. We've lived our whole lives with it here and we haven't seen anything. Can you show us its power?"

Many in the crowd joined in this call to see the power of Anizi.

Ibrahim spoke now, a little annoyed at the stubbornness of some in the crowd.

"We can't turn on its power like that. Can you turn the rain on and off when you want? How can we make a thing from heaven perform when we want it to and stop it when we are finished with it?"

His logic and annoyance caused the crowd to become quiet and some of them looked somewhat embarrassed.

Rasin then spoke quietly, "It was your belief and passion that has brought Anizi to life for us, Selim. You have taken what was hidden and forgotten and brought it before us renewed. Now each of you must decide about Anizi for yourselves. Will it be part of the life of the tribe? What part do you want it to play in our future? No-one can answer these things for you."

Selim responded, "As Rasin has said, what you believe about this sword is up to you. We have the writings of Ziasudra and the Jewish writings that you can read so you can decide for yourself, if you want to. What I have experienced with Anizi seems to fit with the stories we have heard about it. In the end, you will need to believe what I have seen and felt and have passed on to you about what the sword did for me. Am I not trustworthy?"

More discussion went on and finally the crowd dispersed. Some went to Selim and told him how they believed what he had said and thanked him for reviving this part of their tribe's heritage. Afari was very proud of Selim and told him so on their way home.

"You have matured, my desert sheikh. You spoke like a leader today. No, you spoke like a king. And I know how kings speak," she said to him as she locked her arm in his.

He smiled at her and in his heart he realised that parts of the boy that existed in him a year ago had slipped away and that he had gained more than a wife and a famous sword. He was growing into the very things his father was and wanted him to be.

The following year was a blessed year for the tribe. Ansim had twins, a boy and a girl. They were lighter skinned than Ansim but not as pale as their father. The tribe's women adored them as the girl had large blue eyes and ash blonde hair, and Ansim had lots of offers to care for them. In his heart Ishkuz remembered Ibrahim saying that some from the past who owned Anizi had seen a higher number of twins born in their families.

Sekeen and Ishkuz worked together on making their own Scythian bow. They tried many different types of wood, though wood was scarce in the desert. They spent a lot of time working out how to bend the wood so that it matched Ishkuz's memory of the bow. Finally, they found both the wood and the techniques needed to shape it. The wood held its form after it had been shaped and then Sekeen bound it in strong leather strips. He held it up with his arm outstretched showing the men of the tribe their newest weapon. When Ishkuz used it for the first time he showed its power to shoot further and with more force than any of the bows the tribes had used. The tribesmen cheered and Sekeen and Ishkuz felt the satisfaction of achieving what they had set out to do. Sekeen, in particular, was glad to see that the tribe would have another weapon to protect the fort and its people. Ishkuz was content that he could give something back to the tribe for the way it had accepted him so quickly and easily.

Bashasha had an elegant chestnut filly that looked like her father Faraj but with feminine features and charm. She was the favourite of Afari and it seemed

Afari was the favourite of the filly. She followed Afari around whenever she was in her paddock. Selim accused Afari of making her fat, as she would take biscuits and fruit to her every time she visited. With a flick of her head and dark hair, Afari denied it all.

Aisha was due late in the season because of her visit to Egypt. Everyone was anticipating her foal but no-one expected what she birthed that year. Like Ansim she had twins, a colt and a filly. They were both healthy and strong and no-one had seen a colt and filly look the way they did. They took the best of both parents. There was so much elegance, yet so much strength. Aisha had added depth and length of leg, while Nurai had passed on his short head, large eyes and small ears along with the elegance that he possessed. Both were light on their feet, athletic and fast. The whole tribe was amazed at their quality and everyone who saw them fell in love with them. Ibrahim, with a twinkle in his eye, thought of the first foal that the filly would produce from Faraj and the foals the colt would produce from the mares of the tribe.

"Yes," he thought. "The future is bright."

Printed by Libri Plureos GmbH in Hamburg, Germany